THE PE

Joshua Humphreys has ceased to include fanciful biographies of himself at the beginning of his novels. He has, in middle age, become a serious person. He has begun to think of his future, has stopped smoking his pipe, and now has only a glass of red wine with dinner on weekends. He teaches a course in Ancient Greek history and is undertaking the research that will enable him to share his passion for the culture of Indochina. How boring he has become. He hasn't waved to a man in a tractor since the yogaclown from *The Creative Art of Wishfulness* threatened to sue him for exposing her wellness bullshit. And he doesn't even tell people that Mel Gibson is his uncle anymore. Instead Humphreys and his Ukrainian wife, Vaselyna Pantsov, have begun doing super serious work with dwarf orphans in the Carpathian mountains, and are working to have the patently unfunny term 'dwarphan' outlawed in the EU. After making his fortune anew in the competitive world of camel beauty pageants Humphreys founded a charity that sends ultra-accurate rulers to parts of the world that still suffer from hysterical outbreaks of penis-shrinking syndromes. He also gives considerable monies to research institutes working to cure Pumpkinson's disease. He spent half of 2020 in the slums of Czechoslarabia, working to get those goddam Czechoslarabians to stop giving people eggs after sunset. What little time he now gets to spend in his hometown he devotes to fartshaming the local mechanics. Most recently he travelled to Yemen, where he discovered that the entire country is a prison for genies. He's pushing for a royal commission into why such a high percentage of dog-grooming businesses are run by lesbians. It's suspicious, is all he's saying. And his uncle, Mel Gibson, has just informed him that their family is *not* the legitimate royal dynasty of Cambodia. So uninteresting has life become. Humphreys regrets having so matured, but feared that not doing so would lead to his being alone for the rest of his life as nobody seems to have a sense of fucking humour anymore. You bunch of ninnies.

BOOKS BY
JOSHUA HUMPHREYS

WAXED EXCEEDING MIGHTY

EXQUISITE HOURS

ANGELA'S LASHES

GRIEVE

TO SAVE A FOREST VIRGIN

CHICKEN HATS

IMAGINED TREASURES

THE CREATIVE ART OF WISHFULNESS

THE PETER FILE

JOSHUA HUMPHREYS

The Peter File

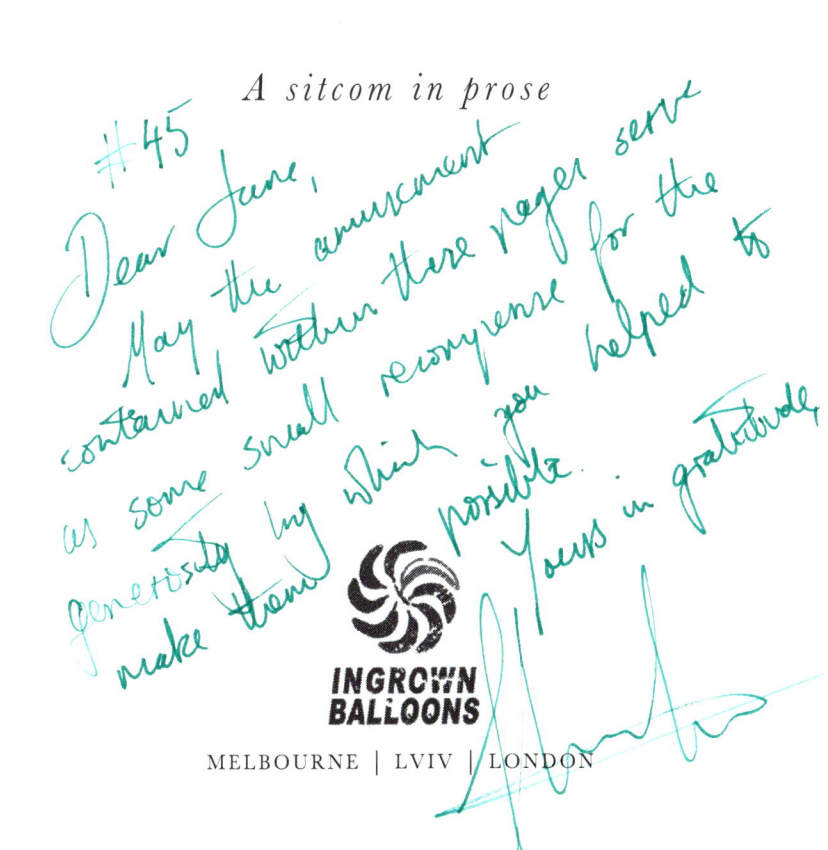

A sitcom in prose

#45
Dear Jane,
May the amusement contained within these pages serve as some small recompense for the generosity by which you helped to make them possible.
Yours in gratitude,

INGROWN BALLOONS

MELBOURNE | LVIV | LONDON

Copyright © 2022 by Joshua Humphreys

The moral right of the author has been asserted.
To whom? I don't fucking know, I just write the books.
I don't have time to assert my moral right to
anyone—but consider it asserted OK?

This book is a work of fictitiousness.
Any references to historical events, pelicans, or places are used
fictitiousnessly. Except for the douchebag on page 146—he was
real. Most of the names, characters, places, and events are
products of the author's spiteful nature and any obvious
resemblance to actual events or places or persons, living or
from Russia, is probably not entirely coincidental.
Page 146 guy can suck an egg, seriously. And just wait till
my stalker gets The Peter File treatment in Season 2.
She's going down.

All rights reserved, bitches.
This book is sold subject to the condition that it shall not,
by way of trade or otherwise, be lent, resold, shunted,
prostituted, snorkelled, licked like a postage stamp, lent to Prince
Andrew at a party, given to a Russian, humped in a van, molested
in a nursing home, or otherwise circulated without the author's
prior consent in a form of binding or cover other than that in
which it is published and without a similar condition, including
this condition, being imposed on the subsequent purchaser.

Whatever the flippety flop that means.

ISBN: 978-8-424-06650-4

Cover artwork by Samuel Humphreys

SAMUELHUMPHREYS.COM

J O S H V A H V M P H R E Y S . C O M

*THE FOLLOWING LUNACY WAS
ENABLED BY THE EXUBERANT SOULS
WHOSE PATRONAGE MADE POSSIBLE
THE WRITING OF THIS BOOK.*

*SO ARE THESE PAGES
DEDICATED WITH
GRATITUDE
TO:*

Agi Makarewicz, Katja Dallmann, Kristy Dye, Katie Haughton, Rebecca Adams, Samuel Humphreys, Caroline Boutros, Natasha Agafanoff, Simone Watts, Mahtab Biermann, Anthony Ogle, Melissa Deskovic, Mark Alexander, Sarah O'Sell, Bronwyn Shipway, Leslie Gonzales, Ninib Bisso, Stella Maxwell, Jessie Garver, Liara Steward, Anthony Conti, Courtney Fleming, Shelley Booker, Michele Metcalf, Liam Brammall, Devon Fortune, Matthew Pratt, Irina Sandaev, Jessica Bowen, Lorraine Fleming, Joseph Yasinski, Alenka Schuller, Lisa Thomas-Tench, Erin Johnston, Vincent Xanthos, Michela Turri, Katee Trinkle, Laura Orth, Claire Cantrell, Kathryn Cox, Muaz Jalil, Heather Gold, Alexandra Gold, Valerie Bennett, Jane Byers, Maria Gomez, Kimberly Wood, Grace Kane, Langley Barnes, Joseph Assenzo, Kathleen Waltrip, Celynna Rightmire, Gary Postma, Carol Silverstein, Marielle Petricevich, Melissa Barker, Fernando de la Maza, Grace Piasio, Sarah Tisdale, Geoffrey Orens, Tania Yorgey, Ashley Decker, Mary Kay Zolezzi Philipa Helliwell, Georgina Lamb, Alyce Cannon, Carol Lague, Cornucopia, Roxanne Holloway, The Noetic Collective, Jennifer Barringer, Jacob Shine, Sarah Anderson, Michelle Simpson, Elisabeth Brown, Aleca Velzeboer, Beatriz Coimbra, Lisa Sproul, Naomi Lawler, Rebecca Tyerman, Devon Foster, Bernadette Giliberto, Tanya Wolfkamp, Alice Barlow, Sarah Englehart, Catherine Flanagan, Wendi Petersen, Paulina Teller, Sharon Griggs, Stephen Gothard, Jane Locke, Lana Alexander, Niramonh Thomson, Jessica James, & Jonathan Shell.

Now enough of the sentimental claptrap!
Let's get to the jokes.

WARNING:

This book contains negative depictions and/or
mistreatment of people, cultures, gender identities,
sexual orientations, sexual orientals, freaks, munchkins,
midges, dwarfs, orphans, dwarphans, hobosexuals,
sexual occidentals, the r-words that rhyme with leotards,
liberal tears, conservative delusions, the debilitatingly ticklish,
eels, Scottish musical instruments, hardware store
employees, yogaclowns, idiots who mouth-breath in saunas,
& the English language.

Because that's what comedy is.

Rather than remove this content, which would
leave a book of around four and a half pages, we
here at Ingrown Balloons want to both assert its
well-meaningness then learn nothing at all from it
as we strive to ensure that comedy doesn't die
with the open society that creates &
informs & cherishes it.

Ingrown Balloons is committed to creating stories
with uninspirational and obviously preposterous
themes that reflect the abiding awfulness &
cruel randomness of the human experience
around entire globe of human world.

To learn more about how stories impact society please visit:
www.suckitupdaffodil.com

CONTENTS

I.	*The Ukrainian Ordinary*	1
II.	*The Chair Man*	47
III.	*The Gum Smuggler*	97
IV.	*The White Kilt*	149
V.	*The Georgian Fencing Parties*	203
VI.	*The Arm Steeler*	257

Now the story of one woman's struggle to discover the truth about her husband's death—

and the buffoon of a family that can't help but prevent her from finding it…

THE PETER FILE

Episode 1

THE UKRAINIAN ORDINAЯY

I

Fiona and Peter Sukhimov were at breakfast on a gleaming January morning, rolling berries around the edges of their plates and smiling into one another's eyes and even, occasionally, forking banana slices into each other's mouths.

Yep, they were in love—and after eleven years of marriage.

'Would you like a burberry, sir?' said Fiona, pressing down on a blueberry.

Peter smiled and gave a content, 'Hnm. What'd he call yoghurt again?'

'Yoga-hurt.'

He, was the waiter who had introduced them. Peter, hiking across Crete on a gap year after medical school, and Fiona, on Greek sabbatical from a detested career—were at breakfast one morning put erroneously on the same terrace table by Dimitris, a dimwitted hotel waiter. Dimitris was also tryingly gregarious, and stood over the two young Melburnians—too polite to tell him of his mistake—as they waited for their coffee. When it arrived with their breakfasts he pointed out their hummy and their newsli, their burberries, then smiled and nodded as they smirked at one another and ate. He soon asked if today they would like to take a walk, and suggested Samaria. 'It's a gorgeous,' Dimitris enthused. 'Near to my old village.'

'A gorgeous walk?' asked a 27-year-old Fiona, quickly enamoured of Greek landscape. 'I'm in.'

'Is a very nice gorgeous.'

'Is it far?' said Peter.

'Yes, is a… ten minoots.'

What Dimitris had meant to say was that Samaria was a gorge, and one that ran for ten kilometres. But halfway down it, just before dehydration had them seeing demons in the cliff faces, Fiona and Peter decided they would look one another up when they got home.

'And when we asked him about it later!' Fiona laughed.

Peter repeated in Greek imitation the phrase that was still dear to them both: 'But the most smart people are the ones who see behind the words that we use, and who undersand the true idea of what is sayed, you undersand?'

'You undersand?' said Fiona, imitating the imitation. 'We really could have died in that gorge! What do you think's the worst thing that's ever happened from someone mishearing a word?'

'Melk!' said Peter and lifted the carton from the table.

'I'd forgotten about melk!'

Annie, their twelve-year-old daughter, bounced down the stairs and through the living room. Fair-haired, lanky, notoriously smiley—she had spent every day of her second-last week before high school playing at friends' houses.

'Would you like some melk, hummy?'

'Did you say melk?'

'Speaking of which,' said Fiona. 'Don't forget Mel's flying in tonight.'

'Think he's grown up at all yet?'

'I don't like our chances.'

Two years younger than Fiona, Mel Dixon was smiling like an idiot-child in the butterfly house of Changi airport—spinning with his arms outstretched in the hope that a butterfly might land on him. When shortly one did he opened his mouth as far as it would go and raised its fingered perch towards his eyes. He moved to transfer the peacock pansy to his nose but the butterfly clapped silently its orange wings and wafted up into an oil palm.

When eventually his elation subsided he whistled *Dear Old Southland* and crossed the shining brown-and-beige floor of the departures terminal. He bent down to take a drink from a water fountain and pressed its button and was squirted in his blonde hair. He dried his chuckling face with his handkerchief and saw that he was standing before a thick placard screwed to the wall. It warned in black outline and red-crossed circle of four prohibitions: No durian, No spitting, No urinating in lifts, No chewing gum. Underneath these it read, 'Fines and canings.' Mel leaned in to inspect the cartoon of a man with his trousers lowered. As he smiled at the lightning bolts striking at its arse somebody bumped into his backpack then said, 'Sorry, mate.' Mel looked over his spun shoulder and called out hopefully, 'Are you Australian?'

But the man strode away.

Mel slung his backpack onto a conveyor belt. He patted his pockets front and back and front as he shuffled along between two old Singaporean ladies. He was relieved to trigger no sound over the threshold of the metal detector. The young woman watching the x-ray screen said something to the tiny-waisted man restacking plastic tubs behind her. So Mel's backpack was palmed and lifted and he was asked if it was his. He nodded and smiled and said, 'Mm hm.'

'What is...' said the elongated boy as he slid a hand into its side pocket. 'This?' he shouted, and thrust aloft a three-pack of chewing gum.

'That's... woah,' said Mel. 'That's not mine.'

'You smuggle gum,' said the guard in a high voice.

'What? No, I don't smuggle gum.'

'Yooouuu smuggle gum.'

'I can't chew gum, I have sensitive teeth.'

'Is your bag? Is your gum.'

Two tiny-waisted young men with locally manufactured machine guns were waved over; shortly Mel found himself locked in a room with them.

'You smuggle gum,' one repeated for the eleventh time and jabbed his fingers at the packet's green plastic. 'Fine four thousand dollar. Or five cane.'

'Five what?'

The other young man, or he could have been old—it's hard to tell nowadays—smacked a thin bamboo stick onto the table. 'Four thousand dollar. You pay now?'

'Four thousand do—. I don't... I don't have that. Surely this is a misunderstanding?'

'Yooouuu smuggle gum.'

'No, listen, I can't chew gum, I have sensitive teeth.'

'You smuggle gum!'

So in disbelief was Mel ordered to stand, and to place his hands on the table—shouted at to allow the lowering of his trousers. The first blow of the cane was first and foremost startling. Of all the ignominious postures he had assumed in Asia this by far was the most shameful. Not even thoughts of the butterfly house could sweeten the sting of the third. In the prelude to the fourth whack he thought of himself as a prisoner of war. The silence that followed the fifth brought a kind of violated relief.

And he was photographed in front of a height chart holding three packets of gum then in handcuffs escorted onto his flight.

Peter presented from his white coat's pocket a lollipop to Mason, his morning's first appointment, and waved him and his mother goodbye. He lowered an elbow onto the high desk behind which Liz his receptionist sat and said, 'Poor kid's gonna limp like a hunchback for five years. But look at that smile.'

'Kids really are Brazilian.'

Peter tilted back his head. 'What's that?'

'It's like you always say: kids really are Brazilian.'

'What I say? What are you talking about?'

'That's what you say,' Liz insisted, her brightness dimmed by a century of isolated inbreeding.

'What's what I say?'

'That kids, they really are Brazilian.'

'I don't say kids are Brazilian. Unless they are Brazilian.'

'Peter, come on!' she smiled, unsure as to whether he was kidding. 'Whenever you give them a bad diagnosis and they don't cry? You always say kids are so Brazilian.'

Peter stood up from his lean. 'Do you mean resilient?'

'Is that a word?'

'Send Olivia in in two minutes.'

He returned to his consultation room and sat at his desk and signed off on Mason's appointment then opened Olivia's file. He found nothing of note on its second page and was running his capped pen along the margin of its first when a sharp sting in his chest caused him to hunch his shoulders and shortly to clench his teeth. He groaned and dropped his pen; sat back in his chair and pursed his lips. When at last the pain was gone he exhaled a high, 'Haw,' of relief. Then the unprecedented stabbing returned. He thumped at his heart with the base of his thumb and, alarmed by the sharpness and location of the pain, groaned: 'What the hell is that?' He leaned onto his left elbow and growled. He shrieked his receptionist's name then said, 'F--k,' and reached out to pick up his phone.

Before he could manage the two thumb-taps that would have called Fiona he was unconscious.

Fiona settled into an extended and frozen push up as her Polish yoga therapist circled, instructed, interrogated. 'Hesitation in your hips you still hold.'

'Mm,' said Fiona as Agi pressed at them.

'Working on this have we not been?'

'Mm,' Fiona conceded.

'Breathe, to let flow the pranayama that washes hesitation from our soul. In, hold it. Now out let it go.'

As she out let it go one of Fiona's two specially selected ringtones sounded from her handbag. 'Oh that's Pete. I should answer it.' She unfroze from the position and moved with the back of her hand the hair that had stuck to her forehead. She grinned at Agi then silenced the song with a tap of her thumb as she wiped the sweat from her ear with a towel. Then she put the phone to it. To her ear, not the towel.

When later she had picked her ear up off the floor she steadied her shaking hands and called her father.

Geoff Dixon was in his second-floor office at the enormous hardware store which everywhere bore his surname. Able to look out through glass windows over each of its thirty aisles, he was instead scrolling through the autobiographical summaries of women who, like him, were looking for what they called love.

'Hottish, yes,' he mumbled and scrolled. 'But Scottish no.' He clicked on the slideshow which each profile presented beneath its 'Likes'. 'Hottish again. But will you retire to Vietnam with me? Because I cannot take much more of this crap. And do I… want you to retire to Vietnam with me?' At the slideshow's fourth and only unedited image he said, 'Aaaand you are Sibyl Fawlty. Why do you hide the real images behind the filtered ones? We're gonna find out eventually, love.'

His phone rang and he saw that his daughter was calling. 'Punnpkin, what's up? … What? … You're shitting me. … Fi, really? … Oh Fi.'

'What am I going to tell Annie?'

'Have you called the communists?'

'I can't, Dad. I can—I can barely…'

'Fi?'

'…'

'Punnpkin?'

'Beh.'

'Fiona?'

'Glergh.'

'Fi, I'll tell them, all right? … Fi?'

'Drnm.'

'I'll be there in twenty minutes,' and Geoff hung up. 'Hey, Siri?'

'Uh huh?'

'Call the communists.'

'I don't see a communist in your contacts, Geoff. Who would you like to call?'

'Call U-Crane.'

Yuri Sukhimov, Peter's younger brother, came into the front office in his crane-driving uniform and picked up the receiver of a very old telephone. 'U-Crane, how can I be of great and goodly service?'

For as a child Yuri had learnt English from watching the only foreign-language VCR tape which his family then possessed:

Reclined with his elbow on shag carpet and his eyes not very far from a thick convex screen, Yuri rocked a bare foot backwards and forwards and puffed up his chest and said, 'Et cetera, et cetera, et cetera.' Then as the television, so he. Yuri sprung up and circled his family's living room with his wrists behind his back—raised one hand and pointed its finger as he recited: 'You are very difficult woman.'…

'Who's this?' said Geoff.

'Who, who—*who*?' Yuri took off his U-Crane hat and ran his free hand over the scalp which he kept skin-bald, for he also believed himself to be the reincarnation of Yul Brynner. More on that in Episode 3.

'Yuri. I don't wanna talk to you, where's your dad?'

'I am not presently seeing him.'

'It's urgent, Yuri—where's your sister then?'

'She is in heat.'

'…'

'Hello?'

'Mate, that's your sister.'

'Yes. My sister is in heat.'

What Yuri meant to say was that his sister was in their banya, the traditional sauna that occupied most of the rear of the business' premises and whose installation had been the family's greatest urgency after immigrating from Pripyat, Ukraine. They left Pripyat in 1993, a little later than they probably should have, for Pripyat is three miles from the Chornobyl nuclear power plant. It's now a ghost town. It had been a ghost town for seven years before Peter's family left—but more on *that* in Season 3.

Stripping off as he neared the banya, Yuri took a pointy felt hat from a hook on its outside wall and opened its door and found both his sister and father inside.

'Close door! You let in Bannik,' said his father as he slapped a bunch of dried oak leaves against his back.

'Papa, the Dixon man has called for you. He is saying it is urgent.'

As the banya's door closed they heard resume the telephone's antique ring. Yuri's father groaned and rose and handed him the bunch of leaves. With a towel at his waist he came into the office and took off his pointy felt hat and answered the phone. 'What?'

'Arsen, it's Geoff.'

'What do you want?' As Geoff told him the news Arsen's natural scowl dissolved from his face. 'Piter? … No.' The scowl returned as his towel hit the floor. 'No! … My

The Ukrainian Ordinary

Piter?'—and dissolved again. 'My kaminyi.' In vacant shock he returned to the banya and declined the oak leaves. Felt hat in hand he resumed his high seat and stared.

'Papa?' said his daughter.

Soon Arsen said, 'Oleksa. Yuri. ... Piter is dead.'

'Papa, what?' said Alexa, her English learnt later than Yuri's but much more perfectly.

'Piter. He is dead.'

Alexa put her fingers to her hairline and wailed. Yuri said, 'Universe is once again dancing.'

'No!' cried his sister and trembled her sweating head.

'My Piter, how I am loving thee. We must be getting him from bahh-barians.'

'What barbarians?' said Arsen.

'These doctors of pills with their unhuman sacks and everywhere scalpels.'

'You are right. Piter must be brought home. Oleksa, go with your brother.'

'Yes, Papa,' she spluttered.

Outside Melbourne Airport Mel's handcuffs were unlocked by federal police officers and he was returned his suitcase and his backpack. Immediately a plague of journalists recognised and encircled him, for he landed to find—since it's such a long goddam flight—that news of his crime had preceded him.

'How much gum did you attempt to smuggle, Mr Dixon?'

'What?' said Mel, surprised by the renown of his offence.

'Did you *know* gum was illegal in Singapore, Mr Dixon?'

'I did. But I can't chew gum, I have sensitive teeth.'

'Do you consider yourself a kingpin?'

'It's—what? No,' he said to the battery of microphones at his chin.

'What's the street value of what you were trying to smuggle, Mr Dixon?'

'The street value? I don't know—two dollars?'

'Do you think you'll be able to return to normal life now you're a notorious gum smuggler?'

'Notorious? It was three packets of gum. No, it was a three-pack—technically it was one packet of gum.'

Having found in its basement the hospital's morgue, Alexa was relieved to also find that the two people behind its front desk were male. She smiled and giggled and said that she was lost. When they asked which department she was looking for she said she didn't know, but her father was in here somewhere and was complaining about the food and could she tell them a secret?

'I think you probably can, yeah,' said the employee who was goateed and corpulent and amenable to smiling and giggling and especially to both.

She pressed her forearms onto the desk and leaned up and over. 'I've brought him some booze.'

'Did you say…?' began the employee who was clean-shaven and pear-shaped and very amenable to smiling and giggling.

'Boobs?' finished the corpulent.

'Booooze,' said Alexa.

'Are you saying boobs?'

'Booze!'

'I'm hearing boobs. I know that's inappropriate but it's what I'm hearing.'

For though Alexa's accentless English had been acquired through immersion, and though occasionally she did unnaturally elongate a word, she was presenting confidently both sources of their mishearing. She took from her back pocket a plastic bottle and placed it beside her elbow.

'Booze.'

'Oh!' said the pear-shaped.

'Samohonka, ever tried it? It's Ukrainian.'

The Ukrainian Ordinary

'I haven't,' said the corpulent as he inspected the bottle without label while the other stared still.

'Open it up, give it a smell. Best thing about it? No hangover.'

He unscrewed its plastic cap and Alexa placed a shot glass onto the high bench and smiled and giggled. When ten minutes later both men were asleep she opened the door behind her and waved Yuri in. He rolled a wheelchair through to the morgue and was met by a silent field of long blue plastic bags stuffed upon shining gurneys. He read the paper labels affixed to each and eventually found the one denoting his brother. He stood at its end and pulled down its zipper until he could see Piter's chest. Alexa's eyes filled with tears. She exhaled, 'God and the devil,' as she joined her hands at the bridge of her nose.

'They are putting in plastic bag what should be put upon altar,' said Yuri. 'Piter. Miy brate.' He inspected the grooves of Piter's face then put the backs of his fingers to his brother's cold cheek. 'By divine blessing of the superagency of the whole world, who have done this to you? Come,' he said to Alexa, who through tears helped lift Piter out of and over the bag.

Yuri took off his own jacket and buttoned it around his brother and found a white sheet to place over his lower half. Upon the morgue's desk he found in a ring binder a piece of paper with Piter's name on it. This he tore out and ate. Then, grinning as they thought Australians grinned, Yuri and Alexa pushed Piter—with a U-Crane cap pulled down over his face—out of the ground-floor elevator. Nodding and waving to visitor and nurse, they rolled their brother down the corridor—straightened his head when it flopped over then held it upright by the ears—and out through the hospital's automatic front doors. Alexa power-walked ahead to retrieve the car from the street as Yuri crossed the car park whose rates he considered immoral and so refused to pay.

Fiona had been sitting in her car outside Amelia Thring's house for thirty-five minutes. Her eyes throbbed from weeping and her neck ached from crying and her stomach felt empty and enormous. Each time she envisaged seeing her daughter—Annie, smiling Annie who had done nothing at all wrong and was soon to have her day and her future ruined—the throbbing, the aching, the emptiness were shown at once to be meagre as the crying recommenced.

She now realised that all morning, even when she did manage to bring the sobbing under control, the corners of her mouth had been drawn out and down. She thought that if she greeted Annie thusly her daughter would know something was wrong. So she made her mouth as small as it could outwardly go. Then she remembered that even if her mouth betrayed nothing of the news she would shortly have to say the words to her face: 'Dad's d…'—to little Annie, who would always wish that she had the chance to better know so good and kind a man. But it had to be done. To delay much further would be unfair to her daughter—her so, so innocent daughter—for the rest of her life left to wonder what it would have been like to have grown up with a father.

So Fiona wiped her eyes and retracted her lips and clenched her stomach then stepped out of the car and walked up Amelia's parents' drive. She rang the doorbell and pursed her lips and waited. Amelia pulled back the front door and said, 'Fiona! Hello, what are you doing here?' Amelia called out to her best friend: 'Annie, it's your mum.' Annie with wet hair in a swimsuit was already coming barefoot.

'Hi, Mum,' she said casually. 'What are you doing here?' She smiled and took a bite out of some fairy bread. Butter stuck to her cheek as she tried to catch the sprinkles that

The Ukrainian Ordinary

fell to the floor. 'Do I have to go?' Fiona tried and failed to say her daughter's name. 'Mum?' Annie knelt down to pick up each sprinkle with a press of her finger.

'Annie.'

'What's wrong, Mum?'

Fiona sensed that she had let droop her lips. She sucked them back in as quickly and as fully as she could and said, 'Da—'

'Do I have to go? It's only lunchtime, we were going to play Marco Polo.'

'With *no* fish-out-of-water,' said Amelia and both girls laughed.

Fiona stared at her smiling daughter, sun-kissed and butter-cheeked and so kind and considerate. 'Da—' she tried again to say but failed.

'Mum! What's wrong?'

And at last, as though it were the final line in a showtune bouncing from duet to chorus in hastening towards a jubilant climax—and as though Fiona were the musical's female though enfeebled lead—the phrase released itself in whining song: 'Dad's dead!'

The curtains of Peter and Fiona's house all were drawn.

Alexa lit a thick candle encased in red plastic and its glow made glimmer the golden background of an icon of a blue-robed St Luke. She raised the candle to a shelf, where it brought out as creamy the white eyes of a black-faced Virgin encrusted in her bronze frame—a Theotokos in her family's possession since the Hetmanate and one of the few possessions they had brought from Pripyat. She shook out the match and turned to join her family at Piter's side.

Yuri, having dressed his brother in a loose white shirt and grey trousers before laying him out on his kitchen table, his feet at the wall and his head to the icons—annoyed his father by humming, 'Shi-va-ya-na-ma,' as Arsen recited the ninetieth psalm in his own tongue. Alexa dropped sesame seeds from between her thumb and first fingers—along each of Piter's legs, in zig-zag across his body, down one arm and up the other—and Arsen closed with what (if this book could afford subtitles) would have been given as, 'Make us glad according to the days wherein thou hast afflicted us.' Yuri took up a bell and bellowed a prayer to Shiva Nataraja:

'When you dance for the preservation of the world the earth beaten by your feet trembles on the verge of destruction. Mad with joy and life and death, the mountains and the oceans and the earth do dance amid bursts of laughter and sobbing.' With his hand he muted entirely the tinkling then he and his father received palmfuls of sesame seeds.

Together they sprinkled them over Piter's heart, over his neck, his closed eyes. They each put a hand on his body and stood silently until eventually Arsen said, 'Until tomorrow, dear son.'

'Until tomorrow,' said Alexa. 'Dear brother.'

'Amid bursts of laughter and sobbing, humanity dances. Until tomorrow, dear brother.'

In silence they left Piter's side and proceeded through the darkness of the living room and walked out the front door.

A short while later Mel whistled *St. James Infirmary* as he ascended the steps to his sister's porch. He found the spare key still in its pot-plant hiding place and pushed open her front door and lifted his suitcase into her front room and called out, 'Fi?' He dropped his backpack onto the floor and left his suitcase at the bottom of the stairs and went through to the kitchen. 'Fi?'

He turned on its light and clutched his chest: 'Jesus! Pete! You scared the s--t outta me.' With his hand at his heart he made for the refrigerator. 'How are you, mate? I'm famished, is that all right? I had no idea they wouldn't serve food on a nine-hour flight, you believe that?' Mel tapped his fingers on the outside of the fridge door as he rummaged through the vegetable crisper—sang, '*Put a twenty dollar gold piece on my watch-chain,*' until he found and chomped into a carrot. 'Y'OK back there, Pete?' He opened a tub of hummus and used the carrot stub to shovel it into his mouth. 'Having a bit of a moment are we?' he chewed. 'I get that. Five years I was in Asia and I couldn't find a single adventure worth having. World's gotten boring, Old Pete.'

He took a carton of milk from its door then shut the fridge and turned to his brother-in-law, prostrate and serene.

'I'll let you have your moment, don't worry. Just gonna eat this and I'll get ahead of the jetlag. Might go for a run.' Mel leaned back against the kitchen bench and recoiled from a cupboard knob that dug into his cane welts. 'You're very still, Pete.' He lifted his chin and looked down the length of Peter's body. 'Say something! I'll get into that cognac you never let me drink. Pete?' He looked back and up at the red glow of the candle among icons. 'Weirdos,' he whispered to himself. 'I know what'll get you up.' He put down the carrot. 'A nice game of gay chicken with your brother-in-law,' and he lay aside the milk carton.

'I'm coming to get ya,' Mel warned as he crept across the kitchen. 'You wanna find out if lip-feel is hereditary? ... Pete,' he sang as he stood over the table and positioned his face above his brother-in-law's. 'What are you covered in, sesame seeds?' He brushed them from beside Peter's unflinching hand. 'You trying to attract birds here? Or is this a yoga thing? Fiona finally got to you, hey? Well, here I come.'

He began lowering his head. 'I'm not gonna back out, Pete. Pete! I've got flight breath.' He bent his knees as he continued his descent and whispered: 'Haven't brushed my teeth since yesterday. … Peter,' he said when at last he thought that the air from his mouth would be felt as a sure sign of his resolve.

When the stubble above and below Mel's lips was bent by Peter's mouth he saw that too there was little chance of his brother-in-law turning away or sliding out. He relaxed his ugly neck and held his breath and planted fully a kiss on Peter's perpendicular face.

'Told you I'd win,' he mumbled as he held the victorious pose. Still he was almost singing: 'I'm gonna hold 'em here till you admit defeat, mate!'

'Mum, is Dad still alive?' said Annie, half panicked as she and Fiona appeared at the front doorway.

'Mel! No, Honey, he's not.'

'Hey!' Mel mumbled, revelling at the end of a day of large embarrassments in this smallest of triumphs. 'I won!'

'Why is he kissing Uncle Mel?'

'Uncle Mel's kissing him, Honey. Mel! Get away from Pete's body.'

Mel rolled his head and spoke from the corner of his mouth: 'Did you say body?'

'Pete's dead, Mel.'

'Dead?' Mel said as he recoiled, then shortly he regained full use of his mouth as he stood up straight and began to scream.

The Ukrainian Ordinary

II

'I still can't believe it,' said Fiona to her brother. 'We were meant to be together.'

'I know you were, Fi.'

Slumped both at the picnic bench in her backyard, Fiona took a large swig from a wine glass then stared into the same afternoon nothingness upon which Mel's gaze was fixed.

'We were *meant* to meet in Greece. We were *meant* to fall in love.'

'I know you were, Fi.'

'If we were meant to be together, what meaning is there in it ending—in us ending? You can't be meant to be with someone forever who—. Someone who d—.' Fiona banished the consonant to the chamber of her wine glass.

'It's all f----d, Fi. The universe is a bastard.'

'Oh hi, honey,' said Fiona as Annie came through the house to the back door.

'Kid, how you doing?'

'I'm all right.'

'How was Amelia's?'

'It was OK. I'm gonna lie in bed, we were swimming all day.'

'I love you.'

'Love you too.'

Fiona took another swig and lowered her voice. 'We were meant to have Annie, that's the worst thing. We really were meant to be together forever.'

'I know you were, Fi.'

'Will you stop saying that? Don't you have some Eastern wisdom for me or something?'

'Eastern wisdom? Asia's not like that anymore. It's all

neon and face masks. And now I'm back here. Here, with no future what-so-goddam-ever.'

'At least you have the chance to have a future.'

'I was supposed to lead such an exciting life, Fi.'

'At least you're alive.'

'Supposed to go off and find my *thing*.'

'And you still have the chance to.'

'Yeah but…' he searched the wastelands of his mind but settled on a shrug.

'There's no but, Mel.'

'Supposed to be James Blonde. Now look at me.'

Wanting to end the most miserable conversation that she had ever had—even after a week of the most depressing imaginable exchanges—Fiona swigged again then asked Mel to take Annie to pick up flowers for the funeral.

'Pink roses, fuchsias, and sunflowers. You got it?' She handed him her car keys as Annie put on her shoes. 'Annie, will you remember?'

'Oi.'

'And all the bunches have to be in even numbers, you got that too?'

'Yep.'

'Annie, will you remember?'

'Oi!'

Geoff spun his car keys on his finger as he walked up the colonnaded entrance ramp to the funeral home.

'Thank you for coming,' said Arsen, waiting for him outside the automatic doors.

'No worries. Anything to help Fiona.'

'Normally I would bring my daughter, but today she is in heat.'

'Mate, that's your daughter.'

'She is in heat a lot this week.'

'What is with you people?'

The Ukrainian Ordinary

When Arsen knocked on the door of his office the funeral director put down a newspaper whose front page above Mel's mugshot read *Gum Smuggler On the Streets*. 'Arsen, please, have a seat.'

'Geoff, the father-in-law.'

'Brian, good to meet you.' Brian took up Peter's billing manifest and read through its dot points. 'So just some last-minute confirmations, Peter was very organised when it came to his arrangements. The church is taking care of the service, the flowers your daughter's taking care of. We've taken care of the casket, the memorial booklets. I understand there's to be no wake, but there'll be toasts at the burial. Is that correct?'

'Toast?' said Arsen.

'Mm hm.'

'Piter wants toast?'

'It's pretty normal,' said Brian.

'This is Australian thing?' said Arsen, looking to Geoff.

'So everyone can say their piece.'

'Say? You mean eat?'

'What?'

'So they can eat?'

'No, it says here no catering because no wake. And there are no requests as to readings at the service either,' Brian continued, 'but there is a time provision at the burial for various speeches.'

'Peaches?' said Arsen, squinting. 'You are making confuse. He wants toast and peaches at funeral?' He looked to Fiona's father for confirmation. 'This is normal at Australian funeral?'

Geoff nodded: 'Pretty much, yeah.'

Arsen scrunched up his scowl and mumbled, 'Toast and peaches?' then accepted that his son had taken on some of the funerary customs of his wife's peculiar people. 'I can organise peaches.'

'Very well,' said Brian. 'But yes, as I said, everything else is pretty much done. Is this a family trait? Are both your funerals already arranged?'

'I think I've got a while to go yet,' said Geoff.

'We do not make these arranges. Family knows what to do.'

'Have either of you ever thought of designing your own tomb?'

'Tomb?' said Arsen. He frowned and nodded and crossed his arms. 'I will have monument.'

'A monument?' said Geoff.

Arsen pouted and nodded.

'You're a bit full of yourself, aren't you?'

'What do you say?'

The funeral director now became audience to their chronic competitiveness, a hostility momentarily set aside after Peter's death. He sensed the dividends that might be skimmed from it, and inflamed. 'You think ah… yours'd be bigger than his?'

'I *know* mine'd be bigger than his,' said Geoff. '*And* it'd be more deserved—the man rents out cranes for a living.'

'You don't *know* what I have done in my life.'

'You rent cranes and you tell people about your daughter's cycles, you communist.'

'I am *not* a communist! How many times I am telling you?'

'Welcome to the tomb room,' said Brian, walking ahead into an exhibition space lined with samples of stone. Two wide touch screens stood side-by-side at its sparse centre. Geoff pressed at one and after typing in his name was soon dragging wreaths and epitaphs from the screen's edge to a virtual mock-up of his own tomb.

Arsen used his finger as a pencil to sketch the angles of a rectangular plinth. He went to change the screen's language but found no Cyrillic, so he typed out the transliteration of his names. Geoff dragged across an urn then looked over at Arsen's screen—glimpsed the large inscription on his hypothetical monument and said, 'Not even your alphabet.'

'And what?' said Arsen as he leaned across and read the inscription atop Geoff's obelisk. 'That is yours?'

'Of course it's mine.'

'You own alphabet?' Arsen returned to his own screen and was pleasantly surprised when the selecting of a brick texture turned his tomb ochre.

'I could if I wanted to.'

'You are not rich enough to buy alphabet.'

'I bet you I can.'

'You sell hammers and plants—you could not afford half a w.'

'You mean a u?'

'Yes. You couldn't afford a u.'

'I could afford you,' Geoff pointed at Arsen. 'Don't you worry about that.'

'In a million years of selling chairs, you could not afford me.'

'How much do you cost?'

'Three hundred dollars a night.'

'What are you, a prostitute?'

'*You* are prostitute.'

'I could afford you, don't you worry—I just think it'd be a bum deal. Get it?'

'Get what?'

'Arse-en.'

'You are a bum deer. I will take my tomb!'

'I'll take *my* tomb!'

'Hello? I take my tomb!'

While in North Melbourne Yuri and Alexa Sukhimov were meeting with the family priest.

'You can put down the gun, Father.'

In his forties with a thick beard wiry at its wide edges, the

THE PETER FILE

Most Reverend Father Kyrylo Pyanenko had taken up his pistol while going over the sequence of Piter's service. Now pointing the object at Yuri, he squeezed then pulled its trigger.

Yuri looked down at his newly moistened chest. 'Holy water,' said Father Pyanenko, then turned the gun on himself and opened his mouth and squirted. 'Oo, that reminds…' He took three shot glasses and a plastic Coke bottle from a drawer in his desk and poured samohonka as he continued: 'Then, as I remind everyone that God's mercy is infinite and His goodness is beyond measure, Oleksa you will—'

'This is what Piter has been wanting while he lived?' said Yuri, certain that it wasn't. 'My brother was not believing in this morality good God of bringing down hope and mercy. He was believing God burns thread of causality whilst he is dancing, of whichly His hru is being infinite.'

'His what?'

'His play, his lila.'

'Yuri, really you are blaspheming in a house of God.'

'House? House? What house? God is having no house!' Yuri spun a raised finger—'He is everywhere,'—pressed it against the priest's desk. 'And not here.'

'Are you then a Buddhist, Yuri Sukhimov? And was Piter a Buddhist? Is he a Buddhist?' Father Pyanenko at last asked Alexa, thinking she had to be more productive of coherent statements.

'So must I be,' said Yuri. 'As reincarnation of Yul Brynner, tamer of all white elephants.'

'Yul Brynner?'

'Mm,' Yuri nodded.

'Yul Brynner the… Buddhist who tamed elephants?'

'Here we go,' said Alexa.

'White ones. Fifteen of which were bringing to him most auspicious blessings.'

'Yul Brynner owned fifteen white elephants?'

The Ukrainian Ordinary

'King of Siam did, and does—all white elephants in all Siamese land and tributary countries adjacent around.' The priest removed the shot glass from Yuri's vicinity. 'Why are you taking this?'

'What are you talking about? What's he talking about?'

Yuri raised his chin and smiled. 'Yul Brynner, who have died day before I am born, was playing King of Siam, gainer of victory in ten directions, four thousand six hundred twenty five times. At what you are laughing?'

'How much holy water did you have before you came here?'

Alexa shook her head. 'Father, I really wouldn't—'

'He's hilarious.' Father Pyanenko chuckled in baritone as he refilled his shot glass with squirts of his pistol. 'You're hilarious.'

'What you are calling me?'

'Yuri…' Alexa warned.

'Top up?' said Father Pyanenko to Alexa. 'You, my son, could not tame a toy elephant on a feast day, let alone a white one on a Wednesday. Shaving your head does not make you the king of Thailand.'

'And growing one beard is making you *not* wise and holy.' As Yuri stormed out of Father Pyanenko's office he said to Alexa, embarrassed behind him: 'We are stealing one elephant.'

'We're not stealing an elephant, Yuri.'

'Tonight. It is muchly one matter of honour. Without honour, though he own entire globe of human world, man is having nothing.'

'He's drunk, Yuri. He's always drunk, you know that.'

'We steal elephant also with holy water. I will be showing this Christian priest who have divine blessings and infinite goodness.'

As Mel and Annie crossed from a covered car park to one

of Southland's indistinguishable entrances, her uncle still was astonished that Annie was unafraid of starting high school next week.

'Primary school's a breeze, everyone's your friend. But in high school they literally want you to die, they tell you this to your face—it would make them happy.'

They strolled between juice bars and sock emporiums. 'Kids'll torment, mock you, rob you. You're lucky you're not fat.'

'I'm fat?'

'What? That's the opposite of what I said. See, look at this guy.' Together they stopped in front of a person dressed all in silver and wearing a tricorn hat and Pinocchio mask. His left hand rested high on a tall walking stick and his whole body appeared to be seated on nothing but air. 'I bet he was made fun of at school, and now he's an invisible-chair guy. How *is* he sitting there?' Mel rounded the man's lack of seating and searched for signs of structure. 'They'll call you Smell. Smell Gibson. Smell Dix-on. Small Di—.' Behind the floating silver suit Mel saw the florist to which Fiona had sent him. As he neared its entrance he called back: 'You're just lucky you don't have a name that lends itself to ridicule.' He turned in and said to a man snipping stems: 'Flowers for Fiona Sukhimov?' Mel winced and momentarily returned his head towards his niece. 'Fiona Sukhimov,' he said, now pronouncing the surname correctly. 'I think I need sunflowers, pink roses, and fuchsias?'

'Yep, that's them.' The florist pointed over Mel's shoulder to three cardboard cartons set aside on the shop floor. He came out from behind his bench and lifted first the sunflowers onto his arranging surface of paper squares. He pushed each bunch aside as he counted.

'What'd they call you in high school?'

'I beg your pardon?'

'I was just telling my niece that high school's tough. Not

The Ukrainian Ordinary

like primary school, that was a breeze.'

'High school was tough.'

'Mine was Smell. D'you have a nickname?'

'I did.'

'What was it?'

Pressed, the florist stopped counting off the bunches. 'It was Even Stephen, if you must know.'

'Ha. Does it have a story behind it?'

The florist put the sunflowers down. 'Yes. It does.'

Mel waited for him to tell it. Instead he brought over the carton of pink roses. 'Oh,' said Mel, remembering. 'And I have to make sure all the bunches are odd numbers only.'

The florist stared across the bench at his long day's first customer.

'What?' said Mel, confused by the staring.

'You think that's funny?'

'Do I think what's funny?'

'Mocking me.'

'Did I mock you?'

'An odd number of flowers?'

'They're for a Ukrainian funeral, the bouquets have to be in odd numbers. Or maybe it's an even number? Hang on—Annie?' She was moving her head from side to side as she endeavoured to solve the question of the silver person's suspension. 'Annie, was it odd numbers of flowers or even?'

'Even, Uncle Mel,' Annie called in.

'All right, get out.'

'What?'

'You're a bully.'

'Me?'

'You don't think I can count?'

'I didn't say that.'

'Even Stephen can't tell the difference between odd and even numbers? Even Stephen doesn't do Maths F. Even

Stephen isn't *that* dumb. Get out.'

'What's going on?'

'Get. Out.'

'I still need the fuchsias.'

'You will have *no* fuchsia.'

'That's a bit mean.'

'Get out. Now!' The florist, who we'll assume was called Stephen, thrust forward the sunflowers and the roses.

'I just need the—'

'Get. Out!'

Mel slid the two boxes from the table and slung them awkwardly under his arms and was able only with his fingertips to grip their top edges. 'But the fuchsias.'

'Out!'

As Mel wobbled out of the store with every intention of returning for his fuchsias Stephen kicked them across the shopfloor.

'Even Stephen can pronounce vagina with a v! *Even Stephen* knows condom doesn't have two m's. Even Stephen can decide who can and cannot have fffff-uchsias.'

Mel caught his toe on the fuchsia box and the sunflowers knocked against the shop's entrance as he fell out of it. He spun sideways as he lost his balance then stumbled backwards with the cartons now serving as cumbersome wings. He managed to turn to face Annie only as he and the flowers slapped onto the floor. He slid into the empty space where the busker's chair was miraculously not and his shoulder hit the walking stick so hard that it instantly bent. The man drooped upon his perch and trapped Mel between pole and silver trouser seat. In panicked breaths Mel apologised through his nose.

Annie leaned down to take the boxes from under his armpits and asked if her uncle was all right.

'No fuchsia.'

'What happened?'

'We have no future.' Mel's sniffing rose to snivelling. 'I have no future.'

'Of course you have a future.'

'No,' he said as the busker writhed to disentangle himself from the seat that now was visible. Then Mel's huffing subsided into genuine crying. 'No future, Annie.' He lay limp upon his cheek and spread out his arms.

Annie grabbed his ankles and attempted to pull. 'You didn't get all the flowers?'

'I have no future.'

Even Stephen drew down and locked the plastic cage that overnight protected the contents of his store as Mel slowly shuffled himself back from the wreck. 'We have no fuchsia,' Mel stuttered as he stood. 'I have no future.'

'Your fuchsia is what you make of it, Uncle Mel. And if you stop crying you can make it a way less embarrassing one. Come on,' she said brushing at his elbows, 'you'll be all right.'

Annie rubbed Mel's back as he ran the side of his hand across the underside of his nose. 'You're a Brazilian little kid aren't you?'

Having scheduled another extra session of yoga therapy, Fiona walked through to the private room of Agi's studio and for the last time in a long time brought herself to say, 'Pete's dead,' before collapsing onto Agi's shoulder.

'Oh Fi,' said Agi and embraced her. 'Poses for that we have.'

When later Fiona had stopped sobbing she was instructed to lie on her front with her arms and legs out and her palms facing upwards.

'This the corpse pose is.'

'Wait, what?'

'Shhhh... avasana. Relax with attention, and a blanket we use to give the feeling of protection, as back up you open the body, and yourself, to the world.' Agi let fall an airline blanket over Fiona's body. 'Now, as you breathe, remember any and all emotions to let arrive.'

'Like a train?'

'Shhhh… avasana. Of kindness and of love breathe out words, first to yourself… Out breathe them.'

Fiona hissed five syllables of gibberish in order to move the routine on.

'Then to person whom you have lost.'

'To Pete?'

'Shhhh… avasana. My dog died last year, and these the words are that got me through—to hear them you would like?'

'Yes.'

'Shhhh…shit,' said Agi. 'Ow, I bit down too far.'

'Are you OK?'

'Shhhhh… avasana. Death is a natural part of life.'

'Death is a natural part of life,' said Fiona, repeating her instructor's intonation.

'Rejoice for those around you who transform into the life force.'

Fiona mumbled the long mantra into her mat.

'Mourn them do not. Miss them do not. And train yourself to let go of everything you fear to lose.'

'Train,' said Fiona, having forgotten the name of the pose in which she lay. For the first time since Pete's death she approached something like a state of relaxation. 'I like that. Mourn them do not.'

'Shhhh… avasana.'

At Dixon Hardware Geoff inspected his Burmese giant water bug, one of several enormous insects which he kept in jars of preserving fluid on the shelf behind his desk. His assistant, Margaret, whom he knew he was shortly to fire, had asked for yet another day off. As he always did Geoff was using the beetle to block out the rambling reasons which Margaret gave for her requests.

When he sensed that she had finished he put the specimen down and granted her wish and spun the jar so that the insect's back could be viewed completely. Then he asked Margaret whether she thought it was possible to buy a letter of the alphabet.

'What do you mean, like a foam F? Or an inflatable D?'

'No, no, an actual letter—who owns the alphabet?'

'Haven't got a clue. Does anyone own it?'

'The language is English isn't it? So… England? Or what about the dictionary, can you buy letters from the dictionary—who owns that?'

'The dictionary'd probably sell words wouldn't they?'

'Oh yeah. Well it's the Latin alphabet. Maybe a Latin country owns it? Brazil, or Mexico?'

'I can call an embassy?'

'No, don't bother them, I'll think of something. Hey have you ever thought about why an *m* isn't a *double-n*?'

'How do you mean?'

'Well two *n*'s are a double-u, right?'

'Right.'

'So an *m* is a double *n*.'

'So my… coffee mug would be a nnug?'

'Yes! And garden mulch—'

'Would be nnulch.'

'You'd be Nnargaret.'

'Nnadge at the club. Oo, and a garden gnome would be—'

'All right, that's enough. I do need to buy a *u* though. I'll figure it out. Righto, Nadge. I'm off on that date with Sybil Fawlty.'

In the late hours of that night Alexa in high heels walked past the closed entrance to Melbourne Zoo and knocked on the passenger-side window of the car to which Yuri had directed her. Within, two security guards were watching cartoon pornography on their phones.

'Right love,' said the greasier-haired one on the passenger side.

'I'm lost,' Alexa smiled, and waved to the greasy-haired one on the driver's. He leaned across and lowered his head and asked what she was looking for.

'Well now I don't know, I feel like I've found something here. Do they give you guys the keys to the place?'

'Of course, what if there's an intruder?'

'You have keys to the whole zoo?'

'Oh, we've got keys,' said the greasier-haired guard, and held up and jangled them. He slid them along their ring as he named each one. 'Butterfly house. Great Flight Abery. Bonobo forest.'

'Even to that big green gate there?' He spun the ring's largest key around and by it hung the rest as he grinned and bounced his head up and down. 'That's the biggest… key I've ever seen. Is it scary inside? Are all the animals making noises—the lions roaring?'

'Be scary for a young lady like you to go in all alone.'

'No, I'm not a-scared of the dark! Plus I have liquid courage, plenty of it.' Alexa took a plastic pint bottle from her handbag and leaned her elbows onto the window sill. She dangled the bottle inside the car and swung it from side to side. 'Anyone up for some… booze?'

'Did you say…?' began the greasier.

'Boobs?' finished the slightly less so.

'Booooze,' said Alexa.

'I'm hearing boobs. I know that's inappropriate, but it's what I'm hearing.'

'Booze,' said Alexa and unscrewed the bottle's cap.

When ten minutes later the 'men' were asleep Alexa opened the car door and took the keys and threw them to

The Ukrainian Ordinary

her brother.

Inside, Yuri threw one leg over a guard rope then jumped down into the dry garden above the three thick cables which fenced off the enclosure. He took a few fast bounds then turned in and jumped and landed with a thud onto packed dirt.

On the far side of its enclosure an elephant raised its head as it roused from sleeping. Yuri boomed, 'Yun khun, Tiruvasi!' and walked calmly towards the animal. It came onto its front knees then shuffled its front legs in as it rose to fully stand. Yuri planted his feet and put his fists at his hips and smiled in the moonlight—and nodded proudly as the animal lumbered towards him.

THE PETER FILE

III

With his fingers intertwined and his elbows on his desk—behind him a wooden Ukrainian clock and humiliating photographs of his commercial rivals and a picture of his Spetsnaz detachment, the survivors of which all went on to become steel magnates—Arsen held a knuckle to his lips and stared across his office to the wafting fins of his aquarium as Denys, his tea serf, poured a cup of mountain tea. Surrounded by flowers—even-numbered bouquets of sunflowers and wreaths of pink roses and countless potted fuchsias—sadness reddened and moistened his eyes, for today was the day of his eldest child's funeral.

He unclasped his fingers and lowered his hands to touch his cup on both sides as Denys bowed his head and backed away from his master. The door bells rang, though the office's sign was flipped to closed. Denys kept his gaze averted as he changed the direction of his shuffle and came round the desk and reversed towards the door. Shortly he pulled in by the leash a sheep.

'What is this?'

The animal was stunned to be in Arsen's office. The bell at its neck jangled as it planted its front hoofs and tensed its neck and bulged its eyes. 'It has a note, my lord,' said Denys in his whiney voice. He transferred the note from the sheep's collar to Arsen.

'*I told you I could afford a evve,*' said Arsen, reading. 'What in the devil is an evve? Denys, what is evve?'

'I know not, my lord.'

'Leave it. Leave me.' Denys dropped the leash and again lowered his head and walked backwards through the office's side entrance.

'Papa, why do you have a sheep?' said Alexa as she came

in from its front in a long black coat and with her braided hair in a thick halo.

'I do not know. Where is your brother?'

'He'll meet us there.'

The sheep was already neck-deep in popping fuchsias and silky sunflowers. 'We cannot leave it here.' Arsen watched it munch on roses the concentration of which no ungulate had ever dreamed. 'We take the truck.'

Mel walked into the vast mustiness of St Mary Star of the Sea and beheld between high white arches two crowds of people standing either side of a tiled aisle. 'What, no chairs?' He accompanied his sister and niece to the front row. 'Where are the chairs?'

'Where are the fuchsias?' Fiona asked, unable to see any in the technicolour apse as she moped through lingering incense smoke.

'No fuchsia.'

'You had one job, Mel.'

'No future. Why are there no chairs—how long's a Ukrainian funeral?'

Alexa's heels sounded at the church's entrance as she pulled her veil over her face. She unbuttoned her coat as she neared the altar and lowered it from her shoulders and in a strapless black cocktail dress took a place at Mel's side.

'Hello, Mel,' she said as she folded her coat over her arms. 'It's been a very long time.'

'Isn't that..?'

'What?'

'Isn't that dress a little inappropriate for a funeral?'

'I'm in heat, give me a break.' She turned and surveyed the faces behind her. When she caught the eyes of a group of three males with their fingers clasped she smiled and winked and squeezed her raised hand together in a wave.

'Where's your terrifying brother?'

'He's on his way.'

'Well stay standing next to me, would you? I want to be as far away from him as possible.'

Arsen's shoes came heavily down the aisle but soon were drowned out by the clacking of the sheep's hooves as it tried to get traction on the polished floor. By its leash Arsen pulled the animal around to the front row and hugged Fiona with one arm. 'Your face is raining. What is wrong?'

'I'm trying to hold it in, I'm sorry. Why do you have a sheep?'

'I could not leave it in office, it starts to eat Piter's flowers. Where are the fuchsias?'

'No fuchsia,' Mel announced as his own father arrived and shook Arsen's hand.

'Why you are wearing skirt to my son's funeral?'

'Why'd you bring the ewe here?'

'The what?

'I told you I could afford one.'

'Afford what?'

'A ewe,' said Geoff and pointed to it.

'You call me sheep? Not today, fucking hell. Not today, man in dress.'

'Mum, why is there a sheep here?'

'I have no idea, honey.'

'Take sheep,' said Arsen and handed its leash to Geoff, who passed it to Annie as he embraced his daughter. The animal leaned against Annie's hip and she struggled to stand still as Father Pyanenko ascended the ambon of white marble. He squirted himself in the mouth then rested his pistol on the front ledge of his podium and placed his palms on either side of it. Of the podium, not the pistol— no wait, actually it's both. Ahem. His amplified voice called the shuffling church to silent attention:

'Welcome all, to the memorial and funeral of Piter

Arsenovych Sukhimov. As per Piter's wishes we will have a combined Australian and Ukrainian service, beginning—as he wished—with a eulogy from his wife. Fiona?'

'Love you, Mum,' Annie whispered, and yanked at the sheep's leash as Fiona with a bowed head stepped forward.

'Love you too,' said Fiona then stepped through the marble altar rail. She put the two pages of her oration onto the brass lectern and cleared her throat as she beheld the hundreds of eyes from which she felt strangely estranged. Her sadness softened as she looked down to her daughter, to her brother, her father. Her numbness was warmed even by the sight of the Ukrainian family among whom Pete had always seemed a sane and comprehensible outlier.

'Thank you all for coming. Many of you will know that Pete and I, we met fifteen years ago in Crete, because of a very lucky mishap, that turned out to be the beginning of a beautiful sequence of happy-family-making coincidences. It turned out we lived only a few streets from each other— which we didn't find out until we looked each other up, after our day in a gorgeous gorge. When Pete volunteered for a year in Ukraine, he flew all the way home for one night, just to see me. And that was the night our Annie was conceived. We were *meant* to have our beautiful daughter, just as we were meant, to be together. Pete and I always knew that the world made sense if he and I were together, because it meant that the world had a 'meant to'. And without a 'meant to'…'

Hearing her words aloud she now felt them to be drained of truth. She read silently through the next sentence and found that it, and so her entire eulogy, had no connection to her new absence of feelings. She lifted her head and hesitated to speak—pushed the pages of her speech together then from their top folded it down over itself and pressed it closed. 'I…' Fiona now knew only what she no longer believed. 'We…' But what she no longer believed did not feel like a sentiment worth presenting at her Pete's funeral. 'The…' She remembered the only piece of advice which, among the past week's freeze-dried tidal wave of consolatory words, had alone given her solace.

'Death is a natural part of life.' She found that she was able to precisely recall Agi's sentiment. 'Rejoice for those around you who transform into the life force. Mourn them do not. Miss them do not.' The emotional necessity of its final line had been painful to concede. But in reaction to the absence of the feelings she expected to be having, she had hardened to its command. So she urged rather than advised it: 'And train yourself to let go of everything you fear to lose. Pete, I love you. Thank you everyone.'

Slow applause dripped from both sides of the standing crowd as Fiona left her speech on the lectern.

'That was beautiful, Mum,' Annie whispered as her mother returned to her side.

'Thanks, honey.'

'I didn't know you like Star Wars.'

'I hate Star Wars, honey, you know that.'

Father Pyanenko returned to the ambon as several flat-hatted deacons held thick candles and slung censers around him. He squirted his pistol into his open mouth before turning his heavy bible to its bookmarked place. 'Let us pray to the Lord, Lord have mercy.'

'Why'd you quote Yoda in your speech?'

'You know I see a yoga therapist, honey—you remember Agi.'

'Agi's a Yoda therapist?'

'Yo-*ga*, honey. With a g.'

'But that was Yoda.'

'Yes, Agi told it to me.'

'For you are the resurrection and the life and the repose of your servant, Piter, O Christ our God.'

'Sick Yoda quote,' Mel whispered.

The Ukrainian Ordinary

'Don't make fun, you know the yoga helps me.'

'And to you do we send up glory, with your eternal father…'

'Mum, the quotation you read out is from Yoda.'

'Yo-ga, honey. With the breathing and the stretching.'

'No, that's Yo-da. He tells it to Anakin.'

'What's an Anakin?'

'…and your all-holy, good and life-creating spirit, O Christ.'

Arsen and Alexa sang with everybody else: 'Amen,' and Fiona sensed that she was supposed to do likewise. 'Amen,' she caught up, then returned her ear to Annie as Mel held out his phone, already playing the scene to which Annie was referring. She watched the little green Jedi's mouth move with the video's captions.

'See, Yoda,' said Annie.

'Through the prayers of our holy fathers, Lord Jesus Christ, have mercy and save us.'

Mel leaned out and smiled: 'Much to learn you still have.'

'Goddam it. I'm firing my yoga therapist.'

The entire standing congregation now mumbled in low harmony all around her: 'Amen.'

Father Pyanenko gave a long trigger-squeeze into the back of his throat before continuing. 'We pray for the repose of the soul of the servant of God, Piter, departed from this life; and for the forgiveness of his every transgression, voluntary and involuntary.' The choir now joined the service, and took rather a long time to sing, 'Lord have mercy.' Fiona clasped her fingers and lowered her chin and, retreating from her surroundings, tried to make sense of her inability to deliver her tribute.

'To he who by his unutterable wisdom has fashioned man out of the dust, let us pray to the Lord.'

'Lord have mercy,' sang the choir and, habitually, Fiona—and as the final word in their refrain quietened there seemed to sound somewhere outside a brassy squeal.

'To Him who brought Piter into existence as a being fashioned according to your image and likeness, let us pray to the Lord.'

'Lord have mercy,' the choir sang, and the same noise squealed underneath the entreaty—this time as though possessing a heightened urgency and a greatly increased proximity.

'Make Piter to be now forgiven in this present world and in the world to come. Let us pray to the Lord,' Father Pyanenko said, and his suggestion was answered instantly by the clearest and loudest squeal yet as there appeared at the church's doors the trunk, then the head—then the very large body—of an elephant. The censers stopped jangling and the deacons watched the congregation turn to investigate so organic a sound. Fiona beheld the animal lumbering down the aisle with Yuri, wearing a gold-encrusted and feather-adorned cowboy-hat, smiling between its ears.

The separate crowds of mourners parted further than the girth of the interruption required as Yuri rose and fell with the elephant's gait. When it reached the altar rail Yuri yelled a long, 'Yaaaa,' and the elephant flicked its ears and stopped walking. 'Map luong!' Yuri shouted, and was rocked sideways as the elephant lowered one knee, then was brought to upright again as it lowered the other. He stood onto its head then leapt onto the floor—put his fists to his hips and proclaimed:

'As sign of respect to my brother, whom I have most dearly loved, I am bringing him tribute of one elephant, ancient mount of Indra Protector of the East.' He took one fist from his hips and shook his pointing finger at Father Pyanenko. 'Even though *he* says I cannot.'

'You,' said the priest. 'Ill-behaved heathen.' He waved his pistol in the air and shouted from memory a verse not traditionally included in any church's funeral liturgy: 'As Elisha was walking along the road some boys came out of the town and jeered at him: "Get out of here, bald man!" they said.'

Yuri took off his hat and shook his father's hand then kissed his sister then with a bow presented himself to Fiona.

'"Get out of here, bald man!"' the priest shouted. 'Before a bear came out of the forest and *ate* the bald man.'

Yuri turned to the altar and stepped back to stand beside Annie. He looked down at her and grinned then raised his eyebrows. Then he yelled, 'Bon!'

The sitting elephant raised its trunk and pointed its nostrils at Father Pyanenko, who resumed the service as his assistants stared across at the animal: 'So sprinkle me with hyssop and I shall be clean, wash me and I shall be whiter than snow.'

'Soong!' yelled Yuri, completing the command, and the elephant sprayed the holy contents of its trunk over Father Pyanenko.

As Peter's casket was lowered into his grave Yuri filed through the crowd and came to stand behind Mel. 'M word!' he said into his ear.

'Yuri,' Mel said nervously after turning and returning his head. 'That's very funny.'

'What have you said?'

'Do you people not believe in chairs?' Outdoors, Mel was standing again.

'The earth is the Lord's,' said Father Pyanenko in the wind, 'and the fullness thereof—the world, and all that dwell therein.'

'What news from Siam? You still are there one photographic priest?'

'I left that job two years ago.'

'You are dust, and to dust you will return.' Father

Pyanenko asked for the fuchsias that were to be strewn over the coffin. Fiona shook her lowered head and the priest repeated his question.

'No fuchsias,' Mel admitted loudly and publicly.

'Did someone say no fuchsias?' said Father Pyanenko.

'I have——. We have... no fuchsias.'

'All right then,' said Father Pyanenko. 'Present the sacrificial sheep!'

'What? Grandpa!' Father Pyanenko shot himself in the mouth then laughed his baritone laugh. 'He's kidding,' Geoff said to his granddaughter. 'I think.'

The funeral director ceased his crank-winding and disconnected the straps from the frame of his lowering device. When he had finished rolling them up he stepped back into the crowd and nodded at Arsen. Arsen yelled, 'Peach!' then looked at the faces of all who were gathered to lay his son to rest. 'Peach!' he yelled again, almost as a question. He soon concluded, as he suspected they might not be, that none had been brought. He pulled out the two that had been all morning in his jacket and walked uphill and handed them to the priest.

Father Pyanenko stared first at Arsen then at the fruit now in his hand. Shortly he bit into one and washed it down with holy water. Turning to stand beside him, Arsen addressed the audience. 'Now we have had peaches, I know at Australian funeral it is customary to make toast. So on table behind you, you have toasters with enough of bread for everyone. Please wash your hands after throwing dirt, before making toast.'

As the crowd slowly rearranged itself into a kind of procession, and as they filed along with each a handful of soil to contribute to Peter's burial, a separate and smaller queue seemed to form in front of Mel. He looked from side to side to see if one was forming before anybody else. Then he leaned over to take in its growing length as one

The Ukrainian Ordinary

Ukrainian after another took up his hand and looked him in the eyes and said something unintelligible. With his hands behind his back Yuri came to Mel's side. An old lady whose moustache Mel thought he recognised as belonging to one of Peter's aunts now handed him an envelope then pressed his hands together and smiled. She repeated what Mel thought was the same phrase, then left the envelope with him as she went to make toast.

'What are they saying?' Mel whispered to Yuri.

'Kontrabandyst zbroyi.'

'And what the hell does that mean?'

'They are calling you smuggler of gun.'

'Gun? Ohhh,' said Mel, the queue somewhat making sense to him. A man sporting a buzz cut and a leather jacket shook his hand then passed him an unsealed envelope.

'Kontrabandyst zbroyi.'

'What is this, cash?' said Mel as he bent the packet.

Yuri listened to the wider mumblings in his mother-tongue then summarised: 'They have been seeing you in newspaper.'

Mel smiled as an old man kissed the back of his hand. 'I didn't smuggle guns, Yuri.'

Yuri grinned. 'And I am never selling tank to terrorist. It is one good thing to show to smuggler of gun that you are respecting him. Unless smuggler of gun is you.'

'I didn't smuggle guns, Yuri. I smuggled gum.'

'Mm,' Yuri nodded.

'You're not hearing me. I smuggled gum.'

'Yes, this is what they are thinking.'

'Yuri, not guns. Gum-m. Chewing gum.'

'You are smuggling chewing gum?'

'Accidentally.'

'You are one idiot.'

'You're an idiot.'

'What you have called me?'

'Nothing. Sorry.'

'Why you are smuggling gum? You can buy in shop.'

When his own queue had dispersed, Mel was followed by Yuri down to the trestle tables laden with peaches and toasters and loaves of sliced bread. 'Why's your dad making everyone make toast?'

'This is Australian burial custom, is it not?'

'It is not. Your brother's gonna get a yeast infection in there.'

With no condiments to moisten anyone's bread the Australians present had reasoned that the toast was some kind of ancient Ukrainian bread-offering. The Ukrainians had reasoned that it was yet another bland Australian tradition. But when eventually their toast popped up each mourner returned to Peter' grave to frisbee their bread onto the dust. Annie stood at the end of the table closest to the elephant—now tethered by a chain to a tree—and held the sheep's leash under her foot as she hurried to feed it as much toast as one of the appliances could supply. Mel took the last crust from a plastic bread bag and stuffed into it the several envelopes that he couldn't fit into his pockets.

'This is not your money.'

'They gave it to me.'

'But you are not smuggling gun, M word.'

'Yes, M word, you're very funny.'

Yuri's jaw clenched, firmly and visibly. 'What you have called me?'

'What?'

'You should not be calling me funny.'

'Funny looking. Funny sounding. Funny smelling.'

'Give to me that bag.' Yuri reached for Mel's outstretched hand and caught the end of the bread bag.

'It's mine.'

'Return to them their money, you did not smuggle gun.'

The Ukrainian Ordinary

'I got whipped in the arse for this money, thank you.'
'Give to me.'
The bag was surprisingly Brazilian as they yanked it back and forth.
'These communist idiots are the ones that can't read, it's mine!'
'Give to me pretending money from gum or I will be cartooning you!'
As again Mel had the bread bag pulled from his chest, then laboured to remove it from Yuri's, its bottom tore open and its contents flew and fluttered across the cemetery. Several of its envelopes hit the ewe in the head. The sheep's leash slid out from under Annie's foot as the animal bolted. The elephant turned a concerned glance towards it then spooked as the sheep ran under its legs and sprinted from trunk to knee to trunk. It sounded a frightened trumpet-call and reared and its chain clinked to taut. The elephant's impending break-out panicked even those guests whose toast was almost done. With a dry and open mouth, Father Pyanenko found that his pistol ran out of holy water as all fled from Peter's graveside.

While Yuri calmed the elephant and attempts were made to recapture the sheep, Fiona descended the cemetery's slope and approached its quiet road. When Father Pyanenko passed out and was driven away only Arsen's ute and her father's convertible Mercedes now remained. Feeling still a bulging emptiness in her stomach she sat on a bench and stared across the lawn at distant walls of plaque and barren fields of headstone. She slumped and slouched and the corners of her mouth again drew out and down. Her tongue pressed against the inside of her teeth as she held back a fit of tears. Dejected breath from her nose seemed to deflate her until her head drooped. She groaned and closed her eyes and shook her head and moved her fingertips to her forehead. Then something was dropped in her lap.

She looked up and saw that the car from which it had been dropped was already driving away. She looked to her right for anything or anyone who might be watching what had just happened, then ahead for the same. Finding no one she darted her head back to her lap and found that a manila folder was now in her possession. She flipped it over and saw on its front a familiar logo: a blue circle over a pointed star upon a wreath, all topped with a red crown. She lifted its front cover and saw there her husband's face—a passport photograph was paperclipped to a document which upon momentary inspection was some kind of record. It listed the date and place of Pete's birth, his height and eye colour, his occupation, her own and Annie's names.

When she reached its bottom she found underneath only one other, almost blank, sheet of paper. Again she looked up and peered across the cemetery; scanned the direction in which the car had sped then searched over both shoulders for anyone who might be watching her. Finding no thing or person out of the Ukrainian ordinary, she took up the document from its folder and brought it closer to her eyes. She peeled up the first page then folded it back and read through on its second—sparse and fragmentary—three very peculiar phrases.

IN THE NEXT PETER FILE...

...Mel returns to Southland to apologise to Even Stephen the florist, and ends up staring uncomprehendingly into his future:

'Thanks again, Stephen. And I am sorry, really.'

As he walked out of the shop holding a conciliatory

fuchsia, Mel found that while he had been explaining their argument the silver-painted busker had again set himself up on his invisible chair. Mel tilted his head sideways then drew it back up as he mentally traced what *had* to be under the man's glove, his sleeve, his coat. He leaned his head to the other side and laboured to discern an outline of a frame in the drapes of the chair man's silver suit. The busker recognised Mel and shooed him away with a flick of his Pinocchio nose.

And Mel, his fuchsia in both hands, stared on.

…Geoff manages to buy Arsen a *u* that he more fully comprehends:

Arsen came naked from the banya into his office and as he raised his felt-hatted head was startled by a cardboard cut-out of himself. 'What is *this* now?' Newly positioned beside his desk, he stepped over arrangements of roseless bush and mangled sunflower to approach the thing. He inspected its waving arm and recognised the uniform of his own business and, standing face to cardboard-face with it, found that it was life-sized.

'This is me? Why this is me?'

He leaned around to inspect its rear and found scrawled on the back of his head a single word: 'You!'

…Alexa returns with a friend to the zoo's car park and, deciding that after a harrowing week she needed her mounting tension relieved, knocks again on the window of the car in which two security guards were watching cartoon pornography:

'So what do you two say?'

'You again,' said the greasier as he wound down his window.

'Would you like some… boobs?'

'Did you say…' he began.

'Booze?' finished the greasy, winding down his window to leer at Alexa's friend.

'Boooobs,' Alexa repeated.

'I'm hearing booze.'

'Boobs!' said Alexa.

'I know that's inappropriate, 'cos we're on duty, but I am hearing "booze".'

…as Yuri says goodbye to the elephant:

Standing upon packed dirt in the moonlight he passed a length of sugar-cane to its mouth and rubbed his hand against the bristles above its trunk. 'I have not either lightness nor darkness in my heart, Tiruvasi, for Siva dances always.'

Tiruvasi transferred lightly from one front foot to the other and twitched her ears as she trunked from Yuri's palm his last length of sugar cane.

'Siva is dancing, Tiruvasi, but who, who, *who*—have killed my brother? I will be finding out.'

Episode 2

THE CHAIЯ MAN

I

With varying degrees of reluctance Fiona's family were sitting silently in Arsen's kitchen over glistening bowls of borshch.

Annie leaned down to finish the last of her first helping as her grandfather placed before her a welcome second. Fiona herself stared out to the garden and had not yet picked up her spoon. Mel looked into his bowl and whispered from the side of his mouth to his father, who was ladling suspiciously through his own:

'This isn't soup, it's just things floating in water.' With the back of his spoon Mel pushed his floating things around their water. 'All parts and no whole. Story of my life. And I was supposed to have such an interesting story too.'

'Mm,' said Geoff. Having managed to obtain at his son-in-law's funeral neither peach nor toast he was interested only in soon eating something that wasn't suspended in purple liquid.

'Supposed to go off and find my *thing*. You know what I figured out on my way home? … Dad? … Dad?'

'What?'

'Know what I figured out on my way home?'

'What?'

'I'm an adventurer without an adventure.'

'Are you now?'

'An adventurer without an adventure.'

For in five years of searching for his thing Mel had tried just about every adventure that Southeast Asia still had to offer. Flying on from Kuala Lumpur to Penang he there took up residence in a green-shuttered Straits Eclectic and on its top floor taught English to Chinese Malays:

'So we can't say that a subject is *overcome* by an object, unless that object changes the state or action of the subject. Does that make sense?' Mel looked down to Lim Soong, his most fluent student, in the hope of receiving a nod of comprehension. But Lim Soong looked unwell. Halfway through the semester he and some of the other boys had taken to trying to out-spice one another at the Indian restaurant across from the school-house. Cross-legged among his classmates, he and Khoo Chiow, his chief rival in both academic achievement and consumption of curried heat, had less than an hour ago shared a madras containing four chillies' worth of spice. Lim Soong squinted and gripped at his stomach and looked to Khoo Chiow, who was grinning triumphantly.

'Who can tell me if in this sentence the subject *was* overcome by the object, in this case an emotion? Lim?'

But Lim Soong threw up a thick gush of almost-glowing red onto the shin of Mel's linens, the regurgitated curry burning his toes as it spread through the basin formed by the upturned edge of his chappals…

In Laos Mel used the savings from the International School to buy a decent camera after deciding it would be a pretty noble thing to document before they disappeared the traditional ways of life of that country's hill tribes:

Strolling one day through a Khmu village he saw ahead, among featherless chickens and naked children, that most photogenic—and profitable—of subjects: a wood-foraging woman in traditional dress with a woven basket hanging from a strap across her forehead.

He smiled and greeted her in Laotian as she came up the path. She looked up and with deranged eyes smiled back. Her exposed teeth redoubled Mel's desire to capture her:

with gums receding almost to her jawbone her lips too were purple, and Mel saw that she was, at that very moment, chewing the leaf which perpetually dazed her. He put his camera to his face and said, 'Is this OK?' and nodded. She smiled on, unaware of most of what happened between her day's six naps; seemingly she had given consent. He leaned back and clicked away as the woman leaned forward to spit. Mel refocused as she reached into the folds of her clothes and pulled out a dirty Coke bottle of rice wine. She swigged from it, spat, swigged again. But then her lips slammed shut and blew out like a trumpet player's. As Mel side-stepped around the wrinkles of her forehead the woman could hold her lips no more—and ejected a large wad of highly bankable purple onto the crotch of Mel's elephant trousers...

While in Thailand he stuck it out for two years as an imitation priest, officiating at technically Buddhist but outwardly Christian weddings:

As a three-woman choir sang, 'Ave Malia,' he stood beneath a Styrofoam arch in the white-lit shop which his employer rented between a nail salon and a plant nursery and recited his own liturgy. 'May you feel no rain from the uncle bear god in the sky, for each of you will be shelter for the other.'

The only part of the job requiring any real application was the correct pronunciation of the couple's names. Standing before their extended families it was ruinously inauspicious for a couple's fake priest to fudge their names at the unofficial ceremony that had nothing to do with either's religion. So he had, he thought, mastered most of the silent syllables and high-sung endings of Thai surnames, and after the first six months stopped preparing for his daily adventures. From beneath his robe he now held out a palm to the groom and said, 'So do you, Thaporn Khrohamyangrai, take Donut Gkanpachun...' He broke off.

His manager had forgotten to transliterate the names as Mel preferred—an 'f' for soft 'ph's and double 'p's for hard ones. Was it Gkanpachunfai or Gkanpachunppai? His instincts told him the latter, for he rarely came across f's in surnames. He looked again at the name then smiled up at the bride, who also appeared to be struggling. The gaudiness of her wedding dress had been partly a matter of taste, partly a matter of concealing a bulging stomach, as under no circumstances could her dozen aunties know that she was pregnant. She sweated and forced a grin as she contracted her height in pain.

'Take Donut Gkanpachunpai,' Mel announced, deeming the 80-20 chance worth taking. There was no commotion; he had chosen correctly. '…to be your lawfully wedded wife?'

'I do.'

'And do you, Donut Gkanpachunpai—are you all right?'

And the very-soon-to-be Donut Khrohamyangrai threw up milky white fluid directly onto Mel's magenta cummerbund…

His final adventure—that which he had quit before deciding to return home—was as a bagpiping faux-Highlander in Singapore:

Playing jigs and reels at the weddings and receptions of nostalgic functionaries, Mel stood between palm trees and with sweat-soaked fingers blew through *The Drunken Piper*.

He had long been nearing his capacity for tropical humiliation. It seemed now that at every wedding a table of uncles plied itself with scotch before staggering over to mock him. Some reached in to lift his kilt, a family heirloom that he had found vital to his interview process. Some slapped him in the sporran or waved their hands in front of his face as though he were a beefeater. Some poured whisky into his drones to see if it affected the sound. And if one more person threw—.

Then somebody's laughing and drunken uncle did, in curaçao blue all over Mel's family tartan of white cloth sparsely checked with grey...

'I was supposed to be James Blonde,' said Mel, staring into the lumps and chunks of his steaming Ukrainian purple. 'Now I'm an adventurer without an adventure.'

'Too bad, ay?'

'Dad.'

'I'll tell you what,' said Geoff. 'If you agree to stay home for a few years, I'll make you the chairman at the hardware store.'

'Chairman? Really?'

'What's family for?'

'That's nice of you! Thanks, Dad. And I'll stay, I'm not going back to Asia.'

'Monday morning, 8am.'

'Chairman,' Mel said softly to himself. 'I'm going to do you proud, Dad.'

'Y'all right there, kid?' said Geoff to his granddaughter, fallen back in her chair and clutching her distended belly.

'Mm,' Annie moaned ambiguously.

'Too much purple?'

'Mm,' she nodded.

'Do you—' And Annie sent a shower of chunks suspended in purple mush onto the chest of Mel's white shirt.

II

'You're sad that Dad doesn't get to see your first day?'

Annie stared out the car window and nodded.

'At least you get to have your favourite sandwich for lunch.'

Annie stared out the car window and nodded.

'Fish fingers! Remember how much Dad hated them?'

Annie stared out the car window and nodded.

'Why *did* he hate fish so much?'

Annie shrugged.

'Oh, honey.'

'Are people going to make fun of me?'

'Make fun of you? Why would you think that?'

'Uncle Mel said everyone makes up mean nicknames for you.'

'Oh don't listen to him. Your uncle was called Smell long before high school, trust me. He used to dry worms in the sun then see how long they'd stick to his body. You're going to love it, Annie. You'll meet so many interesting kids, you'll make so many new friends. I know it's tough to start something new without your dad, but…'

Fiona had not yet reconciled herself to the truth that life had to go on.

'The heart's Brazilian?' said Annie, helping her along.

'What's that?'

'Something else Uncle Mel said. The heart's Brazilian.'

'He means resilient but he's right. And you're the most Brazilian kid I know. Now, you all set?'

Annie tapped the backpack in her lap. 'Yep.'

Fiona put a hand behind her daughter's head and lowered her gaze. 'I love you.'

'I love you too.'

Annie took a deep breath in then pulled back the door handle and pushed out the door and quickly disappeared behind bushes and iron bars. Fiona let out the breath that she had held since Annie's inhalation then looked to the back seat. The file that was handed to her after Pete's funeral had fallen into the footwell. She stared down at it for a time then turned her body in her seat and reached for it and almost had a hand on it when a knock sounded on the passenger-side window. Fiona recognised her friend and fellow mother-of-a-12-year-old, Pinal Connelly. She smiled and waved and lowered the window.

'Hi Fiona, how are you?'

'I'm good. You just dropping Inika off?'

'Yes, just dropped her off. It's so exciting to see them grow up.'

'A bit sad, but…'

'Why don't you come round for some morning tea?'

Annie sat beside a girl who had introduced herself as Floyd after seemingly everyone in the classroom paired off with kids whom they appeared to already know. So the two new acquaintances awaited—in the classroom familiar to them from orientation day—the arrival of Ms Conrad, whom they had also met on that morning of prefatory newness.

Shortly in walked their teacher, and with a water bottle and a textbook in hand Ms Conrad wended through the double tables to her desk at the front of the room.

'Good morning all! Welcome to Year 7. If you don't remember, I am Ms Conrad, your homeroom teacher for the year. I hope you're all as excited as I am? Because high school brings you into the next stage of your development as assertive, mindful, radical allies. We're *all* here to help one another, to discover our authentic identities, and to use them as best we can to facilitate change. And in order to best be ourselves this year, we'll need iPads.' Ecstatic, she reached into the large box that already was on her desk and stacked thin packages onto one hand and continued her introduction as she handed them out. 'These are courtesy of the department of education—don't open them just yet—and each one shoots in 4k at 60 frames per second. I'll tell you more about the year's first big project next week, but make sure you look after these as you would your own minds—*don't* open them just yet, thank you. And now that we all have one, the first thing we're going to do is introduce ourselves.' Ms Conrad moved the empty box to the floor and pointed to the back corner of the room. 'Would you like to tell everyone your name?'

'Me?' said the young boy seated furthest from both his teacher and the classroom door.

'Please.'

'Wigbert Boychoir,' he said, turning his raised his hand into a wave as he looked around the room.

'Welcome, Wigbert.' Ms Conrad pointed to the boy beside him. 'And you?'

'Micky le Dongringer,' said the boy, and held up one of his thumbs.

'Moonlight Wang,' said the girl on the next table over. And, 'Sophat Urinporn,' said the girl with whom Moonlight had come from the same primary school.

So it was just as her Uncle Mel had told her. The whole system was rigged to get everyone's names out in the open and these poor kids, the year's first victims, had fallen for it straight away. The introductions gained speed as they leapt from one double table to the next:

'Ahmed Baboun,' said the first boy on the third table in the back row—his admission followed by, 'Darth Dumpleton.'

'Mai Phat Phun,' said Mai Phat Phun.

'Boobesh Rapeelam.'

'Are these names for real?' Annie mumbled under her

breath to Floyd.

'Celery Flintstone!' announced the girl in front of Annie.

'Hi everyone, I'm Jayne-Jane Slutszky.'

'These *can't* be real names,' said Annie and leaned over to Floyd, whose time had now come.

She put her elbow on the table and rotated her palm in order to wave as she too looked around the room and gave her full name: 'Pinkish Floyd.'

And then it was Annie's turn. She nodded and felt that even if her Uncle Mel were right, and these children would soon be wishing her dead—her name couldn't possibly be on a list of prime mockery targets here.

'Annie Sukhimov,' she said with a soft k and a long i.

'Well that's an interesting surname!' The sound of her teacher's voice made Annie's heart sink—on hers alone did Ms Conrad pounce?! 'Where's it from?'

'My dad was—. Is… My dad's family's Ukrainian.'

And so it was. Three years after emigrating from Pripyat her grandfather set up a crane-rental company named, he thought rudimentarily, U-Crane. Operating successfully for 25 years, Arsen—after thriving in a new country—wanted now to retire and thought his best chance of doing so was his daughter. In her mid-thirties and wanting increasingly to be free from both the proletarian stigma of working with cranes and the commanding influence of her family—in fact wanting to somehow, anyhow, go into business for herself—Alexa was anxiously disinterested in moving from U-Crane's only customer relations assistant to its chief customer relations officer.

'It's the same job, Papa!' The argument had resurfaced in the banya, out of which Arsen now followed her. 'Why can't Yuri take over?'

'It is foolish to pass your burdens to your son,' said Arsen, wearing nothing but a felt halt. 'But to your daughter is not so a problem. You are not happy with promotion?'

The bells over U-Crane's front door interrupted their script. Arsen growled and took his robe from its hook and went through to see who it was. 'What? What!?'

'Ya sent me a crane without a driver,' said a customer with beady eyes and sunburnt lips.

'Yes?'

'What use to me is a crane without a driver?'

'Sir, what is the name of my company?'

'U-Crane.'

'Yes,' Arsen grinned. '*Not* Me-Crane. Not She-Crane.' Arsen pointed to Geoff's cut-out of himself, frozen midwave at the end of his desk: 'Not *He*-Crane. U-Crane. You hire crane, you operate crane.'

'I can't operate a crane, mate—that's why I hired you.'

'You hired me for having crane. You want somebody to drive, here. List of operators in Melbourne.' Arsen offered him a single piece of paper. 'I-Crane, Novocrane, Frasier Crane.'

'I've hired from We-Crane before,' said the customer. 'They gave us an operator.'

'We-Crane? *We*-Crane! Sons of unclean transactions. Sir, look at picture behind me.'

Arsen pointed his thumb in the direction of the largest of the photographs on the wall between his steel shelves. It was of Anastas Migranyan, the Georgian who was his chief rival in Melbourne's crane-renting industry. The image showed Migranyan outside the embarrassingly modest home into which he had recently had to move from a far more immodest one. With a taped box in hand Anastas was captured surprised, ashamed, and grieving at the appearance of a camera-wielding Arsen. 'This means how poor is boss of We-Crane. You want to hire him, you get worse crane in all Australia.' Arsen flapped the piece of paper that still was in his outstretched hand: 'Novacrane is lazy, Frasier Crane is strange. If you want great operator, good operator—and best price—call I-Crane.'

'I-Crane?' said the customer, taking the sheet from Arsen's outstretched hand.

'I-Crane.'

Believing that it enabled him to better communicate with the dead, Yuri was asleep in the morning sun on the freshly transplanted grass of his brother's grave.

Shortly after sleep had overtaken him he stood by and watched as Piter rode a tank down the street. His brother, dressed as a priest, was trying to save Anastasia from a giant Mexican walking fish, and as his she-nephew ran ahead of the lumbering axolotl journalists ran out from their houses. From all over the tank's body camera bulbs flashed in order to blind them before they could get to her. Soon their number was too great and the flash bulbs couldn't keep up, so Piter ordered the tank's milk cannon to fire. When it had sent several journalists sliding into the gutter its pressure began to drop. Piter turned to the crate of baby bottles behind him and with them refilled the cannon's reserve. The milk recommenced firing as Fiona, beneath her husband in the body of the tank, refilled the bottles from her own breast. She passed them up to Piter as quickly as she could milk, but as Yuri found himself standing atop a Ferris wheel the cannon's pressure became entirely insufficient for keeping the sprinting journalists at bay. Yuri yelled to his brother that he needed horses; Piter couldn't hear his high and distant voice. So Yuri climbed down the Ferris wheel but then was at the docks amid rows of stacked shipping containers. He turned to see the height from which he had climbed and found that the wheel had turned into the fiery enclosure of Shiva Nataraja. Turned again, Yuri ran in the direction of his pursued she-nephew and milkless brother. He pulled out the pistol which he often kept in the back of his trousers but as he brought it forward it turned into a garfish and fell from his hand. It flopped towards then into an open shipping container—emblazoned with the Cyrillic of his father's name and filled with oranges. Yuri knelt and rummaged at the base of a mound of round fruit and soon he heard the unmistakable growl of a bear. He leaned back and looked left and heard the same growl coming also from his right. He dug his arms deeper into the oranges that were rolling out around him. As he hurried to retrieve his gun every orb into which he pressed collapsed into its own juice. When shortly he located the weapon he put his fingers around its butt but struggled to pull it out, for the bottom of the container was magnetic. At last he yanked the weapon free then stood and turned and found that he was in front of his brother—on a quiet bridge in a white-flowered park whose green lawns and pink river were coloured as though with wet chalk. Everyone around him wore black suits and carried a lace parasol; his own and Piter's were three-tiered. As they began to stroll Yuri asked his brother where Anastasia was. Piter returned no answer as they descended the bridge. In the distance Yuri heard a faint digital melody and sensed that he and his brother were walking towards the military parade from which it was sounding. Piter said, 'Tato yie,' as the pace of their stroll was hampered by the stickiness of overheated asphalt underfoot. Looking around at the white petals of frangipani trees Yuri turned to watch a water dragon slither into the pink river. He was in Siam, and the distraction meant that he missed the suited passer-by who lowered his parasol and jabbed it into his brother's side. Yuri turned to find Piter's face dripping with Bangkok sweat. He watched the assassin run up over the bridge and away as the digital melody loudened. 'Piter, shcho stalosya?' Piter pulled down the runner of his parasol and lowered its tiers and looked calmly into Yuri's eyes. He began to hum the melody which a baritone choir had taken up and whose low frequency began to shake the white petals from the trees. Then Yuri woke up.

He blinked and squinted as he rolled his head. He clapped his tongue against the roof his mouth and stood and found that several families were staring at him, distracted from the placing of flowers and the stroking of headstones by the sight of a man rousing and rising from sleep in a graveyard.

Yuri answered the vibrating phone whose ringtone had brought him out. 'What?'

'Is this I-Crane?' said the customer standing at Arsen's cardboard cut-out.

'This is I-Crane, how can I be of great and goodly service?'

Pinal Connelly poured a cup of masala chai for Fiona, seated uneasily on the couch which looked across the living room to a large photograph of Pinal and her husband.

'It only hurts so much because we were meant to be together.'

'And what makes you say that?' Pinal took her own full cup from its tray and sat in an armchair.

'Our whole... everything, was coincidences. Pete and I met because a Greek waiter accidentally sat us together. When we got home we found out we lived three blocks away from each other. We both grew up without a mum. And Annie was conceived the night Pete flew back, from Ukraine, just to spend one night with me. The world made sense when we were together—it made sense *because* we were together.'

'Fiona, we need to address the elephant in the room.'

'I'm sentimentalising? And need to start moving on?'

'No, Ganesh.'

Both women looked to the yellow-trousered green-haloed icon of Ganesh, enthroned upon a teak table by the window—for Pinal had taken her husband's surname thirty years after leaving her native northwest India.

'We should not grieve for what is unavoidable.'

'Is this from Star Wars?'

'No,' urged Pinal. 'It's very old.' She put her hand to her chest. 'Ganesh puts us in touch with both the past and the future, because there was *never* a time when I did not exist, nor when you did not exist.'

'This sounds like Yoda. Is it Yoda?'

'It's Krishna.'

'The green one?'

'The blue one. And as there was not a time in which Peter did not exist, there also is no future in which he shall cease to be.'

'So Krishna says… Pete still exists?'

'All of Hinduism says it. And it's the oldest religion in the world.'

'So Pete's just… elsewhere?'

'Holy cow.'

'I know, I'm sorry—it sounds silly. I've been having some pretty crazy thoughts lately.'

'Nandi!' Pinal pointed to the other end of the room, where beside the doorway lay a Nandi in dark bronze, gazing serenely up at a photograph of Pinal's family. 'Nandi shows that you can respect and adore what you love, simply by waiting, and by watching.'

'Watching what?'

'As the dweller in the body passes through childhood into youth, and from maturity to old age—so at death we pass into another kind of body.'

'Are you talking about reincarnation?'

'A monkey's uncle!'

'Which one is that?' Fiona searched the room for an icon

The Chair Man

resembling a primate.

'I burnt myself on the bloody tea,' said Pinal and blew on her fingertips.

'So there never was a time in which Peter did not exist?' said Fiona, trying to make sense of the statement's implications. 'And there never will be a time when he... won't exist?'

'I hope the kids are OK at school,' said Pinal, putting a hand on Fiona's knee. 'Do you think they're OK?'

Annie's first activity on the first day of her first year of high school had been to write out her year's, her youth's, her life's aspirations—then to stick them under her photograph on the wall among the parade of portraits which Ms Conrad had placed at waist height around the room.

Pinkish Floyd returned to her seat as their teacher now moved onto their year's second activity. She stood at the whiteboard and wrote out in red marker and capitals, 'THE MODERN ALLY.' Then she pointed at Kibble Cooch-Hunt and called out his name.

'Yes, Ms Conrad?'
'Guilty.'
'Of what?'
'Clea Torres?'
'Yes, Ms Conrad?'
'Guilty.'
'I am?'
'Blanche Yuraiholl?'
'Yes?'
'Guilty!'
'Of what?'
'Through centuries of cistemic racism, discrimination, and economic exploitation your families have all committed crimes the nature of which now require generations of

reproach, repentance, and reparation.'

'Huh?' said Blanche Yuraiholl. 'Mine?'

'Annie Sukhimov?'

Gripped with shy hesitation, slowly Annie said, 'Yes?'

'Guilty!'

'I am?'

'You are. We all are. And internmelising the three Rs is the very first step towards a more just, a more equitable and a more inclusive Australia.'

'Wait, what am I guilty of?'

'Centuries of oppression, exploitation, and trans-exclusionary logocentrism.'

'Huh?'

'You, your family—all our families—murdered, raped, and stole, to get this country from its traditional owners.'

'My mum's family grew the first oranges in Victoria, is that what you're talking about? And my grandpa helps to build the country every day, he owns a—'

'Annie, you *can't* say that.' Ms Conrad had almost scowled. 'This country was built by genocide and slavery and we've inherited that legacy. Saying your grandfather helped to build this country disminishes the supordinate role forced upon margarinised communities.'

'Wait,' said Annie, her shyness lifting as she thought through the assumptions of what she was being told. 'So we have to… be guilty of what you say our families did, but I can't say what my family's actually doing?'

'Thank you, Annie, for bringing us back to the three Rs: Reproach,' said Ms Conrad and tapped the ends of her first fingers together. 'Repentance,' she said, and tapped at her middle finger. 'Reparation,' and Ms Conrad held up her blossoming fist to the class.

'But my family *are* helping to build the country.'

'Annie, you can't say that.'

'But they are, both sides.'

'Annie Sukhimov, do not talk back to me!'

'But Ms Conrad!'

'Sit down, child!'

'My grandpa owns a hardware store!' Annie shouted to her teacher's pulsating eyes. And so he did…

Mel whistled *I Whistle a Happy Tune* as he looked up to admire his own surname stencilled in huge white letters against a warehouse-front of blue corrugated iron. It was through the 'Hardware' beside that surname that Annie's grandfather was helping to build the country—by supplying the tools and materials with which Australians tame and shape the land and build upon it their dwelling places.

Mel straightened the knot in his tie and wriggled his ugly neck and swung his briefcase forward as he bounded, whistling still, towards and through the entrance to Dixon Hardware—Geoff's third attempt at business. His first had been in sporting goods, a venture which initiated Geoff's fondness for attaching his name to his own companies…

Standing on the street outside his newly opened store, its name stencilled in yellow against black-painted brick—the O in 'Dixon' a red football—Geoff stood among the foot traffic that he thought was his most valuable stream of potential custom:

'Dixon Balls!' he bellowed as he spun a football on each palm. 'All your Dixon balls, right in here! You there? Take a look! Dixon Balls *are* the best, and ours *are* the cheapest. Come inside, take a look—at aaalllll our Dixon Balls!'

Forced to spend her entire Saturday with her father, Fiona in a Jewel t-shirt—braces on her teeth and beads in her hair—called out, 'Dad, you can't hear what you're saying.'

'Come in and try Dixon Balls!' Geoff yelled at a woman with a perm, a lycra one-piece and child-in-a-football-jumper betraying her ripeness for partaking in a sale.

'Today's special, Madame, an extra pair of Dixon Balls *free*, when you grab any other two Dixon Balls. Any balls you like, Madame, grab 'em while they're cheap. It is *madness* in here, with more Dixon Balls than anyone could possibly bounce or squeeze!'

His athletic venture was followed by a foray into pet care, after Geoff took over then rebranded a cattery for what he thought was a steal.

'Dixon Pussies!' he yelled, standing on the street beside a towering inflatable cat. 'Your kitten left satisfied and smiling here, by Dixon Pussies!'

Forced to spend her Sunday morning with her father, Fiona with short bleach-blonde pigtails—wearing a choker chain and a skirt rolled up at the waist—called out, 'Dad, you really have to be hearing that!'

'Sir, what will you do with your cat on *your* next family vacation?'

'We get the neighbours to feed it.'

'Why not try Dixon Pussies!? For your next family vacation, Sir—your cat will find only the softest and the warmest home-away-from-home in Dixon Pussies!'

'At, Dad! Say *at*—not *in*.'

Eventually Geoff took his daughter's advice and stopped spruiking outside his store, and after a few slow years Dixon Hardware now teemed with customers from Monday to Sunday and from early morning until early evening.

Mel in his suit and tie was overcome with nostalgia as he approached the customer service desk. Actually let's not say 'overcome'—he didn't faint, or even stop walking, which would have been him being overcome by it. Let's say he was nudged a little by it. Mel in his suit and tie was nudged a little by nostalgia—there we are—as he approached the customer service desk. In his late teens he had regularly terrorised the back offices after school while waiting for his dad to finish work and had spent the

The Chair Man

summer before university working in the store's loading dock. Unfazed by nostalgia's nudge, Mel waited his turn at the front desk and when shortly he was greeted he asked the employee if he was a manager. He pointed to his name tag and said that he was. 'Oh good,' Mel said, 'I'm the new chairman.'

'Oh cool! Come with me.'

The day's customer service manager left the low enclosure to which he was casually confined and walked Mel past the check-outs and the paint desk and a towering aisle of ladders. Eventually he turned down one of the more distant aisles and stopped and turned around halfway down it.

'Here we are.'

'Where we are?'

'Aisle 27. It's all yours.'

'And where's my office?' said Mel, looking around for his final administrative destination.

'This is it, brah. You're the new chair man, right?'

'Right. So... isn't my office in the back? Upstairs?' Mel pointed to the rear of the store, and the maze of rooms and toilets in which he had passed so many after-school hours.

'Dude, most people have to work here for weeks before they're put in charge of chairs.'

'I don't understand.'

'What's to understand? You're the new chair man, this is aisle 27. Chairs.' Mel looked at the stackable plastic seating which crowded the bay beside him then surveyed the length of the aisle. It passed from rows of folding seats to stacks of flat banana lounges to bags of folded camping chair. He was overcome—actually this time—with disbelief. For both sides of the entire aisle of blue and yellow scaffolding, and two tiers above the floor of ready inventory were filled with—.

'I don't think you understand. I'm the new chairman.'

'I understand that perfectly.'

'Can I—is my dad here?'

'I don't know, is he? Have you lost your mummy too? Did you escape from your pram? What's in the briefcase, a guide to selling chairs?' The young manager, whom Mel was beginning to dislike, stepped to a high-backed outdoor chair and pointed: 'Legs, arms, and this… is the chair's back. If you have any other questions check out Dixon Hardware's Guide to Choosing Chairs.' He passed Mel a pamphlet from a plastic container drilled to the scaffolding.

'Dad?' said Mel as he unfolded it and found a catalogue of chairs. 'Dad!?'

Geoff pulled his Mercedes C-Class into the car park of the yacht club to which he had belonged since Dixon Hardware began turning a substantial profit. Singing along to Pinkish Floyd's *Money* as he searched for a parking space, he shortly found that rarest of sights, even in The Ship Club's car park: a woman. Her car keys dangled from her hand and Geoff thought that probably she was about to leave. He slid down his window as he pulled up beside her and asked her if she was.

'Just up there.'

'That's a shame, isn't it?'

'Is it? Why's that?'

'I was hoping to ask you a very important question.'

'And what might that be?' the woman smiled.

'Have dinner with me some time.'

'Woah that was fast—and not a question.'

'I am *not* getting any younger.'

'You know what?'

'What?'

'I'd love to.'

'Well that's great.'

'But.'

'Always a but.'

'Something I should tell you if we are gonna go out. To save any embarrassment down the track.'

'And what's that then?'

'No, I shouldn't. I'm not really—' The woman lowered her sunglasses and began to walk off. Geoff implored her: 'I'm old enough to have heard it all! Trust me.'

'I've had people be judgmental about it before.'

'No judgment here—what's your name?'

'Marnie.'

'So, Marnie… You have a what? A husband? A mental disability?'

'No, no, it's nothing like that.'

'What is it then? A sex addiction?'

Surprised to find someone who so quickly guessed the weakness about which she was so insecure, Marnie grinned and tilted her head in confession.

'Wait, really?'

'Embarrassing, right?'

'Not in the least,' said Geoff, saying each word distinctly. 'What kind? If that's not too personal a question.'

'Oh, any sects really. Hindu, Buddhist. Muslim.'

'Hindu sex?'

'Mm, my favourite!'

'Are ahh… Muslims into sex as much as the other ones?'

She smiled and shook her head as though telling a familiar joke: 'Not as much as the Christians! But I do like to try all the sects, every group gives you a different experience.'

'D'you say groups?'

'Wouldn't be sects if it was just one person.'

'That's true I guess. Well, Marnie-with-a-sex-addiction—what are you doing… tomorrow night?'

'You really don't mind about the…'

'No, I don't mind at all.'

'Then let's do it!'

THE PETER FILE

Fiona was on a bench between date palms in St Kilda's Botanical Gardens—a hot breeze blowing firmly at her cheek and trams dinging beyond the bushes behind her. She had brought from the recesses of her car the file that had been thrown to her after Pete's funeral, and through the remainder of her morning had vacillated between thinking about it, and about what Pinal had said about reincarnation. She looked down to the file, now seeming to shout at her from the bench. She lifted its cover and could see the right half of the phrases printed on its second sheet. With her thumb she lifted that page's bottom corner and again pondered the existence of a police profile on Pete—Pete! She let the dossier's cover fall and mumbled as she contemplated again whether Pinal's assertion was a truth or a belief: 'Nor is there any future in which we shall cease to be?'

With bright flaps of its wings a yellow butterfly announced its arrival. It darted around the greenery, with each flit picking itself up off the breeze, before finally settling among some oleander. Fiona smiled and sounded a pleased grunt as the butterfly descended to a spike of lavender that was almost within her reach. She gave another, higher, hmm of contentment, then went on making inferences from Pinal's quotation. 'At death, then, we pass into another body—another kind of body?'

Fiona could see the butterfly's antenna bend forward as it stepped lightly over the petals and leaned up to reach the pollen. The insect backed out of one flower then sprung into the air as a grey cat pounced from within the greenery and snapped shut its teeth. Standing between Fiona and the lavender, the cat's lips smacked together as it gnawed with a yellow wing dangling at its chin. Fiona sighed and huffed as the cat brought the rest of the butterfly into its mouth. For a time it licked the side of its paw. Then it looked up at

Fiona and ran its tongue along its top lip. Then it seemed to wink.

'Did that ca—?' said Fiona to herself, and looked around to see if anybody else had seen it do so.

Arsen walked into U-Crane's front office from the premise's rear just as a customer came in through the front door. Not expecting to find anyone there, Arsen untied his blood-splattered rubber apron and threw it to the floor behind the desk.

'I tried calling but nobody answered. I need to rent a crane.'

'You have come to the right place! I am Arsen.'

'Ben.'

'Denys!' Arsen implored the man to sit then squeezed a towel along each of his bloodied fingers. 'What kind of job do you have?'

'I'm projects manager for Melbourne Zoo. We need to redo the elephant enclosure, but it's too far from any of the main gates, so we'll have to lift everything over.'

'Oh, simple, simple! Tea?'

Denys carried in a tea tray from his quarters and if this book could in any way afford subtitles they would show that Arsen said in Ukrainian, 'Get Oleksa ready.' Denys nodded as he placed the cup and teapots in front of his master then bowed and backed out of the office.

'Ben, I prefer to do business in banya. Do you know what is banya?' Ben began shaking his head. 'It is like sauna, but traditional Ookrainian. How is your tea?'

'It's very earthy.'

'Yes! Come! I show you banya.'

He led Ben through to U-Crane's rear then handed him a felt hat.

'You're ah… taking it all off?'

'Honesty is very serious matter for Ookrainians. Here

now you can see I have nothing to hide.' So Ben untucked his shirt.

Arsen held open the door and Ben in his underpants went in ahead of him. 'Oh, sorry,' said Ben, turning shyly from the doorway.

'No, no, go in! Ben, this is my daughter, Oleksa. Sometimes she is coming to banya for her stress.'

'You steam naked with… with your naked daughter?'

'We say in U-Crane, family who bathes together, stays together. Nastrovye!' Arsen handed out shots of the ice-cold samohonka that Denys had brought in.

'Nastrovye!' said Alexa, turning to Ben. She slapped the wooden bench at her thigh and Ben, with his eyes fixed on her braided and woven hair, turned about and sat nervously beside her. 'What kind of work do you do, Ben?'

'Shh, sh, daughter. Banya is silent place, so your soul can find calm. Wait, I can hear telephone.' Arsen stood and turned an ear towards the office. 'Is ringing. I come back.'

For the first time in a long time Alexa was excited to be in the banya with a prospective U-Crane customer. Normally her father's clients were older, fatter, sour-smelling. But Ben—Ben was younger, handsomer, and much less rapey-eyed. And as Alexa sniffed she found he smelt neither of smetana nor unreachable sweat. He even smelled, Alexa was elated to sense, as she thought a man ought to.

'Your wife won't mind us being in here naaaked together?'

Though nervous, Ben too was excited to be in the presence of a woman outside a nightclub, and one to whom he had not been forced to talk by the married friends who lived vicariously through his perpetual loneliness.

'I don't ah… have a wife. You can put a towel on if you want.'

'I what?'

'You can put a towel on. I don't mind.'

This no man had ever said to Alexa Arsenovna Sukhimova. 'Ben, you're a gentleman.'

'Where's your dad from?'

'We moved here from Ukraine.'

'And the business is called U-Crane? That's pretty funny. Everyone saunas naked in Ukraine?'

'Papa's right, there's honesty in nudity. Look at me. Do I look like I have anything to hide?' Ben glanced at her thigh then turned away and stared upwards as Alexa ran her fingers from her collarbone down to her knee.

'Nn nn.'

'See? We have nothing to hide?'

'Does that mean you're an honest woman?'

'Too honest, Ben, for this world.'

Alone in this world at Dixon Hardware, Mel had cleared a shelving bay of all its stock before nestling into an outdoor dining chair, one ankle on his other knee and his head tilted against his fingertips—his eyes wide, focusless, desperate.

'Are you the chair man?' A customer had searched the whole aisle for assistance before locating, and bringing a chair back to, Mel. Mel moved his horrified eyes towards him. 'Is this marquee adventurer powder-coated or resin-coated?'

'Resin-coated?' said Mel, not knowing whether it was coated in anything at all.

'These solid shank wrap rivets. Are they easily replaceable?'

'Huh?'

'The wrap rivets, do you know if they're easily replaceable?'

'What's a—' Mel moved his head from his fingertips and searched for what the man was talking about. With his fingernails he had pulled out a little plastic thing from the side of the chair's leg. 'I don't know.'

'And the carry bag—is it made from 100% sustainable polyester?'

'Are you serious?'

'What?'

'It's a chair, man.'

'I thought you were the chair man.'

Mel returned his forehead to his fingertips then tensed his ugly neck as he slid his hair into his hands. The customer walked off and Mel looked slowly up to the high ceiling.

'Rough day?'

A woman in a dark blue pants suit stood over him and smiled. Her hair was long and curled at the shoulders and a pearl earring hung at each earlobe.

'My life is over.'

'I'm sure it can't be that bad,' the woman cackled.

'I've searched for adventure from one corner of the globe to the other. James Blonde. And now James Blonde is here, a chair man.'

'At least you're not a blind guy.'

'That's true I guess. Who are you?'

She reached out and took his hand and smiled again. 'I'm the vice president.'

'You are?' Mel's shoulders came up from their hunch as hope lightened his gaze.

'I used to work as a travel agent, had a *pretty* amazing life, till it all came crashing down. Then I started working here. Within weeks I was vice president.'

'So you know my dad?'

'Who's your dad?'

'Geoff.'

'Dixon?'

'Yes!' Mel almost shouted, relieved that at last somebody was about to acknowledge who he was.

'Walk with me.' The vice president waved Mel on with a finger. He stood and was led up the aisle of chairs towards the rear of the store and the offices. A long middle section divided all the aisles into two. 'See?' said the vice president, pointing ahead. Beyond the end of his own half-aisle a man in grey trousers and khaki jacket, with very large sunglasses over his eyes, pointed a ball-ended stick at some curtains and explained their fabric to two customers. 'Blind guy.'

'He works here?'

'Pretty good at what he does, too. And down here's the man of steel.'

In the next aisle over, a man's blue t-shirt and jeans were, strangely, complimented by a red cape as he held up a steel fence post and explained its composition to a customer. And did he have red underpants over his—.

Mel looked back as he walked on: 'Wait, he calls himself that or you call him that?' He followed the vice president into the next aisle—its own open section of a row of steel and wooden benches backing onto a row of kitchen counter tops. A customer turned from one of the benches and was relieved to have found a staff member. 'Admiring the twin-start acme thread?' the vice president said to him.

'It's a pretty nice vice,' said the customer, his hand on its closed jaws.

'Three-inch throat, integrated anvil, captured safety jaw. It is a *very* nice vice.'

'Hmm,' pondered the customer as he twirled its handle.

'What do you think?' said the vice president to Mel. 'Should he buy this vice?'

'Wait. You sell vices?' said Mel.

'I'm The Vice President,' said the woman, and swivelled her head and winked at him.

'You sell vices,' said Mel and ran the balls of his palms from above his eyebrows to under his chin. 'You're The Vice President. And I'm the f----ng Chair Man.'

Annie threw her backpack into the footwell of her mum's

car and slid into the seat after it. 'So? How was it?!'

'It was OK.'

'OK?!'

'It was good.'

'What'd you learn? What'd you do? Who'd you make friends with?'

'Mum, are we criminals?'

'What?'

'Grandpa, Uncle Mel, you. Are we criminals?'

'No, we're not criminals. Why—. Did you—what did you do?'

'I didn't do anything. But my teacher spent the day telling everyone that we're guilty. She put our photographs on the wall, and asked us to write down our aspirations, and gave us all iPads. But then the rest of the day was about how guilty we all are and something called overcoming whiteness? Are we white? Should we not be?'

'Hm,' said Fiona. 'What do you want for dinner? Sushi?'

'Oo yes please!'

Unhappily Mel was watching *Doctor Dolittle* on Fiona's couch when they came home.

'How was work?' said Fiona as she went through to the kitchen.

'I'm the chair man,' said Mel without looking away from the television.

'And how was it?'

'I'm not the chairman. I'm the chair man. Dad's got me selling chairs.'

Fiona smiled from the kitchen doorway. 'Really?'

'My life is goddam over.'

'Oi.' She mouthed silently: 'Not around Annie.'

Mel nodded then shouted, 'How was school, kid?'

'Good,' said Annie from the refrigerator.

'That's good. What's for dinner?'

'Sushi!' Annie yelled.

'No,' Mel drawled. 'Sushi makes me sick, even the smell of it.'

Fiona tilted her head at him. 'We haven't always been able to have sushi, Mel. Pete hated fish. So to celebrate Annie's first day of high school we're having her favourite meal, aren't we, honey?'

'Can we get the platter?'

'It's a lot of sushi,' Fiona warned.

'Leftovers!'

'Seaweed,' said Mel. 'Raw fish. Eel! Really, it makes me sick.'

'Then you'll have the tempura vegetables. Oh, I have the Ukrainian memorial service tomorrow. Something about one week after—. You know. Do you want to come? It's at U-Crane.'

'Will Yuri be there?'

'I assume so.'

'Then no way. That guy terrifies me.'

'I *love* Uncle Yuri,' said Annie as she sat beside Mel on the couch. 'He stole an elephant.'

'Ah! But can he talk in crab or pelican?'

'What?'

'Like hell he can. I've ridden an elephant before.'

'You're really scared of Uncle Yuri?'

'So did you get made fun of?'

'I didn't actually. There's a kid in my class called Ichabod Cowpys.'

'There's what!?'

'Annie, you want to call Tran's Sushi House?' Fiona threw her her phone.

'Can we not have sushi?'

'Ask for extra sashimi rolls, and tempura vegetables for your scared uncle. To be honest though,' Fiona said to Mel as Annie put the ringing phone to her ear, 'I understand what you mean. He's not very in touch with reality.' She bulged her eyes and said, 'And the things Pete told me he's done!'

'Just imagine it,' said Mel, pointing to the television.

'What?'

'Chatting with a chimp in chimpanzee.'

III

Fiona sat in a towel on the lower bench of U-Crane's banya, beside a small half-barrel brimming with what a very naked Arsen told her was kutya. Seated on the other side of the barrel, with Yuri and Alexa nude behind him, Arsen stirred the mixture with a long wooden ladle and looked into its rolling globbiness.

'In other times we use kutya to offer to God for good weather. In these times, we drink kutya like Piter is feasting with us.'

Arsen took up a bull's horn and filled it with the kutya. He raised it in both hands and said, 'My son, Piter, my kaminyi—you are with your beautiful mother. My wife and son now together.' He put the horn to his mouth and raised slightly its end in order to allow him to drink. Then he thrust the horn upwards, sending what he hadn't drunk to the ceiling. Most of it fell and slapped onto the ground; Piter's family looked eagerly from beneath the brims of their felt hats at what had stuck, and seemed to analyse it. Arsen pointed at the adhesive remainder. 'Every poppy seed is one egg that a chicken will give. Every grain is new cattle we will have. Yuri?' He refilled the horn and passed it back. Fiona watched Yuri hold the thing out and intone:

'Brother, with whom we are sharing sacred feast, the movement of your soul is blessing us with fearful joy of eternally renewing matter and blessed be you in whichever body you now have taken.'

He drank from the horn then passed it down to Fiona. Arsen nodded as she moved it towards her mouth.

'Should I say something?'

'Piter hears what is in your heart.'

She felt a deep and familiar sadness, then tears amassing

in her sinuses as with two hands she put the horn to her lips. Finding that the kutya was not quite a liquid she sucked in a mouthful and chewed and tried to make sense of its muted flavours as she passed the horn to Alexa. She too said a prayer to her brother then handed the vessel down to her father who after a long moment of silence said, 'Come. Now we feast.'

As they filed out of the banya Fiona saw on Yuri's bare back his tattoo of a dancing figure whose encircling border reached from blade to blade of his shoulders—and whose several arms indicated it might have been taken from Pinal Connelly's living room. Outside they stood in robes before the ewe turning on a spit. Alexa held a long plate in both hands and rocked from the balls of her feet to her heels.

'You seem happy,' said Fiona, almost as a question.

'I know, I'm sorry.'

'No don't be sorry. The last thing I want's for people to pretend to be sad around me.'

'Well I am sad. But I'm happy too—I have a crush.'

'Well that's exciting.'

'He's the nicest handsomest man I've ever met. He's not old, he doesn't smell. He told me to put a towel *on!* I think—. No, that's silly.'

'What?'

'I think I love him. Never have I so wanted to entrust my fate to a man's honour.'

'That's…'

'This guy is just… Mm!' Alexa moaned and came again onto the balls of her feet.

'It's great to hear.'

'Alexa, plate!' said Yuri as he passed a full one from beneath the spinning ewe.

'Yuri, can I ask you a question?'

'Questions are best way for absolutely knowing.'

'That prayer.'

'Mm?'

'Whichever body Pete's now taken. That's Hinduism, right?'

'It is truth of Shiva's Dance.'

'What's Shiva's Dance?'

He stopped carving and pulled down the top half of his robe and turned his bare shoulder to his sister-in-law. 'Nataraja, destroyer of every matter through creation of every matter. He is dancing, and world is playing along. No morality good God of mercy and hope. You can see his hand that is raised?'

'With the palm out?'

'It is gesture of best reassurance. There is not one time to worry, Fiona, for within circle of Shiva's dance, he is reminding us there was no time when we were not existing.'

'And no future in which we cease to be.'

'You are knowing it!' said Yuri and smiled.

'It's reincarnation, right?'

Yuri replaced the shoulder of his robe and resumed his carving. 'As dweller in *this* body is passing through childhood to old age, at death we are passing into one other body.'

'Can I ask you another question?'

'These are dispelling ignorance that is leading to rebirth.'

'Pete.'

'My brother.'

'He wasn't involved with… all this, was he?'

'All what?'

'With U-Crane and… and you?'

'Was he being involved with me?'

'Did he—. Was he—.'

'Ask of me your true question.'

Fiona nodded as she came out with the gist of her inquiry: 'Did Pete ever steal a tank?'

'So your meaning is revealed. Our destinies were muchly different—Piter was one doctor, and family man, and now you, Fiona, are more family than before. If there is anything you are needing, make sure of that you ask to me, for which to fulfil would be my honour.'

'Thank you, Yuri, that's very kind.'

'It is duty of brother to look after brother's family.'

Fiona's brother had that morning added to his hovel-office a plastic outdoor table, for he would not—he resolved—spend another day merely sulking in a chair. Spread out before him now was a handful of *Dixon Hardware's Guide to Choosing Chairs* and a pen and a pencil taken from one of The Vice President's benches. And there Mel sat, brooding in a cushioned round rattan chair.

'Do you know how much this Ultimate Explorer veighs ven it is folded?'

Mel's eyes moved scornfully from the customer to the chair in her hand. 'When it's folded?'

'Mm,' said the young woman, East German and bespectacled.

'Well let's see.' Mel leaned up from his cushion and put his elbows on his desk. 'Fold it.'

She pushed down the cloth seat and did.

'Pick it up.'

She raised it from the ground with both hands.

'That's how much it weighs when it's folded.'

'OK, smart arse. I'm taking it on a expedition and ze expedition has a per-person veight limit. I couldn't find its veight in ze pamphlet.'

'Did you say expedition?'

'Yes.'

'What kind of expedition?'

'A boat trip to Antarctica.' The woman leaned in and whispered into the cold-floored office in which Mel now stood intrigued: 'Actually I'm going vailing.'

Mel lowered his head and raised his eyebrows towards the woman's short greying hair. 'I've actually done some adventuring myself.'

'Oh yes? Vair to—ze gardening section?'

'No,' said Mel, offended. 'I'm a gun smuggler. Across the Malaysian border.'

'And vot do you smuggle? Pricing guns? Vorter pistols? Glue guns? Sounds super dangerous—sit back down, chair man.'

The purported whale-hunter's condescension stung Mel with an embarrassed sadness that he had not felt since the day he wore a Dixon Balls t-shirt to school. He lifted his hands from the plastic table and slouched as he fell back into his spinning chair and stared across the aisle with overcomedness until shortly his phone rang.

'Fi, what's up?'

In the botanical gardens Fiona had again returned to thoughts of Hinduism and her husband. Beside the pleasant accompaniment of oleander and lavender she had folded back the manila folder's cover and was—one, two, three—glancing at the sans-serif fragments which increasingly puzzled her—three, two, one. As she contemplated the first phrase—the only which might, because of his job, plausibly pertain to Pete—she felt a soft warmth at her leg. She looked down and saw what she assumed was the cat from yesterday. It ran the length of its grey body along her calf then turned and rubbed its cheek against her shin. She leaned down to see if the animal would let her touch it. It did, and she scratched at its cheek and felt it rumble as it purred. Then she returned to upright, and to the document on her lap.

She brought the profile back over and sighed and shook her head—stared at her own name, and at Annie's, and tried to remember if Pete had ever shown any inclination towards his family's inveterate brigandry. As she stared on and thought she was certain that he hadn't, she heard a meow.

The cat had wrapped its tail into a neat arc around its paws. Looking to its right, casually it meowed again then turned its head and looked left. Shortly it looked straight on, shining its green eyes up at Fiona. And it winked.

'It did wink,' said Fiona to herself. 'You winked again.'

The cat meowed then sauntered off, towards the gate through which Fiona had entered the gardens. She looked to the lavender and the oleander and remembered yesterday's butterfly, and the wink that she was certain had followed its death. The cat meowed again and now Fiona decided to follow it.

It led her to the park's gate—or rather she just followed it there—and turned in the general direction of Fiona's home, intriguing her almost to the point of hope. Then she remembered that she had to pick Annie up from school. She took out her phone and walked behind the cat as she called her brother.

'Fi, what's up?'

'Can you pick Annie up from school?'

'Hello to you too.'

'Yes, yes. Can you?'

'I should be able to. What time does she finish?'

'Ten past three.'

'Can I bring her back to the store with me?' And Mel was hung up on.

An announcement sounded everywhere overhead: 'Could The Drill Sergeant please go to the loading dock for an urgent delivery.' Mel thought he recognised the voice. 'Drill Sergeant to the loading dock.'

'Dad's here,' Mel said to himself, and stood from his dejected stupor.

The Chair Man

Geoff had spent most of his day in The Olde Curiosity Shop—the store in the city that sold stuffed pelicans and taxidermied eels and antique scientific instruments and which specialised in his beloved insects. He held his latest acquisition to the light, admired the luminescence of its green thorax and ridged carapace, then made space for it on his shelf.

'Dad?'

'Cheirotonus peracanus,' he said as his son came in in a suit and tie. 'Malayan Scarab—what are you wearing?'

'We need to talk about my job.'

'Y'enjoying it? You're not doing very well at it.'

'I don't want to be a chair man, Dad.'

'You told me you were looking forward to it.'

'I thought you were making me the chairman.'

'We don't have a board. Why would I make you the chairman?'

'Who runs the business then?'

'We have me as president, we have a vice president, and that's it.'

'Couldn't you make me the vice president?'

'What do you know about vices?'

'The same amount that I know about chairs.'

'You're still in the papers, you know that, right? I had to get The Man of Steel to shoo away two photographers last night. Isn't this better than being a gum smuggler? Speaking of which, you ever thought that an m should be a double n?'

'Huh?'

'Two u's is a w, right? Why isn't an m two n's?'

'I don't know what you're talking about.'

'That makes you a gunn snnuggler.'

'Dad, I can't be the chair man. I'm an adventurer, James Blonde. Years I was travelling the world for adventure—'

'Mel.'

'Dad.'

'I'd love to help you.'

'Good,' said Mel, glad to be making progress in his inevitable climb to chairman.

'But I don't care. And if you'll excuse me, I have a date.'

Geoff stood from his upholstered captain's chair and was watched by his disbelieving son as he walked out of the office.

'They haven't made fun of you at all?'

'Nope,' said Annie, spinning in her uncle's work chair. 'You're getting made fun of at work more than I am at school.'

'Not your first name? Not the second name?'

'My name's boring at school. There's a girl called Boobesh.'

'You're kidding me?'

'We have a Moonlight Wang. And an Ahmed Baboun.'

'These are names?'

'Mm hm.'

'Mel Dixon would be untouchable.'

'Not if they found out he's a chair man,' Annie smiled and spun herself again. 'This isn't a bad future, Uncle Mel. People always need somewhere to sit.'

'People need somewhere to sit. D'your mum tell you to say that?'

'Nope.'

'It's not what I'm supposed to be doing, Annie.'

'You get to sit down all day. You get to hang out with Grandpa. And it smells like a sausage sizzle.'

'A sausage sizzle,' Mel said with scorn. 'I was supposed to be James Blonde, kid. James Blonde. Now look at me. Never make plans, Annie, I tell you. And don't look forward to any future—and definitely don't think your life's gonna be any good, because it won't, and you'll just be disappointed.'

'I think,' Annie began slowly, spinning still in the chair, 'you should make the most of it. Every day's an opportunity. Think of how many people you're meeting—how many people you *will* meet. I think you should treat every customer as a unique and interesting soul.'

'It this the crap they're teaching you at school?'

'And it's only temporary. You're not going to be the chair man forever.'

'No I am not.'

'Plus your job doesn't define who you are. Otherwise Mum would be nothing. Same with Auntie Alexa.'

Her Auntie Alexa was trying to find out from her grandfather who would be attending the evening delivery to U-Crane's latest job.

'Good, Oleksa! You are interested in your proper place.'

'I'm not, Papa, that's not why I'm asking. I just want to know what time you're getting it there.'

'Why you are dressed like this?'

'Like what?'

'Like you are going to have blackmailer buy you caviar in hotel.'

'This is how I always dress.'

'But not when I need you to.'

'Don't start, Papa. I've done every job you've asked for the last year, even after the assaults. Is it just you and Yuri going?'

'Who else would be going? Denys?'

'And from the zoo? Who's the construction manager?'

'Ahhh! You are wanting to know if Ben will be there.'

'No, I'm just curious.'

'Ben will be there, Sashenka. But I have warned you about mixing business with leisure.'

'Pleasure.'

THE PETER FILE

'What is pleasure?'
'Exactly.'

From a distance at which, she thought, any unfamiliar cat would have fled, Fiona watched her grey Korat criss-cross footpaths and with its tail in the air traipse along garden beds—still in the direction of her, even its, home. When it turned off the road which led to their street she froze with anticipation. When it turned down her street she couldn't decide between shaking and nodding her head. Amid an astonished mixture of both she said, 'Pete.' When then the cat turned up their driveway she was almost—almost—overcome by nerves.

She walked ahead of the animal and held open her front door but found it reluctant to go inside. The cat, not the door. The cat stalked along the doormat, rubbed itself against the brick of the entrance, stalked back again.

'Come on,' Fiona urged, taking it for granted that the animal wanted to go—even return—inside. She said in a high and enticing voice: 'Come on.' Still the animal wouldn't step over the threshold and onto her, or his—their!—carpet. She made sure the door would stay open then went to the refrigerator. When she returned with a slice of leftover sashimi she found three cats now prowling over the doormat. She looked beyond them and saw two more coming up her driveway.

'So many Peters.'

So she went inside to get more sushi then put one piece on the threshold and walked backwards as she laid a sushi trail across the carpet, all the way through the living room to the kitchen table.

Geoff had so far detected not a single fatal flaw in Marnie's personality. Sitting across from her at Tran's Luon House, by the time dessert came he had found that she was, most importantly, very interested in spending part of her year in Vietnam. She also thought she could remember having some Scottish blood in her family tree. And she even loved to snorkel.

'I just love snorkelling,' said Geoff. 'Feels so free, it's what I'm most looking forward to there. So's there anything else I should know before I retire and we up and move to Vietnam?'

'Hmm...' said Marnie, having to think, for she had already revealed much that was usually reserved for men she had known a lot longer. 'I once got arrested for taking a leek,' she said as she lifted her spoon through their shared three-coloured dessert.

'In public?'

'The supermarket, yeah. Oh,' she said and licked her spoon clean. 'There is *one* other thing. But I don't usually tell men this until further down the track.'

'Well you don't have to tell me everything, we have time.'

'This one'll come up in the bedroom sooner rather than later.'

'Oh will it now?'

'Why wouldn't it?' said Marnie, smiling.

'Why not indeed. Go on then.'

'I'll know if you judge me, I'll see it in your face.'

'I bet you I won't. Out with it.'

She leaned forward and stared into his brown eyes. When it seemed that his gentle smile had grown permanent she entrusted him with another admission: 'I have a pea fetish.'

Geoff turned his ear to her. 'What's that now?'

'I have a pea fetish.'

Geoff clenched his cheeks and pressed his tongue against the outside of his top teeth. 'I thought you had a sex addiction?'

'I do, have a sects addiction. And this is part of why I like the Hindu sects so much—they put pea in all their food.

But the fetish is kind of… above all that. It's the only way that I can… finish. Is it a deal-breaker?'

'I guess it explains the supermarket story. A pee fetish?' Geoff thought ahead to what satisfying her might entail. Quickly he decided that he would at least try this new addition to what was a plentiful but rudimentary set of sexual experiences. 'Well, you only live once, right?'

'No! Not according to the guys I'm meeting tomorrow. The Hindu sects always include rebirth.'

As Mel made Annie carry his dry-cleaned shirt in from the car he pushed down on her backpack in order to hinder her from walking comfortably up the driveway.

'So your mum told you about the worms, huh? I only did that to gross her out.'

'Sure you did, Uncle Smell.'

'Told you about that too, huh?'

'But promise me tomorrow you'll be OK with being the chair man? I don't like the idea of you being sad all day.'

'Don't you worry about me, kid—we're the ones who worry about you.'

'I'll be fine.'

'Then so will I. Deal?'

'Deal,' said Annie.

Mel held open the door for his niece and as he stepped in after her they both were greeted by the sight of Fiona prostrate on her kitchen table and being crawled upon by cats.

'Mum?'

'Fi, what the hell are you doing?'

Slices of leftover sashimi were arrayed on her thighs and California rolls covered her stomach and unagi encircled her breasts. 'Oh, hi!'

'Mum, why are you covered in sushi?'

Half the cats were seated and leaning down to gnaw, half

were stepping over her limbs and licking their lips as in a frenzy they strutted and meowed along the kitchen table.

'I think Dad's been reincarnated as a cat, honey. It's one of the grey ones, but I lost track of which one.'

'Fi, why are you naked?'

'It's the only way I could get him into the house.'

'Him?'

'Pete! Come say hi, honey.'

'Mum, this is really weird. And Dad hated sushi.'

'But it's fish, cats love fish.'

'Dad hated fish, too.'

'But he's been reincarnated as a cat,' Fiona insisted, stretching her neck out to look back at her daughter. 'Come and say hi, honey!'

'Mum, this is *really* weird.'

'If the cat was Pete wouldn't it hate fish?'

'I did think that. But I don't really know how it works.'

Arsen had made himself chicken soup for dinner. The Veryovka Choir sounded from speakers in his living room as he crossed from stovetop to kitchen table and first placed an empty bowl and cutlery in front of the chair beside his—a place always reserved for the memory of his wife.

Arsen lilted back to the table as a wailing soprano cried out over the violin beneath her, record-crackles sounding in between intercessions of full choir. Beside the vacant bowl, now opposite Arsen as he sat, was the cardboard cut-out of himself, slotted in at the table after he had brought it home from work.

Arsen looked to the empty chair at his elbow and sighed and moaned, 'This song,' he said, in very expensive Ukrainian, 'I wish we could dance together, Leza. One more time.' He took up his spoon and began his dinner—tore his bread roll in half and placed the smaller piece in his dead wife's empty bowl. Then began the feminine harmony and whistling flutes of *Oi Harna Ya, Harna*. The turtledove to which the singer compared herself, horlitsya, was the source of the pet name by which Arsen had always called his wife: Holubka. He looked again to the vacant chair and smiled as a tambourine joined the song's chorus and the swing of the harmony picked up. 'My Leza,' he said forlornly, then stood and by the shoulders picked up the cardboard cut-out of himself. He turned it around so as not to be looking at his own face and put his arm around its waist and held its waving hand—and waltzed around the kitchen table. He nuzzled the cardboard's neck and remembered what his Holubka's perfume smelled like. He closed his eyes and thought that he could feel on his cheek how soft had been her hair, taste how good had been her varenyky, how exquisite always felt her p—

'Papa?' said Yuri.

Mid-dip in the centre of the living room, Arsen halted his whirling and stood up straight and turned to face his children.

'What the hell are you doing?' said Alexa.

Arsen realised that they were looking at two of him and threw the cut-out to the floor. 'I…'

Sitting on the edge of Marnie's bed and facing her en suite in a t-shirt and his boxer shorts, Geoff guzzled water from a two-litre bottle, for he did want to please her and assumed that that would entail performing at fullest volume for as long as possible. As Marnie readied herself in the bathroom his still-socked feet rested on all the towels that he could find in her cupboards. Foreseeing a ruinous amount of liquid, he had overlapped them on the carpet of the bedroom into which she now stepped, wearing a bra and black-lace garters.

'So…' she said as she leaned against the bathroom door.

'Who's ready to put the pea in my mouth?'

'In your mouth?' Geoff said, then gulped. He finished the last of the water then slowly screwed its cap back on.

She reassured him: 'We don't have to do that if you're not comfortable. Would you prefer to put it on my leg?'

'Uummm… Could we not do the mouth tonight—save that for another time? This is very new to me.'

'My leg it is then,' and Marnie ran her fingertips along one of her thighs. 'You ready to put that pea on my leg?'

'Yep, I think so.'

From the bathroom Marnie pulled in and unfurled a green bag. 'Here we go then.'

'What's that?'

'Why are all my towels on the floor?'

'Are they—' Geoff squinted. 'Are they peas?'

'Mm hm,' she nodded as she slunk towards him. 'You ready to put 'em on my leg?'

'You have a pea fetish?'

'Mm hm,' she nodded, and ran a fingertips across his lips.

'Oh, I can put that in your mouth!' he mumbled.

'Good!' Marnie growled, then straddled—and with rising enthusiasm, kissed him.

'Did it… talk to you?' Wrapped in a blanket on the picnic table outside, Fiona was trying to rationalise the sushi incident to her brother and herself.

'No,' she admitted. 'Just winked.'

'I don't think cats can wink, Fi.'

'I am absolutely certain that cat winked. Twice—two days in a row.'

'Even if it did wink, it wouldn't be winking *at* you.'

'That's why I thought it was so strange. It looked directly at me, I swear—then it winked. After one of the mum's from Annie's school mentioned reincarnation, *and* after Yuri mentioned it at Pete's memorial. I miss him so much,

Mel—Annie?' Fiona's daughter came outside from the kitchen and at the end of the picnic table leaned forward and put the side of her temple on her mum's shoulder. Fiona wrapped her arm around Annie's head and rubbed her hair. 'Honey, I think I might see if you can stay with your uncle for a bit.'

'Sleep in Uncle Smell's room?'

'Your Uncle Yuri. Just for a few days while I get my head and my heart figured out. Would that be all right?'

'Maybe the heart's not so Brazilian after all?'

'Maybe not, honey.'

Lights whirled orange on the roof of the flatbed truck which Arsen always drove ahead of his cranes when delivering them to U-Crane jobs. The Ukrainian national anthem played very loudly from speakers between the lights:

'*Never perished is Ukraine, nor her glory and freedom!*' sounded in its own language through the warm air of a summer dusk as Yuri drove the truck-mounted crane through Royal Park. '*Fate shall smile once more,*' was sung by a baritone choir as he wound his arms in turning the truck's enormous steering wheel. '*And our enemies shall vanish like dew in the morning sun.*'

'You look…' said Ben, as Alexa emerged from her own car and in a blue and yellow dress crossed to the zoo's entrance.

'Mm?' she said, and spun the sides of the dress. 'I like your uniform.'

'It's just a tucked-in shirt.'

'But look at this looogo, it's so official.'

Alexa stood beside him and watched as the orange lights and Slavic choir neared: '*Soul and body shall we lay down for our freedom.*'

'That kind of looks like a rocket launcher,' said Ben as the crane rolled down the hill and came round a roundabout and followed Arsen to the zoo's north-eastern wall.

'It's actually only a small adjustment to make it one,' said Alexa as they set off after the vehicles.

'To show that we are brethren of the Cossack nation!' blasted before the anthem's chorus repeated itself while Arsen parked his car. He stood behind the crane and guided Yuri back with his raised hands until it was in position—close enough to the zoo's wall to still allow for its outriggers to plant.

Fiona arrived too as Yuri in his I-Crane uniform hopped out of the cab.

'Yuri, hi.'

'Fiona,' he said, emphasising as always the first syllable of her name.

'Yuri, I have a favour to ask.'

Slowly he bowed his head.

'Could Annie stay with you for a week or so? I'm kind of struggling with what's happened. Her being at the house I think is just a reminder of—. Pete's…'

'It is destined to be so.'

'Thank you. And what about… Well you know.'

'What?'

'The ahh…'

'The what? Tell to me.'

'Your struggle with alcohol?'

'Struggle? Struggle—what struggle?' he beamed. 'I am very naturally one alcoholic, it is no struggle. And I am looking forward to goodly spending time with Anastasia!'

'As head of U-Crane's customer relations,' said Alexa, 'I'll probably have to visit the job site a few times.'

'Mm hm,' said Ben.

'Zoo Crane!' Arsen shouted when suddenly he made the connection. 'Oleksa! Zoo Crane!'

'Do you think you'll be around when I visit?'

'Oleksa!'

'What, Papa?'
'It is Zoo Crane!'
'Yes, Papa! So do you?'
'Probably I guess. I'm here most days.'
'Zoo Crane!'

As Geoff struggled with the annoyance that had replaced his consternation…

'Put more pea in my mouth,' Marnie whispered into his ear before lying back and pushing her hands against the bedhead.

'Why are you saying it like that?'

'Saying it like what?'

'One at a time. Can't you say, "Put *those peas* in my mouth"?'

'But I *like* it one at a time. Oh, Geoff—put that warm pea on my leg.'

Geoff opened his fist and looked at the pea that he had been asked to hold until it defrosted. Marnie lay still as he reached down and balanced the warmed pea between the top and bottom of her garter. It rolled off when shortly she shuddered, then she grabbed Geoff by his hair and shouted, 'Pea all over me!'

'Peas!'

'Please! Pea all over me!'

'Say peas!'

'Please! Please put pea everywhere! Geoff, pea on me!'

IN THE NEXT PETER FILE…

…Mel decides to really try enjoying being the Chair Man:
'Hi there! Can I help you?'

'I think I just need six of these and I'm set,' said a middle-aged woman who had made straight for the stackable

The Chair Man

plastic chairs.

'Is this man harassing you?' said The Blind Guy swinging his cane. He had all morning been crossing to Mel's aisle in order to joke with his customers. The woman walked off with six chairs in hand and The Blind Guy said, 'Lunchtime?'

He dropped his lunch box onto Mel's plastic table and put his sunglasses on top of his head. 'I tell you, sometimes the wife's sandwiches make me wish I had no taste instead of no sight.'

Mel smiled and shook his head as The Man of Steel came down the aisle in his cape and jocks and brought with him an employee whom Mel had not yet met.

'Chair Man, this is The Drill Sergeant,' said The Man of Steel. This other co-worker—in a green shirt tucked into green trousers and sporting a cavalry hat with a golden tassel at its crown—unholstered an electric drill and placed it beside The Blind Guy's lunchbox. 'Where you from, private?'

'Goddam it!' Mel said as he threw onto his desk a clear-plastic container of leftover sushi.

'What's that?' asked The Blind Guy.

'Sushi,' he said and pushed it to the far corner of the table. 'My sister packed me leftover sushi. I hate sushi.'

The Man of Steel opened its lid and took up a piece of unagi. 'This is eel.'

'Oh God.' Mel's shoulders convulsed as he huffed through his nose and shook his head and trembled his palm towards his lunch. 'Eel makes me vomit.'

'Hi, which one of you's The Chair Man?' said a man in a brown suit, newly arrived in Mel's aisle.

'That'd be me,' Mel groaned with his hand at his stomach.

'Would you like to see a stool sample?'

'What?' said Mel, looking up and scrunching his nose.

'Smell that,' said The Man of Steel, and passed a piece of unagi under Mel's chin.

'Can I show you a stool sample?' The man raised and presented to Mel an open briefcase, into which Mel promptly threw up.

…Annie tries to make friends in the schoolyard:

She replaced the elastic band around her empty packet of leftover sushi and dropped it into a bin. Three of her classmates were sitting under a tree, reading each a paperback on their laps. Tired of spending her lunch hour with the relentlessly kind Pinkish Floyd, she crossed the down-ball courts and approached them.

'Isn't it crazy what Miss Conrad was saying this morning about herstory?'

'Oh she's a nutjob!' said one of the boys as they all looked up from their reading.

'How are we gonna survive a whole year of that crap?' said another.

'Right!? Thank you! I'm Annie. Annie Sukhimov.'

'I'm Vajeen Vajones,' said the boy to her right.

'Elvis Pterodactyl,' said the boy in the middle.

'Hi, I'm Martin Luther Ching.'

…and Fiona, eating lunch in the garden of Tran's Sushi House, halts her California roll halfway to her mouth when she hears a high and long meow that sounds a little too familiar:

'Fiona?'

Episode 3

THE GUM SMUGGLEЯ

I

'Uncle Yuri, what are these?'

Asleep on a reed mat in his bedroom (which should probably be referred to as his reed-mat-room—the only bed was in the guest room), Yuri woke to the sight of Annie in pyjamas under a hat that was much too big for her and holding in both hands an umbrella. He smiled and answered her as he rose. 'No, no, no, Anastasia. These you must not touch.' He lifted the hat from her head and took possession of his... most prized possession.

'They're so detailed, what are they?'

'Hat is responding only to his owner. And this, was gift to me by my milk brother.' At the centre of the bookcase in Yuri's living room a sword rack and a hat stand... stood empty. He brushed the hat's bird-of-paradise feather as he returned it to its ivory pole and with both hands placed the umbrella back in its... well, its place. 'It is said that a nyangfa inhabitates certain umbrellas from the East—a spirit for watching over dynasty. If umbrella is safe, we are safe. So these we do not touch, OK?'

'Sorry.'

'No, Anastasia! Never apologise. You can be doing no wrong, you can be only doing.'

'What's a nyongfa?'

'Come! We are making you ready for day of schooling.'

Side by side in her uncle's bathroom, Annie was just able to see herself in the mirror as Yuri handed her his toothpaste then lathered his scalp. 'Ewww!' she said as she squeezed the tube over her toothbrush.

'What is matter?'

'It's purple.'

'Mmmm?'

'Why is it purple?'

'It is flavour of buryak. Organical best remedy for making teeth strong and clean, and breath all-day fresh. You are not using such a thing?'

'It's toothpaste, right?'

'It is toothpaste.'

'Why is it purple?'

'What unalike colour can buryak be?'

'Will it stain my teeth?'

'Ah! There appears fun of brushing teeth.' Yuri put aside his razor then squeezed a strip of the paste onto his own toothbrush and ran it under the tap. 'It is one race that in we must hurry, because if we are taking too long, *then* have purple mouth for rest of day.' He poised his wrist at his cheek. 'Ready?'

'Oh God.'

'Go!'

With fear in her eyes Annie swivelled her toothbrush over the outside of her teeth and looked up at her uncle, trembling his wrist as he drew his toothbrush from the back of one side of his mouth then shoved it into the other. As she lifted her elbow to reach the back of her bottom teeth Yuri swallowed and returned his toothbrush to the tap.

'De hoo ha hah—' said Annie with an open and purple mouthful. She leaned down and spat. 'Did you just swallow that?'

'Mmmm.'

'That's disgusting!'

'It is organical.'

'And that's disgusting!' she said, pointing to the river of

The Gum Smuggler

purple in the sink.

'You have beaten stain, this is good. They are not excellent days whereon stain beats you.' Yuri took up his razor and drew its blades from his forehead. Watching wide strips appear in the foam Annie said, 'Why do you shave your head?'

He wiggled the razor under the running water. 'Yul Brynner also was Ukrainian, and he have died day before I am born. So his spirit have inhabitated my soul, and is forming part of who I am.'

Annie scrunched up her nose and said, 'You're weird.' The plastic razor handle stopped halfway along Yuri's scalp. He raised a displeased eyebrow then turned it slowly to his niece. She looked up at him and spread a toothy grin.

'Come, I must be making one stop on way to school.'

Mel walked into Dixon Hardware determined to take his niece's advice and to make the very most of today. He turned down his aisle and when he came to his outdoor table in its shelving bay gleefully pulled it out from its awning of stacked boxes. He centred his spinning chair and leaned up and planted his elbows and clasped his hands and thought of how many people he was about to meet, and nodded. He neatened his fan of guides to choosing chairs and made parallel his pencils and thought how beautiful an opportunity indeed today certainly was—the very first day of the rest of his life. And happily he awaited the arrival of the day's first unique and interesting soul.

'Good morning!' he rejoiced when eventually it came down his aisle. The opportunity said, 'Good morning,' as it strolled past Mel's desk in its quest for wooden folding chairs. It glanced back as it neared them. Then the unique and interesting soul reversed to Mel's niche and squinted and pointed. 'Are you that gun smuggler?'

'Am I what?' said Mel and smiled on.

'That gun smuggler—aren't you him?'

Mel grinned and moaned and wobbled his head at the opportunity.

'You are! You're that guy that got caught smuggling guns.'

'Gun,' said Mel, looking away from him.

'It is you, right?'

'Gunm.'

'Gun? You smuggled—what, just one?'

'Gum-mm. I smuggled gum. But actually I didn't—I can't chew gum, I have sensitive teeth.'

'So you didn't smuggle guns?' said the opportunity, understandably confused.

'Gunm.'

'You didn't smuggle… *the* gun?'

'Gum.'

'You did smuggle it?'

'Chewing gum.'

'Ah,' said the unique and interesting soul as he patted his pockets. 'I don't have any, sorry.'

'I smuggled gum, all right?'

'You smuggled gum? Like chewing gum?'

'Technically no, it was planted on me.'

'Look, are you that gun smuggler or not?'

'You came over to me, man!'

'And have you got any?'

'Guns? No.'

'Gum.'

'I can't chew gum, I have sensitive teeth.'

'Why'd you smuggle it then?'

'Are you gonna buy a f-----g chair or what?'

'Not now, you swore at me.'

Mel grunted and shooed the opportunity as though it were a pigeon. When it had flitted away he came out from behind his table and with the sole of one foot scuffed the concrete floor. He gritted his teeth and shook his jaw and shortly leaned against the beam above his chair. He loosed his ugly neck and hung low his discouraged head.

'Hi there, sir, are you the chair man?'

'Yes,' Mel snapped, already tired of the day's mostness. 'Waddya want?'

'Would you like to see a stool sample?'

'What?'

'I have some stool samples in my car, I'd love to show them to you if you have the time.'

'That's disgusting!' Mel stood back from the scaffolding and reversed towards the Blind Guy.

'Shall I bring the stool samples in to show you? Hello?'

'You are sad for death of father?'

Yuri knew Annie to be much more talkative than she presently was. He looked across the car as she stared out the window. 'I miss him.'

'This is best outcome, and goodly way for it to be. To be making you feeling less sad, Anastasia, remember that a broken man is one tragedy. A dead man *should* be one tragedy. But dead broken man is not tragedy. Be much thankinging that your father was not broken, and for that he have died living good life of free man—life of Cossack.'

'What's cossack?'

'You are Cossack. Someone who feels what is true, and says what he feels. And who cuts out tongue of man who is telling him how to feel, or what to say.'

'I don't get it.'

'Hold on, Anastasia.'

'For what?'

In one violent motion Yuri pulled into the kerb and brought the car to a stop. 'I will be back in sharply one moment.'

Annie watched her uncle round the car's front and call out to, then rush, someone working in a yard of stacked tyres. As Yuri put on leather gloves the person whom he was attempting to corner dropped a tyre and hurried inside.

Outside a police station Fiona held in her hands the folder whose delivery and contents had been perplexing her since Pete's funeral. She ran through the various phrases which beyond the station's doors she might have to say— the unspeakable statements that even when silently admitted still brought tears—all of which she might now have to utter to a stranger. But this too had to be done, or she might spend the rest of her life wondering why Pete had been of interest to, of all people, the police. She closed her eyes and momentarily bowed her head. Then she ascended the station's front steps.

She took in the rows of plastic chairs and the two windows with holes drilled through them as though containers for small animals. At the window on the left a woman stood behind her teenage son and talked through holes to a uniformed officer. 'All I said was I thought I heard a snigger in my backyard,' said a handcuffed old lady as she was brought in behind Fiona, and taken straight through doors that had to be unlocked from the inside. Another police officer came out and rose to sit on the cushioned stool behind the other window; eventually he looked to Fiona and said, 'Morning.'

'Good morning.'

'How can I help?'

'So. After my husband's funeral last week, this was handed to me. Anonymously.' With both hands she placed the file on the counter. The officer told her to push it through and Fiona slid it into the metal recess.

'Its first page is a biography—I guess it's a police report?' The officer opened its cover. 'But the second page is just those three phrases. I don't think Pete ever did *anything* illegal, but I was wondering if you could tell me what the

The Gum Smuggler

phrases mean? I can't…'

'*Who* gave you this?'

'I don't know, I was looking down, I was at the… at the funeral—and I was looking down and it was dropped onto my lap. I looked up and a car was speeding away.'

'Didn't get its license plate?'

Fiona shook her head.

'The phrases sound like gibberish.'

'Well I thought that too. But he's a paediatrician, which could be the first one, right? And he's Ukrainian, which might explain the third one?'

The officer twisted towards a computer screen and tapped at its keyboard. 'Fiona Sukhimov?'

'Suk*hi*mov. Wait, how do you know that?' Fiona leaned forward and tried to see the screen in front of the officer as from the room adjoining the enclosed space a man wearing sunglasses and a blue shirt and tie came out. He approached the officer at the window and leaned down to whisper in his ear. In turning his head Fiona saw the top of his own ear had a wedge missing. Then without looking up he walked on and disappeared through another of the station's locked doors.

'Sorry, Madame—not really anything we can do for your husband.'

'No, he's—.' Fiona closed her eyes and swallowed the thought of admitting it out loud. 'I don't want you to help him, I want to know what those phrases mean.'

'What phrases?'

'In the file.'

'What file?'

'Did you—You just slid it into your lap. Can I have my Peter file back please?'

'I beg your pardon?'

'You just slid my Peter file into your lap—can I have it back please?' Fiona leaned in and raised her voice: 'Hello, that's my Peter file!' With the raising of her voice came the

THE PETER FILE

silence of the station's chatter. The woman at the window beside her looked at Fiona and put a wary arm at her son's shoulder.

'Madame, is your husband a paedophile?'

'What? He's a paediatrician.'

'We can investigate a paedophile.'

'Can I have the file please?'

'What file, Madame?'

'What's going on here? Why is my name on your computer? And who just came out and spoke to you?'

'Spoke to me?'

Fiona stood back from the counter and huffed impatiently through her nose. 'A man came out and whispered into your ear, then you started trying to get rid of me.'

'What'd he say?'

'Just give me the Peter file, please.'

'Madame, are you drunk?'

'Drunk? I just want my Peter file back.'

The pair at the next window had left and an elderly man had taken their place. He too now stared across at Fiona.

'Tom, we got any paedophiles in lock up?' The officer at the other window shook his head.

Fiona pleaded slowly and sternly: 'Please give me my Peter file.'

'Which paedophile, Madame?'

'The one in your lap!' she snapped, now made anxious by the ordeal.

The officer looked down at his lap and put his hands in the air and leaned back.

'I can see it, right there. Give it to me.'

'Ohhh.' The officer returned her file to the counter and passed it under the window. Fiona snatched it and turned around and on her way out passed someone shouting as he was brought in in handcuffs: 'You don't understand, I was playing the fiddle *for* children!'

The Gum Smuggler

Yuri yelled down to the man who was cowering against the front window of his own office: 'Who, who, *who*—have killed my brother?'

'Yuri, I haven't heard anything. Not from the heavies, not from any Georgians, not from anyone.'

Yuri rose to standing and stepped across and looked out the window closest to the office door. He smiled and waved to Annie, watching and waiting in the car. She raised her hand as Yuri stepped back to the window whose view was blocked by columns of tyre. 'Somebody have killed my brother, and I will be de-dicking you if you do not tell to me who.'

The man fumbled at the top button of his overalls in an effort to prevent more blood from getting on his white t-shirt. 'How I can tell you what I don't know, Yuri? What do you want me to say?'

Yuri crouched down and smiled as he bounced on his ankles. 'Who have killed my brother?'

The man put his wrist under his nose and continued pleading. 'I haven't heard a thing—not a whisper, not a rumour. You know I'd tell you if I knew *anything*, Yuri, please.'

Yuri slapped the man's arm from his face and again rose to standing. 'Who have killed my brother?' he said calmly, and without giving him time to replead his ignorance he sent his fist onto the man's face. 'Who have killed my brother?' Again he punched him, before instantly repeating: 'Who have killed my brother?!'—and at last Yuri knocked him out.

II

More than halfway through her first week of high school, Annie was several times a day discovering a large and confusing incongruence between her textbook and her teacher's lessons. Each of Ms Conrad's periods seemed to bring a new, and longer, divergence from what Annie could clearly see she was supposed to be learning.

'So I just want to reinterate,' said Ms Conrad, twenty minutes into an unbroken monologue, 'that press freedom is a form of white privilege—and anyone who says that privilege doesn't exist, is actually exercising their privilege in saying it.'

Annie put her hand up and whispered, 'Ms Conrad?'

Ms Conrad welcomed the inquisitiveness. 'Yes! Annie!'

'This is maths?'

'I'm sorry?'

'This is—all this is maths?'

'Do you not think this is important?'

'Oh I didn't say that. It's just—you came in with a ruler and we all have our protractors out. You said at the start this was a maths lesson.'

'I'm getting to the racism of maths—worry not, child. Understanding privilege is necessary for understanding how maths has been used to oppress people and communities of colour.'

'And that's algebra?' said Annie, looking at the headings and subheadings on the first pages of her textbook.

Ms Conrad looked down at her desk and shook her head. 'Do not get me *started* on algebra. Did you know algebra was invented by Muslims? And stolen by Europeans, just like how Europeans stole this land? Actually that's a great idea. Today in maths we're going to learn about Islam—

thank you, Annie—the religion of peace.'

Each day more enamoured of Ben—Ben, who had asked her to put clothes *on* in the banya—Ben, who had refrained from stroking her sweating neck and who in two brief conversations had betrayed not a single sign of lustfulness—Alexa emerged from the shade of the freeway and between concrete pylons descended the grassy bank of Moonee Ponds Creek.

As though it were a holy object she held upon both hands a wreath of wild flowers. A frame of green wicker threaded with poppies and daisies and cornflowers, she knelt down and held it over the tea-coloured puddle which she had chosen as the closest flowing body of water to Ben's place of work.

'Oh Ben, my crush,' she said to herself. 'I entrust our fate to the waters of the land. And now that you are my crush, may I be yours, and may love flow into our lives as these blossoms on a stream, and soon.'

She released the disc of flowers and reached down to take a poppy from it before clasping her hands and watching it drift away. She thought about how romantic it would be if Ben himself recovered it from the torrent, for whomever found a wreath so cast was destined to become her lover.

It's a Ukrainian thing.

Momentarily the wreath caught too much concrete and stalled; shortly it span in and wafted around the bend— where a man who had recently fallen from river dandy to creek tramp was surprised to have so delicate an object hit his bare feet. With gloved hands he lifted it from the water. On the freshness of its flowers he reasoned that it had only just been set adrift. He walked up the concrete river bed to perhaps catch a glimpse of, surely, she who had released the splendid token. In blue coat tails and a puffy shirt he watched Alexa ascend the river bank before crossing under the freeway to her car.

He took off his grey top hat and held it to his chest and said, 'To our next meeting, Magnolia, and soon.'

Thinking that at last he had lost the man who had returned to Dixon Hardware to show him samples of his stool, Mel went back to his aisle of chairs and to his day of trying to perceive customers as something more than seat-seeking nuisances.

'Mel?'

'Yeah?' he said, suspicious of being thusly addressed at work.

'Drew,' said the man and pointed to himself. 'Fluckinger.'

Mel squinted then recognised him. 'Flucking Fluckinger? Shouldn't you be grooming a child somewhere?'

'How did you know?'

'How'd I know what?'

'About my new business.'

For Drew Fluckinger, at high school in a band with Mel called The Four Skins—but that'd take too long to flash back to—then vaguely his friend into their first year at university, had recently started a new venture:

…In a purple top hat he stood outside the enclosed trailer that he'd had custom built and there twirled a bejewelled cane as he addressed the accompanied parents who neared him.

'Let *us* groom your child, Madame!' But the woman grabbed her son at the shoulders and hurried on.

'Manicure and a haircut, little girl?' he said to the next child to walk by, whose father then emerged from a 7-11. 'Let Drew's Mobile Child Grooming attend to all your bodily needs! Care for a little grooming, little girl? Sir, how would you like to have me groom your child?' The father pushed Drew by the shoulders and pinned him against his own trailer. 'People like you should be castrated.'

The Gum Smuggler

Twirling thusly for two months, Drew's child-grooming business was proving far less lucrative than he had projected…

'Steve Blackman told me you're a chair man now?'

'Scam Steve Blackman? How does *he* know that—wait, did he say chairman or chair man?'

'What do you mean?'

'Scam Steve Blackman.'

'Hey, how bout lunch tomorrow?'

'I'll be eating lunch tomorrow.'

'With me?'

'I don't think so.'

'Come on, Mel! Old time's sake. I could really use a chat about something—money actually.'

'I have to work, Drew, I don't have time.'

'On a Sunday?'

'There's no rest for a chairman.'

'I'll come in next week then, we'll have a snag from the barbie.' Drew pointed his thumb back to the cafeteria adjacent to the nursery section. 'I hear Dixon sausages are pretty tasty—I'll catch you.'

'Mel?' Fiona sang at length.

'What!? Oh.'

'Calm down.'

Mel sighed. 'What are you doing here?'

'I just popped in to see Dad, is that all right?'

'Sorry. Long day.'

'I'll leave you to it,' and she did.

'Maggie's farm, hey brah?' said someone who had taken Fluckinger's place.

Mel repressed the urge to dispel the young man and his Led Zeppelin t-shirt. 'What?'

'Tough job working at Dixon Hardware, man. I hang out in the next aisle, I'm a pot dealer.'

'Www—. Should you be telling me that?'

'I think they're gonna fire me but. I haven't sold a pot in four weeks.'

'Oh yes, very funny. You're a pot dealer, who sells pots in the gardening section. Vice President's over there, I'm the chairman, and you're a pot dealer. Ha ha, ha.'

'Ah *you're* the new Chair Man!'

'Chairman.'

'Nice to meet ya, Chair Man. Hey you got any ideas on how to sell more pot? I could use some help from an exec.'

His Burmese giant water bug and new Malayan scarab both on his desk, Fiona's father was hunched over as he switched from admiring one to inspecting the other.

'Hi, Fi.' Geoff rose and hugged his daughter. 'How you doing?'

'I'm OK. How's the new girlfriend?'

'Mm.'

'Everything all right?'

'She has two fetishes I'm not really OK with. Or not with the way she says them anyway. Have you ever heard of a pea fetish?'

'Dad!'

'You're right, sorry. To what do I owe the pleasure?'

'I want to show you something, and ask you what you think about it.'

'You haven't taken up painting or anything, have you?'

'What?'

'You're not about to show me something you've painted? Or potted, or woven or anything?'

'No.'

'Good.' She placed the manila folder on her father's desk and pushed it towards him. 'What's this?'

'It was dropped into my lap at Pete's funeral.' Geoff opened its cover as Fiona talked him through its meagre and confusing contents. 'The first page is a police report, right?

The Gum Smuggler

Which is—I mean, it's Pete. And the second page, I just... None of it makes sense, they're like cryptic crossword clues.'

Geoff turned the police report over and put his forearms on his desk. His head lowered as he read the three phrases that had been baffling Fiona. Then he went through them with her one by one:

'*Great at breastfeeding.* Hmm. ... Can you just be good at breastfeeding? There aren't competitions are there? I've seen Japanese... ahh. ... Did Pete do research in breastfeeding?'

'Not that I know of. His research was paediatric cardiology.'

'Great at breastfeeding,' Geoff repeated, similarly perplexed by the fragment. 'Could it refer to a kid maybe? Like a kid that gets the milk out quickly?'

'I mean, it could. But what does that have to do with the other two?'

'*Retarded eel magnet.* What the *hell* does that mean? Can an eel be... differently abled? Are eels magnetic? You have electric eels. Or!' he said with his mouth covered. 'Is the eel retarded or the magnet's retarded? That'd make it an eel-magnet—but what the hell's an eel-magnet? Or a nnagnet. Maybe it's a technical term, like fire-retarded?'

'That's retard-ant.'

'Retard-ant?'

Fiona nodded.

'I've always wondered about that. So maybe it's a retardant eel magnet—an eel magnet that retards something.'

'But it does say...'

'Retarded.'

'Yep.'

'A magnet for retarded eels?' He shook his head and concluded: 'That doesn't make any sense. A broken eel magnet? What the f--k is an eel magnet?'

'And why is it below "great at breastfeeding", behind a police report? Pete never did anything wrong, he shouldn't have a police record at all.'

'*A juiced scud*,' said Geoff, reading the final phrase from her scantily printed page. 'Scud's a missile isn't it? A Russian one. Was Pete involved in anything… Russiany?'

'His brother maybe, but not Pete.'

'Juiced like, amped up? Like a juiced athlete? Loaded—or nuclear!' Geoff lowered his voice. 'Fi. They *are* communists.'

'They're not communists, Dad,' said Fiona, dismissing his most frequent misconception of her in-laws. 'And a nuclear missile couldn't possibly have anything to do with Pete. It's Pete! But you see, right? None of it makes sense.'

Geoff repeated the three phrases, as though in quick succession they might reveal their own meaning: 'Great at breastfeeding, retarded eel magnet, a juiced scud.' He put his fingers to his lips. 'It's very strange, Fi.'

'It is strange, right?'

'*Who* gave it to you?'

'I have no idea. I was sitting on a bench after the burial and it fell in my lap. When I looked up a car was driving away.'

'Take it to the cop shop?'

'I did. They… well they kind of dismissed me. It's like they were trying to confuse me, or deny the file even existed.'

Geoff closed the folder and inspected its cover. 'This is AFP, you know that right?'

'It's what?'

'The logo,' said Geoff and tapped at it. 'That's not local, that's the federal police.'

'Which one's the federal police?'

'The airport.'

After school Yuri took Annie to U-Crane.

'You have never been in banya?'

'It's like a sauna?'

'How have your father not taken you? It is fine Ukrainian tradition.'

The Gum Smuggler

'Annie!' said Alexa, neck deep in a cauldron suspended on an iron frame over a fire pit.

'Hi, Auntie Alexa. What are you doing in there? You look like someone's trying to boil you like Bugs Bunny.'

'Anastasia has come for her first ever banya.'

'Oh, come here then!'

Alexa stood in the water and Annie averted her eyes from her naked aunt. 'Come, Nastyusha—you can't go in with your hair like that.' She waved Annie over then reached a foot out to the steps of the cauldron's ladder; Yuri took off his clothes and put on a pointy felt hat and went into the banya. Alexa's breast now came frighteningly close to Annie's face as she asked her to stand up straight. Alexa's breast then swung into Annie's forehead as she separated three sections of her hair. Alexa's breast jiggled at Annie's ear as she tugged and twisted at the weaving of a braid.

When the weaving was complete Alexa took a pin from her own braid and tucked Annie's into itself then fixed it into place.

'Now you are ready for banya.'

'Thanks,' said Annie, frozen and staring into the low distance.

Alexa's breasts formed a momentary headrest as she pulled Annie in for a humid hug. Her aunt implored her to take off all her clothes and soon with her elbows close and her wrists crossed Annie walked shyly into the banya.

'Hi, Grandpa.'

'Anastasia!' said Arsen from the centre of the top bench. 'Look at your hair! You look beautiful.'

'Grandpa, why is everyone naked?'

Arsen chuckled. 'You think it is strange?'

'Mm hm,' said Annie, straining to keep her eyes on the ceiling.

'This is who we are, Nastyusha—no disguise, no costume. Who can you be more honest with than family? And this is who you are.'

Annie sat with hunched shoulders on the front edge of the lower bench as Arsen leaned down and stirred the wooden ladle through its bucket. 'Now in banya, here is beer and water. Special Ookrainian mixture. Take the spoon, and throw it on the rocks.'

'Me?'

'Take.'

She took the ladle from her grandfather and dropped its mixture onto the cage of stones beside him. A hiss sounded through the banya and shortly Annie's head felt even hotter and she thought she could smell crumpets.

'Australian city is not in nature. But here with branch we return to forest,' Arsen slapped Annie on the back with his bunch of leaves. 'And with beer, we return to field. With smoke of water going through, we are part of the rhythm of life. My granddaughter, are you OK?'

Annie's face had turned red and she was shaking and squeezing her hands.

'Nastyusha?'

'It's so hot, Grandpa.'

'You will get used. But quick, go outside and jump in ice pool.'

'Ice pool,' said Annie and stood and hurried to reach such a thing, but stepped desperately aside as Alexa's breasts came in.

'Close the door,' Arsen called down and Annie pushed it shut behind her.

Yuri continued. 'He is saying again and again that he is hearing not one word from anyone. Not heavies, not Georgians—not north Pole norther south Pole. I am thinking I am believing him. In his eyes I can see he knows I was about to—'

Annie reopened the door. 'Grandpa, I'm going to stay out here.'

The Gum Smuggler

'OK, Nastyusha. Just close the door.'
'Can I go into the Bugs Bunny thing?'
'Yes, close the door—you'll let Bannik in.'
'Let what in?'
'Anastasia, close the door!'

But it was too late. The whirring in the steam-filled cabin, which Annie hadn't previously noticed, suddenly ceased and the banya fell eerily silent. Yuri looked to his father and both seemed to wait for something. Alexa too sat perfectly still, her eyes half-rolled back in her head in frightened anticipation. Then there came from behind the caged stones a deep and echoey cackle.

'Out!' said Arsen and rose from his seat and stepped down. 'Quickly, go.'

Standing all of them naked, Yuri and Arsen in pointy felt hats, the four Sukhimovs stood outside the banya and stared through fogged glass as inside the room's light began to flicker.

'What was that noise, Grandpa?'
'That was Bannik.'
'What's Bunnik?'
'Bannik's a goblin,' said Alexa.
'If he get into banya, we cannot go into banya.'
'Did you say a goblin?'
'One *angry* little man,' said Yuri. 'With old white hair and pointy fingernails like seller of fortune.'
'He throw boiling water. He will scratch Yuri's back with claws. He will *squeeze* you and Oleksa.'
'It's a Ukrainian thing,' said Alexa.

'Grandpa, that can't be real!' Annie stepped forward and opened the banya's door. The same echoey cackle sounded then turned into a loudening hiss as it seemed to rush for the door. Annie slammed it shut and gave a short and frightened hoot as she stood back.

'It is Bannik. We have to get rid.'

III

At dawn the next day Alexa, in a loose white dress, walked the very short distance to the park nearest her home.

At the park's centre was a kind of oval bowl, sloping gently down from its wooded outskirts to a flat lawn. Amid magpie song and an early morning breeze Alexa crouched and ran her fingers through the grass. It was, as she had hoped, dewy. She slid her dress's straps from her shoulders and let it fall to the moist ground. She smiled and closed her eyes and whispered, 'Oh, Ben. May my crush be mutual, and ours—and the gentle waters of the passing night invigorate it.' She unhooked her bra but decided against getting completely naked. 'May you find me young, and beautiful, and fruitful—and your affection for me be quenched as the morning grass by dew.'

And Alexa lay on the ground and tumbled down the hill and—in the hope that it would increase her youthfulness, her attraction, her fertility—rolled through its grass glistening with fresh dew. It's a Ukrainian thing.

Her whispered prayer had been loud enough to wake the only man still asleep in the park. He lifted his boater hat from his chest as he stood in the clump of bushes that he had twice that week defended as his own. He rubbed his eyes with the backs of his fingers, unconvinced that he was really looking at a topless woman rolling through the grass of the park's inverted hill. 'Marian?' When still they beheld Alexa tumbling around the bowl, now back and forth along its longest slope, he brushed the leaves and the dirt from his Norfolk jacket and put on his hat.

'A woman as green as the grass!' he said, and stepped further behind his clump of bushes so she wouldn't spot him watching. 'Just the luck of a travelling salesman. Marian!

The Gum Smuggler

'What are you wanting for lunch today? Big speech? Little speech? Tiny speech?'

Yuri strolled through the produce section of a supermarket and put a nectarine, an apricot, a plum into a plastic bag. Annie passed him the bread roll she had chosen from an assorted wall of them and he put it on top of the speeches as together they neared the supermarket's entrance. Then he walked out with them—through the wide space between eight self-serve checkouts.

Annie hesitated to follow him. Quickly she concluded that her uncle wasn't going to look, let alone turn, back. She hurried through the herd of people scanning their own groceries and whispered when she caught up to him: 'Uncle Yuri, we didn't pay for our shopping.'

'We are never paying for shopping.'

'You just stole it?'

'Anastasia. In order to steal, one must be stealing from someone. What is name of person from whom we have stealed?'

'From the supermarket!'

'Supermarket is one person? Who are its parents? Company that is owning supermarket also is owning all gambling machines in whole country. It is wrong to steal from casino?'

'I'm pretty sure it is. What if we get caught?'

'Australian people are so in love with their consumering, that no one ever will be thinking I am not paying for onething—that we, are not paying for onething.'

In the dairy aisle of the same store Geoff and Marnie were in search of some smoked salmon for the homemade breakfast they had conceived while flicking tepid peas off the bedsheets.

'Here we are,' said Geoff and looked up to browse the

selection. 'Scottish or Tasmanian? Smoked or plain? Rolled? ... Marnie?'

She opened a freezer door behind him.

'Cured or smoked, I guess. ... Marnie?'

Having torn open a plastic bag she held out a handful of orange and yellow cubes as Geoff turned around. 'Will you slide the carrot between my—oo, that almost sounded dirty. Will you slide the carrot over my chest?'

'What?'

'Or rub the corn inside my arm?'

'I thought you had a pea fetish.'

'I do!' she smiled and bulged her eyes.

'But you're what—turned on by a frozen corn bag? Is it frozen vegetables in general?'

'I'm all worked up from lying in bed this morning.'

'Speaking of which... For someone with a sex addiction I would have thought morning sex might be on the table.'

'You wanna have sex on a table? We can do that. Oo, rub this corn on my collarbone. Or! D'you wanna take a leek?'

'Marnie?' A bald man in an orange robe and blue jeans had recognised her while putting tofu into his basket.

'Oh my god, Ajahn Chah! What are you doing here?'

'Just shopping.'

'Here?'

'It's a supermarket.'

'Geoff this is Ajahn Chah. Ajahn Chah, Geoff.' Geoff broke from staring at the folds in the man's scalp and robe and nodded and shook his hand.

'Well I'll see you tonight, right?'

'Definitely!' said Marnie.

Geoff stared at all the folds as Ajahn Chah went off down the aisle. He grinned and said, 'Who's that?'

'He's the leader of one of my group sects.'

'That guy?' Geoff stared for a moment at the aisle-end down which the Buddhist hunk had turned. 'What exactly

The Gum Smuggler

are you involved in, Marnie?'

'Oh it's nothing too crazy—I thought you were OK with it? We just go into the forest and they bring me as close as possible to nirvana.' She smiled in recollection: 'They have this monkey there who likes to watch. But when your eyes are closed he—'

'A monkey?'

'He's adorable, but he is a little cornbag. Here, put this pea on my neck.' She lifted her dyed-dark hair from her shoulder and tilted her head and held out a bag of frozen peas.

'Peas,' said Geoff.

'You're so polite. Please.'

'You want peas on your neck in public?'

'Please,' she moaned. 'That talk of table sex got me hot under the colour.'

'Marnie...'

'Geoff, put the pea on me.'

'Peas.'

'Please!'

'Marnie, we need to talk.'

'Do you *want* to take a leek?'

'Same company also is mining coal,' said Yuri. 'Coal! Like Charles Dickens in year 2561. *And* they cut down forest, Anastasia. It is wrong to take from company that is destroying earth that is yours?'

Again Annie shrugged. Her uncle's arguments were beginning to make sense but still the sight of him walking through the self-serve checkout without paying made her uncomfortable.

'They are stealing your future—destroying nature of environment that is your inheritance. Your father was having forests. Your father was having clean air for breathing. He would have passed them to you, but cannot because supermarket. It is volcanic corruption. You call it supermarket. I do not see what is super about it.' He handed her the plastic bag as she left his side to round the car. 'Now, make lunch on way to school.'

Fiona walked into the ground-floor section of the international airport which her phone had told her housed the public office of the Australian Federal Police. Among all the grey and the beige and the plastic she searched for a sign pointing in that office's direction. Then shouting erupted at the arrival hall's centre.

Fiona turned towards it and beyond a pylon saw a man wearing a kind of tunic, and who had only a single tuft of hair that looked like a giant sperm had swum into the top of his head. Holding a luggage trolley between himself and two police officers he stepped right, stepped left—pushed it towards them and turned to sprint away—only to find that two other officers had surrounded him. He collided with their embrace, which immediately turned him back around. Swarmed by eight knees, he found himself prostrate, floor-cheeked, handcuffed. He was picked up by his arms and Fiona followed his escort to a door which until it was opened, and this odd person shoved through it, had been invisibly flush with the terminal wall.

She came to a counter and a window with holes drilled through it as though it were an otherwise airless rodent's container. Above it was the blue and white-lit logo now familiar to her from the folder she had been carrying around for almost a week. Behind it sat an officer in dark blue uniform.

'Good afternoon, hi.'

'How can I help?'

'So my husband recently… he passed, and at his funeral this was dropped into my lap.' She held both pages against the glass. 'Its first page is a police record, but then the second page is these three phrases.'

'What's your husband's name?'

She said it then spelled his surname as the officer twisted to a computer screen and tapped at its keyboard.

'Died of a heart attack?'

'What?'

'Who gave you that file, Madame?'

'Does it say he died of a heart attack?'

'Could you pass it through here for a sec?'

'They never did an autopsy, why does it say he died of a heart attack?'

A voice called out from the depths of the office: 'Sergeant Cullen?'

The officer turned an ear but when no further words came he told Fiona he'd be back in a second. He rose from his stool and went through a door with opaquely frosted windows. Fiona was attempting to read his computer screen when shortly he came back out and took his seat.

'Could I see that file for a second, Madame?'

'Can you tell me what its phrases mean?'

'Just pass the file through, I'll see what I can find out.'

'Why does Pete have a federal police file? And does it say he died of a heart attack? Is there a man with a chunk out of his ear back there?'

'Pass the file through, Madame.'

'It's *my* Peter file,' she said and reassembled and closed it.

'Madame?'

Fiona stepped back from the window with her file in both arms at her chest. 'It's my Peter file.'

'Madame?' Did you say paedophile? Was your husband a—Madame?' She turned and walked to the furthest possible corner of the terminal. She found a spot that gave her a clear view of the office and watched the invisible door. Shortly a man emerged from it, in a blue shirt and tie, and Fiona squinted to try to see if he had a chunk missing from his ear.

She thought that almost certainly he did and muttered, 'What the hell is going on?' as behind him there burst from the door he who had just been shoved through it—naked with his hands still cuffed at his back. He leapt onto a file of luggage trolleys and frolicked over their handles. As he neared its end an officer positioned herself to catch him. He jumped sideways onto a baggage carousel and its movement took his feet from under him. He fell over and had his cheek streaked with conveyer belt before rolling through luggage onto the hard floor. He rose onto his knees then stood onto bare feet and sprinted in a zig-zag as he bounded through the terminal—cackling as automatic doors opened and he fled into the daylight.

Fiona tried to relocate the man with the wedge out of his ear. She could find no familiar figure among the people returning to wait for their luggage. Then her phone rang.

She said, 'Hello,' then shortly: 'She what?'

'And when I wrote out the list of different types of public transport,' said Elvis Pterodactyl and stared down at his desk, 'I put trains, and monorails, and cable cars. But I forgot trams. So I'm sorry.'

'Well, thank you, Elvis. But it is trans-exclusionary, not trams-exclusionary.'

As Annie's classmate nodded and looked up from his desk it now was her turn to confess a thought crime. She had spent the last twenty minutes scouring her mind for what might be accepted as one, for nobody in Ms Conrad's class was permitted to assert their own innocence. Unable to continue the gapless transition from Vajeen Vajones' confession to Elvis' she stared in contemplation as Ms Conrad immediately called upon her.

'Yes, Ms Conrad?'

'Your last thought crime?'

The Gum Smuggler

Annie had to wing it: 'My... dad just died. ... And I'm starting to think the world has no meaning. Which my mum says is a bad way to think. So... that's mine.'

'So Annie, we don't actually say "dad" or "father", we say "non-gestational parent".'

'What do we say?'

Ms Conrad repeated herself, slowly and clearly: 'Non, gestational, parent.'

'Why do we say that?'

'Calling one of your parents your dad is thought-violence. *That's* your thought crime for the week.'

'But my dad did just die.'

'No, your non-gestational parent died.'

'Yes, my dad.'

'Annie, we can't say that.'

'I can't say my dad died?'

'Don't raise your voice at me, child.'

Annie, with her hair still in a braided kind of halo, now found herself unable to remain seated as she defended a statement whose repetition, and cruel denial, was beginning to upset her.

'Two weeks ago,' she announced, 'My father died.'

'Annie, you cannot say that.'

'I can say that—I can say whatever I want. And I'm saying that two weeks ago my father died.'

'Annie, you need to de-centre yourself. Check your privilege and sit down, child.'

Annie's feebleness was gone, and with it her quiet. 'Two weeks ago, Peter Sukhimov, my father, died.'

'Some children don't have fathers, Annie. Using that term is thought-violence against those who don't have gender-normative families.'

'If they don't have fathers how were they made?'

'Sit down, child!'

'My dad died,' said Annie, her voice shaking.

'You may say that that your non-gestational parent died.'
'My dad is dead.'
'You *must* say, that that your non-gestational parent is dead.'
'Anybody who tells another person what to say, Ms Conrad, should have their tongue cut out. I am Anastasia Sukhimov, and two weeks ago my dad died.'
'Principal's office. Now!'

Alexa arrived at Melbourne Zoo with the handwritten letter on which she had all of last night worked and throughout that morning rewritten. She slung the construction permit at the neck of her large-sleeved sundress and showed it to the attendant at the zoo's front entrance.

'Ben!' she said when eventually she found him.
'Hi?'
'How are you?'
'I'm good. Just at work.'
'I have something for you.' With both hands she held out an envelope.
'This is for me?' The poppy she had saved from her wreath—then pressed between two books and inserted into the envelope—fell to the ground as Ben extracted and read her letter. 'You… entrust your fate to my honour?'
'If you'll let me. Can I admit something?'
'OK…'
'I have a crush on you.'
'A crush?'
'Do you… have a crush on me?'
'Oh you're the crane girl!'
'Yes!'
'Alexa, right?'
'Alexa! Do you have a… a crush on me?'
'I mean… I don't not have a crush on you.'

The Gum Smuggler

'My crush!' she smiled, and put her hands to her chest and stepped in and kissed him on the cheek. 'I was thinking maybe…'

'Wanna get dinner some time?'

'Yes! Oh, my crush! Nothing would delight me more!'

'It's a date.'

'A date!' said Alexa and pushed his hard hat back and kissed his cheek again. 'What about tonight?'

'Tonight?'

'Tonight!'

Their second embrace was rendered very brief by a loud crack and a crash then a trunk-squeal—as into the elephant enclosure's moat fell a thin concrete slab. Above it a loose cable swung from the boom of a crane whose arm came slowly back over the zoo's wall.

'What the hell's happened?' said Alexa as she and Ben made for the emergency door.

'It's the bloody driver,' said Ben. 'He's hopeless. Third precast he's dropped in two days.'

'Where's he from?'

'I don't know, he barely speaks English.'

'Which company?'

Ben and Alexa came through the zoo's wall as the crane's cab swung slowly around.

'Frasier Crane.'

Inside, a chubby man with a large forehead and bulging eyes wore huge headphones as he pulled back one shift-stick and pushed forward another. In tennis shorts and a white polo shirt—cable-knit jumper tied at his shoulders—he looked to Ben and smiled and waved. 'That was close one!'

'Nooo,' said Alexa. 'No, no, no, no, no. Frasier Crane are the worst,' and she called her father.

Admitting that only Finns matched Ukrainians in banya expertise, Arsen sat over some mountain tea with Jan

Hämäläinen of Finnished Saunas.

'You are shaying it is a problem *behind* the rocksh or *under* the rocksh?' said Jan with meaty s's.

'It is both.'

'I don't undershtand how thish can be poshible. It's an electrical problem, or a ventilation problem?'

'It is neither I think.'

'Well that *ish* imposhible.'

'Come, I show you.' At the banya's door Jan pulled his overalls back from his shoulders then took off his shirt.

'What are you doing?'

'A Finn cannot go in a shauna with his clothes on. It is bad luck.'

'You are just to repair. It's not hot.'

'Nevertheless.'

'What?'

'It's not on.'

'No, it's not on—why you are taking off clothings?' Arsen held open the banya door and scowled as Jan took off his boots then pulled his boxer shorts from his feet.

'Nice saunamyssy,' said Jan and pointed to the rack of felt hats on the banya's outside wall as he stepped through to its silent and room-temperature rear.

'Everything was normal, we were sitting there, around 82 degrees, then bang! It stops and start to make loud noise. We run out, light goes off—then flashing. Now not work.'

Jan knelt in front of the vertical cage filled with stones. He took a torch from his plastic toolbox then searched for a point of entrance to the banya's stove. Arsen averted his eyes as Jan leaned very far forward and twisted and jiggled. He was relieved when his phone rang. 'What?'

Alexa told him about the near-accident.

'So why do you call me? You want to take over U-Crane, this is what you must deal.'

'You need to let this go, Papa. You know I want to make

my own money, use my own brain.'

'Silly complications, Oleksa. Who is operator?'

'Frasier Crane.'

Arsen grunted. 'They are idiots. Tell Zoo Crane man about radio show. And how only they eat egg salad—and who they hire. F-----g Byelorussians! Oleksa, you *know* what to do, don't call me for this.'

The repairman screamed and fell forward as he had his arm pulled into the rear of the stove. Arsen hung up on his daughter and hurried to the depths of the banya. Jan extracted and beheld his arm, now bearing three crimson scratches from wrist to elbow. 'What in earth is in there?'

'What do you find? You scratch arm on screw?'

'Shcrew? That was alive, sir! You need a bat-catcher or shomething. That was a kind of an animal in there. A bad animal.

'Bannik,' Arsen lamented as the repairman hurried to take his clothes to the front office.

With rebloodied hands Yuri unflipped his phone. 'Fiona. What am I owing this great and goodly pleasure?'

'I need you to come to Annie's school.'

'Yes, I will be picking her at 3 and 10 o'clock.'

'You need to come now.'

'Now, now—now?'

'Annie's in trouble, and the principal doesn't believe you exist.'

'Exist? I am existing, and flourishing. I will show him who is not existing. Five minutes.' He closed his phone and pointed down at the mangled face cowering between his feet. 'You are very difficult man. But today, lucky.'

'Soil yourself!'

Standing on a podium of stacked bags of soil mix and haranguing with a smile each customer who walked into the gardening section, Mel pointed to a customer among shelves of plastic and ceramic plant pots and shouted again: 'Madame! Yes, you there—soil yourself!'

He had taken The Pot Dealer's plea for help as further impetus to his niece's sermon—truly an opportunity to assist a colleague who if not in full possession of a unique and interesting soul was at least more so than the savages who needed chairs. 'You there, Sir!' A man turned from counting stacked saucers. 'Soil yourself!'

'Excuse me?'

'Today only, free soil with any forty-dollar purchase of pots, saucers, *or* planters.'

'Oh OK. Thanks.'

'*You're* the guy helping out The Pot Dealer!' said The Drill Sergeant, come to investigate Mel's inter-aisle altruism.

'I am!'

'Me and The Vice President think you're doing all right!'

'Thanks, Drill Sergeant' said Mel, surprised by the kindness. 'Good afternoon, Sir—soil yourself!'

'I beg your pardon?'

'You the guy helping out The Pot Dealer?'

'Hey! I am!' said Mel from his dais. 'Soil yourself, Madame! Today only, free soil with any forty-dollar purchase of pots, saucers, *or* planters. Who are you?'

Beneath a sailor's cap the man wore a t-shirt printed with crossed belts of rifle ammunition. 'Counter-revolutionary.'

'Of course you are!' said Mel and gave a feeble laugh. 'Let me guess—you sell counters?'

'Kitchen counters, bathroom counters—all your benchtop needs—at *revolutionary* prices.'

'This store, I tell you!'

'Hey, Counterrevolutionary!' said The Drill Sergeant. 'This is the new Chair Man.'

'The Blind Guy told me! The Blind Guy tells me you're a bit of an adventurer, Chair Man.'

The Gum Smuggler

'That I am, Counterrevolutionary. That I am. Good afternoon, Madame—soil yourself!'

The Pot Dealer returned to his own section: 'Chair Man!'

'Pot Dealer!'

'There's a dude with purple teeth in your aisle, Chair Man. Says he wants to talk to ya.'

'Tell him I'm busy.'

'Yeah I told him that. He told me to stick butter in my mouth and get f----d by a baker.'

'Jesus,' said Mel, instantly ceasing his search for new customers to shout at.

He stepped down from his podium and enthusiastically The Pot Dealer took his place. Normally disinclined to talk to customers, he now mounted the soil mix, for he could not remember ever having sold so many pots.

Waiting on one of the soft chairs looked down at by the several people staffing the school's office, Fiona's file was open on her knee. Again she was meditating on the three phrases of its second page, wondering how, or if, they might be related to one another and what possibly they could have to do with Pete—Pete! Who according to the federal police died of a heart attack? It made less sense now than before she had inquired after it. She closed the folder and put it aside and took up her phone. She typed, 'Breastfeeding competition,' into the top bar of an internet browser and was returned a single result: a video from a Brazilian prison in which such a thing was annually held. She watched babies scramble over inmates as cats over sushi-laden bodies then typed 'eel magnets' into the same. The phone's rainbow-wheel was spinning when her name was called and Mr Blodgett the school's principal waved her into his office.

'I do have a diversity conference in ten minutes,' said Mr Blodgett. 'How far away's Annie's uncle?'

'He's around the corner, he'll be five minutes.'

'I guess we can start.' He showed Fiona into his office and had her sit in one of the chairs facing his desk. 'So there was an issue today with Annie's language. I understand her non-gestational parent recently died?'

'Her what?'

'Your partner.'

'My husband? What about him?'

'I understand he died recently, if those were his pronouns.'

'He d—. Yes. He did.'

'I'm sorry to hear. But this morning in Ms Conrad's history class, Annie used some pretty upsetting language, and refused to stop using it when she was asked not to.'

'Wait, where's my Peter file?' Fiona darted her head from one corner of the desk to the other.

'Your what?'

'The Peter file, where is it?' Fiona leaned over to inspect the area around one ankle then the other.

'What are you looking for?'

'My Peter file,' Fiona almost shouted as she twisted in her chair.

'Are you saying…?'

Yuri rounded the corner which led to the school's office and through a large window saw Fiona writhing and searching. 'Oh there he is.' He banged on the window then gave Fiona his customary greeting of a bow of his head and a flourish of his hand.

'That man's a paedophile?' said Mr Blodgett.

'That's Annie's uncle.'

'Annie's uncle's paedophile?'

'What?'

Fiona stood up and stepped out and was relieved and relaxed to find her file on the table beside the soft chair. Yuri came into the school's office and followed Fiona into the principal's.

The Gum Smuggler

'Yuri, this is Ken Blodgett, Annie's principal.'

Yuri puffed out his chest and folded his arms. 'Why you have called me away from urgent business of most important day?'

'Fiona tells me you've been looking after Annie the last few days.'

Yuri raised his chin and awaited the man's point.

'This morning in Ms Conrad's history class Annie was telling everyone—'

'My she-nephew is taught history by a comrade?'

'Ms Conrad, yes.'

'Already I am not liking this.'

'And *in* Ms Conrad's history class, Annie refused to apologise for saying her father has just died.'

'My brother's death was not her fault. Why should she be apologising?'

'We try to create an inclusive environment at Elwood College, and that means taking into consideration the dynamics of all our families.'

'This is a puzzlement. Why you are calling me here? Fiona, why am I called here?'

'As I said, we try to create as inclusive an environment as possible, in line with our diversity—which we're *very* proud of—and that does mean we use gender-neutral language wherever possible. If you could both start using the term "non-gestational parent", instead of "father", or "dad"—I'm sure Annie'll fit much better into Ms Conrad's learning scheme.'

'I am finding much confusion. It is my brother who have died, but more it was Anastasia's father. She will not be hugging him for rest of present life.'

'Yes. See, Ms Conrad won't be tolerating that kind of language in her class. *We* can't tolerate that kind of language in the school.'

'You are not liking way that I am speaking?'

'Not you, Annie. Ms Conrad, as I said, told me that—'

'A comrade tells my she-nephew she cannot say her father has died, and you are calling me for coming here? Annie has stated what is scientific fact.'

'Well facts are expressed by language, Yuri, is it? And the facts don't change, just the language we use to express them. As I said, inclusivity is key.'

'What is this in-clu-sivity? I will be entertaining no unscientific notions as yours. Fiona's husband have died. My brother, have died. To Anastasia her father have died. If you are disrespecting his memory another more time, you shall see who is existing and who is not. Good day.'

And without unfolding his arms Yuri left.

Mel found in his aisle a large man in a faded-blue ski jacket crossed at the chest with a rainbow of muted colours. When he was close enough to read the text above and below the oversized logo on its breast—Tonny Halfmaker—the man said, 'You. You are in charge of this?'

Mel found himself unable to instantly reply, for the colour of the man's teeth was extraordinary. 'I... I sell chairs, yeah.' His hair too was bewildering: short and parted in the middle and pointed at the sides and brushed slightly forward.

'You are chair man?'

'I wouldn't go that far, no.'

'Where is chair man? Who is in charge of this?'

'This is my aisle. Are you looking for a chair?'

'You are chair man?'

'All right, I'm The Chair Man, OK? Does that make you happy?' Mel raised his voice and spoke both to himself and the store: 'I admit that I'm The Chair Man.'

'You are chair man?'

'Yes!'

The man thrust from within his jacket a stack of 50-dollar notes into Mel's hand. 'I need guns.'

The Gum Smuggler

'Hm?'

'Guns. I need.'

The resurgence of what was becoming the central joke of Mel's life deflated him. 'No, listen.' He put his chin in his hand and sighed and shook his head. 'No guns, OK?' He returned the cash to the man's enormous hand. 'I never smuggled guns.'

'You are chair man?'

'I said I was.'

'Dobre, I need guns,' and the wad found itself again in Mel's possession.

'Gum.'

'Hm?' said the man, and began searching his pockets.

'Gum-m.'

'I don't have, sorry.'

'No, I smuggled gum.'

'Ohhhhh,' said the very round man, and in accepting the encodement bulged his eyes: 'I need *gum*.'

'No, idiot, look.'

'What?'

'I'm not a gun smuggler. I accidentally smuggled gum-m. OK?'

'You are making confuse.'

'I am not a smuggler of any kind, do you understand? No smuggle.'

'No, no smuggle. You have, I buy.' Into Mel's hand went the slab of money once more.

'You're not understanding me, guy. Listen, no smuggle. No guns, no gum. I didn't smuggle anything—on purpose. I am *not* a gun smuggler.'

'OK. But you have?'

'No, I no have.'

'You are chair man?'

'I'm not admitting it again.'

'I need gun.'

'Gum.'

'I no have gum!'

'Please go away. I don't have guns, I don't have gum. I can't chew gum, I have sensitive purple. Teeth. I have sensitive teeth.'

'You are making confuse.'

'No guns, all right?'

'You are chair man?'

'Please, go away.'

The man raised one eyebrow and appeared to attempt to touch his nose with his chin. 'Your doctor brother was more better at you than this.' And he returned the money to his jacket and walked off.

'My what?' The stripes on his jacket grew smaller as he walked to the front of the aisle. 'Did you say doctor brother?' Mel called, then walked after him as he turned towards the cash registers.

'Hi,' said a unique and interesting soul, leaning back from her browsing. 'I have a question about the Elba resin bistro chair.'

'Peter?'

'Does it come in cappuccino?'

Fiona followed Yuri's striding from the school's office, across the outdoor basketball courts to its front gate.

'Yuri, is there a chance that Pete's death wasn't random?'

'Why do you ask of me this?'

'I just have a weird feeling. Something's not adding up.'

'I am knowing my brother was murdered.'

'Murdered? What do you mean, you know?'

'I have seen it in one dream. His death was no accident, it was ah-ssassination.'

'Assassination? Who—wha—I mean… why?'

'Shortly I will be knowing these out. If person who is involved is of known and interest to you, you also will be

The Gum Smuggler

knowing. But this I am thinking will be un-likely.'

'And what have you been saying to Annie?'

'About this? Not one such thing.'

'Have you been telling her that nobody can tell her what to think or say?'

'I would never,' said Yuri, dipping his head as he placed his knuckles at his hips.

'This morning she told her teacher that anybody who tells someone else what to think should have their tongue cut out.'

Yuri raised his chin and laughed. 'I have merely told to her some truths of which she was not previously sure. If you are telling truth to most people, they will not be hearing it. But Anastasia is intelligent. I can educate her according to ancient lines, she is like magnet to many truths.'

'Magnets!' said Fiona. 'That reminds me.' She took out her phone and dragged down the open browser page and waited for its results to refresh.

'As for my brother, I am certain I am sure it is because my father's past, and that my brother fought for liberty— and that ASIO spies had something very much to do with ah-ssassination. You are not listening.'

'Hm? I am.' Fiona looked up from a screen that was showing her fridge magnets of cartoon eels. 'I was looking something up about Pete—did you say Asian pies? Wait, what's liver tea? You're not giving Annie liver tea are you— is that a Ukrainian thing?'

Then Yuri's phone rang. 'I have had enough of this machine! What? ... Sister. ... Yes, I am able... Very well.' He snapped his phone in half and threw it into a bush. 'I cannot today pick Anastasia up from school. I must to work, but you can place her at my home, she knows where is spare key.'

'You think Peter was assassinated?'

IV

'Then she sent me to the principal's office because I kept saying "dad".' With towels at their shoulders Mel and Annie descended the wooden steps behind Brighton's beach boxes. 'Don't you think that's weird?'

'I've never really thought about it,' said her uncle.

'If you had kids they wouldn't be allowed to call you Dad. They'd have to call you "Non-Gestational Parent".'

'If I had kids I'd be worried about them calling someone else Non-Gestational Parent.'

Fiona was in a marquee adventurer on the ledge of her family's peach-and-lime-striped beach box. At her knee her Peter file was open to its second page; she was no longer staring at it, but rather beyond it, in a confused and circular stupor. When chatter heralded the arrival of her daughter she tilted her head in Annie's direction. 'Hi, honey! How was the rest of school?'

'Good.'

Mel unfolded another marquee adventurer and placed it beside his sister. 'Annie, you wanna get an ice-cream?'

'Oo, yes please.'

'Here's five bucks, get whatever you want.' When she was gone Mel said, 'Watcha readin'?'

'I have had the strangest day.'

'So have I. I have a question for you.'

'Mm?'

'Was Pete involved in anything... Russiany?'

She turned her head from the beyonds of her knee. 'Why do you ask that?'

'Someone came into the store today and asked for guns. Then he said that my doctor-brother was better at selling them than I was. Is Yuri a doctor? Because if he's not, the guy was talking about Pete, selling guns.'

'That is strange. Yuri thinks something's off about Pete's—. He thinks something's off too. But it makes no sense, Pete was the kindest most harmless man in the world. He also said something about Asian pies and liver tea, so... I'm worried about what he's feeding Annie. And telling her.'

Ice-cream in hand, Annie came back behind the beach boxes and when she heard her own name stopped to listen in the thin corridor formed by the sides of her own and the adjacent one.

'The guy definitely said doctor?'

'He had a thick accent, and purple teeth, but he definitely said doctor. I told him I didn't sell guns but he kept persisting, then eventually he put his money back in his pocket and he said, "Your doctor brother was better at this than you." Yuri's not a doctor, right?'

'Yuri is not a doctor. He sold a tank to a terrorist, but he is not a doctor.'

'God, he's terrifying.'

'He really is,' Fiona conceded.

'Five dollars wasn't enough,' said Annie, poking her head out from the corridor with her cone behind her back.

'What do you mean?' said Mel.

'For an ice cream. They're $5.50.'

'For soft serve?'

'Mm hm.'

'*That's* outrageous,' said Mel, and handed his niece another five-dollar note.

Yuri was outside the zoo and inside the cab of a U-Crane crane. For half an hour he had been offloading flat sections of concrete from the back of a truck, strapped to cables by two men, as Ben and his assistant manager beyond the wall guided him in their placement—all talking to one another

THE PETER FILE

on walkie-talkies.

'And how is Tiruvasi?' said Yuri as he brought the empty arm back to the car park.

'Who's that?' said the man beside Ben.

'You are seeing elephants?'

'We are,' said Ben.

'Tiruvasi is thoughtful and dignified one, and elephant with most gentle curiosity.'

'What are you, an elephant whisperer?' said the assistant manager into his walkie talkie.

'What?'

'I don't see no thoughtful elephants here, mate.'

'I forget. You see chang as only instrument, and cannot be forging genuine bond with onething more noble than yourself.'

'D'you say its name? How do you know its name?'

'I have been riding her many times.'

'Same way I ride Dave's mum?' said one of the men waiting beside the truck.

'Yeah keep it up,' said Dave, tired of his mother's rideability being alluded to no matter what job he worked on or with whom.

'They let you ride the elephants here?' said Ben.

'Absolutely not,' said a zookeeper who happened to be walking by.

'Zookeeper says you can't ride them.'

'Ah!' said Yuri as he watched the attaching of a new slab to his load block. 'First you must be taking them out of zoo.'

'What the hell are you talking about, buddy?'

'Tiruvasi was most happy to be leaving horrible place that does *not* resemble jungle.'

'We have! We've got an elephant whisperer, boys!'

'Or a bullshit artist.'

Yuri paused the latest slab's wall-crossing and leaned out

of the cab. He yelled as loudly as he could, 'Tiruvasi! Pai!'

Tiruvasi swished her tail and flapped her ears and turned to the front of the enclosure.

'Elephant is walking towards you?' said Yuri to his walkie-talkie.

Ben turned around. 'How'd you know that?'

'Tiruvasi, ngham!' Yuri waited a few moments. 'Elephant is near to water?'

'It fucking is,' said the surprised manager beside Ben.

'Tiruvasi, bong ngham! Bong!'

'Did he just make it drink?' said Ben.

'Funny guy this guy,' said Dave.

'What have you said?'

'Hilarious,' said the man beside him.

'Where do you find these blokes, boss—comedy clubs?'

'Tiruvasi, suong!' Yuri yelled as he stepped out of the crane. The elephant raised its trunk from the water and poised it in the air. 'You are believing me now?' he said into his radio as he approached half the men in the conversation.

'Bald, and funny,' said Dave as Yuri paced towards him.

'Bong suong!' The elephant seemed to smile as it sprayed a trunkful of water across the strip of garden above her enclosure.

'You wanna get back in the cab there and finish the job, buddy?'

'Then we can all go and ride Dave's mum.'

'You should not be addressing strangers, with whom you are having no familiarity, as though they are your equals. And why you are disrespecting honour of Dave's mother?'

'What?'

And Yuri punched first Dave then the man who had been standing beside him.

Arsen had offered Danylo Petreschenko, the only Ukrainian sauna repairman in the state, double his usual fee to come and look at U-Crane's banya. Danylo had already had his day's fill of mountain tea so Arsen took him straight through to the problem, where—if this book could afford goddam subtitles—they would have had the following conversation:

'You are sure it's not Bannik?'

'Sure it's not what?'

'Bannik.'

'What is Bannik?'

'You're a Ukrainian with a banya, and you don't know Bannik?' Arsen pouted and shook his head. 'If it's Bannik, Sir, and you say it's not Bannik…'

'It's the heating pipe, I'm sure. We were sitting there, my family, and it was working fine, 82 degrees. Then my Anastasia poured water and it broke. There was a big bang.'

'You did not hear a snigger?'

'I thought you could not say this word anymore?'

And as this book's author realised that that joke only works if they were conversing in English, Danylo carried his tool box warily across the banya's threshold and in overalls entered the woody calm of its unheated benches. He looked back to the thermometer nailed to the wall and sniffed. He neared the caged stones and lowered and turned his head in order to listen for signs of life. When he heard none he placed his tools on the lower bench and knelt.

Arsen tidied the felt hats on their rack and turned and leaned against the banya's outside wall. Shortly the screaming started. 'S--t.'

A loud hiss sounded from within, as though air were being sucked into the banya. Then a tool was thrown onto other tools and there came a scraping noise and at last a deep and echoey cackle. With three gashes torn from the front of his clothes Danylo stumbled out of the banya and fell into the space beneath the cauldron.

'You lie, Arsen Sukhimov! You have a Bannik—a bad

The Gum Smuggler

Bannik! I will spread word to the whole country: no repairman will come to U-Crane!'

'You don't want to come in?'

'No, thank you,' said Mel. 'Your uncle Yurine scares the bejeezus out of me.'

'Uncle what?'

Mel watched the windows of Yuri's house for any sign that he was home. 'I call him Yurine, but not to his face. Does he still think he's the king of Thailand?'

'He showed me his magical umbrella, is that what you mean? But he called it an un-brella.'

'He's so strange. And terrifying.'

'He's not terrifying.'

'He's *terrifying*. The things I've seen him do, Annie. I'd never call him Yurine to his face—you know why?'

'Why?'

'Because he'd punch me in the face.'

'He would?'

'What! You are doing outside my home?!' With both palms Yuri banged on Mel's window. When he saw that he had both scared the bejeezus out of him and made him scream like a girl, he leaned back and laughed and put his fists to his hips. Shortly he leaned in and repeated his question. Reluctantly Mel wound down his window.

'It would be my pleasure to be receiving you in my home, M-word. If I am remembered correctly, never have you been one guest of my royal hospitality.'

'Just dropping Annie off, thanks. You got everything?'

'Yep. Thanks, Uncle Mel.'

At dinner Annie saw that Yuri's knuckles were abnormally swollen and in parts the same colour as the soup he had made her.

'What happened to your hands?'

'I have punched men in face.'

'Man?'
'Men.'
'Why?'
'Some men are needing to be punched in face.'
'Like Uncle Mel?'
'He is not needing to be punched in face. He is merely needing to lead life of man, not life of boy.'
'Did you sell a tank to a terrorist?'
Yuri grinned. 'Who have told to you this?'
'Someone asked Uncle Mel today if he had any guns and then they mentioned my dad. But it might have been gums? Are paediatricians dentists for kids? Why would someone ask Uncle Mel for gums and mention my dad?'
'Who was this person? Were they saying guns or gums?'
'They asked Uncle Mel, so it'd be gums right? Or gum?'

Alexa returned to the zoo in high heels, wearing a long yellow dress and with her hair in a halo braid, and found Ben standing precisely where she had that afternoon left him.
'My crush!'
'*My* crush! You look so beautiful,' said Ben, surprised.
'Really I'm your crush? Oh Ben, you melt my heart.'
'I won't be much longer—you OK if I don't shower before we go out? I have a change of clothes in my car but there are no site showers here.'
Ben was still working because of the slowness of the driver now unloading the truck. He was from Novocrane, and Ben's late and last resort after calling the police on Yuri.
'Of cooouurse, my crush,' said Alexa. 'All that's important is that we get to spend time together.'
Inside the U-Crane crane's cab the Novocrane driver had a vacant smile on his face and stared off into the distance as he moved the panel's controls.
'Go!' said Ben impatiently into his radio. The second-last slab of concrete had been unstrapped beside the elephant

The Gum Smuggler

enclosure but the crane's boom failed to retreat.

'Hm?' said the driver into his radio.

'Go, goddam it. One slab left—pull it back, come on!'

'Hmm?' the driver smiled. 'Hmm,' he conceded to himself, and pulled a lever and rather enjoyed spinning in the cab as the boom came back over the zoo's wall. The men whom Yuri had punched in face lifted and joined the straps that at last fixed the final slab to the crane's hook.

'Go,' said Dave into the radio. When the driver stopped giggling he spun himself again as the crane raised the concrete into the air and moved it to the wall.

'Come on!' said Ben, this slab taking even longer than the last. 'This is it then we're all done.' As at last the day's final task glided over the zoo's wall, Ben looked up and urged Alexa to stand back. She sidestepped until Ben's hand stopped waving at her. 'Easy now, then done!' he said as the slab hovered over his head.

'He say done?' said the Novocrane driver, then answered his own question: 'Yep. Done!' With his head tilted and a numb grin on his face he hit the crane's emergency release button. 'Done,' he repeated with relief, and leaned forward and moaned a kind of laugh. The load line ran free from the boom and Alexa screamed as the slab of pre-cast concrete fell to the ground.

'My crush!'

Looking on from the trees of Royal Park, the River Dandy who had recently fallen to Creek Tramp, and the newly homeless Travelling Salesman—both in fancy hats and outdated clothing—clapped their hands and said, 'Yesss,' when shortly Alexa came screaming out of the zoo's emergency exit.

After a successful teeth-brushing race Yuri brought to Annie's bedside a plate of cheese. 'This is kozeloho. In your language I think is cheese of goat.'

'I just brushed my teeth.'

'Before bed is more important to have small meal of only cheese. Cheese is making dreams more frequent and more clear—and most true.'

He ate a slice from the plate and Annie took one and nibbled at its edge.

'Oo it's strong.'

'Kozeloho gives most divine auspicious dreams, a form of truth, Anastasia. Are you paying attention to dreams? Often what we see with eyes closed is more true than what we are seeing with eyes open. Finish plate of cheese and I read one bedtime story?'

Yuri turned on a lamp and switched off the bedroom's light. He sat on the edge of her bed and opened to its first page the book he had brought in. Annie nibbled at another slice and slid down her pillow and chewed as Yuri read:

'My friend Sasha, Or I will say, Nastyusha. *I love this book as a monument to a struggle in which I have sacrificed much, but not the courage of knowledge—'*

'Are you the king of Thailand?'

Yuri took a moment to answer. 'Me?'

'You.'

'I am none such thing.'

'But you are Yul Brynner?'

'His soul have been reborn in me—he have died day before I am born.'

'And he played the king of Thailand?'

'King Of Siam, four-thousand six-hundred twenty-five times. Phra Mongkut, one grandson of His Majesty Yodfa Chulalok, returner of Emerald Buddha and most scientific mind.'

'So then you…'

'Would like you now to be sleeping.'

And, content, Annie closed her eyelids and soon fell to sleep with a gentle grin at her mouth.

The Gum Smuggler

IN THE NEXT PETER FILE...

...While looking at stool samples Mel is paid a visit by a very menacing figure:

Standing suddenly before him as Mel turned from stacking stools, a man with a wide moustache under a flat-brimmed Stetson, spoke in a voice both gruff and accented: 'Ladies and gentlemen, I'm The Soil Baron.'

Mel looked over his shoulders for the ladies, or the gentlemen, whom the man thought he was addressing.

'You have a great chance here, Chair Man, but bear in mind you can lose it all if you're not careful. I've heard tell that you're trying to get between me and my soil—passing it on at a discounted rate in order to help The Pot Dealer. Yes, I make it my business to be here and to see the work that's being done in my aisle. If you go on demeaning my soil by using it as a... as a gimmick, Chair Man, I will break you and I will beat you.'

'Me?'

'This, is the way that this works.'

...Geoff breaks up with Marnie as she takes another leek:

'I just can't get past the group-sex addiction,' he said as she slid the vegetable into the crotch of her yoga pants.

'Oh, you should come along! You'll see how harmless it all is, really. Tomorrow there are three monks coming from their forest sects.'

'Do you see what I mean, Marnie? Sex with monks.'

'It's better than the sects without monks, trust me. And these ones are slowly dying out—completely unprotected sects.'

...Annie leaves her toothpaste on for too long:

'Do not ever leave bathroom when brushing teeth,' said Yuri at his bookcase. 'You will be losing track of time—hurry! Go!' Annie's eyes bulged and she turned and ran back to the bathroom.

'Show me?' Yuri said when later she hesitated to get out of the car.

'Nn nn.'

'Come, Anastasia, I am certain I am sure it's not so bad. Show to me.'

For the first time since leaving the house Annie parted her lips. Her entire mouth was purple—almost black at the gaps between her teeth and violet near her gums and streaked with pink along the grooves of each tooth.

'Is it bad?'

But Yuri was unable to tell her that it wasn't.

…And Fiona again loses the dossier pertaining to her husband:

'You punched a kid in the face?'

'He made hun of my heeth,' Annie mumbled outside the principal's office.

'Why would he make fun of your teeth? Wait, where's the Peter file?'

'Wha?' said Annie, refusing still to open her mouth.

Fiona searched the office's long counter then rummaged through the magazines on the table between the soft chairs. 'I had it with me on the way in, have you seen it?'

'Heen wha?' Annie vowelled through closed lips.

Fiona hurried outside and asked the first adult she found: 'You haven't seen a Peter file have you?'

'What?' said the immediately concerned parent.

'I had it with me when I got out of the car. It *must* be on the school premises. Never mind.'

Rounding the corner which led to the path between the ovals she asked another: 'Have you seen a Peter file?'

'A paedophile?'

'What? Why would I ask you that? We're at a sc—ohhhh!'

As she searched the grass on either side of the path she came across another meandering adult. 'Hi, excuse me, you haven't seen a… a file pertaining to a Peter have you?'

'Seen a what?'

'A file, pertaining to a Peter.'

'I don't understand the question.'

'It's a file.'

'Right.'

'Pertaining to a Peter.'

'So it's a… a Peter file?'

'Yes, all right? It's a Peter file. I'm now aware of what it sounds like, but it's *my* Peter file, I need to know where it is, have you seen one or not?'

'Have I seen a paedophile?'

'Between here and the car park, yes?'

'Should I call the police?'

'Oh they won't be any bloody help.' She turned to the crowd coming and going from the school's office. 'Attention parents of Elwood High,' she yelled. 'Have any of you seen a Peter file? It's on the school grounds, I'm not exactly sure where, but I really need to find it before the kids get out of class.'

Episode 4

THE WHITE KILT

I

It was the weekend and Annie with purple teeth asked her Uncle Yuri about washing some clothes.

'But you are being here only too few days.'

'But I'm only having too few school dresses. I've worn them all.'

'How many times?'

'Once! I'm not stinky.'

'I once am wearing same suit of clothes for three hundred days.'

'That's disgusting.'

He grinned and asked why.

'Uncle Yuri, I can't go to school on Monday wearing dirty dresses. I'll smell.'

'I am not having latest technology of machine for washing clothes. You must go to mat.'

'OK.'

'What?'

'Will you take me?'

'You cannot go?'

'I'm twelve.'

'And, and—*and*? When I was twelve, Anastasia, I am starting new school, in suit for skiing, *in* different country.'

'Which country?'

'This, country,' he said, raising his hand and pointing a finger at his feet. 'But before you are departing, tell to me some things that pertain of your Uncle Mel. I am not very well getting to know him.'

Her Uncle Mel was at Dixon Hardware, wearing a very large gold chain over an oversized flannel shirt, and with a goatee drawn in black around his mouth. After only a few minutes of helping the Pot Dealer with a 'Pea Yourself!' promotion he had been threatened by the Soil Baron with a breaking and a beating. So he struck a friendlier deal with Henry Sprinkler:

'Where your hose at?' he said to a customer, and with one palm pushed fake US dollar-bills from the stack of them in his other.

'Excuse me?'

'Where your hose at?'

'I... What are you talking about?'

Mel pushed his women's sunglasses to the top of his head. 'This weekend only spend forty dollars on garden pots and get a 15-metre hose set free! Where your hose at!'

'Mel Dixon,' was declared slowly and clearly behind him.

'Good God,' Mel said, immediately recognising another school friend.

'As I live and breathe.'

'Steve Blackman?' Mel squinted. 'It's like a high school reunion this place. What are you doing here?'

'Just popped in on my way to work.'

Mel inspected Steve's outfit of trench coat over a suit and tie, his brown leather gloves and massive watch. 'Where do you work?'

'On Wall Street.'

'Ah. I'm a chairman now.'

'So I keep hearing.'

'It's weird you work on Wall Street, no?'

'Why?'

'You were the shiftiest kid in school.'

'F--k yeah!' he said, proud of the recollection.

'Your whole family had a catchphrase.'
'But here I am!'
'Got any hot moneymaking tips then?'
'Of course! Invest in eels.'
'In eels?'
'You wanna make money fast, you invest in eels.'
'Eels make me vomit.'
'Trust me on this one,' Steve winked.
'You're saying eels, right?'
Steve looked at his watch. 'Look, Mel, I got a feeling something's about to happen with aluminium, I gotta run.'
'Chair Man to the service desk.' Mel raised his ear to the ceiling and the announcement. 'Chair Man, to the service desk.'
'Yeah I gotta run too.'
'I'll see you round?'
'Yeah, if you... come back to the store I guess.' Mel started on the long walk from the nursery to the customer service desk. From the end of his own aisle he saw the almost unmistakable back of Yuri's head; his pace slowed as the girl behind the desk pointed—then Yuri turned and strode towards him.

'We are going for goodly one drive.'

Arsen Sukhimov hung up on the fifteenth sauna maintenance company that he had that morning called. Having resorted to asking if he couldn't fly in the men of a Tasmanian company, they too declined the job when Arsen revealed precisely where it was. Word had spread from Thredbo to Hobart that there was a Bannik in Melbourne, and that that Bannik was in U-Crane's banya.

Between calls made, Arsen was also having to deal with calls answered—an infuriating torrent from equipment hire companies and onsite rental groups and construction firms all looking to buy U-Crane outright.

Again his phone rang. 'Listen you son of a goat rape,' he said before asking who was calling. 'You cannot march in and take over U-Crane! Call me again, I flatten *you*!'

Alexa came slowly in from an entire morning spent in the cauldron. Staring, she fell back into the leather arm chair which faced her father's desk and whimpered: 'Crushed!'

'Oleksa! Please can you help?'

'Crushed! I have nothing to live for, Papa.'

'God and the Devil. Oleksa, you have job, you have work to do, please can you help?'

'There's no point. My crush is goooone.'

'This is worse than Boryslav coming! You are better with people, Dochka, please? I answer call from journalist—journalist! He is coming to U-Crane to make interview of my story. But what is my story? It was accident, they are happen. Oleksa!'

Her arms dangled over the sides of the chair and her chin sat heavily on her sternum. 'Crushed.'

'Oleksa, please!'

'Call Geoff,' she moaned at the ceiling.

'Geoff?'

'He's had to deal with bad press before.'

…Standing on the street outside his slowly failing sporting goods emporium, Geoff bellowed to the foot traffic which seemed to dwindle with each day's spruiking:

'Come inside, little boy, and grab two Dixon balls—grab three if you like. Here! Catch my Dixon balls!' Geoff threw him the first then handballed him the second. 'Feel the bumps and the grooves on those Dixon balls, and get *excited*!' Both bounced into the street as the boy's mother pulled him hastily out of Geoff's reach. 'The deal of a lifetime, are Dixon… Balls.'

Having a late and unhealthy breakfast at The Ship Club, Geoff was doing everything in his patronly power to keep a new waitress at his table. Her hair was shining, curly, and auburn, and when she brought over his third coffee Geoff asked if she was by any chance Scottish.

'How'd you guess?'

'Hottish and Scottish! Look at us, ay? A couple of old Scots at The Ship Club. We're a rare breed, Heather.'

'I'm pretty sure half this room is half Scottish.'

'Ah!' said Geoff. 'But! How many of them know their clan tartan? And how many of them wear it to every formal occasion?'

'A man in a kilt—do you really?'

'Wanna know what colour my tartan is? It's white.'

'They don't have white tartans,' said Heather, playfully sceptical.

'They have one, and I'm allowed to wear it.'

'How do I know you're even Scottish? You have dark hair and brown eyes.'

'I beg your pardon!' he smiled before his phone rang. He beckoned Heather to excuse him. 'What do you want?'

'Geoff. I need your help.'

'Oh do you? Wait, Heather, listen to this.' Geoff put his phone on speaker and placed it on the table between them. 'Arsen, answer me one question: where am I from?'

'What?'

'Where am I from?'

'You are Australian.'

'What's my background?'

'How the f--k should I know?'

'What'd I wear to Pete's funeral?'

'You wear dress. To my son's funeral—you want lady-crown for this? I need help, Geoff. You have heard of accident?'

'What about it?'

'I have journalist who is wanting my story.'

'Yeah?' said Geoff, not seeing what help he might provide.

'How do I make him write good story?'

'Ohh. Umm... well journalists are all about favours. Do him a favour. Is it a him?'

'It is him.'

'Put him in your sauna next to your daughter.'

'What if banya is not working?'

'Put him next to your daughter in a public sauna.'

Arsen grunted. Public saunas hovered around the top of his exhaustive list of local dislikes. 'Which one is good?'

'Oo, I know a great one,' said Geoff, and grinned at Heather and pointed down at his phone. 'It's called The Rainbow Room.'

'Rainbow Room?'

'That's the one.'

'OK, thank you.'

'What's family for?' and Geoff hung up. 'So I have another question for you, Heather.'

'Mm.'

'Would a young lass like you ever have a drink with an old laird like me?'

'Not voluntarily. But I will tell you what—I can't resist a man in a kilt. Wear that white kilt of yours, and I'll go out with you.'

'Not a problem, Heather,' he almost sang in an almost Scottish accent. 'I just have to get it off my son.'

In the passenger seat of Yuri's car, Mel had taken off his gold chain and unbuttoned his shirt and smudged the goatee across half his face. Unsure of where he was being driven—for Yuri refused to tell him—he looked out the window and whistled *Beau Koo Jack* as they left the city. When shortly he didn't know the next part of the song he sucked his cheeks against his teeth and tossed a clicking sound from one side of his mouth to other. The car turned with a long and rising bend then seemed to cruise along the edge of a sprawling valley. Soon Mel felt ill from all the winding. To distract him from his churning head he took up his whistling at the last part of the song he could remember.

'You are producing eggs?' Yuri inquired of his passenger.

Mel turned in from the window. 'What?'

'You are producing eggs?'

'Do I produce eggs?'

'Mm.'

'No.'

'So you are not one bird?'

'No.'

Yuri grinned across the car. 'So shut the f--k up.'

The whirring-by of trees replaced the whirring-by of slightly more distant houses as Yuri eased the car around another hairpin. Mel sucked in his stomach and leaned forward. 'Yuri, I feel carsick.'

'What is cassick? You mean Cossack? You are not Cossack.'

'Carsick. Driving in the car, it makes me nauseous, I feel like I'm gonna throw up.'

'It was not your destiny to survive beyond size of one child. I am needing petrol, we will pull over.'

Yuri stood at the car's petrol tank after telling Mel to go inside and pay. Mel kept an eye on him as he searched the aisles of the service station for anything that might enable him to protect himself. The most wieldable object he could find was a 1.25-litre bottle of Sprite. Behind the cover of a rack of air-fresheners he held one by its neck and swung it as though bludgeoning an attacker—held its base with both hands and thrust it as though into that same weirdo's eyes. It was not ideal, and not at all sharp, but it would have to do. As he waited in line he wondered what form Yuri's assault would probably take. As he reached the counter he scanned its many products and thought about being punched, or tortured, or even—wait, was that a possibility?

So he grabbed a packet of condoms from a display case and placed it on the counter and said, 'Number five.'

That morning had been the first since Peter's death on which Fiona found the energy to use her membership at the St Kilda Sea Baths' health club. Though usually she jogged on a treadmill today she felt more inclined to a gentler session on a stair machine.

She put her phone on the ledge beside its control panel and pushed in her earphones and hit the machine's idiotically large start button. On the beach below, a volleyball tournament was being played; Fiona took her first heavy steps and watched through the floor-to-ceiling window as people in not a great deal of clothing jumped into and out of sand. She was searching for her workout playlist when the sweating woman on the machine beside her said, 'Way too hot to be out there today.'

'What's that?' Fiona took out an earphone.

'I said it's way too hot to be playing volleyball out there.'

'Mm, it's a scorcher,' said Fiona.

'I was supposed to be down there today actually, with my late husband.'

Fiona had almost reinserted the earphone. 'What's that?'

'I was supposed to be down there today, with my late husband.'

'I'm a widow too.' Fiona's hand had made it to her heart as she brimmed with an unfamiliar comfort.

'Pardon?'

'I'm a widow as well,' Fiona reassured her.

'Oh!' said the woman, shaking her head. 'No, my husband's not dead, I'm so sorry. He's running late, he's my… running-late husband—I'm so sorry.'

'Oh it's fine. *I'm* sorry. I just—it's fresh, I haven't really talked to anyone about it yet.'

'Did you want to?'

Fiona had ceased trying to master the stairs. 'I don't really know. Even just saying any of the words makes me well up with tears.' She lifted her phone from the machine's ledge and showed its screen to the woman.

'Is that him?'

'No, it's just a picture of him.'

'You look so happy together.'

'We were. We really were.'

'I was just about to finish up, but maybe we could get brunch some time? If you wanted to talk about it?'

'Actually I think I'd like that.' Still in her hand, Fiona's phone vibrated. She mouthed an apology to her new friend and answered it. 'Hi, honey.'

'Mum, I'm at a laundromat and I don't know how to work anything. I think they need coins but I don't have any.'

'Crushed!' Alexa wailed, her chin still pressing heavily against her slumped body. 'Never again will I love.'

'Listen you, you…' Arsen boomed into his telephone. Unable to find a sufficient insult he trailed off.

Alexa lamented in a whisper: 'Who but Ben could be worthy of holding my fate in their hands?'

'You are nothing but a… Fffff… You are just…'

'A deaf hillbilly,' Alexa moaned to herself.

'No, *you* listen! Yes, you—you…'

Alexa looked up from all her slumping and moaned again: 'Call him a deaf hillbilly.'

'What?'

'Call him a deaf… hillbilly.'

'You are deaf hillbelly,' said Arsen into the phone. 'Yes, that's right. Oh *I* am dumb ass? Well you are a… Nmn!'

'Call him a window-licker,' Alexa said from her wallowing, 'rampant with lice.' Arsen's eyes bulged at the complexity of the phrase. Alexa pulled her limbs in from their dangle and sat upright and broke the phrase into two:

'A window licker...'

'You are a window-licker!'

Alexa rose and came to her father's side. 'Rampant with lice.'

'Who is rampened with lies.' Arsen smiled then silently chuckled as the hollering through his telephone became yelling through his telephone. 'That was good, he is angry.'

'Tell him his grave will be f---ed on by turtles.'

'Turtles will f--k on your grave!' said Arsen, beginning to enjoy himself.

'And your sons will drink soy milk from a hooorse penis.'

Arsen covered the phone's mouthpiece. 'He has two little boys.'

'Say it.'

'Your sons will drink soy milk. … Yes, Davit and Erik. … From a horse penis. … Oh yes? F--k *your* dead wife with a moccasin, you We-Crane… We-Crane…'

'Rat!' Alexa whispered.

'Shchur! You are rat! I hope you get *crushed* by one of your We-Cranes!' Arsen's shoulders rose with his voice as he slammed down the receiver. 'This f-----g asshole!'

'Crushed,' Alexa whimpered, then sank her shoulders and wailed: 'Crushed!'

'That was fantastic, my daughter! You have strong imaginations.'

Alexa put the side of her hand to her forehead and returned to the armchair. 'Never will I love again, Papa. We were oh so perfect together. No love could burn as brightly as what we had.'

The bells on U-Crane's door jangled as someone came through it. 'Arsen?'

'What?!'

'I'm Jason Getzkwarsh, from the Herald Tribune.'

'Journalist, journalist. Come in.'

With forlorn curiosity Alexa lifted her head from her

chest to see who had entered the office. As it fell back down she yanked it back up. The journalist come to interview her father was tall, thin, not balding, and about her age. She sat and gathered and tidied her hair into a ponytail—stood and extended to him her left hand. 'I'm Alexa, director of customer relations.'

'Jason.'

'Jason,' she exhaled, and felt no ring as his hand shook hers. 'Will you excuse me for a second?'

'Righto.'

Alexa turned and tightened her ponytail as she went through the rear door of the main office and to the supply cupboard in her own.

'So I am thinking I have better idea for interview,' said Arsen. 'Today I am very tired, from so many calls. What if tomorrow we have interview? Have you ever taken Ookrainian banya?'

Alexa held back the cupboard's metal doors and took the top frame from a tall stack of bracken wreaths. From the other side of the cupboard she held up a bunch of wilting daisies—inspected their petals and chose the least decomposed and pulled them from the bunch and dropped the others. Then she threaded a long stem through the wreath and intoned, 'May this be the first, tiny, seedling in a vast field of affection. Oh, Jason.'

'Well Uncle Mel was working at Grandpa's work but everyone around him was really small and Chinese I think? Then Uncle Yuri came in, and he had *his* eyebrows shaved off too, and I was a little bit scared of him because he looked so strange. But we were all on our way to help *you* fight a bear.'

'A bear? That *is* a weird dream, honey.'

'And it's not even the weirdest. Yuri and I eat cheese before bed to make them weirder. Is this where people laundry money?'

Annie and Fiona were at a long white wooden bench in the centre of a St Kilda laundromat, transferring her school dresses from her backpack to two plastic baskets.

'Laundry money?'

'Uncle Yuri said I should start learning how to laundry money.'

'He means launder, money, honey. And he shouldn't be telling you that.'

'He said it's important to have money the government can't steal.'

'Well it's not stealing, it's called tax.'

'Yuri said politicians tax people to pay for voters' sex-change operations. We learnt about them at school.'

'This really isn't what you should be talking about with your uncle. Oh honey, no. No, no, here…' Fiona took out the red t-shirt that Annie had thrown in with her light blue dresses. 'We have to separate the whites from the colours.'

'What did you just say?'

Fiona threw the t-shirt into the basket containing Annie's black underwear. 'See?'

'Excuse me?' now came obviously at them as a young woman stormed from the far end of the bench to stand at Annie's side. 'How could you say such a vile thing?'

Fiona asked what the young woman was talking about.

'Slavery caused the deaths of more indigenous people than capitalism, Christianity, and colonialism combined. And you want to return to what, the British Empire?'

Annie's eyes searched the bench for a distraction as her mother jutted her confused face sideways and said, 'Huh?'

'How are you so ignorant? Everyone's welcome here, and you want to separate your "white master-race" from all the "coloured" people? And you're teaching this to your daughter? I feel sorry for you.'

'I was talking about our clothes.'

'What century are you living in?!'

'Whites,' said Fiona, and held up one of Annie's paler crop tops. 'From colours,' she concluded, lifting the red t-shirt from the basket into which Annie had moved it. 'Is that all right?'

'You should watch your language,' said the young woman and wiped the foam from the corners of her mouth.

'You should separate other people's business from your own.'

When finally Yuri stopped the car Mel opened the door and fell with his carbonated weapon onto gravel and lay flat on his back.

'Walk.'

'I feel so sick.'

'Walk,' Yuri demanded as he stood over him.

Slowly Mel stood up. 'Where are we?'

'In forest.'

'Why are we in forest?'

'Walk.'

Mel closed his eyes and groaned from the nausea. With his Sprite bottle under his arm he turned to the direction in which Yuri was thrusting his chin. Ahead a path wound past a picnic table and into the trees and as they left the car park, and shortly the path, Mel pleaded back from the forest, 'Please don't kill me.'

'Shh.'

'I'm Fiona's brother, your sister-in-law.'

'This is making you my sister-in-law?'

'Fiona's your sister-in-law, we're family. Please don't…' Mel turned and planted his feet and with both hands pointed the bottle's lid at Yuri. 'Don't kill me!'

After a moment of condescending bewilderment Yuri slapped the bottle down and grabbed Mel by his shirt and returned him to face the bush. 'Walk, fool.' He frisked him as he pushed him on and presently found a curious square in the pocket of his jeans.

'What is these?'

'Nothing.'

'These are—this is having price tag of petrol station. You are purchasing at petrol station?'

'Please don't rape me.'

'Why in earth would I be raping you? I am not one raper.'

'Then what the hell are we doing out here?'

'Wait. You are buying condoms because you are thinking I am raping you?'

To this Mel made no answer.

'It is true you are calling me Urine?'

'What? I would never.'

'It is true man have come to you and asked for guns?'

'That did happen, yes.'

'Why?'

'I don't know.'

'Why—why?'

'I don't know! He came to my work and he asked for guns. I said I didn't have any, then he said my doctor brother was better at selling them than I was. Are you a doctor?'

Yuri stood up straight and put his knuckles to his hips—raised his chin and furrowed deeply his eyebrows. 'Describe to me this man.'

'Well he looked… you know.'

'How—how?'

Mel turned back and saw that Yuri had stopped walking. 'He looked Ukrainian.'

'And what does this mean?'

Again Mel tilted his head to the side. 'You know…'

'I do not.'

Mel brushed his hair down his forehead and split it in the middle then hunched his shoulders and frowned and dangled both hands in the air. 'Ukrainian.'

The White Kilt

'This is what you are saying Ukrainians are looking like?'

'I...' Yuri pressed a finger to his own chest, 'am Ukrainian.'

'He had purple teeth. His breath smelt like a corpse. And he was wearing a Tonny Halfmaker jacket—what is that?'

'Tonny Halfmaker? This is famous brand in Odessa. It is possible he was Ukrainian. We must be finding who he was.'

'Can we get out of the forest and find out who he was?'

'First we return to raping.' Yuri held his hips and stalked in a circle. 'You are thinking... I am beginning to rape you... but then am whispering to your ear, are you having protection?'

'I don't know what I was thinking.'

'You are preferring safe rape?'

'Well yeah. If that was an option. Wouldn't you?'

'Nobody who is raping is raping safely. You think gangs of Turks when they are raping are asking first white woman if she is wanting safe-rape?'

'Ah, excuse me!' said a voice from the eucalypt forest's edge. Mel smiled and Yuri scowled at the interruption as from the tree line there emerged three men with binoculars at their necks. Each wore a royal blue t-shirt emblazoned with the word *Twit*. 'What did you just say?'

Yuri watched them stride from the thicket as another yelled, 'Did you just imply that males of the Islamic faith are more likely to commit sexual assault than those of other ethno-religious backgrounds?'

Yuri pressed his knuckles against his waist and widened his stance.

'We're Twits, and you've just used a phrase that relies upon—'

'And perpetuates! Orientalising and barbarising stereotypes about recently arrived migrants.'

'A source of outrage,' said the third Twit to plant his feet at Mel's side. 'How do *you* know they don't ask the woman if she'd like to be safe-raped first?'

'No, no, Daniel—that's not what the outrage is about.'
'It's not?'

With a backpack of clean laundry Annie walked with Fiona along the harbourfront, eating hot chips from a paper packet in her arms as she regaled her mother with stories of her uncle's strangeness.

'He has an umbrella that he says is magical, but he calls it an un-brella. Does he mean umbrella, or is that something different?'

'You really never know with Yuri.'

As they stepped from the pier to the artificial jetty they passed a procession of parked masts and gently clunking hulls. 'Look at all these big boats. Didn't Grandpa have a boat?'

'He did, good memory—that's why he joined The Ship Club. We used to go out every Sunday, the whole family. I didn't like him though when he had that boat—boats change people.'

'They do?'

'Yeah I don't like people who own boats, there's something about them. All that money just sitting there, the competitiveness. There's really something wrong with boat people.'

'Excuse me,' said a young woman who looked a lot like Grover from Sesame Street. She turned her very thin neck as Fiona passed, then her body followed.

'Actually no, I *hate* boat people! There was this—'

'*Excuse* me!' the young woman repeated, ensuring now that Fiona knew she was being spoken to.

Fiona turned back. 'Me?'

'What did you just say?'

'When?'

'You *hate* boat people?'

'Oh! Yeah, I hate them.'

'That is so offensive.'

'Is it? Why? I used to be a boat person.'

'Um, I'm sorry? Did you come here on a rickety fishing vessel, risking everything to make a better life for your family?'

'What are you talking about?'

'How are you *even* comparing yourself to a refugee?'

'Please leave us alone,' said Fiona as she turned from the intervention and walked on. 'You can't say anything in public anymore,' she remarked to Annie.

'Ms Conrad says we can't say breastfeeding.'

'That's strange.'

'It is, right?'

'Why did she say you can't say breastfeeding?'

'Umm, because it negatively impacts on people who don't define themselves in binary gender terms.' Two people in blue t-shirts had been standing at the water's edge with binoculars at their eyes. Alerted to Fiona's bigotry by the Grover who took issue with people who took issue with boat people, both turned in and walked towards Fiona and Annie with their binoculars at their chests.

'Excuse me!' said the Grover as all three Twits now manoeuvred to prevent Annie and Fiona from going around them.

'Are you teaching your daughter to say breastfeeding?' said she whose eyes bulged with the veins of her tiny neck.

'The term "breastfeeding",' mumbled a young 'man' with a mullet from behind a surgical mask, 'implies that people without breasts can't properly care for their children.'

'Does it?'

'Say chestfeeding please.'

'Ahhh… no,' said Fiona. 'I'll say whatever I want to say, thank you though.'

'Little girl, don't listen to your gestational parent, she seems to think it's 2020. The correct term is chestfeeding.'

'Please don't speak to my daughter.'
'Will you say chestfeeding, young person?'
'Please don't talk to my daughter,' Fiona insisted.
'Chestfeeding.'
'*Chest*-feeding.'

As the Twits began to chant they began also to stalk towards Annie. Fiona put an arm out to shield her from the apparent birdwatchers and shortly was having to step backwards as they were chanted at: 'Chestfeeding. Chestfeeding. Chestfeeding!'

Surrounded at a turn in the boardwalk Annie and Fiona soon had nowhere to go but over its edge and into the water—'Chestfeeding, chestfeeding,'—when with a rustle and a thud a pelican landed beside them and raised its beak and spread its wings—'Chestfeeding!' The three chanters turned to the very bird that they had earlier been watching. It lifted and flapped its wings and plodded towards them as they were themselves corralled back across the pier and to the water's edge. They looked at the lack of footing behind them. One said, 'Easy, big fella.' The pelican glanced back at Annie then returned to her harassers. 'Careful not to misgender the pelican, Meg.' It leaned its long neck over until its head was fully sideways, then it opened its beak and flapped its wings and rushed the twits off the boardwalk and into the bay.

Wings lowered, the pelican now wiggled around and nudged at Annie's chips with the edge of its beak.

'Thank you?' said Fiona.

The White Kilt

II

Perplexed by yesterday's rapeless morning with Yuri—and unable to see it, though he really was trying to, as containing the seed of an adventure—Mel was slumped at the desk in the centre of his aisle when The Weed Killer came and said he needed his help.

'I'm not in the mood, Weed Killer—what the hell happened to you?'

His face was smeared with mud. 'It's The Soil Baron.'

'That guy's weird.'

'He threatened to bury me underground.'

'I'm sure he doesn't mean it like that.'

'Can't you do something to help?'

'Weed Killer, I'd love to, but I've got my own stuff to worry about right now.'

'Mel?'

'Morning, Dad.'

'Mel, I need the family kilt.'

'The what?'

'The white kilt you took to Asia.'

'I didn't take that kilt to Asia.'

'It's a family heirloom and I trusted you with it, and I need it back. Weren't you bagpiping in Singapore?'

'I didn't take that kilt to Asia, Dad.'

'Mel, do you know where that kilt has been?'

'Yes, Dad, I know where it's been.'

Geoff broke into recitation, and his accent: 'As the Dixons at the Firth of Clyde bought a family's berth of tickets.'

Mel groaned. He had been retold this pseudo-poem innumerable times and was, even after half a decade of not hearing it, exhausted of its contradictions.

'To where and why none knew at all—'

'Dad, it says they bought tickets, they have to have known where they were going.'

'Now South Australia bound.'

'There we are.'

'The last grandmother Dixon, of the town of Auchinleck, came tearing down the gentle rise—'

'I've woven this dear grandson,' Mel said, hurrying his father along.

'From the hair of our last yak.'

'They don't have yaks in Scotland, Dad.'

'Take the kilt, dear Dougie! Wear it loud and proud and grand—and hide our ugly necks now Doug, with mem'ries of your land.'

'Yes, we all have ugly necks.'

'Mel, that kilt is…'

'Dad.' Mel put his hands on his father's shoulders. 'I'll look for the kilt. Maybe Fiona has it at her place. If I didn't take it to Asia and you don't have it, she's the only one with a house.'

'I don't know what I'll do if we don't have that kilt.' Geoff left the aisle of chairs and Mel turned towards his desk and saw Yuri striding past the marquee adventurers. Frightened by the thought of being unsafely raped in a forest, Mel hastened across the gap between his aisle and that of The Blind Guy, into whom he now walked.

'Damn it, Blind Guy, move!'

The Blind Guy widened his arms and waved the end of his rubber-ended cane. 'Who's talking?'

'I know you can see goddam it, let me go!'

'Chair Man? Is that you?'

Yuri grabbed Mel by the scruff of his shirt and pulled him from The Blind Guy's embrace.

'Tonight we are going for dinner.'

'And what, this is an invitation? Let me go.'

'You must meet man.'

'Why do I have to meet man?'

'Because man will be knowing guy. I must know and be meeting guy. It have been arranged.'

'Hm,' said Mel, and thought ahead to a caperish kind of an exploit. He shook off Yuri's rough wooing and said, 'This sounds kind of like an adventure.'

'At restaurant there will be hoooorse,' said Yuri, very slowly.

'Whores?' said Mel, very quickly.

'You are okay with this?'

'Good looking ones?'

Yuri chuckled. 'No! I will be having dinner with ugly hoooorse! Of course good looking!'

'Then I'll be there with bells on!'

'With bells on?'

'With bells on, Old Cock!'

Arsen arrived in his best Tonny Halfmaker tracksuit and allowed his daughter—her hair in a halo braid and wearing nothing under her trench coat—to walk ahead of him through the low brick entrance of The Rainbow Room. Inside he found Jason Getzkwarsh of the Herald Tribune, waiting amid dim lighting and padded walls. 'Interesting choice of venue.'

'This is proud Ookrainian tradition. Banya is where your soul can find calm.'

Arsen insisted on paying for everyone and asked a shirtless man in a bowtie for three tickets. The man leaned out of his booth and looked Alexa up and down then said the changeroom was unisex and directed them to it.

As they came back down a corridor lined with pictures of naked and starving men Arsen said, 'So Jason, I go into banya naked, my daughter goes into banya naked. Nudity in banya is big matter of trust. You can see I have nothing to hide, and see U-Crane have nothing to hide. But you,

Australian, don't need to.'

Inside he sat upon shimmering tiles then unravelled the knot at his hip; Jason hung his towel on a hook and sat in swim-shorts on the bench beside his and Alexa unravelled the knot at her chest and sat naked beside Jason. All relaxed and shortly three men came in and spread themselves out across both levels.

'See,' Arsen whispered. 'Is normal to be naked in banya.'

'I've tried lemon juice,' said one of the men at full volume. 'But my boyfriend said he didn't notice a change, even after a fortnight. And it kind of stung.'

'You have to apply it twice a day for at *least* three months. Trust us, it works.'

Arsen looked down at their enfolded hands and whispered, 'Shh.'

'Excuse me?'

'Banya is silent place,' Arsen whispered.

'Umm, please don't shoosh my husband.'

Arsen scowled and leaned his head towards Jason then let it fall back against the steam-room wall.

'How do you apply it? With a sponge?'

'I get Brad to apply it with an eye-dropper.'

'I love helping him *and* I love his anus. It's the best of both worlds.'

'Sshhh-sh!'

'You *don't* shoosh us!'

'Papa, can I talk to you outside?' Alexa retied her towel and Arsen grunted and shortly both stood between naked photographs.

'You might want to leave, Papa.'

'Leave? We are just starting meeting.'

'This isn't a regular banya, Papa.'

'Is public sauna,' Arsen frowned. 'Recommend by Geoff.'

'Well it's not quite public.'

'What do you mean, Sashenka?'

'It's a sauna just for…' She pointed her thumb at the photograph behind her.

'Just for what? Talking?'

'For gay men.'

'What?'

'I'll talk to Jason, I'll straighten everything out.'

'Dixon Balls. I will get *him* for this.'

Despite neither sharing Arsen's prejudice, as the conversation in the Rainbow Room sauna continued Alexa and Jason discovered that they both were anusphobic. So they decided to get some lemon squash and take a nice stroll along St Kilda beach.

'I can assure you that U-Crane has the most modern and comprehensive safety measures in place. It really was just an accident.'

Jason put his pen to his notepad. 'Would you say it was a freak accident?'

'No, there were no freaks there. In fact the man who got crushed was…'

'Are you OK?'

'I am. He was just… He was a good man.'

'I'm sure he was.'

'Are you a good man?'

'I think I'm all right.'

'You seem like a good man. How about tomorrow I show you a U-Crane worksite? And maybe after we can get a drink?'

'Oh I'm not sure a drink's a good idea.' Alexa looked up into his eyes and moved slightly over so the late morning's sunlight shone fully off her hair. 'You really look so young,' said Jason, inspecting the smoothness of her face. 'You said you're thirty-four? There's not a wrinkle on you.'

'Do you want to know the secret?'

'What is it?'

'Hooorse milk.'
'Whore's milk?'
'All over my face. Twice a day if I can.'
'I think we should—yes—go and inspect a U-Crane sight, and go for a drink afterwards.'
'So it's a date!'

While further along the beach Fiona was having a sunlit brunch with a woman she hoped might be a new friend.

'Wine with brunch?' said the waitress at their side.

'Oo yes please!' said Fiona.

'Red or white?'

'Oh, I much prefer whites,' said Fiona, and was returned the waitress's much-lowered forehead before without writing anything down she walked off.

'Did you see that look?' said Suze from the health club, leaning in. 'That was a sneer!'

'That was more of a snigger.'

'Umm, excuse me?' said another waitress, whipping her head to their table and bulging her eyes as she too now stormed off.

'What was *that* look?!' Fiona smiled.

'You'd better be careful with the s-word around here.'

'Evidently. So can I ask you a strange question, Suze?'

'There are no strange questions between friends.'

'Oh that's nice of you to say. Do you believe in reincarnation?'

'Absolutely.'

'You do?'

'Both my parents died a few years ago. My dad was a landscaper, and every time I see a tree I think of him, especially a banksia—our surname's Banks.'

'And you think they've been reincarnated *in* something?'

'In something?'

'Never mind. So you have a daughter, right?'

'I do, Janie. And you?'

'My little Annie, yeah. She just started high school.'

'So did my Janie! Do you have a picture of her?'

'I do!' As Fiona tapped at her phone she said, 'She seems really sad since her father…. you know.'

'Oh, she's drop-dead gorgeous, Fi!' said Suze as Fiona held out her screen. 'How did her father die?'

'He dropped—' Fiona closed her eyes and gulped. 'He—'

'I'm so sorry. I didn't…'

'It's OK. I'm OK.'

'Well this is Janie anyhow.' Fiona smiled at Suze's phone screen. 'We were planning on having another one this year, but I think she might be too old—I think *I* might be too old. Luke's business is really taking off and another kid would just—we'd never be able to get to Crete.'

'Crete in Greece?' Momentarily Fiona saw the Sfakian terrace bathed in sunlight and the hotel's chairs and the glowing sea and her waving, smiling, dashing, Pete.

'Yeah, Luke's dying.'

'He is?' said Fiona, lowering her voice.

'He really is,' said Suze as she swiped at her screen.

'Of what, can I ask?'

'Of what?'

'Is that too private?'

'He's dying to get to Crete.'

'Oh.'

'Oh god, Fiona, I'm so sorry—I didn't even think.'

'No, no, it's OK. I'm—. I'm still sensitive about it all.'

'I do need to watch my language, I'm trying not to trigger anyone. The last time I heard the s-word I nearly had a heart attack.' Fiona's bread paused in her mouth and again she closed her eyes, and sighed. 'Please don't tell me that's why Peter dropped dead.'

'I think I'm gonna go, Suze—is that OK? I'm really sorry.'

'No, don't go! … I'm trying to be inclusive when I speak.

… Fiona? … I'm so sorry, I'll do better.'

While on his lunch break Mel sat reluctantly across from Drew Fluckinger, the second schoolmate to discover his new occupation, at Dixon Hardware's public cafeteria.

'Dixon sausages are pretty damn good!' said Drew, chewing on his first ever mouthful of one.

'*What's* going on with this child-grooming thing?'

'It's dying, that's what's going on. And I'm getting more and more depressed every day, I'm playing the fiddle practically all the time—you remember I play the fiddle?'

'Oh I remember.'

'That keeps me getting me into trouble too.'

'So Drew, why don't you stop calling it a child-grooming business?'

'But that's what it is, I groom children! And I'll have to write it off completely if I don't make a few grand soon. I'll have to sell the truck, all the child-grooming equipment, declare bankruptcy. In the next couple of weeks if…'

'Hm.'

'What?'

'You remember Steve Blackman?'

'Of course, he's who told me you're working here.'

'Well I ran into him here as well. He works on Wall Street now.'

'*He* works on Wall Street?'

'Right? And he told me to invest in eels.'

'In eels?'

'He said plainly: If you want to make money fast, invest in eels.'

'How do you invest in eels?'

'I have no idea. But that's what he told me.'

'You trust Steve Blackman? His family was the shiftiest family in school.'

'I mean, if he works on Wall Street, right?'

Drew squinted. 'You remember what everyone used to say about his family? What everyone used to *chant* about that family?'

Mel and Drew now said in unison—its melody inscribed in their adolescent memories—precisely what used to be chanted about Steve's family: 'Never trust a—'

Arsen was at Café Beztsihan, a name that translates to Café Gypsyless—for its owner, like most of his compatriots upon arrival, had been elated to find himself in a land without them.

One of the last businesses on Fitzroy Street still owned and operated by a human being, that elated human being was Maksym, a Carpathian who after the disintegration of the Soviet Union brought the foresty tendencies of his oblast to Melbourne. Charred-oak wainscotting ran half way up cream walls around small spruce tables and chairs, and Beztsihan's wide front window opened onto the footpath from a long wooden bench—behind which Arsen and some of his oldest, and oldest, friends huddled around a pair of tables as Maksym demonstrated the latest addition to his business: a grey rounded cube.

'Hey, Siri?'

'Yes, Maxim?'

'Turn on the front lights.' Slowly they all came on. Arsen looked up at several newly glowing lamps. 'Actually, Siri, turn them back off,' and she did.

'That is amazing,' said Arsen, astonished.

'Yep. Hey Siri?'

'Hi?'

'Play kobzari.'

'No worries,' said the female voice, and shortly there sounded throughout the café an accordion whose tune all in Arsen's circle recognised. They leaned back from the device and prepared to sing along—swayed like drunken pirates as they bellowed in Ukrainian lyrics that really were hideously expensive to subtitle:

> *'Mother, what will happen to me if I get captured in a foreign land?*
>
> *Well, my dear, first they'll bend you over a haycart and shove ducklings up your arse.'*

When Arsen opened his eyes to prepare for mother's explanation of what they would do second he saw Fiona walking by—her own eyes swollen and red from holding back tears. He called out her name and beckoned her to the open window.

'What is the matter, child?'

'Nothing. I'm all right. How are you?'

'Me? Phone calls, all day from journalist, from We-Crane—and I cannot banya, Fiona. Do you know what this means? Banya is broken, and I have never been so stress.'

'Why don't you go to a public sauna?'

Arsen scowled.

'No good?'

'This morning we go to public banya. The men, Fiona. They look at me like piece of meat—and the things they say. My daughter should not hear such things—*I* should not hear such things.'

'Try the Sea Baths, they have a great sauna in there.'

'It is sauna for chomosexuals?'

'No. I'm a member.'

'I have question: what is background of your family?'

'Background?'

'If I am Ookraine Australian, what is your family?'

'Oh, we go back a ways. But we're Scottish.'

'Like Braveheart and orange people?'

Fiona's phone started ringing and she saw that it was her father calling. 'I have to run, Arsen, I'll speak to you later?' Instead she walked, back towards the beach. 'Hello?'

'Fi, do you have the family kilt?' Her father was in his basement astride an open box and rummaging through the contents thereof.

'The what?'

'The contents thereof.'

Wait, that's me not him.

'The what?'

'The family kilt—you know the one I'm talking about.'

'Do I?'

'As the Dixons at the Firth of Clyde bought a family's berth of tickets—'

'Oh Dad, please, no. I don't have the kilt, all right?'

'Do you have any idea how important that kilt is to our family, Fi?'

'Dad, I have other things to worry about right now.'

'It was woven from the hair of our town's last yak. By our ancestor who was hanged for weaving it.'

'By her ugly neck, I know. I haven't seen that kilt in forever, Dad.'

'Do you know what her last words were, Fiona?'

But Fiona had hung up. Nearing the boardwalk, she had spotted a pelican very near to where one had yesterday interceded on Annie's behalf. It was standing in the breeze at the jetty's edge with its beak resting on its chest. Fiona approached it and said to it softly, 'Hello?' It shuffled its feet as it turned to face her.

'It's you, isn't it?'

The bird lifted a wing and turned its head and momentarily preened itself.

'Pete?'

It raised both its wings then flapped open its beak as it honked. Fiona felt emboldened. 'Thank you for yesterday,' she said as sweetly as she could.

Its wings still raised, Fiona reached out to touch the animal and found that it allowed her to do so. She put her fingertips to the top of one of its elbows—if birds elbows have—then stroked its feathers.

'It was a really nice thing you did. But I know you were just protecting our daughter. Thank you.'

She withdrew her hand and nodded then turned and walked away. Shortly she heard the same honk—and looked back to see the bird waddling after her.

As Mel came up the hill towards U-Crane's office he said, 'Dad, I don't care about this f-----g kilt!' and hung up on him. As he turned the doorknob the door was opened from within. Alexa in a white dress embroidered at the chest with red flowers—hair in a halo braid—was surprised to see him.

'What is that, a wreath?'

She looked down at the fully woven garland and said that it was. 'Things are finally falling into place, Mel. All I need is something that allows me to make my own money, and I'll be at happiness at last.'

'You want a money tip?'

'Do you have a money tip? Aren't you a chair man now?'

'A chairman, yes. But, you should invest in eels.'

'In heels?'

'Eels.'

'High heels?'

'What's a high eel?'

'My shoe.'

'That's a heel.'

'I should buy more?'

'Eels!'

'Eels?'

'Yes.'

'Vuhor!'

'What?'

'Eels!'

'Yes! I have a friend who works on Wall Street. He told me if I want to make money fast, I should invest in eels.'
'How do you invest in eels?'
'Yeah he didn't tell me that part.'
Again Mel's phone rang. 'Hello?'
'Meet me at Tran's Luon House.'
'Yuri?'
'They have changed time and location. Tran's Luon House, in half of one hour.'
'Eels you say?'
'Eels.'

Walking side by side along the boardwalk, Fiona was having to defend the pelican from a succession of people who appeared angered by their unsegregated waddling.
'Shoo,' said yet another woman and flicked the backs of her fingers at it.
'Hey!' said Fiona. 'Don't you shoo him.'
'Mum what are you doing?'
'Annie!'
'Mum, you look insane.'
'This is the pelican.'
'What pelican?'
'The one that saved you.'
Annie stared at the bird then at her mother. 'How do you know?'
'Mm,' she admitted, looking down at the thing as it knifed its beak through a paper bag of tepid chips. 'What are you doing here alone?'
'Uncle Yuri's busy, I just went for a walk. I have a question, Mum—what's liberty?'
'Did Yuri make you drink it?'
'Huh?'
'What is he feeding you?'
'Was Dad into what Uncle Yuri's into?'

'What do you mean?'

'Did he believe in dynasties? And magical umbrellas?'

'Why don't you ask him?'

'Ask Yuri?'

'Ask your dad,' said Fiona and lowered her head towards the pelican.

'Mum.'

'I know it sounds crazy, honey, but think about it. It flew down to protect you. It let me approach it, and touch it—and talk to it. Why else would it do that?'

'It's a pelican.'

Fiona bulged her eyes with embarrassment. 'He'll hear you.'

'But it won't understand me, because it's a pelican. I can't be here while you hold hands with a bird, Mum.'

Annie walked off and Fiona knelt down and took up the shredded packet of chips and was followed along the boardwalk, first by the pelican whose head she occasionally stroked, then by three Twits in blue t-shirts, astonished all that somebody was able to get so close to a pelecanus conspicillatus.

Mel walked through the high glass doors of Tran's Luon House and at a table in the corner spotted and waved at Yuri. As he walked among closely packed clothed tables he found himself unable to look away from the large horse that was standing calmly in the corner.

'Where are your bells?' said Yuri as Mel reached their table.

'What bells?'

'You have said you will be wearing bells.'

Yuri had on over his shirt a kind of shawl covered in sleigh bells. The lift of his hand from his lap as he reached for a glass of water sent his whole sleeve jingling.

'Why are you wearing bells, man?'

'We are having proud tradition of bell-wearing in Ukraine.'

'And why is that in here?'

'It is good looking, no?'

'It's a horse.'

'There is nothing so handsome as a hooorse.'

'Why is there a horse in a restaurant?'

'I have told you there would be hooorse.'

'I thought you said whores.'

'Whores? We are having job to do. Oh he is here,' said Yuri, jingling as he stood to receive the man who had just walked in. With his fringe brushed forward to his eyebrows and a very prominent underbite and, for some reason, his fingers dangling in the air, Mel said, 'I told you that's what you look like.'

When the man had jangled Yuri's hand they sat in silence and took up menus.

'Wait, this restaurant only serves eel?'

'It is Tran's Luon House,' said Yuri.

'So?'

'Luon is meaning in Indochinese language eel.'

'F--k.'

'What?'

'Eel makes me vomit.'

Annie was home alone for the evening at Yuri's.

When she finished the borshch he had left her she went into the living room and passed his bookcase then remembered what was resting therein. She stepped backwards then turned to her uncle's bookcase—stared at his heavy umbrella and his flamboyant hat. Shortly she reached out and lifted with both hands the parasol from its sword rack. She inspected its bands of gold then found and untied the ribbons which encircled it. It loosened, and Annie shook it then put its top on the floor and made sure that its handle would stand against the bookcase. She turned her inspection to the ivory pole. A kind of black cowboy hat into which a golden spire had been stuck, its brim shimmered with gilt over a thick and bejewelled chinstrap.

Cautiously she lifted it with both hands and placed it on her head. She jiggled her ugly neck to have the hat rest comfortably, then pulled the chinstrap down over her face until it dangled against her throat. With a straight back she lowered herself down and picked up by its golden handle her uncle's golden parasol.

'What *is* this stuff?' she whispered. She slid the umbrella's runner out and shortly in her hand bloomed its three silken tiers. She held it upright and shimmied her shoulders and said, 'Hello?' Then the umbrella seemed to whisper, 'Hello?' back. Annie yelped and threw it to the ground and pulled herself out from under the hat as she shoved it from her head. With wide eyes she stared at the shimmering regalia and hoped that it wouldn't make another sound.

'This *really* isn't the guy,' Mel mumbled, the restaurant so loud as to enable him to speak to Yuri without the eel-enjoying oaf hearing him.

'No, this is man. Man will be knowing who is guy.'

'And this isn't soup.' Mel had ordered the one dish on the menu that didn't contain eel. He lifted his spoon from the depths of its bowl. 'It's things floating in water again.'

'Try this.' Yuri's arm jingled as he passed a full ladle of wet eel across the table. Mel's chin thrust forward and the nape of his ugly neck squashed into his shoulders as he gagged. He put the back of his hand to his mouth and shook his head and looked across to the horse. 'Get it away,' he managed to say before snapping his shoulders up as he tried to prevent his body from vomiting.

'You are knowing who is this man?' said Yuri to the oaf, and jangled in Mel's direction.

The man looked out from underneath his spiked fringe. 'He is Australian.'

'He is.'

'He is your friend?'

'He is not,' said Yuri as Mel began to nod. 'He is smuggler of gunm, to whom someone have come to ask to buy.'

The oaf leaned towards Mel. 'You sold?'

Mel looked down at the man's eeled chopstick and closed his eyes and shook his head as he fought a pang of nausea worse than his carsickness.

'We are wanting to know who have asked to buy.'

'Nobody can buy gum without clearing with Georgians.'

'So it *is* the Georgians,' said Yuri.

'Wait, did you say gum?'

'Gum? I don't have.'

'Who are the Georges?' said Mel.

'Georgians. From Georgia. We must go to Georgian fencing party. There we will be finding man.'

'Not guy?'

'This is guy.'

'No, this is man.'

'This is not man.'

'You think I am not man?'

When the oaf-man-guy had finished his eel he zipped up his Tonny Halfmaker and nodded and left.

'This is beginning to feel… adventurey, don't you think?'

'No,' said Yuri as he jingled Mel the bill. 'But you are not such enormous hood of penis. The night is juvenile! Would you be wanting to come with me now for cruising for hose?'

'Cruising for hoes?'

'For hose, yes.'

'Hell yes!'

After returning her uncle's hat to its ivory pole and fluffing up its silken feather to resemble her memory of it, Annie turned to the umbrella that she would have sworn had just said something to her. She took one step towards it and waited in case it made another sound. When thankfully it didn't she closed her eyes and picked it up by its conical tip and hastily slid down its runner. She tucked in its gilt folds as neatly as she remembered they had been and when she was confident Yuri wouldn't be able to tell she had conversed with it—or it with her—she raised the retied object to its sword rack then dropped it and ran to the other side of the living room.

Still jumpy, she sat in Yuri's only armchair and raised her feet onto a four-legged stool. With no television in the house she looked down to the side table, where several bearded men glared up at her from the cover of a book entitled 'Russian Thinkers.' A jagged bronze snake's head protruded from its top; Annie lifted the book onto her lap and opened it (the book, not her lap) to Yuri's curved prayer dagger. Before her now lay the title of an essay and two long epigraphs. She read the first and didn't know what it was talking about but in the second she recognised a word—Cossack. And in one of those instantaneous quarter-hours in which we take up the thread of history and become ourselves its weaver—in which invisibly we are handed by those whose intellect we admire the treacherous torch of reason—Annie read, and was enthralled by the exotic fates of romance, revolution, and Europe:

'They were at one in placing the ideal of individual liberty at the centre of their thought and action.'

While in the late dusk Alexa emerged from the concrete pylons of the freeway and descended the grassy bank of Moonee Ponds Creek.

As she lowered with both hands the wreath she had prepared she said, 'Oh, Jason Getzkwarsh, my love. Here do I entrust our fate to the waters of the land. May love flow into our lives as these blossoms on a stream, and soon.'

Looked upon by both the river dandy and the travelling salesman, both with hats in hands and heads a-shaking—

Alexa cast the wreath into the trickling water and with her palms against her chest watched it struggle to float away.

With an elbow resting on his car's windowsill, Yuri turned the steering wheel as he slowed outside a construction site and pulled into the curb. 'There they are.'

Mel searched the barely lit compound of dirt, puddle, and portable toilet. '*Where* are they?'

'So much hose.'

Yuri yelled as he walked a spool of black hose back towards the fence: 'So much hose!'

'Your bells are gonna get us caught,' Mel whispered. 'You sound like Santa's sleigh.'

The site's fence rejumped, Mel stood at the mound of hose and said, 'Can we roll this spool on the ground?'

'Pool? What pool?'

'Spool.'

'Pools? What word are you saying?'

'This is a spool, goddam it.'

'This is hose.'

'Can we roll the hose on the ground? They're heavy.'

'Rolling will be making too much noise. We lift. Come—come!'

Mel squatted as they pushed another wooden spool to one side to get a hand under it. As they lifted in unison Mel said, 'Ow, wait—wait! Oh God.' He dropped his side of the spool and stood up straight and was afraid to breathe.

'You have pulled your cage?'

'My what?'

Yuri jingled his fingers to his chest. 'The cage for your more important organs.'

'My ribcage?'

'You have hurt? We can roll, but we must make hurry.'

'Curry?'

'Hurry! Roll!'

III

The following afternoon Fiona was at a picnic table with the pelican that she had convinced herself was that with which, or whom, she had yesterday held hand to wing. Though decreasingly was she certain that it, or he—or she for that matter—was the reincarnation of her dead husband, for whatever its pronouns were it was proving hopelessly unable to help her with her Peter file.

She hid the parcel of hot chips by which she had lured it from the pier and placed before the bird's beak the second, unintelligible, page of her folder.

'Which of them's *more* important?' she said to the pelican, then pointed at the page. 'Breastfeeding?' She leaned down and looked the animal in its dumb eye. 'Breastfeeding?' she repeated, then shook her head. 'All right, what about the eel magnet?' The pelican stepped back from the picnic table and raised its wings and craned its neck then let fall its gullet.

'No, no, I need you to focus—can you focus please?' She tapped at the picnic table. 'Down here. Hello?'

While Alexa walked into the office of Radchenko Capital.

Resting upon its brown carpet was a beige desk with rounded corners; resting behind that desk was a man in a Tonny Halfmaker tracksuit—his hair brushed down his forehead and his fingers dangling in the air, for Alexa had walked in while he was struggling to figure out what to type next. He relaxed his raised wrists and let protrude his underbite then asked Alexa what he could do to her.

'You help people invest in cryptocurrency?'

'Crypto, yes.'

'There's a cryptocurrency called Eelcoin?'

'Eelcoin, Eelcoin.' The man scrolled through a browser

window on his computer. When he got to its very bottom, then moved back up just a little he found it. 'Eelcoin, tak!' He read to her from its financial profile. 'Eelcoin is crypto based in Holland operating on—'

'I want twenty thousand dollars' worth.'

'What?'

'Is that the way it works?'

'You want twenty-thousand dollars Eelcoin?'

'Yes.'

'That is lot of money for crypto I have never heard.'

'Nevertheless.'

'What?'

'Nevertheless.'

'Never… wa the—Never what?'

And she dropped onto his desk a paper bag containing all but a sliver of her life savings.

'To what do I owe the pleasure?' said Geoff as Arsen sat opposite him and began inspecting his office.

'I want to thank you for help with journalist. You do not offer people when they come to your office?'

'Offer them?'

'As Ookrainian we drink samohonka, tea, even coffee, when businessmen are meeting.'

'Oh, I can get you tea or coffee. Which one do you want?'

'Coffee, please.'

Geoff went to the tearoom and Arsen took from his breast pocket a vial of poison and sat waiting with it in his closed hand as at the touch of two buttons Geoff received two coffees. 'Thank you,' said Arsen as shortly one was placed in front of him. 'So, you are Scottish? You do not look Scottish, I thought they are orange people.'

'Not all of them.'

'You would like to look more Scottish?'

'Look?'

'Tell me about these bugs. In Ookraine is worst possible thing to have bug in office.'

'The bugs?' Geoff spun and rolled his chair to them. Arsen uncapped the vial with his finger and thumb and held its lid between his first two knuckles. 'All extremely rare, and expensive. You couldn't afford one.' Geoff stood and lifted a jar from its place on the shelf. 'This one here's a Bengali phasmid, a stick insect to you.' Arsen watched him spin a jar and behold its contents as he leaned across the desk and upturned the vial into Geoff's paper cup. He leaned back into his chair and slid his hands to his lap as he recapped the vial then returned it to his pocket.

'And how is search for new vife?'

Geoff put the jar back in its place and spun back to his desk. 'It's not going great. Last woman had a pea fetish—you ever heard of that?'

'How can someone be so unlucky with women?' Arsen smiled, then lifted his coffee to his mouth.

'And how was the Rainbow Room? And the journalist?'

'My daughter is meeting today, to show him U-Crane safety at building site.'

After signing the waiver with Radchenko Capital which invested her meagre wealth in Eelcoin, Alexa met Jason Getzkwarsh at the only job to which a U-Crane crane was currently attached—a construction site in Windsor.

Above rolls of rebar and spools of hose a Frasier Crane driver wore a fluorescent tabard over his white polo shirt. The gloved workers who manned the truck bed of girders each wore a yellow tabard that matched their yellow hard hats, and the three men guiding and unstrapping the payload wore tabards branded with the names of their contracted employers—while the writer of this story greatly enjoyed repeatedly using the word 'tabard'.

'See,' said Alexa. 'All up to the strictest safety codes,

always.'

She signed in at the foreman's office with her full name and added that of Jason Getzkwarsh. She put on a hard hat and gave this writer another chance to use the word tabard before leading Jason down into the concrete outline of the site's sunken foundations. She walked as though on a tightrope as the crane brought across another iron log.

'You know it's an interesting name you have.'

'Jason?'

'Getzkwarsh. Where's it from?'

Unanswered, Alexa turned and saw Jason staring up at the girder that was coming over. It had been brought to a halt, high—but quite directly—above him.

'Jason?'

Finding it odd that the girder was no longer moving he looked down to Alexa and frowned. 'Why's it stopped?'

'Jason, move,' she said and waved him forward.

'What?' he yelled, unable to hear her beneath several jackhammers.

The river dandy and the travelling salesman both came up onto their tiptoes as with bloodlust they gripped onto the site's fence. Alexa looked up at the girder, now swaying in the wind, and strode back across the foundations as Jason cupped his ear. 'Huh!?'

'Jason! Get out of the way!'

'Huh?'

'Get out of the way!' she yelled as she pulled him on by the wrist. The jackhammers paused. 'I thought I might lose you!'

'Lose me? What do you mean?'

And the river dandy and the travelling salesman sighed and returned to flat-footed.

While for the first time in a long time Mel was finding himself flirted with.

'Wait, don't sit on that.'

'Why not?' said a woman with shoulder-length blonde hair.

'It's the display chair, it's dusty. I'll get you a clean one.'

'Oh, thanks. Yes, I wouldn't want to sit on that, I don't like to be dirty in public. … Do you?'

'Do I what?'

'Like to be dirty in public?' The woman ran the firm curls of her hair back behind her ears and smiled into Mel's eyes. He found he had to put his whole ugly neck into swallowing the saliva that was accruing in his mouth.

'I guess not, no.'

'I like to be squeaky clean on the outside. And keep the dirty for the—. Well. Are you OK?'

After a pause in which something other than his mind took control of his mouth he blurted: 'I'd like to see your dirty insides!'

'I beg your pardon?'

'I'll get the chair down.' Mel shook his head and turned to the bay of marquee adventurers and pushed onto his tiptoes. As he reached up he was hit by a sharp pain in his side and came back down wincing.

'Are you OK?'

'Yep,' he hissed with a tensed jaw. He pressed his fingers into his side and said, 'I've got a niggle.'

'Oh they're the worst. In your cage?'

'Is everyone calling it that now?'

'Why don't I try one of these?' She lifted from a stack of marquee adventurers all but one of them and pulled out the bottom, clean, one. 'It's perfect,' she said. 'Comfortable, light, it's got a drink holder. You really pointed me in the right direction here. Is it possible you're this kind *and* this knowledgeable, and this handsome?'

Mel pointed to himself. 'Me?'

The woman slowly nodded.

'Of all the chair departments in all the world.'

'Only because I know someone on Wall Street.'

'I know someone who works on Wall Street! There's ahh… there's a bit of a thing going on here isn't there?'

'I think there might be a bit of a thing going on, yes.'

'What would you say to—'

'Mel!' Mel turned to see his father careening down his aisle. 'Mel, we need to talk.'

'Dad, I'm with a customer.'

'Have you found the kilt yet?'

'Dad, I'm busy,' said Mel with clenched teeth.

'I need that kilt and I need it now.'

'Dad, can you not see I'm busy?'

'With what? We haven't sold so few chairs since we had the fat Chair Man. Excuse me, ma'am, I'll have him back in a second.'

Geoff pushed his son along the aisle. 'I need that kilt, Mel, where is it?'

'Dad, I was with a customer.' He looked back to find she had left. 'A good-looking customer, goddam it.'

'Where is that bloody kilt?'

'Dad, I haven't seen that thing since I wore it to Fiona's wedding, all right?'

'Fiona's wedding?'

'Yes.'

'There'll be photos of it.'

'There are photos of it.'

'This I can use!' and Geoff pulled out his phone and called his daughter.

'Look, I understand they're *all* a bit confusing,' said his daughter to a—perhaps *the*—pelican. 'But if you can narrow it down to just one? And I can look into that one properly.' Fiona put her palm on the open folder and implored the pelican to return its attention to the page. 'What about a juiced scud? Pete? A juiced scud? Nothing?'

And her phone rang.

'Fiona, where are your wedding photos?'

'My wedding photos? Dad!' she frowned. 'I'm—. This isn't easy for me, why would you ask me that?'

'I need to look at them, where are they?'

'They're in the house. Under the coffee table.'

'In the living room? Hello? … Hello?'

Fiona returned her phone to the picnic table and took a chip from the hidden packet and placed it above the Peter file. This seemed to refocus the pelican's attention; it stretched forward and turned its head sideways to grab it.

'What if I say them to you quickly in order? Pete, are you listening?' The pelican left the corner of the table on which Fiona was trying to get it to focus and waddled in search of the seemingly endless, but frustratingly concealed, source of chips.

'Please just tell me what happened to you, Pete.'

'I would like to be having one refund on this hose I have purchased here only two days ago.'

'I'll call Henry Sprinkler,' said the woman behind the inquiries desk.

'What are you doing here?' said Mel, still searching Dixon Hardware for the woman with blonde hair and dirty insides.

'I am getting for this hose, that I have *purchased*, one refund.'

'You know this is my family's business, right?'

'Last night was gay. Were you finding it also enjoyable?'

'Apart from the eel. It was pretty much an adventure.'

'No. But I am thinking today of cruising for proper hose.'

'How much hose do you need, man?'

'Not that hose, smuggler of gum Mel Dixon. Hose.'

'Hoes?'

'Yes.'

'Actual cruising for hoes?'

'Yes,' Yuri smiled, and flashed his eyebrows towards his scalp. 'You would be liking to join me?'

'Hoes, right? Not hoes,' said Mel, and grabbed a garden hoe from a nearby rack of them. 'We have hoes here—you're not gonna go out and make me steal a bunch of these are you?'

'Smell, who you are thinking that I am? Cruising for hose. With long, tight legs.'

'Hoes?'

'Yes!'

'Somebody call for Henry Sprinkler?' said the middle-aged man who had recently been made by Twits to change his name from The Illegal Irrigant.

'This gentleman,' said the refund woman.

'Eyyyy,' said Henry Sprinkler to Yuri, and in his leather jacket held up a thumb and smiled at him. Then he swung his thumb to Mel before moving it on and smiling into a non-existent camera, and saying at length, 'Eyyyy.'

When satisfied that U-Crane was following industry protocols and that probably the zoo incident had been, though it had involved no freaks, one of their accidents, Jason Getzkwarsh and Alexa left the construction site and went to find that drink.

'Oh, we're passing the Mongohhhlian grocery store. I need more hooorse milk.'

'From me?'

'You want to come in?'

'Or on.'

'I'll be just a second.' On her way to the counter at the store's dim rear she grabbed two bottles of milk from the yellowing refrigerator. Outside she unscrewed one of their caps and took a swig then dipped a finger into its top before patting the milk onto her cheek.

'What are you doing?'

'You want some?' She redipped her finger then went to apply it to Jason's cheek.

'No,' he said, recoiling. 'Definitely not.'

'This is what I was talking about—this is how I look so young.'

'You really shouldn't drink that. And you *definitely* shouldn't use it as a cosmetic. Cows are forcibly impregnated, for months they're injected with antibiotics, then their calves are taken away and they're milked with machines till they bleed.'

'Not these guys, this is hooorse milk.'

'It's why I live a vegan lifestyle.'

'Vegan?' said Alexa, suddenly sickened.

'Mm.'

'You didn't tell me you're a vegan.'

'I didn't? I usually tell people a few seconds after I meet them. So what about that ahh… whore's milk?'

'Here,' she smiled, and again failed to find his cheek.

'No, the whore's milk.'

'*Whore's* milk? What's whore's milk?' She scrunched her nose. 'Why would I put that on my face?'

'Actually I'm sorry, I shouldn't use that word. It's a patriarchal term for women who exercise their right to select whichever sexual partner they choose.'

'Huh?'

'It's my unintended feminine minimising, I'm trying to be better—can you forgive me?'

'I have no idea what you're talking about, Jason.'

'You're not woke?'

'Not what? Wait, you said you're a vegan?'

'One day we'll be so numerous that we can force *all* of society to think properly.'

And the woven flowers of Alexa's hopeful heart withered as instantly she discarded her plans to tomorrow morning roll around naked in dewy grass.

Geoff too was soon to be disappointed.

After taking Fiona's wedding album from underneath her coffee table he brought it to The Ship Club and presented it at the bar to Heather.

'Look what I have.'

'What's this?'

'Proof,' he said, and pulled open its heavy cover to a double page of photographs, one of which showed him and his son at Fiona's side, both of them wearing kilts. 'That, is the kilt,' he said, putting his finger beside Mel's image.

'It's a black and white photo,' said Heather. Geoff flipped through the album's pages and found that all were either black and white or sepia. 'For all I know, that kilt's orange. Or pink.'

'But that's the kilt, Heather! That's the white kilt. Hang on, I'll call my son.'

'Here it is,' Yuri announced as they neared the Acland Street boutique in which, Mel had been repeatedly assured, hose would so abound that they'd be able to practically window-shop for them.

Yuri stood before several mannikins and their several costumes, his head rolling with wonder. All were dressed in thick tights, some green, some orange, others with one leg red and the other yellow. 'So much hose,' said Yuri with his knuckles on his hips. 'It is biggest and most glorious range of hose in entire Melbourne city of Victorian state.'

Mel's tongue pressed against his bottom teeth. 'You're an idiot.'

'Not at all, come! It is my treat. Would these be your first hose, or you have had one hose before?'

As Yuri bounded into the store Mel overheard something far stranger, though much more familiar, than the thought of trying on skin-tight man-leggings: 'You're not gonna believe what I just saw,' said an astonished boyfriend returning to his seated girlfriend. 'There's a woman walking her pet pelican.'

'Her pet what?'

Fiona had given up on trying to get the animal to tell her which of the Peter file's phrases was most important and instead was stealing a few more precious moments with the spirit of her husband that she believed the bird contained. Mel left Acland Street and walked up to the beach and along the boardwalk, where shortly he was saddened to recognise a woman who was being followed by several excited Twits and a handful of filming onlookers. 'Fi?'

His sister was stroking the back of the pelican's head as the pair of bipeds strolled over a grassy hillock. 'Fi?' he said louder.

'Mel.'

'What the f--k are you doing?'

'Oh,' she said, her brother's voice making instantly obvious the unacceptable oddness of her afternoon. 'Oh, I don't know.'

'Is this Pete again?'

'I guess not.'

'You can't be doing this in public, Fi, you'll get committed. Shoo!'

'Oh don't shoo him,' Fiona moaned with no real concern. 'Shoo!'

The pelican squatted and lifted its wings and began to run then flapped as it flew away. Fiona stepped up onto the seat of a picnic table and turned and sat on its bench. She put her elbows on her knees and her head in her hands. Mel winced as he sat beside her and put a hand at her back.

'I think maybe Pete was killed—murdered.'

'What?! Why?'

'At the funeral. A file was dropped into my lap.'

'A file?'

The White Kilt

'Pertaining to Peter.'

'A file pertaining to Peter? You mean a... Pe—?'

'You don't want to call it that, trust me. But I took it to the police, and they dismissed me. And, they said his cause of death was a heart attack. But Yuri stole the body before an autopsy could be done—how would they know that?'

'That might explain why I had to have dinner with Yuri last night.'

'You had dinner with Yuri?'

'And some Ukrainian oaf. At Tran's Luon House. Luon means eel in Vietnamese. I had to eat dinner in a literal house of eels, Fiona.'

'Eels make you vomit.'

'Tran's eel made me vomit all right. I got the only thing on the menu that *didn't* have eel and even that made me vomit. Turns out Tran's anything makes me vomit.'

'Excuse me?' said a Gonzo-looking woman who had recently committed herself to leaving very few innocuous comments unattacked.

'What?' said Mel, looking up from his conversation.

'What did you just say about trans people?'

'Tran's people? Who are they?'

'Umm, a heavily oppressed minority, who attempt suicide three times the normal rate of other queer people.'

'Huh?' said Mel, as his phone rang. 'Dad, what do you want?'

'Do you have any colour photos of you in the kilt?'

'F-----g hell, Dad! I don't have any photos of any damn kilt, all right? Stop calling me about this!'

After a contemplative pause Geoff tried to call his daughter. He quickly heard the long beeps of a busy tone and at last admitted to Heather: 'I don't think my white kilt exists.'

'Well that's too bad for us, isn't it?'

'Say what was that, Geoff?' said another Ship Club member, being led to his table by a waitress.

'My white kilt, Jock. It doesn't exist.'

'Well it's *about* bloody time someone said so. Hey, Lawrence,' he called to his friend on the far side of the room. 'Hear what Dixon just said? Say it again, Geoff, so Lawrence can here ya.'

'My white kilt doesn't exist!' Geoff admitted throughout the club. 'My white kilt doesn't exist. Heather, I tried.'

As The Ship Club broke into *For He's a Jolly Good Fellow* Geoff inspected the inside of his forearms. 'You know I never thought I had this many freckles. See this?' he said to Heather and held them out to her. 'I swear I didn't have this many freckles yesterday. Will you admit freckles as evidence?'

Fiona's phone rang and she looked at its screen then silenced it.

'Dad?'

'Dad.'

'Why's he so obsessed with being Scottish all of a sudden? I'm sick of hearing about this white kilt.'

'Um, excuse me?' said a burgeoning young woman with a surgical mask over his face.

'What?' said Mel.

'Did you just say what I think you said?'

'I don't know, what do you think I said?'

'Can you just go away please?' said Fiona. 'We're trying to have a private conversation here.'

'There's no such thing.'

'Please leave us alone,' Fiona pleaded, and the young woman hissed like a cat and walked on. 'You know it's funny you mention eels.'

'Why?'

'The Peter file has—the file, has Pete's police record, and

then three phrases on a piece of paper, and that's it. But one of the phrases is "retarded eel magnet".'

'What the hell is an eel magnet?'

'I have absolutely no idea.'

'Actually that *is* weird.'

'Why?'

'Yesterday at work I ran into Steve Blackman, you remember him?'

'Shadiest family in school.'

'Right. He works on Wall Street now, and he told me to invest in eels.'

'How do you invest in eels?'

'That's what I said. But maybe that's your eel magnet—money. What are the other phrases?'

'Great at breastfeeding.'

'Um, excuse me?'

'Can you be great at breastfeeding?'

'It's chest-feeding!' called another Twit from across the lawn as slowly they encircled the picnic table.

'I don't think you can.'

'And the third one?' Fiona turned and took up her Peter file. As she opened its cover its pages slid out and fell to the ground. Mel stepped down to retrieve them but stumbled forward in pain.

'What's wrong? D'you hurt your back?'

'No, I've got a—' He stood and grimaced and tapped at the side of his torso. 'Oo it hurts.'

'What's wrong?'

'I've got a niggle in my cage.'

A nearby Twit lowered her binoculars and said to her Twit friend, 'Did he just use the n word?'

'From dragging hose across the ground.'

And they were joined by the infuriated Groverish Twit as Mel returned to sitting and bemoaned:

'What a life this has become. I'm *sick* of hearing about

our white kilt. That got ruined by Asians. I'm having open discussions about safe rape in the forest. I go cruising for hoes but end up having to drag them across the ground—I'm throwing up from Tran's anything. And I've got a child groomer asking me for help but all I can do is give him financial advice from a Blackman. But I don't trust him, because—well, you remember…'

And Fiona joined in the chant whose classroom melody was inscribed into her mind too:

'Never trust a Blackman!'

'No!' said one of the Twits, so enraged she crapped her pants. 'Just no!'

'Oh, these bloody people,' said Fiona.

'Who are they?'

'They're like the language police. They tell you what you can't say and then they snigger at you.'

'Did you just use the n-word *again*?!' said one of them, blue-haired and jack-booted and face-masked.

'It was the s-word!'

'I want your names and addresses now, I'm calling the police.'

'Suze?'

'Fiona?'

'You're a Twit?'

'And you're a racist. I should have known from what you said at brunch. "Preferring whites." Using the s-word willy nilly. She works out at the gym there,' Suze said to her accomplices and pointed to The Sea Baths.

'What's going on?' said Fiona, confused by the aggression that surrounded her.

'Just wait'll they hear what kind of a person she is.'

And as a squad of Twits stormed the front desk of the Sea Baths and demanded they cancel the membership of one Fiona Sukhimov—and as a young man in a polo shirt from behind his keyboard cancelled it—there walked in behind them three other Sukhimovs as Arsen, Yuri, and Alexa pushed through the turnstiles and followed the signs to the steam room.

In the misty dark they looked for an empty space among plastic benches. They found that they had to slot themselves in rather far apart from one another and Arsen could find no place on the top row. Yuri too was distressed at having to sit on the lower bench where the air was barely warmer than the outside evening's.

'Hot in here, ay,' said the tattooed young man now beside him.

Slowly Arsen turned his head and said, 'Banya is silent place.'

Alexa was uncomfortable untying the knot in her towel in front of so many fully clothed people. Feeling constricted, she spun its top edge around her torso and jiggled her arms. 'This is un-natural.' Two nattering women left the door ajar as they came in from the pool; Yuri stepped forward and pulled it closed as they neglected to lower their voices in discussing which lives matter.

'Shhh,' said Arsen as the young man beside him stood and in the centre of the steam room bent slowly down to touch her toes. Arsen stared at its bicycle shorts and frowned. 'This can not last a long time.'

IN THE NEXT PETER FILE...

...Geoff wakes up not only feeling Scottish but looking it:

Lying in bed he looked to the new freckles on his arm and found that overnight they had redoubled again. 'What the hell,' he said as he beheld the orange-spotted insides of his forearms then the caramel-dotted backs of his wrists. He turned on the bathroom lights and stood over the toilet and found that too his penis was covered in small dark circles. 'Woah, that's not good,' he said, then washed his hands. He blinked and looked up to the mirror over the basin and there froze his face.

Overnight his eyes had turned blue and the lids around them were now pink to the point of translucence. He blinked and trucked his face towards its reflection. His eyelashes had grown invisible and his eyebrows barely discernible, for they were the same colour as the dots and spots and blotches which covered his face and his lips.

He ran his completely freckled fingers through hair that now was wiry rather than wispy and which had turned entirely and undeniably—and he really hoped not irrevocably—orange.

…And this book's author asks his bird-loving brother if birds have elbows:
'Yep.'
'Really?'
'Shoulders too.'
'Do they have wrists?'
'You're making fun of me aren't you?'

Episode 5

THE GEORGIAN FENCING PARTIES

I

'It is like gulag in here.'

Scowling beneath his pointy felt hat, Arsen was so close to so many people at so many points of his skin that he had to tuck in both elbows to be able to thwack his dried oak leaves at his body. The tucking meant he could only reach his shoulders, and as he flicked at them a young man came into the steam room and sang, 'Four words: and just like tha-at!'

Arsen leaned forward and slapped the screamer with his leaves then pointed to the sign on the wall—a cartoon of somebody talking, encircled and crossed out with a red line.

'Sorry, man.'

'Shh,' Arsen hissed and slapped him again.

'Eels!' Alexa seemed to lament. 'Eels!'

'Shhh!' said Arsen from his low and chilly bench.

'You don't understand, Papa. I've lost everything—everything! I'll turn thirty-five and I won't have a cent to my name. It's aaall gone.'

'Good,' said Arsen. 'You can focus on taking over U-Crane.'

'I don't want to take over U-Crane, Papa, I don't! Eels! How, eels!'

'Are you saying heels?' said somebody in the darkness, and was angrily shooshed.

The man seated beside Alexa descended to the rectangular

floor and in tiny shorts attempted with both hands to touch the ceiling. He arched his back and inhaled so loudly that the hiss of the tepid steam coming into the room could no longer be heard. As he placed the sole of one foot against the knee of his other leg he exhaled even loudlier—inhaled again as he put his pointed hands together then bent slowly, fully, over.

'What is this?' Arsen mumbled. 'What is this—sit down!'

'Just gettin' a few stretches in mate.'

'Shh!' said Arsen, and thrust his leaves at the no-talking sign.

'I'm sorry, do you own this place?'

'Get out,' said Arsen.

'Get out!' said Alexa, wanting to banya in miserable peace.

'And close door behind you, is *freezing* in here.'

'Papa. I am needing from you to be organised one meeting with Georgians.'

Arsen grunted and nodded then scowled as a woman leaned down to the steam vent. From a small vial she extracted an eye dropper and squeezed it over the basin that caught the excess water.

'What is this?' said Arsen.

'It's essential oil of spearmint, with just a *hint* of eucalyptus.'

'Shh!' said Arsen and pointed to the sign. 'Now banya is smelling like chewing gum?'

The woman leaned down again and pinched the eye dropper once more. Arsen threw a ladle-full of his beer-and-water at the minty basin. 'Get out, get out!' he said and lashed at her until she left.

'Eels!'

'Are you saying eels?'

'Shh!'

Somebody came in and sat beside Yuri. When he had

steadied himself he put a safety razor to his cheek. Yuri turned to scowl at him as he drew its blades down his face. The razor scraped against the front of his chin then he flicked the thing out towards the floor. As he returned it to his face Yuri grabbed his wrist.

'You are bahhbarian?'

'Am I a barbarian?'

'Or one barber? You are in wrong place, barber man.'

'I'll stop,' he said, wanting to defuse the unexpected tension.

'Ohidno.'

He rested his razor on his knee and leaned back and closed his eyes. Then as somebody came in and stood at the banya's centre—and exhaled as he too extended his joined hands to the ceiling—the sauna-shaver started whistling.

'Banya is silent place!' Arsen shouted. 'God and the Devil!'

Then the woman beside Alexa farted—wet, long, and seismic.

'I'm done!'

'I'm done!'

'Not even misery's making me happy in here!'

Arsen gathered his paraphernalia and Alexa pulled down their magnetic no-talking sign as she descended to the wet floor. Yuri pushed open the door and Alexa followed him out and Arsen jolted back to those still seated:

'So your soul can find calm!'

II

Fiona was on a log at Collingwood Children's Farm, where she could sense that she was a less than ideal brunch date. Pinal Connelly was eager to discuss their daughters' progress in settling into high school. With Yuri still looking after Annie, Fiona was unable to compare her experience to Inika's. But Pinal sensed what was wrong.

'It's only been two weeks, Fiona. Grieving takes longer than that, much longer. Sometimes years. If you would like to talk about it, I'm here to listen.'

'You're a great friend, thank you. It's just… It's manifesting in very odd ways.'

'How so?'

'You won't judge me?'

'In India you would have to shave your head to express your grief.'

'That's a good point.' Slowly Fiona told Pinal of the sushi incident and of Annie being cornered on a jetty then rescued by a pelican. 'Couldn't it be that the pelican was shielding Annie from harm? You said, right, there's no future in which we cease to be?'

'If Peter was pure and virtuous, Fiona, he would be reincarnated as a higher being than a pelican.'

'He *was* so pure, and virtuous. I miss him so much.' Fiona's ugly neck seemed to lose its tensile strength. Her head fell sideways and her attention faded into a despondent stare—beyond the farm café's umbrellas and in the direction of several cows that were munching on hay at a trough.

'Fiona?'

'Mm,' she moaned.

'Are you seeing Peter right now?'

'Hm?' She returned her head to upright. 'What? Oh no. No, Pete I think would pick an animal more interesting than a cow. No offense.'

Pinal shook off the hate crime and said, 'Why don't you go to the zoo? It has the widest range of animals—you can see there if Peter is turning up again.'

'I think that might be fuelling the crazy.'

'Or speak to an animal medium,' Pinal shrugged.

'What's an animal medium?'

'Someone who can communicate with animals. Talk to them, tell you what they're thinking, and what they're saying.'

'That sounds like the last thing I need. Oh, Pinal, am I crazy? I'm crazy, aren't I?'

'There is a temple in India where people let rats drink from a tray of milk. But before the rats are finished the milk, they take the tray and drink, the leftover rat milk.'

Fiona's body convulsed as though she were Mel presented with eels.

'There is no crazy, Fiona, there are only different ways of perceiving the unseen. But maybe you should spend some time with family. Family's the only thing that helps to heal something like this.'

The second youngest member of her family was two aisles over from his own and helping out Madame Tran at the Nail Salon.

Having received an order of bullet-head nails which not for the first time weren't pre-sorted by length, she had heard that The Chair Man was uniquely amenable to helping his co-workers. So Mel sat across from her at a low marble table with a large white lamp between them, sorting out thousands and thousands of nails.

'You have girlfriend?!' said Madame Tran as she held a nail against the 50mm standard. Finding that it was a 45mm one she slid it across to Mel.

'No, no girlfriend,' said Mel, accruing shorter nails into a pile of three hundred and sixty.

'But you so handsome!'

'Thank you, Madame Tran.'

'Hair look so good! Blon!'

'Your hair looks good too.'

'Noooo! My hair just Vietnamee!'

Mel reached 360 in his count then slid his pile towards the edge of the table and flunged them into their plastic container. 'Is that lunch yet?'

'Lunchtime, OK!'

Mel walked with Madame Tran to the cafeteria and saw there, seated at one of the plastic tables—wearing French cuffs under a three-piece suit—Steve Blackman. 'What are you doing here again?'

'Heyyy, Mel! Just on my lunch break. I tell you what, are Dixon sausages the best thing y'ever put in your mouth or what?'

'You're taking your lunch break at Dixon Hardware?'

'Where else would I take them?'

'Where's your office?'

'Come, I'll show you.' Steve wiped his mouth with a napkin and stood and walked towards the front of the store. 'Come on!' He waved Mel on then turned down aisle 26. In the aisle onto which his plastic-tabled office backed, Mel stood at the beginning of a long succession of painted aluminium siding, of slotted-sleeper retaining walls, of pre-moulded imitation rock wall. Steve Blackman strode ahead and drew his hand in an arc from the aisle's first bay to its last. 'Waddya reckon?'

'I reckon we're in aisle 26.'

'She's a beauty isn't she?'

'Steve, do you work on a street of walls?'

'Flat out today too.'

'You told you me you worked on Wall Street, Steve. You

The Georgian Fencing Parties

told me to invest in eels.'

'F--k yeah. 360% increase in price over the last three years. That's unheard of, Chair Man.'

'Steve, I told everyone I know to invest in eels. I told Drew Fluckinger—I told my sister's sister-in-law, to invest in eels. What the hell have you done?'

'Eel futures or eel dividends?'

'You don't know anything about money, you work on a street of walls, Steve—you work in an aisle of walls!'

'I know a lot about eels but. A kilo of baby eel was three hundred dollars three years ago. Thirteen-hundred now. What's the matter, Chair Man? I told you I work on Wall Street.'

'I thought you meant Wall Street in New York.'

'How would I work there and live here?'

Mel clenched his jaw and shook his head as he took in Steve's aisle.

'Calm down, Chair Man! I'll tell you what, I know exactly how to make it up to you. Remember the blonde who was in here last weekend? She asked about you. I'll get her to come in again. Sound good? Mel?'

At the end of Wall Street Mel had found a man with his back to the aisle, crouching and gripping at the edge of a sheet of shed-wall around which he wasn't so much as looking as peering. 'What are you doing?' Mel shouted.

The man stood from his suspicious kneel and pouted and shook his head and said, 'Nothing,' as he relaxed into a casual wander and quickly was intercepted by The Vice President.

Fiona emerged from the aisle of chairs down which she thought she might run into her brother. So she carried on past The Blind Guy to the back of the store and her dad's office.

'Isn't this a nice surprise,' said Geoff.

'What the hell happened to you?'

'What do you mean?'

'Your skin's glowing.'

'Oh yeah,' he said rolling his arms around in front of himself. 'I think the communist poisoned me.'

'What? Why?'

'I sent him to a sauna for homosexuals.'

'And he what—made you a redhead? Is that possible? Is it permanent?'

'I bloody hope not,' he said, and took off his flat cap and revealed a large ball of orange hair. 'I look like a leprechaun.'

'Can you—put your hat back on would you? Can you pick Annie up from school for a while?'

'Of course, what's up?'

'Oh Yuri's been doing it, but I'm worried about what she's learning from him. I'm really struggling, Dad, I think I might be losing my mind.'

'Why d'you say that?'

'I befriended a pelican on the weekend.'

'You what?'

'Then my gym membership got cancelled because I used the s-word. I can barely concentrate on anything, I've become a bad friend, a bad mother. I need a Dad hug.' She stood and pouted and held out her arms.

'Fi, grieving takes time. Trust me, I know. Do you want Annie to stay with me?'

Fiona stepped to the side of her father's desk and jangled her wrists. 'Is that all right?'

'Of course. But if you wanna be this miserable, go and hang out with the communists.'

Arsen lowered his head as he entered the office of Father Pyanenko, who took two shot glasses from his top drawer and filled one from his water pistol. It ran out of samohonka after covering only the bottom of the second. He took a bottle from his second drawer and pulled the plastic cap from the pistol's rear and slowly refilled it.

'Father. I need you to make exorcism.'

'Another?'

'It is banya. There is…' Arsen sighed before admitting it: 'There is a Bannik. My family cannot go in, we cannot make business. I cannot relax, not think. You have no idea what public banya is like, Father.'

'You have a Bannik.' Father Pyanenko topped up his shot glass then held it out to Arsen. Arsen met the glass with his own and both drank. 'Theeere is only one way to get rid of Bannik. And it is no Christian matter.'

'I will do anything.'

'You must consult a Rain Woman.'

'Ergh,' said Arsen and scowled. 'There is one here?'

'I will check,' said Father Pyanenko. He leaned up to the centre of his desk and said, 'Hey, Siri?'

'Hi, Father.'

Arsen looked down at the grey cube which he hadn't noticed among Father Pyanenko's books. 'I know this woman. She can turn on lights.'

Father Pyanenko nodded and lowered his head to the contraption. 'Siri, find me a Rain Woman.' Arsen leaned forward and waited for what wonder the thing would perform next.

'You want to rent Rain Man, Father?'

'No, no—get me a Rain Woman.'

'Rain Man is a 1988 film starring Tom Cruise and Dustin Hoffman.'

'It is also talking enciclopedia?'

'Would you like to rent it now, Father?'

'No, idiot. Find me a Rain Woman.'

'Did you say Rainbowman? There's a male escort service in Southbank—should I call the Rainbow Room?'

'No. Father, you do not want this.'

The phone at the far corner of Father Pyanenko's desk let out an electronic bleat; the voice in the grey cube said, 'Would you like me to answer that, Father?'

'Yes, Siri. Tell them I'm in a meeting.'

'It can answer phone?' said Arsen. 'I must have her.'

Nearing the end of a long day of irrelevance, Annie found herself unable to any longer focus on the pages that she was using to ensure she didn't have to focus on what Ms Conrad was spouting. For the first time that day she put down her book-within-a-book and looked up at the whiteboard as Ms Conrad went on.

'There are 58 different genders according to the Centre for Mental Health Research, and really you can never know—and you should never presume—which one your friend, let's call them Tommy, is going to reveal themselves as. So what do we think we *say* to Tommy when they invites us to their reveal party?'

'Ta da!' said Martin Luther Ching, very loudly.

'Thank you, Martin, that's enough.'

'Chinese burn!' Martin yelled again, and threw back his head in mischievous laughter.

'We have to remember that a gender reveal party is one of the most important rituals in all of our lives, and it's important that when we do arrive, we're willing to sacrifice everything to their's party. All right, it's nearly three o'clock which means I have an announcement! At the start of each year the whole school always holds a short-film competition, which anyone from any year level can enter. This is part of why we were given iPads on our first day. If you choose to, from today you have two weeks to film and edit a three-minute movie about anything you'd like to explore that celebrates our Three Theses: diversity, inclusion, equality. All entries are judged by the school's film and art teachers, so get your filmmaking dreams out and your directors' eyes working. There'll be entries from every year level, but I think the freshness of your minds, my dear class, along with the ruthless orthodoxy that I enforce, will mean you have an equally—equality—good chance of winning one of this year's prizes.

'That's all for today. Pack up your things and the bell's about to ring. I'll see you all tomorrow!'

Where Annie was used to meeting Yuri after school she was surprised to find her grandfather's car. 'Hi Grandpa! What the hell happened to you?' she said as she put on her seatbelt.

'Nothing. What do you mean?'

'Did you dye your hair?'

'No.' Geoff had put a palmful of gel in his hair after finding this darkened it to auburn. This he had combed back under a flat cap. 'What do you mean?'

'It's red.'

'No,' he scoffed.

'What's this music?'

'Never heard this song?'

'Uh uh.'

'Slim Dusty!' Annie pressed with both hands at the button that would have raised her window but found that it did nothing. 'Can you wind my window up please?' She slunk down her seat until she couldn't be seen from without as Geoff sang:

'*Where my mummy and daddy are waiting for me, and the pals of my childhood once more I will see*. ... So what'd you learn today?'

'There are fifty-eight genders.'

'Genders? Fifty-eight are there? I've only heard of two. Oh and the ahh... the ones that are kind of in the middle.'

'Ms Conrad said I should be thinking about which one I identify as. Because I've been assigned a socially constructed gender by my interpersonal relationships.'

'Said all that did she?'

'Don't you think it sounds dumb?'

'Me?'

'When I told Uncle Yuri he told the principal he should be tied in a sack and steamed over stinging nettles.'

'He's a hot-head, that fella. Strange too, with that bald head, the pantaloons.'

'Did Australia have freedom when you were young?'

'Freedom?'

'Have you ever read Alexander Herzen?'

'What's that, a book? Books'll do you mischief, Annie.'

'What's liberty?'

'Very big words, Little One. I'll tell you what I reckon? There's only one thing that matters in life—wanna know what it is?'

Annie nodded.

'To be able to retire comfortably. Y'earn a good living, y'eat some decent food, you get to watch your grandkids grow up. And anything that doesn't get in the way of that, I could care less. Oo, ya ready?'

'For what?'

Geoff pointed at the centre of his dashboard and leaned towards his granddaughter as he drove and sang: '*Oh, there's a track winding back to an old-fashioned shack…*'

'Are we going to where I think we're going?'

'Sure are,' said Geoff, and shortly turned his car in to park outside USA Sweets. 'Anything you want and as much as you want of it.'

'As much as I want?! Red liquorice?'

'Anything you want, Little One.'

Fiona had taken her father's indifferent advice and invited Alexa to the beach box.

'I want to kill your brother.'

The Georgian Fencing Parties

'How much did you lose?'

'Who's *he* to tell me to invest in eels?'

'Maybe he was joking. He hates eels, they make him vomit. How do you even invest in eels?'

'What a destiny I have ahead. I'm so so tired of being in heat for my father.'

'Wait, what?'

'Taking those disgusting men into the banya, just to get him business.'

'Oh phew! You're sick of being arm candy?'

'Sick of what?'

'Being arm candy. Looking good so people want to rent cranes from you.'

'That's what I am—arm candy! I don't want to be that anymore. I'm tired of making men jiggle. All I want is my ooown business, that makes my ooown money. To be free.'

'I have a weird question for you, Alexa.'

'Ask, please.' Alexa took another sip from her champagne and dangled her wrists over the arms of her camping chair. 'This is so nice, Fiona.'

'Would you come to the zoo with me?'

'The zoo!' Alexa wailed, then threw back the last of her drink. 'Oh, the zoo! It's where I lost my crush. My crush! He was…' She held out her glass to Fiona for a refill.

Seeing tears newly in her eyes Fiona said, 'I guess that's a no to the zoo.'

'Anywhere but the zoo! Fi! I'll turn thirty-five and I'll have no job, no money, no husband.'

'When's your birthday?'

'Tomorrow!' Alexa moaned and flopped her head over the back of her chair.

'What?! Happy birthday for tomorrow!' Alexa moaned and again urged Fiona to fill her glass to the top. 'We should have a beauty afternoon! We could get our nails done, our hair?'

'I'm booked in tomorrow at the hair saloon. Will you come? That'd be so nice.'

'The hair salon?'

'The saloon.'

'Vidal Sassoon? I don't—'

'Sassoon's Saloon, you know it? Then I'm having a party tomorrow night. Please come!'

'Ohh, I don't know how much fun I'd be at a party. I've been a bit… weird, since… since Pete.'

'Please come! It'll just be me and my girlfriends. And it's my birthday, which means I get so drunk I pass out for a whole day. But it's been a tough year, the assaults, then the… the animal place. This one'll probably be two days! Please come, will you?'

'Hello you buy nail?!'

Mel was again opposite Madame Tran at the Nail Salon, hunched over a mound of nails and sorting the flat-headed from bullet-headed. Madame Tran at the Nail Salon too was occupied with the task but was having to sell nails as she sorted: 'Hello you buy nail?!'

Mel looked over his shoulder as a man in a branded and torn aqua polo shirt browsed the display rack across the aisle.

'He steal nail.'

'He does?'

'He steal nail.'

There came a 'Psst' from behind Madame Tran. Mel looked up and saw Steve Blackman peeking through from his street (aisle) of walls.

'What do you want?'

Steve said through the shelving: 'Someone here that wants to meet you.'

'The blonde?'

Steve grinned and nodded. 'Meet you in your street,

The Georgian Fencing Parties

buddy.'

'Two minutes. Madame Tran, how do I look?'

Mel stood and put on his blazer and presented himself to her. 'Show me hand.' He splayed his fingers and Madame Tran turned her lamp to them. She inspected closely their ends. 'You OK.'

'Mel, this is Tess. Tess, Mel. And I've gotta get back to Wall Street, so I'll leave you two to it.'

They smiled and shook hands and smiled some more as Steve left them alone in Mel's aisle. 'Need another marquee adventurer?'

'I'm afraid this visit's purely personal,' said Tess.

'Shall we take a walk, through the gardening section, or you hungry? The cafeteria's just there.'

'Steve did say I should eat Dixon sausage while I'm here? I don't think he hears himself speak sometimes.'

'We'll forego the sausage. So what does Tess do for work?' They rounded the end of aisle 27 and strolled among seedlings.

'Tess, works on the sock market.'

'The stock market? Wait, not the same way Steve works on Wall Street?'

'No, no,' Tess smiled. 'I *actually* work on the sock market.'

'As like a day-trader?'

'Mm,' she reflected. 'Yeah we're not open at night.'

'And what if tomorrow night, since you won't be working, we got a… drink in the city?'

'You move fast. That sounds like a fant—'

'We are meeting again tomo—'

'Shuddup.' Mel thrust out his arm sideways and held his index finger to Yuri's face. 'Tess,' he calmly said. 'Please write down your phone number for me.'

'Tomorrow we must be—'

'Ah!' said Mel, and reasserted his finger as Tess wrote on a piece of paper from her handbag.

'Call me?' she said as she handed it to him.

'Tonight,' said Mel. 'I will call you tonight.'

Tess smiled then winced at Yuri as she left the gardening section and Dixon Hardware.

'What have I now been witnessing?'

'You have now been witnessing, my terrifying friend, me getting the phone number of a very beautiful woman, who works on the stock market.'

'For you I am most happy. For her I am much concerned. But. Man have telled me that tomorrow guy will be at Georgian fencing party. Have you been before to Georgian fencing party?'

'Surprisingly, I have not. But I fenced at uni.'

'So you can bring own equipment? This is good. Georgians will be liking.'

'Why a fencing party?'

'Georgian people are most festive. I think they are even having Circus Olé.'

'Cirque du Soleil? That is impressive. Things are finally looking up, Yuri my boy!'

'What is your meaning?' said Yuri after glancing at the ceiling.

'I might still be a chairman, but I have parties to go to, dates to go on—dates with beautiful dames. And, you didn't tell me not to call you my friend. Adventures, Yuri. I am finally having adventures.'

'It is not adventure. We will be finding out who have killed my brother. Then we are killing him.'

'Wait, what?'

'What the f--k happened to you?' said Mel as he came into his father's living room and found Geoff beside Annie in front of the television. 'Sorry,' he said to his niece, a rope of red liquorice dangling from her mouth. 'What happened to you?'

The Georgian Fencing Parties

Geoff looked up from his phone and, surprised to see his son, said, 'Ah.'

'D'you dye your hair?'

'He didn't always have red hair, did he? I told you, Grandpa! Uncle Mel, want some liquorice? Look how much Grandpa let me get.'

Annie pointed back to the kitchen table, covered in paper bags brimming with knotted red ropes of the stuff.

'You look like a leprechaun.'

'You know the words to *Road to Gundagai* don't you?'

'I guess so.'

'Been teaching it to Annie, giving her some culture.'

'I learnt the words, Grandpa. It's just not a good song.'

'Can I go to the basement, get some of my old stuff?'

Geoff tapped triumphantly at his phone and said, 'Dinner is on its way. You hungry?'

'What are you having?'

'Sushi!' said Annie.

'Nnn—nn nn,' Mel called as he descended. 'No thank you.'

Downstairs he looked over the assortment of boxes and tubs and the enormous striped plastic bags that all lined the walls of his father's basement. Under a wooden bench he recognised the blue end of a sports bag and opened its front zipper. He tugged at a patch of white fabric then unfurled an old Dixon Balls t-shirt—the two words in its name vertical and side-by-side with a basketball and a tennis ball at their base. He shook his head as he recalled the social carnage that had followed his wearing it to school. Then he found that the remainder of the bag indeed contained the thicker white fabric for which he was looking. He slid it out and opened it fully and pulled out his mesh-fronted helmet—returned it to its compartment and said, 'Ah ha!' as he pulled out a long nylon bag. He unzipped its bottom corner and pulled open its flap and found there the grips of his épée, his sabre, his foil.

He pondered for a moment, then decided that a party full of Georgians—and what's more his new friend—might think him a try-hard or a show-off if he brought all three. So he would take only his épée—gripped at its handle and nestled his fist into its domed guard—looked upon its blunt tip as he flailed it from side to side.

'You didn't find the white kilt down there did ya?' said Geoff as Mel stomped back up to the living room.

'Is that dinner already?'

'Press of a button,' said Geoff, and changed the channel.

Two plastic bags were open on the coffee table and from them had been taken two plastic trays and countless plastic tubs. 'Want some sushi, Uncle Mel?'

Annie held out a black and white log filled with green and orange. Mel sniffed and said, 'What is that?'

'Unagi,' said Annie then sang: 'Eee-el.'

Mel's shoulders tightened as his head momentarily pressed towards his chest. He turned aside and clenched his teeth and shook his head.

'What are you doing with that crap?' said Geoff.

Mel asserted proudly: 'I… have a party to go to.'

'With an s-word?'

'It's called an épée, Dad—you know that. And yes. I have a party to go to with an épée.'

III

After spending his entire morning practising, Mel followed the noise coming from behind the address that Yuri had given for the Georgian fencing party. He thought upon the years of lonely training proudly carried out, the tournaments scantily attended—a decade of esoteric labour that had long come to little but which was about to culminate—and so soon after his homecoming—in a kind of social debut. Wearing his full white suit and holding his meshed helmet in one hand and his unsheathed épée in the other, he passed through a front lawn of parked cars and went in through the side gate.

Ahead, at the end of a narrow walkway formed by two brick houses, he saw a host of thickly-haired and darkly bearded men all facing the same direction, their elbows rising and wrists falling as they hammered nails into upright planks of wood. Mel emerged at the corner of the backyard and stopped beside a verandah; a long trestle table was there being laid with food by women in black dresses and red head scarves. On the far side of the backyard five other men wore silver-lined tuxedos and played large guitars as they bounced up and down on a trampoline—while ahead a steel-and-wooden symphony of nails being thumped into palings clammered on.

'What in Buddha's name you are wearing?' said Yuri, halting his own hammering to come over and greet him. 'Where have you been—fighting with one sword?'

'No, Yuri. Not fighting with a sword. You said this was a fencing party.'

The band on the trampoline neared the end of a song and all bent their knees to stop their bouncing before saying in unison, 'Olé!'

'It is Georgian fencing party.'

'I thought you meant this fencing,' said Mel, and flailed his épée into a clump of balloons.

'Fighting with swords?'

'Fencing, Yuri.'

'Yes! Come!' said a Georgian now at Yuri's side.

'Mel, this is Giorgi. This is his home, and this… will be his fence.'

'You can put the sword down here if you want,' said Giorgi and pointed to a table in front of the verandah.

'It's an épée,' said Mel as he laid it beside his helmet.

Then Giorgi led him towards the far end of the long half-built fence. 'Yuri tells me you are a chairman.'

'Did he say chairman or chair man?'

'Hm?'

'Can I ask you a question?'

'Please, tell me!' said Giorgi as he escorted Mel across his backyard.

Mel leaned across and said, 'Breastfeeding.'

'What's that?'

'Breastfeeding,' Mel repeated, and nodded.

'What about it?'

Mel glanced at the backs of the heads of the fence-builders behind whom he was being walked. Then he said, as though he had been misunderstood, 'Breast…'

'All right!' said Giorgi as they came to an empty place on the fencing line. 'Roman, this is Mel.'

'One thousand two hundred twenty three nails,' said Roman, and nodded with most of the top half of his short body.

Giorgi held up a hammer then rattled a packet of nails and handed both to Mel. Roman beside him placed the tip of a nail against a paling then with three diminishing strokes drove it into the wood. He knelt down to the packet at his side and said, 'One thousand two hundred twenty two nails,'

The Georgian Fencing Parties

as he took out another.

'I've never built a fence before,' said Mel, surveying the long line of men wearing tool belts around their tracksuits.

'One thousand two hundred twenty one *nails*,' said Roman.

'Breastfeeding,' said Mel.

'Yeah,' said Roman in two descending syllables.

'Breastfeeding?' said Mel, sensing momentarily that he had cracked the code.

'Yeah,' said Roman, and rolled his head towards Mel's feet.

'What can you tell me about it?'

'One thousand two hundred—two hundred and twenty nails,' said Roman after hammering in another.

So Mel turned to his right, where the upcurled moustache of a young man in a tight black polo shirt dripped with sweat as he flunged his hammer at a succession of nails. Mel said, 'Breastfeeding,' to him and was replied to in a thick Georgian accent: 'How are you, mate? I am George.' George threw his hammer to his left hand and offered Mel his right.

'Breastfeeding,' said Mel.

'What's your name?'

'Breastfeeding?' said Mel, and nodded.

'Did you say breastfeeding?'

He stared into George's eyes and said, 'Eel magnets,' and nodded.

'Hm?'

'Hello, Siri?'

Fed up with answering phone calls from competitors wanting to buy him out or taunt him, Arsen had gone to an electronics store and found a box bearing a near-enough likeness to the device that he had seen turn on the lights at Café Beztsihan and answer Father Pyanenko's phone.

After taking out the flat-bottomed orb and placing it at

the centre of his desk he leaned towards it and smiled and said again, 'Hello, Siri?' He blinked and waited. 'Siri?' he said louder. Still the device made no answer. He lifted it from the desk and held it to his mouth. 'Hello? Siri?' His front door bells rang as Fiona arrived to pick up Alexa for their salon date. 'Fiona! Do you know what is name of this? I thought it was Siri, but maybe is Silly? Is Silly a name for your people? Simi? Hello, Simi?'

'Oh, I've seen those, I don't understand them at all. You need a young person for that stuff, Annie knows about it.'

'Where is she?'

'She's with my dad.'

'Siri, call Geoff.' Arsen held his breath as he waited for the orb to respond. 'Siri, call Dixon Hardware.' He grunted and picked up the receiver of his telephone and began winding its dial.

'Oleksa!' he called out as he approached the halfway point of the phone number. 'Oleksa! Fiona is here.'

'This place is weird,' said Annie to her grandfather.

'You think so?' said Geoff, holding a wombat's skull in front of his face as he turned to—to face her.

'See!'

Geoff put down the skull and picked up and inspected a flamingo's head, the bottom half of its beak removed and a considerable length of its throat plastinated.

'Do you think I could film in here?'

'Film?'

'I have to make a short film for school and I'm going to make mine about my family. You said you know the owner?'

'Want me to ask if you can film?'

'Yes please.'

Geoff crossed The Olde Curiosity Shop's vanilla carpeting and asked the younger woman (younger than him, not his granddaughter) if his granddaughter might film in the store.

The Georgian Fencing Parties

She said it was fine and Geoff gave Annie a thumbs up. Annie raised her tablet and pressed record and panned across the shop's bat skeletons and bone hour glasses and meteorite fragments and emu eggs—turned it past a rack of naga-headed walking sticks to her grandfather, now leaning against the shop's sales desk. Slowly she walked towards him, holding the device as still as she could.

'So you ever been to Vietnam?' said Geoff.

'A long time ago,' said the finger-tattooed woman. 'Beautiful country.'

'Not a fan of snorkelling by any chance are you?'

'I am! It's one of my favourite things to do on a date.'

'On a date?'

'Isn't that why you brought this over?'

'This? Why?'

'It's a snorkel.'

'This is a snorkel?' he said as she took the flamingo's head from him.

'Mm hm, it's Mayan,' she said and raised it to her chin.

'Oh you don't need to put your mouth on it,' said Geoff, having carefully observed the shoddiness of its taxidermy.

'It's fine, it's sterile,' and she put the flamingo's mouth to her own and exhaled. 'See, look,' she mumbled, then flapped her tongue in and out of its upside-down skull.

Geoff scrunched up his nose and lowered the bottom corners of his mouth. 'Never mind.' His phone rang as he retreated. 'You. What do you want?'

'I need help of Anastasia.'

'So?'

'Please can you bring her to U-Crane?'

'Why would she want to visit that hellhole?'

'She likes it here.'

'I doubt that very much.'

'Ask her.'

Mel sat in a folding chair at the long Georgian trestle table and shook out his wrist and rotated his elbow as behind him Circus Olé bounced mariachi. 'Not quite the adventure I had in mind, Yuri.'

'Why is it so that you are using this word with muchly repetition?'

'Adventure's what I'm meant to be doing, Yuri, that's why. I'm James Blonde, I'm not meant to be hammering nails into a fence all day.'

'Do you not like to be fencing?'

'This isn't fencing, idiot. This is building a fence. I spent my afternoon trying to talk to Rain Man.'

'You are knowing of such men?'

'What men?'

'Men who are making it rain—your culture is having these?'

Mel shook his head then leaned up to the table and searched for something that might not taste of beetroot.

'Why you have been saying to everyone, "breastfeeding"?' Mel pulled with his front teeth at a piece of cheesy bread. 'Giorgi is thinking I have brought village pervert to fencing party. You do *not* get invited back to Georgian fencing party if you are saying to everyone "breastfeeding".'

'The guy who mentioned Pete's definitely not here.'

'Of this you think you're sure you absolutely know?'

'What?'

'You think you are absolutely sure he is not here?'

'I looked at the faces of every man building that fence. He's not here.'

Giorgi whistled loudly at Circus Olé and waved his hands to get them to stop. Again they silenced their instruments and ceased pushing down against the trampoline. Slowly and silently Giorgi walked the length of his verandah, humming a low note in order to gather the attention of all who were feasting beneath it. When he reached its end he intoned a word. Then he appeared distressed as after a warbling introduction he loudened his voice and sang a dirge whose opening lines, if this book were in any way able to afford even one goddam subtitle, would have been given as:

'My father was killed in battle,
Germans shot my mother in the open field.'

Mel chewed away at his cheese-bread and nodded as Giorgi was joined in standing by most of his fellow fence-builders, and shortly even by Yuri in his singing. Mel looked up and was surprised that Yuri knew the words:

'My sister is now enslaved,
They cut my eyes out with a knife.'

Finding the hastening melody jovial and its choral aspect rousing, Mel bobbed his shoulders from side to side and began to nod with the bouncing beat. Yuri tapped him in the back of the head and furrowed his eyebrows at him as he sang:

'But through the slot of my machine gun,
I sense the evil of my enemies.
And with lead I kill them all
As they come to rape our daughters.'

Mel shook his head back up at Yuri and turned up his palms, thinking that at the very least he was being polite. The song came to its most upbeat stanza yet:

'My cousin ate my grandma
So we boiled her thighs with beets.'

And Mel felt the urge to clap along, and did so, as Yuri both sang in baritone and bulged his eyes at him with urgent insistence:

'All the mud and the blood and the snowfall,

Had made cannibalism an inaccurate form of revenge.'

And Yuri grabbed Mel's wrists and held them closed and shook his head.

Geoff told Annie that he had to go back to work and sent her on her way, out of the car and into U-Crane's front office.

'Nastyusha! I am happy to see you!'

Annie dropped her backpack on the armchair and said, 'Want some liquorice?' She held up two ropes of it. Arsen opened his mouth as Annie came around his desk and sat on his lap. She placed one between his teeth then put the other at her own lips.

'Do you know what is this, my granddaughter?'

'I know these.'

'You can make it work?'

'Is it on?'

'It is out of box.'

'You have to turn it on first, Grandpa.'

'Ah.'

'Then you have to connect it to Bluetooth.'

Arsen bit off some liquorice and held the remainder of the rope in his hand. 'To what?'

'Bluetooth.'

'From radiation?'

'What?'

'Blue-tooth is first sign of radiation. One of your teeth…' He tapped a fingertip at his incisor. 'It's turning blue, and if you do not get away it falls out. Then you grow ear from your cage.'

'Are you joking?'

'Joking? This has happened to Poroshenko the fencer. He has now all blue teeth, and four ears. No more he can build fence.'

The Georgian Fencing Parties

'Give me your phone?' said Annie, and Arsen lifted the olive green telephone from the far corner of his desk. 'Not that kind of phone, Grandpa. A smartphone, an iPhone.'

'I don't have this.'

'OK, well we can use your computer.'

Annie leaned forward and held Arsen's mouse and right-clicked an icon. Then she lifted up his new orb and held down a button on its underside and waited for it to make a noise. When the noise came she returned the device to the centre of the desk and said, 'Now try it.'

Arsen leaned around his granddaughter and addressed the orb: 'Hello, Siri?'

'This one's Alexa.'

'What?'

'Siri's a different company.' Annie whispered: 'You have to say "Alexa".'

'Alexa?' Arsen whispered. 'That will make confuse. What if I want to call Oleksa?'

'Hello?'

Arsen gasped. It was alive.

'See.'

'But if I am needing to call out for Oleksa?'

'Mm hm?' said the contraption.

'This *will* make confuse. Hello, Alexa?'

'Yes? Who am I talking with?'

Arsen looked to Annie. 'It ask human questions?'

'Tell her your name.'

He leaned down and said, 'Arsen Oleksiyovych Sukhimov.'

'Not your whole name, Grandpa, just your first name.'

'Arsen,' he said cautiously to his desk.

'Did you say your name is Arson?'

'Tak, yes.'

'Could you say your name one more time?'

'Arsen.'

'And just one more time?'

'What, you are deaf? It is deaf?'

'It's learning your voice, Grandpa.'

'It can learn?' Annie nodded. 'What do you want?'

'If I could get your name just one more time?'

'Arsen.'

'OK, Arson. How can I help you today?'

'This! Is what I remember! Thank you, Nastyusha. But I don't need until phone rings.'

'Can we go in the banya, Grandpa?'

'Oh, Nastyusha, banya is broken. And the Rain Woman does not arrive until tomorrow.'

'What's a rain woman?'

'In Ookraine it is woman who make spell on field for harvest. But in here I think they make spell for business. She will get rid of Bannik.'

'Spells like a witch?'

'Mm,' said Arsen, not wholly granting the comparison. 'Not evil. She is like babusya.'

'I wanna meet her!'

'Then you stay with me. Tell me, does your grandfather Geoff look different?'

Fiona and Alexa walked through the swinging wooden doors of Chapel Street's Hair Saloon and were smiled at by a young woman behind a laptop: 'Howdy pardeners!'

The empty centre of a two-storeyed brick warehouse was covered in sawdust. Hairdressers all wore petticoats and corsets with ruffles for sleeves and in the far corner stood a pretty good-looking horse, tied up with its muzzle over a water trough. An unpolished upright piano sat covered and unplayed beside the receptionist.

'Alexa Sukhimov, for two.'

'Right this way.'

'Oh, I miss playing,' said Alexa as she ran her fingers along the top of the piano.

The Georgian Fencing Parties

'You play?'

'Mm. But I'm so depressed all year I don't want to. It's even that I *can't* play.'

'You Ukrainians are so talented,' said Fiona as she and Alexa had black plastic capes tied at their necks. 'We always tried to get Annie to play an instrument but she never took to it. Mel plays the bagpipes—you ever heard such a racket?'

'You should meet Boryslav. He plays the accordion like nobody I've ever seen—like nobody Ukraine's ever seen.'

'Who's Boryslav?'

'He's a friend of the family. He once caught syphilis on purpose so he'd go mad, so he'd be able to play the accordion like Panini.'

'Where's he?'

'Where's Boryslav?' Alexa looked up at her frightened reflection. 'Boryslav is always coming.'

'Isn't this nice though?' said Fiona as she and Alexa were eased back into basins.

'It is nice,' said Alexa. 'Thanks for coming.'

As they relaxed into having their hair washed somebody sat at the piano and started to play. Alexa turned her head to the new noise and saw too that somebody had begun milking the horse.

'Why would they have such a giant animal in here?' said Fiona.

'That's not so giant,' said Alexa.

'No?'

'It is not a large horse,' said the Very Eastern European woman with her fingers in Fiona's hair.

'Is animal medium,' said Alexa's hairdresser.

'Animal medium?' said Fiona and rolled her head back.

'Eleven litres milk per day.'

'That's a medium animal,' said Alexa.

'Animal medium,' said Fiona.

'Do you sell the milk?' Alexa asked.

'We have at front of store.'

'Alexa, you're smiling,' said Fiona as she was returned to upright and spun to face the saloon mirrors. 'It makes me happy to see you smiling.'

'I'm not smiling. The future's disappearing for me.'

'You are—you're glowing!'

'What?' She leaned forward and inspected the mirror. 'I haven't been near anything radioactive.'

'Glowing's good! You look radiant.'

'Radiant?! I don't have blue tooth do I?' She raised her top lip to Fiona. Returned a strange look, she put her handbag on her lap. 'Here,' she said and handed Fiona two pills. 'Iodine. They'll prevent the blue tooth.'

Annie lifted her backpack onto Arsen's kitchen table and took out another rope of red liquorice.

'No, Nastyusha,' said her grandfather. 'No more sweets before dinner. And take bag off table, we eat there. Put it in living room.'

Annie returned the rope to the paper bag that still was full of them and put that inside the backpack that still was full of *them*—then put her backpack on the coffee table in the living room.

'Come. We make the varenyky you love.'

'Yes!' said Annie, instantly excited. 'With bacon and potato?'

'Any kind you want. First go to backyard, and bring five potatoes and two onions.'

'You mean the fridge?'

'What?'

'Did you say the backyard?'

'Yes, five potatoes two onions.'

'Why are they in the backyard?'

'What?'

'You keep your onions in the backyard?'

'Keep? I grow.'

'You mean buy?'

'Anastasia, I am surprised. And disappoint in your mother. You do not grow these things?'

'Grow?'

'Come, I show you.'

Arsen's stood at the front sleeper of his vegetable garden and pointed to a low row of green leaves. 'There,' he said, and told Annie to step in. 'Dig your fingers into the ground and tell me what you feel.'

'Here?' said Annie with her fingertips at the topsoil.

'All the way in, go.' She pushed both hands down and wiggled her fingers and recognised the texture between them. 'Now lift.'

'They're potatoes!' said Annie as she sifted away the dirt. 'You grow them? And onions?'

'It is no life for a human being if you must buy everything from supermarket.'

'Is that why Uncle Yuri steals things?'

'It is not.'

Aproned at the kitchen bench Annie said, 'Grandpa, can I film us cooking?'

'Film?'

'I have to make a movie for school, I'm going to make mine about my family.'

Arsen looked across at Annie then down at the object that she was already pointing at him. 'Now, Nastyusha, you must listen. When we are pressing dough, we whisper good thoughts to it.' He leaned over and down and whispered into the wad of dough that he was rolling and folding on the bench.

'Grandpa, are you for real?'

'We must make the dough smile, Nastyusha. So we whisper good thoughts only, beautiful thoughts—and varenyky will come out most delicious.' Again Arsen leaned down and spoke almost silently to the dough. Then: 'Come, it is your turn.'

'Me?'

'Come!' Arsen stood back from the bench and urged his granddaughter to take his place. 'Give to me.' He took the flat rectangle from her. 'Get your hands pushing, and push… like that, yes. Now whisper beautiful thoughts.'

Annie leaned forward then smiled at her grandfather. He filmed and nodded as she abandoned her reticence and whispered into the softening dough.

Moving the lenses from sizzling bacon to simmering water, Annie turned and filmed her grandfather as he placed a third setting on the dining table.

'Who else is coming?'

'This is for your grandmother.'

'Grandma Elizabeth?'

'Yelyzaveta, yes. My horlitsya.'

'You put out a plate for her?'

Her grandfather became solemn. 'She is waiting for me. Until I can join her, I remember the meals we eat together.'

'You miss her.'

'Every day.'

'I wish I got to meet her.'

'So do I, Nastyusha. So do I. Come, we eat.'

Mel met Tess, Steve Blackman's chair-seeking friend, in Southbank.

'Where should we get that drink?' he asked. 'This place does take-away negroni.'

'You know, it's a really nice evening,' said Tess. 'Shall we go for a nice troll?'

'Oh good idea, I like a stroll. Your hair looks nice,' he said as shortly they strolled through Queen Victoria Gardens.

'Thanks! I got it done at the Hair Saloon. So tell me about you, Mel Dixon. What have you done with your summer?'

The Georgian Fencing Parties

'I just got back from Asia. This is my first Australian summer in five years.'

'Nice goatee, ya car-salesman-lookin' sneeze rag! Asia, nice. Which part?'

'Did you—. Did you just yell at that guy?'

'Yeah,' she said and grinned. She sipped at her drink and whispered: 'I love a nice troll. What were you doing in Asia?'

'I was trying to find my thing, does that make sense?'

'Turtley. Discovering what you're not just good at, but great at?'

'You get it. You the best at anything, you think?'

'Well… I have been told my tickles are the best there are.'

'Your tickles?'

'Mm hm! Hey Hulk Hogan called—he wants the rest of his haircut back, ya Swede-freak coot!'

As the Swede-freak passed, Mel looked at his balding head, then across at Tess. She was grooving her head up and down with her straw at her lips. 'And the… stock market. Tell me about that?'

'Oh, that's not that interesting I don't think. A lot of cushioning and heel pockets. Sole trading, Bonds. Wear a scarf you no-neck tortilla peasant!'

'What *are* you doing?'

'D'you see that woman's neck?! It wasn't even there. She looked like a Peruvian shepherd.'

'I guess so.' Mel pouted and went on. 'So the vocabulary's pretty specialised then?'

'You pick it up pretty easily. I grew up around it, so…'

At a bend in the path Mel stepped fully into a puddle made recently by a sprinkler. 'Ah, shiite.'

'Oh no!' said Tess. He took off his shoe and inspected his sock. 'What are they, long-staple cotton? Nice. That dual-layer knit'll move the moisture to the outer—they'll be dry in no time.'

'You know a lot about footwear huh?'

'Couldn't have gotten to where I am without it! Ya racoon slut! Ha ha!'

Mel raised an eyebrow at Tess, who he now admitted was yelling indiscriminately, though with much discrimination, at passers-by. His first instinct was to ask if she had Tourette's syndrome, but he decided it might be insensitive on a first date. He sipped from his drink as for a time they trolled in silence and shortly he began whistling both parts to *Weather Bird*.

'You're an excellent whistler,' she said as though consoling him.

'You think?'

'You whistle like an old man.'

'You know, that's the only thing where comparison with an old man's a good thing?'

'What do you mean?'

'If you *drink* like an old man, or you *snore* like an old man—they're bad. But *whistling* like an old man… It's the only one.'

'That is a very perceptive observation, Mel Dixon. Your drink empty too?' She leaned over to look into his cup.

'Shall we… double back and get two more?'

Thinking that their date was going unusually well, Tess ignored her fear of rejection and took a leap: 'Would you have dinner with me tonight?'

'Tonight.' Mel clicked one side of his back teeth. 'I can't tonight. I'd love to,' he inserted quickly so as to reassure her. 'But I have a birthday party with a new friend I've just made. When can I see you again?'

'Oh wait, look at this guy—wait don't look!' she said as Mel moved to turn his head. With both hands she grabbed at the middle of his shirt and smiled into his eyes as they waited for the man to near. She shot her eyes sideways as he passed them then yelled out: 'What are you, a molested

The Georgian Fencing Parties

rooster? You look like you play the violin with your arse, you beef frown!'

The man turned around and said, 'Excuse me?' as Mel and Tess ran off in the direction of one more drink.

Fiona stood at a table in a loud and packed St Kilda bar, surrounded by Alexa and several of her Alexa-looking friends.

'Are you sure you don't mind?' Alexa asked when finally her friends had convinced her to pull out her oldest party trick.

'No, I really don't,' said Fiona. 'I'm fine here.'

'It's one of the things I'm really good at,' said Alexa. 'And I love helping my friends, I'll be back in a couple of minutes?'

Fiona nodded and held her drink's straw to her mouth as she waited for Alexa—the only party guest with whom she could tolerably communicate—to return from asking several men if they minded if her friends came over and talked to them. To her solitary relief Mel now came sideways through the crowd of people. 'Sis!'

'Thank God, where have you *been*?'

'I went on a date,' Mel announced.

'Who, who—who—have gone on date?'

'That'd be me,' said Mel as Yuri arrived to stand across the table from him.

'Was he paying for your dinner?'

'Very funny.'

'What?'

'What's with the earring?'

'You are liking?' Yuri turned his ear to Mel and Fiona and shook his head in order to make what was hanging from it dangle. 'It is most frolicsome sapphire from Sri Lanka.'

'Tell me about the date then,' said Fiona.

'It was great actually—she's amazing. She's very uninhibited. We went for a stroll and she just started yelling at people. It was... freeing. *And* she works on the stock market.'

'Has she given to you one dusty hoffman?'

'One what?'

'One dusty hoffman.'

'What the hell is a dusty hoffman? Do you mean Dustin Hoffman?'

Yuri extended his first two fingers from his fist and explained: 'A dusty hoffman is when lady is giving to you fishfingers out of doors, but then you do not wash fishfingers.'

Fiona's and Mel's mouths flew wide open and both their noses scrunched tight. 'Yuri!' they said in unison. 'That is disgusting!'

'We are both of us men. Are we not susceptible to silly complications of pleasant simplicities? We are out on the town, and no less for birthday of my sister! This is what men are discussing on such occasion.'

'Good God,' said Fiona, appalled still.

Yuri's flip phone vibrated. 'Please be excusing me sharply one moment,' and he disappeared into the crowd to answer it. Alexa now came to stand behind the Dixons. 'Mel.'

'Hey, happy birthday!'

'I forgive you.'

'For what?'

'For telling me to invest in eels.'

'Why forgive?'

'I put my life savings into them.'

'Into eels?'

'It disappeared in eight hours.'

'Why would you do that—how would you do that?'

'Everyone seems to be gone,' said Fiona.

'I told you,' said Alexa. 'I'm the best wing-woman there is. I like being arm candy when it's for my friends.'

'That was man,' said Yuri, returning. 'He have informed to

The Georgian Fencing Parties

me orally that tomorrow at other Georgian fencing party, guy will certainly be attending. Do not be making fool of us again. Bring correct equipment to Georgian fencing party.'

'I can get it from work, don't worry.'

'Now I must to leave. Alexa will have no cake and there must be preparations for Georgian fencing party. I will see you there.'

Yuri nodded sternly at Fiona then left. One of Alexa's friends took his place, and complained to Alexa that her guy had turned out to be a douche. 'You think you can find other one?'

'Just tell me who,' said Alexa, and was gone again.

'Parties with Yuri now?'

'The one today had Cirque du Soleil.'

'Mel, be careful. Yuri's…'

'Strange? Terrifying? Psychotic?'

'I know you're sad about being a chair man, but the adventures that Pete told me Yuri gets up to… You're not made for those adventures.'

'I am,' said Mel, offended.

'James Blonde, you're not—trust me.'

'Who ordered their animal medium?' said a waitress, arrived at Alexa's table with four plates in hand.

'Animal medium?'

'I've got eight steaks coming, is one of them yours?'

'I don't know.'

'Animal medium?' the waitress said, raising her voice so that Mel too might answer her.

'Just put them at the end, they'll be back soon.'

A different waitress returned with a tray of tumblers surrounded by shot glasses and craned her arm back and forth as she placed them around Fiona and Mel. 'These are all for us,' Alexa sang as she returned to the table.

After several more rounds Fiona found that she had to end the night in the bar's bathroom.

'Why eels?' she said to Alexa and the toilet bowl.

Alexa lamented under a hand-dryer: 'Your brother told me to invest in eels. I should have bought heels.'

'It's very strange. And not eel magnets, right?'

'What's an eel magnet?' said Alexa, sipping from a shot glass.

'Your guess is as good as mine,' Fiona slurred, her knees sideways on the floor. 'You're so good at that tonight.'

'Good at what?'

'Getting men for your friends.'

'I'm the best arm candy,' Alexa struggled to sing.

Fiona dragged her legs across the tiles and nestled beside her sister-in-law. 'Have you ever heard of an animal medium?'

'A medium animal?' Alexa shook her head and offered her shot glass to Fiona.

'Animal medium,' said Fiona and refused the drink. 'Someone who talks to animals, communicates with them.'

'Them! My friends use them to talk to their doggos after they're dead.'

'They're real things?'

'Doggos? Mm hm.'

'Animal mediums.'

'Mm! How else do you find out what your last doggo wants your new doggo to be called?'

'You know what?'

'What?'

'I'm going to the zoo.'

'No! No, don't go to the zoo!' said Alexa. 'It's where love gets crushed, Fi. Where true love gets crushed—and eels!'

'I'm going to the zoo. And I'm going to call an animal medium. *And* I'm going to… No wait, that's all.'

'Stay away from the eeeels!' Alexa moaned, then downed the last of her shot.

IV

'It's so bright in here, Grandpa.'

'Yes,' said Arsen, standing over U-Crane's aquarium and pinching fish food along its top. 'I will have no curtains.'

Annie readjusted her squint and said, 'No curtains?'

'I hate curtains. Thirty years I lived behind curtain, I hate them.'

'It's weird you have pet fish, Grandpa.' Annie rested her iPad on the desk and angled it towards him and pressed its screen's red button.

'There is balance in the water, Anastasia. A small change in temperature, change in salt—balance is upset and all fish die. Aquarium is like the world, and the world is like the mind. Balance.'

'You see that in an aquarium? My dad's family thinks a lot more than my mum's. Uncle Yuri keeps talking about freedom.' Arsen mumbled in the affirmative as he reached for the furthest corner of the aquarium. 'Why?'

'Why what?'

'Why does Uncle Yuri keep talking about it?'

Her grandfather nodded as he put down his green net and pinched more fish food. 'Freedom is very important, Nastyusha, the most important of all.'

'Why?'

'Because we have lived without it. Your mother's family cannot understand this. But we—have lived without volya, and for Cossack there can be nothing worse.'

'Oo, what's Cossack?' said Annie, hoping that at last her question would be answered.

'You are Cossack, Nastyusha. Cossack is free man, always ready to fight for his volya—his freedom.'

'Is freedom the same as liberty?'

'Good idea, Rain Woman is late. Denys!'

The door at the side of the office opened and Annie looked across as there backed in, then turned towards her, a short man wearing a padded vest that was everywhere fraying over long and loose sleeves. Annie's face was one of fascination as Denys placed a silver tray at the desk's end then tilted back his disintegrating mariner's cap. She stared at the thickest and flattest nose she had ever seen, at his long and bushy moustache and full and wiry beard—at his deep wrinkles and dusty skin. He turned over two porcelain cups then seemed to whisper something as he filled them.

Annie turned her iPad to the teapot, to the tiny spoons, the sugar bowl. Denys whispered again and Annie thought that he must be talking to her. 'What?' she whispered back before her mouth returned to half open.

Denys turned his hideous neck to Arsen and saw him preoccupied with the aquarium. He raised his voice as high as he dared: 'If I sleep he pours water on me.'

'Hm?' Annie whispered, understanding not a word of what he said.

'If I talk he beats me with frozen chicken.'

Though intrigued Annie was unable to understand his accent, thicker even than her grandfather's. 'What are you saying?' she said, slightly above a whisper.

'Denys!' Arsen turned his head, then his body, to his desk. 'Do not address my granddaughter!'

'Sorry, Gospodin,' said Denys, and was filmed as he cowered backwards out of the office.

'God and the Devil!' Arsen yelled as he fished his dropped fish food container out of the water.

'Who was that, Grandpa?'

'Anybody who does not own a serf, Anastasia, is not a man.'

'My dad surfed.'

'He did, Nastyusha. He did.'

Remembering the touch and sight of her father, Annie felt empty and alone. She rose from Arsen's oversized chair and crossed his office and wrapped her arms around her grandfather and put her cheek to his enormous body.

'Oh, Nastyusha. It cannot be easy.'

'I love you, Grandpa.'

'I love you, Anastasia.'

While in Arsen's living room Alexa eventually woke from her birthday hangover.

In the early hours of last night she had decided in the kitchen that there was no way she'd make it to her bedroom. Knowing that probably she would only manage to get as far as the hallway, she gave up on staggering even all that way and made a fall for the couch. Misjudging the angle, she fell onto the corner of the living room's coffee table and knocked Annie's backpack over—crawled over its scattered contents to clamber onto the couch and there she promptly passed out.

Now as the sun streamed through the curtainless back windows she moaned and squirmed and eventually dared to open her eyes. Unimpressed by the coarse brown of the couch's back cushion she rolled over but put too much effort into it and fell onto the floor. She considered standing up, but found that nothing below her waist was in favour of doing so. She groaned and squeezed her eyes shut then slammed them open. She was looking at the ceiling, which—as she had been certain that she was facing upwards—she considered a victory. She looked down to her toes and saw that she was still in her cocktail dress. Beside its strap she found that a rope of red liquorice had in the night wound itself around her arm.

'Mm!' she groaned, as pleasantly surprised. 'Arm candy,' she struggled to mutter, then with considerable effort lifted her head to her bicep and tried to grab the liquorice with her lips. It was stuck tight. She leaned a little further up then bit into the rope before returning her head to the carpet and, chewing, falling back into the early hours of her hangover.

Annie shook her head and screwed up most of her face as she took her first sip of Carpathian tea.

'Nn nn,' said Annie. 'That's gross.'

'Maybe you need more sugar.'

'And what's volenitsa?'

'A volyanitsa, is someone whose spirit is wild—someone who *lives* volya.'

'Which is freedom?'

'Tak. And someone who becomes rebel when someone else tries to tell him what to think, or what to do—or her.'

'I want to be one of them.'

'You are, Nastyusha,' Arsen reassured her. 'I have seen it.'

The lesson was interrupted by U-Crane's door bells as into its office came a short woman whose head was permanently slanted upon her flabby neck. Her short grey hair appeared wind-blown from her face and her sideburns had been trimmed into oblivion. She wore loose grey trousers and a khaki jacket over a coral-coloured Hawaiian shirt—and said nothing as she presented herself at Arsen's desk.

'You are the Rain Woman.'

'Yeah,' she said in two high and descending syllables.

'Good.'

'Kvantas,' the woman snapped at Annie.

'Pardon?'

'Kvantas!' she shouted again and twitched.

'Yes,' said Arsen. 'She is Australian.'

The woman de-slanted her head and revealed a gap in her large front teeth as she grinned and informed Annie: 'Kvantas never crash.' Then she reached out to squeeze Annie's cheek with her thumb and finger.

The Georgian Fencing Parties

The Rain Woman held a palm up to the door of the banya. Her splayed fingers began to shake; she watched them move and frowned with determination before flunging for the handle of the banya's door.

Annie came carefully out to U-Crane's rear with her filming iPad held still in front of her—just in time to record the same echoey cackle that had last week forced her to evacuate.

'Hold it,' said the Rain Woman to Arsen. He held the door open as she took from inside her jacket a tied bunch of leaves. She dipped them in the water of the cauldron then splashed invisible x's ahead of herself as she crossed the banya's threshold. 'Uh oh,' she shortly chimed.

'What?'

'Nother nail,' she said with a moaning American accent.

'What?'

'One more nail,' she said, re-slanting her head. 'Nother nail.'

'Ergh,' Arsen grunted.

'Is that bad?' Annie whispered from behind her camera.

'What about one more nail?' Arsen asked hesitantly.

'Nail in the coffin,' said the Rain Woman in her descending syllables. 'Uh oh!'

'What's going on, Grandpa?'

'I must go to cemetery. And take there one big nail. And hammer into my mother's grave.'

'To get rid of a sauna goblin? That sounds weird.'

'Uh oh! Here forever,' said the Rain Woman.

'Forever?' said Arsen.

'Here forever—or one more *nail*.'

'Is your mum's grave in Ukraine?'

'It is in Oakleigh.'

'In Melbourne?'

'Yeah,' said Arsen in the voice of the Rain Woman.

'I want to go with you!'

Mel walked through Dixon Hardware wearing a hard hat and with a hammer dangling from his brand-new tool belt.

'Madame Tran, I have a nail question.'

'Show me you!'

'No, no. Nail nails.'

'Oh, nail nail—OK.'

'Which nails are the best ones for building a fence?'

'Hmm,' said Madame Tran. 'You bill fence?'

'I build fence.'

'I thing, if no ask Olympic Fencer, we take this.' She took from one of her racks a tub of long flathead nails.

'Hi, Uncle Mel!' Annie chimed as she and Arsen came down the aisle.

'What are you doing here?' He shook the hand that Arsen extended to him.

'We need a really really long nail, don't we Grandpa?'

'What is longest nail you have?'

'I'm not sure, I'm the chairman. But Madame Tran'll help you out.'

'Hello you buy nail?!'

'Why are you dressed like a builder?'

'I,' said Mel and rattled his packet of nails at his niece, 'have a fencing party to go to.'

Mel followed the noise coming from behind the address that Yuri had given him, and—wearing short shorts belted with tools—went in through the side gate.

Ahead, at the end of a narrow walkway formed by two high brick houses, he saw a host of people in padded white doublets and two-toned tights, shuffling forward and shimmying backwards—all wearing mesh-fronted helmets—as they guarded, and lunged, and goddam riposted.

'You have got to be kidding me,' he muttered as he tipped back his hard hat.

He emerged at the corner of the backyard and stood with

a disgruntled jaw before an entire backyard of pairs of portly Georgians with sabres in hand, shifting one way then the other in chaotic unison. Yuri spotted Mel's entrance and called a halt to his own duel. He took off his helmet and put it under one arm as he came to the front of the backyard. 'Why are you once again attending Georgian fencing party in uniform most incorrect?' He pointed the end of his sabre at Mel's tool belt, his hat—his bare thighs. 'Well, well—well?'

Mel stared blankly at him.

'You are liking my hose? Good-looking, no?'

Annie spotted the Rain Woman's hunch at the bottom of a slope in the cemetery. The woman's arms were stretched towards the sky and her head bowed low as she mumbled and jangled the bells at her neck.

Arsen came to the headstone of his mother's grave, where Annie recognised the Cyrillic she couldn't read. He placed the end of the lawn spike—which he had gotten not from Madame Tran at the Nail Salon but from The Soil Baron— on the grass and held the bolt upright. 'You are ready?'

Annie pressed record on her iPad and nodded and Arsen raised his mallet and held his breath. With all his strength he brought the hammer down onto the spike's head and exhaled, relieved that he had commenced so dangerous, but so essential, a task.

When there were only two inches of spike left to hammer, Annie, lying down and fascinated, filmed her grandfather tapping the mallet rhythmically and softly— one, two, three—before whacking it with enough force to drive it further in.

'The only thing you do not want,' said Arsen, and put his ear even closer to the ground. 'Is hit skull.'

'Because it's your mum?' Annie whispered.

'Because it will make ghost,' said Arsen and banged the

mallet again.

'How do you know if you hit the skull?'

Arsen tapped gently at the head of the spike—one, two, three—and listened for any crunching sounds. When he heard none he struck again, but this time a hollow clunk reverberated through the bolt. Annie looked from the last inch of its length to her grandfather. 'That was skull.' His eyes bulged and he looked up and across the grave. 'Run.'

'What?'

'Run!'

Arsen stood and grabbed his granddaughter's hand and shuffled hastily away from his mother's grave and soon Annie was pulling him along and urging him to hurry as they dashed for the cemetery's closest gate.

When most in attendance were finally exhausted of parrying and flunging, Yuri stood in a corner of their second Georgian fencing party in as many days as this book's author looked up the word "flunging" then went back and inserted it throughout the episode. Mel, beside him—beside Yuri, not this book's author—searched the unhelmeted guests for the brutish man who had at Dixon Hardware approached him in search of guns.

'That guy looks familiar,' said Mel, unsure as to why as he pointed to a short, stocky, slow-witted bald man.

'That is Costanza,' said Yuri.

'George?'

'He is Georgian, yes.'

'But his name is George?'

'Why would his name be George? It is Costanza.'

'Wait, I think that's him.' Mel pointed at the trestle table in front of the backyard's excellent fence.

'Who, who—*who*?'

Mel nodded towards the closer end of the table—'That guy,'—and the bulging doublet of a man who was stuffing

The Georgian Fencing Parties

his face with purple food.

'You are sure?'

The man at whom they both stared turned in from his stuffing and, now facing the house, jammed an enormous dumpling into his mouth. Mel recognised instantly his bonobo hair and the tendency of his wrists to dangle.

'That's him. That is definitely him.'

'I shall return.' Yuri picked up his sabre and strode across the backyard as Georgian Costanza came up to the house. 'How you doin?' He dropped a sandwich to his plate and wiped his hand on his hose before offering it to Mel. 'I'm Costanza.'

'George?'

'Georgian, yeah—but isn't everyone? Hey, let me ask you a question—you ever buy shoes that are *too* grippy? Can you have too much grip on a shoe?'

'I think you can,' Mel nodded.

'I bought these last week, it's like fencing on tar out there.'

'That's happened to me before,' said Mel, surprised that somebody else had noticed the phenomenon.

'It's like the shoe companies are competing for whose shoes have the *most* grip.'

'But now it's like we're all walking around with glue on our feet.'

'You get it! *We're* the victims. Say, did I see you standing with Yuri Sukhimov?'

'Mm! We're good friends, very good friends.'

'What are you doing next weekend?'

'Me?'

'I'm having a boxing party on Saturday. We can always use an extra set of fists.' Costanza thrust one fist over his plate and said, 'We'll get the old tape out,'—hunched his shoulders and ducked and wove—'Put a few heavyweights away. Waddya say?'

'I just met you thirty seconds ago. But I'll have a think

about it.'

'Good,' said Costanza and tapped Mel on the arm. 'You'll have a think. A think is good.' He turned to the rest of the party and smiled. Shortly he returned the wedge of sandwich to his mouth and after a protracted silence said, 'All right,' and he smiled and went in search of more dip.

'We are meeting dealer of arms next week,' said Yuri, stepping up to the verandah.

'It was that easy?'

'Man with whom you have spoken is Ukrainian. Dealer of arms for whom man is working, is not. So he gives to me informations. I do not think you are knowing who is my family. We are most ancient aristocats.'

'Crats.'

'What?'

'You weren't cartoon cats.'

'No, my family is most ancient aristocats.'

'Crats!'

'What is this crats?'

'Aristocrat. You're not a cat.'

'Why you are saying I am a cat?'

'Never mind, man. You said an arms dealer?'

'Yes,' said Yuri and nodded once and folded his arms.

'Now *that's* an adventure.'

'It is *not* adventure.'

'That is definitely an adventure, my man. Finally.'

'Merely we are finding out who have killed my brother— you are looking forward to this?'

At the centre of really the *sublimely* fenced backyard, two Georgians had called a truce to their fencing in order to with helmets in hand stand side by side and start singing.

'Come!' said Yuri, stepping down to the lawn. 'You will be much liking this song. It is for killing Turks.'

Mel followed him down as the remainder of the duellists ceased their flunging and joined the duet's song as they encircled it. Yuri put his arm around Mel and leaned across and himself smiled as he sang in absolutely ruinously expensive Ukrainian:

'When I brought up my horse to defend our home,
An assassin came round to kill me.
But into his eyes I spat samohonka,
For immune am I to its holy burn.'

Though ill-dressed Mel was happy to find himself at the beginning of an adventure, excited at the thought of its escalation—exhilarated by the possibility of its—his!—heroic consummation. Seeing him similarly excited, Mel wondered what Yuri was rejoicing about, then intimated a clap to ask if he should do so. Yuri frowned and shook his head and bulged his eyes as he and the Georgians sang on:

'The Turk's head rolled in a basket
Bare but for its Asian moustache,
For before we chopped it from his rapist neck
We made him eat his eyebrows.'

While Fiona had ventured to Melbourne zoo alone.

She held her hand to the side of her face as she passed the pelicans, ignored the seal which did actually wave at her, thought she heard a giant tortoise click its tongue in order to get her attention. Then she was certain she heard her name come down and out of a tapir's snout.

It sounded again, though this time as a vague but more urgent question: 'Leonie?'

'No,' Fiona asserted, shaking her head and looking at the ground as she walked on. Then she felt a prod at her arm, and heard what had actually been asked:

'Leona?'

She glanced across to a man now walking nervously beside her. 'Who are you?'

'Are you Leonie Sukhimov?'

'Suk*hi*mov,' she corrected. 'Fiona.'

'Peter's wife?'

'Pete's—. Who are you?'

'I'm the Peter file man, keep walking.' They stayed a metre apart as they shuffled through a raucous crowd of family and pram—she intrigued, he anxious.

'You're who?'

'I'm the Peter file guy,' he said and pointed to himself.

'What?' said Fiona, unable to hear him clearly amid the chatter and the crunching on the path beside the giraffe enclosure.

'I'm the Peter file guy!' he yelled.

A pair of mothers stopped pushing their prams and stared as they allowed the man to pass.

'The Peter file, it's me!' he said.

The three mothers in front of them stopped too, and turned back and scowled.

'I dropped it into your lap.'

'You did that? What do its phrases mean?'

'What phases me?'

'Huh?'

'All manner of things phase me, but listen—is it possible to steal an arm?'

'Steal an arm? Is this a riddle?'

'Your husband—did he know anyone who steals arms? He was a doctor wasn't he?'

'A paediatrician.'

'Who's Petey and Tricia?'

'What?'

'Look, did Petey, or Tricia, ever mention an arm being stolen—someone having their arm stolen?'

'How can someone steal an arm?'

'Your husband knew an arm steeler. He was working with him while he was still—wait what was that?' The Peter file

The Georgian Fencing Parties

man's head darted towards a large tree crawling with red pandas. He thought he saw the bushes beneath it rustle. 'We're being watched.' Then he broke from their trajectory (not the bushes') and disappeared into the crowd.

Fiona was left standing high over the bonobo forest. Beyond the logs and hedges which kept visitors from an artificial ravine, several bonobos lumbered across beams and hung from rope nets and rolled on their backs with pineapples between their feet. At the corner closest to the crowd a baby bonobo was suckling at its mother's teat. As it fed, another bonobo lumbered over and looked up and pointed—Fiona thought to her. She pointed to herself. Soon the bonobo pointed to the breastfeeding mother then held up two fingers to the crowd. Then it pointed to itself, and added a third digit to its display.

'Is that chimp counting?' said Fiona to the woman beside her.

'That's a bonobo,' said a zookeeper, carrying buckets of fish on her way to feed the penguins. 'Not a chimp.'

'It's a what?'

'A bonobo. They live in large family groups in the Congo.'

'Can they count?'

'Count? Bonobos can talk.'

'What?' said Fiona, now very serious.

'Linguistically they're the smartest animal there is, other than us. If ever there was an animal we could communicate with…'

The zookeeper moved on with her buckets and Fiona returned to looking down into the enclosure. The bonobo now craned its wrist and its three dangling fingers between itself and, hopefully—seemingly—clearly!—Fiona. Then it added a fourth finger to its count and whacked its chest with its wrist and grinned.

And Fiona called Pinal Connelly to ask whether she had the number of a reputable animal medium.

IN THE NEXT PETER FILE…

…Annie grows impatient of the Rain Woman:

'It's 12:31,' said the Rain Woman, glancing from the television to her digital watch. 'Uh oh.'

'What?!'

'Definitely 12:31.'

'So?!'

'Lunch is 12:30.'

'Lunch is coming, I told you!'

'Four fish fingers,' said the Rain Woman when shortly Annie placed them before her.

'What now?!'

'Four fish fingers.'

'That's all there were in the freezer.'

'Supposed to be eight.'

'Eight?'

'Yeah,' squawked the Rain Woman.

Annie took up the knife and slammed it down at their centre. 'Eight fish fingers, all right? God and the Devil!'

…While Alexa, not halfway through her birthday hangover, zombies her way to the corner shop in order buy the Gatorade that was the first step in her curative routine:

Having put on sweatpants and a hat, and after being too frightened to check herself in any mirrors, she stood in line with her head bowed and—unbeknownst to her—a rope of red liquorice stuck around her arm. In the queue beside hers a rather handsome man said, 'Arm candy.' She was in too much pain to hear or heed him. Then he leaned across and chomped into it.

Alexa recoiled from the touch of his lips on her skin and looked at the man, now smiling as he chewed.

'Arm candy,' he said again, and Alexa pulled the sticky remainder from her armpit and shortly found herself smiling back at him.

…Mel arrives at Georgian Costanza's boxing party wearing baggy shorts and heavy gloves:

'Hey everybody, it's Yuri's friend!' Costanza looked up from pulling a tape gun across the flaps of a cardboard box. Beside him two Georgians lowered dumbbells into boxes of their own.

'Oh, f--k this.' Mel spat out his mouthguard and pulled off his gloves and turned around and went home.

…And at the very end of a very stressful day together Arsen put his only granddaughter to bed:

After tucking her tightly into a blanket, Arsen pushed Annie's leg in from the edge of the bed and sat and smiled and sang her the lullaby that had been whispered to him when he was a child, a song which—IF THIS GODDAM BOOK COULD AFFORD GODDAM SUBTITLES—would have read:

'Sleep, sleep, sleep,
But not too close to the edge,
Or the black wolf will grab you by the foot,
And drag you into the woods forever,
Where he'll put you in a hessian bag
And steam you in stinging nettles.
Sleep, sleep, sleep.'

'What does it mean, Grandpa?' said Annie as her eyes fell closed.

'I'll tell you in the morning, Nastyusha. Sleep now, my love.'

Episode 6

THE ARM STEELEЯ

I

Resuming her vantage above the bonobo forest, Fiona raised her eyebrows and swiped her hands and flailed her elbows.

'I don't think you'll have much luck,' said a zookeeper, carrying buckets by penguins freshly emptied. 'Pedro's been pretty depressed lately.'

'Who's Pedro?'

'That bonobo you're waving at.'

'His name is Pedro?'

'Had to separate him from his wife two weeks ago.'

'Did you say his wife?'

'Did I say wife? I meant partner. Bonobos can't legally marry yet.'

As the zookeeper walked on Fiona's final, desperate, hope arrived. 'So many voices. So many mean, *mean* voices.'

She recognised the Bostonian accent from their phone call. 'Dr Katie?'

'This top doesn't make me look like a Christmas carol does it? Make them stop—*so* many mean voices! Pangolin doesn't know what it's snorting about. You wanted to communicate with one of the animals?'

'I did. Him,' said Fiona and pointed across the moat and into the logs at Pedro.

'With the parted hair?'

'His name's Pedro, but I think you'll be able to call him

Peter.'

'All right, give me a moment.' Dr Katie put away her ear muffs and turned fully to the bonobo forest. She raised a palm and put a hand to her heart and closed her eyes and bowed her head. 'Mm,' she moaned as she nodded. 'He says hello.'

Fiona snapped her head sideways. 'He does?'

'He sure does.'

Dr Katie rocked back and forth as she deciphered what Pedro was telling her. 'He says he sees you, and he appreciates that you see him. Shh!' she said and threw her head to the side.

'Me?'

'The hippopotamus. A fat b-word. I can too!' Dr Katie snapped before returning to her forward rocking.

'Could you ask Pedro if he was recently separated from anyone?'

Katie put her raised hand to her forehead and without opening her eyes said, 'His wife.'

'His wife? Can bonobos get married?'

'See the male in the corner, reading?' Fiona could not. 'That's their priest. Banana bread wedding cake. Oh that's sad, I'm sorry, Peter.'

'Wait, Peter or Pedro? Wait what's sad?'

'He doesn't feel like talking. He's a bit down, he hasn't been able to get aroused lately.'

'Aroused?'

'Oh Peter, I can't say that. No, Peter—that's vulgar.'

'You can say it. We were adventurous.'

'He's been cupping his brother's testicles to get him going, but not even that seems to work lately. Peter, don't be mean.'

'He's being mean?'

'Vulgar too. He says he'll talk to us if you take your top off.'

The Arm Steeler

'Me?'

'Yes, very funny, I'll leave mine on.'

'This doesn't sound like Pete.'

'No, it's a bonobo.'

'But I think it's the reincarnated spirit of my husband.'

Katie stopped her rocking and turned an open eye to Fiona. 'Right, who said that?' she screamed and turned around. 'I am *not* a lazy she-camel! Was that you, red panda?' She darted her head from high tree to high tree. 'You can try to hide the Chinese accent, I know it was you.'

And Fiona put her hands on the log-rail and thought about arousing Pete from afar.

Alexa Sukhimov emerged in an agonising haze from her bedroom. The second and traditionally final day of her birthday hangover was at last subsiding and she thought she could manage the peeling of an egg and its slicing onto toast. She got as far as the end of the hallway before realising she had overestimated herself. She stopped and blinked and looked down at the piano—smiled and remembered how much she once enjoyed playing. She turned to it and in her pyjama bottoms and a singlet sat on its bench and lifted its fallboard.

She looked from the low keys to the high and thought upon her life savings and lamented their loss in eels. She thought about stroking the shoulder of somebody other than Ben, and as she ran a finger down a black key felt the familiar humiliation of being head of U-Crane's customer relations. She readied several fingertips at a chord and raised her elbows and inhaled, and realised that soon, inevitably, she would have to return to performing for her father. Her arms dropped and her breath fell from her. Now feeling something sticky under her arm she looked down and grabbed at her shoulder blade and found there half a rope of red liquorice.

'Arm candy,' she said while looking at her armpit. She unstuck the liquorice from her skin and put it between her teeth and shut the piano's cover. Then she hunched down and placed against it her forehead.

Brunching at The Ship Club, Geoff Dixon was rereading a curious email that he had that morning received from a company called FU Management Group, when a brunette woman with a big smile and sallow eyes said, 'Hi.'

He looked up from the email's request to inspect his business in preparation for an audit.

'I wouldn't normally do this, but I'm at brunch with a friend of a friend, and he told me you're single?'

Geoff slid off his reading glasses. 'Last woman I spoke to tongued-kissed a dead flamingo.'

'Gross.'

'Girl before that had a pea fetish. Yes, I am single. And I think it's time.'

'Time to what?'

'Give up and sell up,' Geoff said and closed his laptop.

'Your hardware store?'

'How do you know about that?'

'Jock told me.' She pointed back to her table, where Geoff watched Jock raise himself out of his seat and wave. 'When I told him I had a thing for redheads he said I should come over and introduce myself. So, I'm Karen.'

'Well first things first, Karen, what's wrong with you?'

'What's wrong with me?'

'You got a pea fetish?'

'Gross.'

'No *peas* fetish?'

'Are they not the same thing?'

'You'd think so wouldn't you? No monk obsession?'

'No what? I am a bad sleeper—is that a fatal flaw?'

'Well that's not too bad I spose.'

The Arm Steeler

'And I have restless leg syndrome.'

Geoff relaxed into his seat. 'Now *that's* something we can work with! I've got a touch of wanderlust myself. Where do you like to travel? Won't you sit?'

'Oo I love Asia. I've been to India three times, Sri Lanka twice.'

'Vietnam?'

'Oh, I'd love to go!'

Geoff's phone rang. 'One second, sorry.'

'Geoff, it's Brian from Greenhaven Funeral Services. Your tomb's ready.'

While a few doors down from The Ship Club two jagged young women stood on either side of the entrance to the public steam room of the St Kilda Sea Baths, and there discussed their very rich and very old boyfriends.

'Why, how often he is wanting?' said one.

'Thankingly only once time per week,' said the other.

'You are lucky. Mine wants four in night times of week. But now I send him to make long beach walk in afternoon, I say for his health. He comes home and is pooped.'

'Pooped? Yours does this too?'

Then a man who won't be properly introduced because he plays only a momentary part in this story came with a towel over his shoulder out of the men's changerooms. As he approached the steam room's door he stopped and looked at the young women who had leaned towards one another in order to obstruct his entrance.

'Closed today,' said one of them.

'What do you mean closed?'

'Closed today,' emphasised the other. An unimportant man came in from an ocean swim and also tried to enter. 'Closed today.'

'All people are equally important,' said you the reader.

'Oh shut up,' said I the author. 'We have a goddam story

to finish.'

'I can see it's on,' said the unimportant man.

'Don't be ridiculous,' said the unintroduced. 'Get out of my way.'

'Do I look like I am fucking round?' said one of the young women and prodded his shoulder.

'Do *we* look like *we* are fucking round?' said the other and prodded the other man's shoulder. 'Today, is closed.'

While behind them both, Arsen pleaded with his daughter to relent:

'Public steam room also is silent place, Oleksa.'

'It's not chocolate, Papa, you don't understand.'

'I understand that your future is in U-Crane. So should you. Why else I have made you head of customer relations?'

'Papa, I don't want to touch old men anymore. I don't want to be in heat for you—I don't want to be arm candy!'

'But you want *money* for arm candy? You don't have to touch, Oleksa. You only have to make them want to touch, they rent crane, and we eat! What is so difficult?'

'Papa, if I have to jiggle for one more man I will kill myself!'

The rubber seals on the steam room's door squelched as one of the young women popped her head in. 'Arsen, phone for you.'

He groaned and stood and at the pool's ledge wiped his ear with his felt hat. 'What?'

'Arsen, it's Brian from Greenhaven Funeral Services. Your tomb's ready.'

At school Annie was struggling to write down the name or nature of a crime committed by one or more of her grandparents. It was her chief struggle in what her teacher prefaced, towards the end of the school day, as her first ever Struggle Session. Having asked her whole class to anomynously write down the same, Ms Conrad now stalked the front of the room with an upturned cap.

Annie looked up from her desk as Sophat Urinporn placed a folded piece of paper into the hat then blankly returned to her seat. Something was off with Sophat, Annie thought—but not only with Sophat. Not merely because of her Uncle Mel's warning had Annie been worried about being made fun of at school. But she had not heard a critical word about her appearance, her odour, her name. 'What about Fanny?' she had thought several times to herself, and had even considered suggesting it to Mai Phat Phun. And except on the rare occasion that she called her mother her mum, at school she had been coddled at every turn—by Celery Flintstone, by Jayne-Jane Slutzsky, by Mickey le Dongringer, and especially by Ms Conrad.

'Annie?' said her teacher.

'Mm?' she said, her lips bubbled together.

'Your anomynous denounciation?'

'I can't really think of anything, Ms Conrad.'

'Annie, you're white.'

Annie's eyes darted uncertainly to the corner of the room.

'Each and every one of your ancestors systematically discriminated against people of colour. They excluded genders, orientals—they probably even murdered them. The best way for you to atone for those crimes is to admit what we've done, even anomynously, and to next time do better hashtag.'

'It just feels like I'd be betraying my family is all. Like breaking a link between generations, does that make sense?'

'Exactly! That's *exactly* what we're trying to do, Annie! Good! To never ever repeat the same mistakes our forefathers m—I'm sorry. The same mistakes our fore-non-gestational parents made.'

'But I love my grandpa, I want to be like him.'

'Love's great, Annie. But you have to love everyone, not just your grandparents.'

'I have to?'

'Mm!'

'But you're asking me to denounce my grandfather. I have to love everyone, except him?'

'Chinese burn!' yelled Martin Luther Ching.

'Martin. … You can still love your family, Annie, and denounce them.'

'But I don't want to, I love them. They made me—they made me who I am.'

Ms Conrad sighed and shook her head and decided to move on from her dimmest student.

'My grandmother,' read Boobesh Rapeelam after unfolding a piece of paper from the hat. 'My grandmother decided to become a homemaker instead of going to university?'

'And who's to blame for that?' said Ms Conrad, much pleased by the confession.

'So… ciety?'

'No, her husband—whoever's grandfather that is.'

'Ah,' nodded Boobesh. 'Then I denounce him!'

Annie turned not only her face but the top half of her body to Boobesh and squinted—for Boobesh was smiling as though she had accomplished something great.

This inordinate positivity was beginning to make Annie feel lonely. Not a single interaction with her classmates had felt genuine; they all seemed, somehow, as though they were kind of simulated. First of all nobody had so much as whispered a pun, a rhyme, a riff, on Boobesh Rapeelam's name. And the day Elvis Pterodactyl flapped his arms as he circled the basketball court—not a single derisive glance had been cast in his direction. Annie would even have welcomed the mocking of her own name—Fanny!—if at least it meant that somebody was being truthful. Cruel but voluntary teasing seemed to Anastasia Sukhimov the better alternative to smiling but forced friendship. 'To mock is to live!' she silently screamed, and felt more isolated still.

While at Dixon Hardware Mel was very much enjoying a lunch date with the girl whose company he was finding more uplifting each time he shared it.

'Sorry it has to be at work,' he said, across from her at a plastic table in the store's cafeteria.

'Oh I understand—you *are* a chair man. Plus there's something about these Dixon sausages that *does* make my mouth feel alive.' Mel furrowed his brow and soon nodded as Tess continued eating the lunch that had been much quicker in the making than his own. 'How 'bout tomorrow you come by *my* work?'

'At the stock market?'

'Mm!'

'Wouldn't it be hyper-stressful to have a visitor there?'

'No, not at all. At the moment I'm really just putting all my profits into my hedge fund.'

'Your stock profits?'

'I guess from selling my stock, yeah.'

'Ready,' sang a low voice in one long bass note.

'It's gonna be the biggest hedge on the street once I've got enough money.'

'Ready,' sang a baritone, joining the larger man beside him.

'What's that?' said Mel as he got up to retrieve his lunch.

'Ready!' sang the tenor, rising to stand on his toes.

'One second,' he called back to Tess as he nodded to the queue of candy-striped barbers arrayed behind the barbecue.

'Rare-dee!' sang the lead, and held up Mel's sausages as all four smiled and held their ready chord until Mel sat back down.

'Why don't you come by in the afternoon, we can go for a nice troll? Or dinner and drinks maybe? Who knows—play your cards right you might get to experience my world-famous tickles.'

'You talk about your tickles a lot.'

'Mm hm!'

'Why haven't I gotten any yet?'

'Oh I don't just give out my tickles to anyone.'

'Well I'm looking forward to experiencing them.'

'Those Dixon sausages were dee-licious. But I have to get moving if I'm going to get back before the market opens. Sorry to dine and dash—I'll see you tomorrow afternoon?'

'Looking forward to it.'

Tess, smelling very strongly of ketchup, leaned down and kissed Mel on the cheek as he bit into the first of his Dixon sausages. He smiled and thought upon how dashing was the addition of new romance to his budding adventure, then about how it was midday and surely the stock market opened hours ago. Maybe she worked with a different market. 'Probably the FTSE.'

'You look stressed, mate.'

'I have been in public steam room. But tomorrow is coming Rain Woman to fix U-Crane banya.'

'I have no idea what you just said.'

'You look Scottish.'

At the far end of the tomb room Geoff and Arsen recognised their respective funerary monuments. As they approached them with proud awe both crossed the exhibition space to inspect the other's.

'What is this word?' said Arsen.

'My name,' said Geoff.

'Your name is Gee-off? What does this mean?'

'It's Geoff.'

'It says Gee-off,' said Arsen, pointing to the two parts of his chiselled name.

'Your name has "arse" in it, you know that right?'

'And my tomb is matching colour of your hair!' Arsen smiled.

The Arm Steeler

'I know it was you.'

'What was me? I make you Scottish?'

'Why's there white bones all over yours? Is this one of your Russian death cults?'

Arsen ran his fingers over the dozens of crossed femurs encircling his plinth. 'Our family for many centuries is white-boned.'

'Everyone has white bones.'

'Not like us, we are aristocats, noability. But all my family was murdered by communists because one fucking serf denounce my grandfather to party committee. They kill them *all*, because they are white-boned. Now, we are proud again.'

'Do you mean blue-blooded.'

'Blood? Blood is red, like your hair.'

'We say the nobility has blue blood.'

'This does not make sense, blood is red.'

'And everyone's bones are white. It's blue blood.'

'Blue blood is white-boned? Why is *your* tomb having so much balls?'

'Dixon Balls, my first business—the start of my whole career.'

'But your balls are not blue, Gee-off. You are not noability?'

'It's blue blood.'

'Balls, here. White bones me, blue balls you. Tell sculptor—Mr Brian! Orange man is wanting balls blue! Or you cannot afford blue balls—you are not noble, Gee-off?'

II

In a pink bikini Fiona approached the bonobo forest and waved shyly as upon her arrival Pedro waddled upright down its slope then came to rest before its moat.

She sighed and tilted her head and felt strangely comforted by the approach and closer sight of him. He had dragged along a box with whose inaccessible corners he appeared obsessed. Fiona smiled as he put the container on his head and craned his neck in order to lick its recesses. When soon he threw the box to the floor he turned his hairy neck and seemed to stare up at Fiona. Then he grinned.

Fiona too came to upright. The bonobo stared on as she put her arms at her side and squeezed them forward against the outside of her breasts. She looked from side to side to ensure that she was alone. Then she squeezed in her arms some more and leaned forward and shimmied her shoulders and smirked. But Pedro looked away, and discovered that he had brought along a box, with whose inaccessible corners he now became obsessed.

Fiona relaxed her shoulders and waited. When soon the bonobo glanced vaguely upwards she waved in order to recapture its attention. With his head very relaxed upon his shoulders he looked in Fiona's general direction; she waved again, but he rolled his head past her then watched himself raise the box over his head. Shortly he threw away his box, and sat with his body parallel to the forest's moat. When a fly caused him to dangle his head Fiona waved again; this time she recaptured his attention. She and Pedro stared long at one another, and when the stare seemed to be holding Fiona again glanced from side to side to make sure that nobody else was around. Satisfied that nobody was, and certain of the bonobo's attention, she arched her back and pulled the bottom of her bikini to her neck.

'Are you flashing a f-----g monkey?'

She snapped her bikini back down and said, 'What are you doing here?' as her brother came to her side.

'What the hell are you doing, Fi?' Fiona cast down her eyes. 'Why are you not helping Annie? And why are you at the zoo, in a f-----g bikini?'

'What does Annie need help with?'

'Why are you wearing a bikini?' Fi pointed across the moat and vaguely down to all the animals that weren't paying her any attention. 'You're not serious—a chimpanzee?'

'It's a bonobo.'

'Which one is it then?'

Fiona pointed to the front corner of the enclosure, where Pedro was passing to his banana-smeared lips whatever his enormous fingertips could scrape from the inside corners of its box.

'You think that's Pete?' Fiona stared and sighed. 'It wasn't the cat. Wasn't the pelican. But it is the... bonobo?'

'They're supposed to be able to use language. And he *did* wink at me yesterday. But then he cupped his brother's balls and raped his sister. The animal medium says—oh, here she is.'

'There is a *very* rude giraffe behind that fence, very rude— the rudest ruminant I've ever met. The cruelty from that cow's mouth! You must be Annie,' said Dr Katie in earmuffs, very loudly.

'What?' said Mel as his hand was shaken.

'Your daddy says hello,' Dr Katie shouted.

'Fi, I know what you're going through is tough. But this,' said Mel and twirled his finger at her bikini, 'is weird. Annie needs you, you can't leave her with the communists forever. She'll end up thinking she's the reincar—. Well.' Mel looked to Dr Katie, again with her eyes closed and a palm raised to the bonobos. 'I'm leaving.' And he did.

'Dr Katie?' Fiona stepped towards her and pulled at one side of her ear muffs. 'Dr Katie?'

'Yes, hun?'

'I need Pete to help me with three phrases, could we focus on them today?'

'Three phrases? Sure, hun, what are they? Tell me and I'll tell them to Pedro and we'll see what he says.'

Fiona took the Peter file from inside her folded coat and rested it on the polished beam that fenced off the bushes above the moat.

'The first one's "great at breastfeeding".'

In U-Crane's front office Alexa sat on the armchair and connected her phone to what she thought was the new speaker on her father's desk. She pressed play on a Prokofiev sonata and sat and stared. Its scherzo was repeating itself when her father came into work. 'Alexa, what is weather for today?'

'You don't have curtains, look outside.'

'Not you. Alexa, what is weather for today?'

'What the hell are you talking about?'

'Alexa, do I have messages?'

'How should I know, Papa?'

'Oleksa, can you turn off music, please?'

Alexa lowered the volume with a button on the side of her phone as Arsen's phone rang.

'Alexa will answer.'

'No I won't.'

'Hello, Alexa? You can answer phone?'

'Papa, what are you talking about?'

'Alexa! Answer phone!' Alexa stared across the office as her father shouted at his desk. 'Alexa!'

The music went silent as Alexa's phone now added to the ringing. She stood up and went through to her office as she answered the call. Arsen's telephone too fell silent. 'Alexa, you did not answer phone, why? Hello?'

'You don't understand,' came Alexa's voice into his office. 'It's called Arm Candy because we have the girls standing in the store but they also have candy wrapped around their arms.'

'Oleksa?' said Arsen to the device through which his daughter's voice was streaming.

'Yes, Arson?' said Alexa, interrupting Alexa's voice.

'Finally! But not you. Why I can hear my daughter?'

'Your daughter? I'm not sure what you mean Arson, who's your daughter?'

Arsen put his ear to the orb as his daughter went on: 'Because I know so many girls, so many, who'd love to find a rich husband, but the problem is bringing them to us.'

'Oleksa?' Arsen said, hoping to be heard by his daughter.

'Yes, Arson?'

'Not you, my daughter.'

'He he, I'm flattered, but I'm not your daughter.'

'So the men come in, they talk to the girls, they taste the candy that's on their arm.'

'Oleksa!'

'Yes, Arson?'

'Not you!'

He was brought out of this deepening entanglement by the sound of his door bells. 'Hello,' he nodded as in walked an obese man with blue-grey hair. He took off gold-framed sunglasses and said, 'You the man to speak to bout rentin a crane?'

'Please, this is me. Sit down. Welcome to U-Crane. Would you like some mountain tea? Coffee?'

'No, none of that. I just needa know what your price is for a week's job, a mobile crane. I've been to We-Crane, I'm tryin to find out the best price.'

'We-Crane? Sir, no. This is not how we are doing business in U-Crane. Sit, please. Do you like samohonka?

Is Ookrainian vodka.' Arsen shouted towards the office's side door: 'Oleksa!'

'Yes, Arson?' said the orb on his desk.

'You shut up. Oleksa, can you come here please?'

'I'm right here, Arson.'

'Oleksa is my daughter,' said Arsen to the prospective customer. 'She is head of customer relations.'

'That thing's head of your customer relations?'

'No, my daughter. Oleksa!' he shouted in the direction of the side door.

'Uh huh?'

'I knew this would make confuse, shut up! Oleksa! Denys!'

Mel came round the last North Melbourne corner before the address opposite which Tess had told him she worked. Whistling *A Monday Date*, though it was a Tuesday, he located the precise address then looked across the street. It was the very edge of Queen Victoria Market, and backed onto a car park.

'That's odd,' he said, and checked his phone, then the street sign above the roundabout, then the address beside him. There was no written or geographical error. He crossed the street and stared at a gold-painted man sitting smugly on thin air as he approached the metal roof and open front of the market. He peered through hanging belts and dangling t-shirts down its last aisle—and two stores in recognised the blonde curls of the young woman whose company now excited him.

'Tess?'

'Oh hey!'

'What the hell are you doing here?'

'What do you mean?'

Standing in an enclosure formed by three trestle tables and stacks of plastic tubs, Tess was picking out matching socks from a loose pile then inserting them one into the other. Mel watched as she placed the new pairs on a pyramid of socks around a metal pole and a handwritten sign: 'Assorted socks: 5 pairs for $10.'

'You work at a sock market?'

'Wanna help me short these?'

'You mean sort?'

'No, short them.' Tess smiled and folded another sock into its matching other. 'I'm shorting my socks.'

'You call this shorting stocks?'

'Socks, silly.'

'You work at a sock market?'

'Give us a hand!'

'Tess, you said you worked on the stock market.'

'I didn't.'

'You said, on our nice stroll—you work in sole trading.'

'Mm!' she said. 'Look at the soles on these babies.' She held up a sock-covered hand and showed him its rubber dots. 'Non-slip, for around the house. I can take my lunch break in a sec, I just have to wait till Dung gets back from hers. We can probably—I could finish early actually, we could go for a nice troll before dinner?'

A customer finished selecting socks and held out a handful of flat pairs. Tess flipped through them and told the woman they'd be fourteen dollars—was handed a five and a ten and told she could keep the change.

'And bonds? Hedge funds?'

Tess made a high-pitched groan of excitement as she put the dollar coin into a money-tin onto whose front she had taped a piece of paper with the words, 'Tess's Hedge Fund'. 'It's gonna be the biggest hedge on my street once I've saved up for it.'

Silently Mel clarified then summarized, then presented his conclusion: 'You work at a sock market.'

'Mm!' she smiled.

But she did have incredibly beautiful hair, and smelt

unusually lovely. The air seemed to brighten when she was around and he *had* sensed a generous cleavage when she came for lunch yesterday. 'The sock market,' said Mel and stared.

'Oh, that's Dung. Shall we?'

'I am needing to talk with you,' said Yuri, now pulling at Mel's arm.

'What the hell are you doing here?'

'We are much needing to talk, now.'

'How did you know I was here?'

'Come!' Yuri pulled him into the crowd of the market.

'Mel?' Tess called out. 'I'll be here.'

'Who is the she-woman?'

'How did you know I was here?'

'When upon one person is depending all knowing who have killed my brother, it is not unreasonable to make sure of knowing where one person is.'

'You're following me?'

'Not me. Walk! … We are meeting arms dealer tonight.'

'Tonight?'

'He is wanting for that you are bringing one thousand units of merchandise, to make sure you are for real.'

'For real? I'm not for real. Wait, does he think I'm a gun smuggler or a gum smuggler?'

'Dealer of arms is not meeting with smuggler of gum.'

'I can't get a thousand guns. I couldn't get a thousand bullets. I can get liquorice bullets—do you want a thousand liquorice bullets?'

'Leave bullets to me.'

'Should I bring gum just in case?'

'Come, we go—we must be preparing for meeting.'

'Wait, wait, wait, wait, wait,' said Mel and shook off Yuri's grip. 'This is really happening?'

'Universe is dancing, as I have seen.'

'We're meeting with an arms dealer—that's a proper

adventure.'

'It is not adventure. Please be stopping your saying this.'

'It's an adventure, Yuri. I'm in. Give me one second though, I have to say goodbye to someone.' Mel walked out of the indoor meat section and returned to the market's leather-reeking front.

'Where'd you go all of a sudden?' said Tess, excited by his return. 'Who's that bald guy?'

'He'd take too long to explain.'

'Ready for a nice troll?'

Mel looked again at the fullness of her lips, the cinching of her waist, the thickness of her curls. Then he took in the sheer number of socks by which she was surrounded. 'I'm so sorry, Tess, I can't tonight. I really want to—really. But I have—it's an emergency. Can you trust me on that? We'll do another night?'

As unhappily Tess accepted the postponement she placed two pairs of thick woollen socks onto her pyramid. 'I guess so.' Now overloaded, the pyramid's top rolled down its side and took with it several pairs as they all fell onto the concrete floor. 'Oh, my socks are plummeting,' said Tess as the pyramid collapsed. 'Could you pick those up for me? My damn plummeting socks.'

'That is a handsome horse.'

Geoff crossed the late-lunch crowded floor of Tran's Luon House and pulled out Karen's chair.

'Why is it in here?' she said as she sat.

'That's a good question, think it's on the menu?'

'They wouldn't bring a—No, surely not. And don't they only serve eel here?'

'Veal? That's cow.'

'What's a cow? That's a horse. I thought they only serve eel.'

'Isn't veal a cow?'

'I thought this was an eel restaurant.'

'It is, isn't it?' said Geoff as he read through his menu.

'Oh good, I love eel.'

'Wait, do they have veal on the menu?'

'They *only* have eel.'

'But isn't veal a cow?'

'But why is there a horse?'

After a very confusing conversation, and one which makes much more sense when read aloud, Geoff said, 'Anyhow, I have been thinking. I *am* getting short on years, so it's best to cut to the chase: how serious is this restless leg syndrome of yours?'

'It's pretty serious actually.'

'Good,' said Geoff, checking that one off his list.

'I beg your pardon?'

'You think we could get to Vietnam by what, middle of next year? Ow—ow! Did you just kick me?' Geoff leaned down and rubbed his shin.

'Sorry,' said Karen, and shimmied her chair to the side.

'That's all right, the table is a bit small. Anyway. Every day I sit at work, at The Ship Club, and all I do is dream about the white sand, the coral reefs, the palm trees, the food. That's my dream.'

A waiter came to their side and told them they'd run out of jellyfish. As he named the remaining specials Karen kicked him in the shin. 'Why you do!?' he shouted as he rubbed the front of his leg.

'I'm sorry!' said Karen, and shimmied her chair around until it was angled at the wall. 'It plays up when I'm cramped in like this.'

'We'll need a few minutes.'

'So you actually want to retire there?'

'I do. And I know it's early days, and it's not practical for someone who's not retired to *move* there. But if I'm spending time with someone I do like it to be on the table that we'll gradually relocate together.'

'Oh, I'd *love* to just pack a suitcase and go!' said Karen and kicked the wall. 'Nothing but bikinis and my snorkel.'

Geoff looked to the direction of the thud and stilled his rattling cutlery. 'Did you say snorkel?'

'Mm hm. I *have* to snorkel, otherwise I can't sleep—I pack it with me on every trip I take.'

'Karen, you're practically perfect,' said Geoff, then looked across to another thud as his cutlery trembled.

So as they used chopsticks to put eel into one another's mouths Geoff told Karen the history of first forays into business—'Dixon Balls will give you a rash—a rush! Sorry! No, not a rash, Madame. Here, hold them! Put these Dixon balls in your hand.'—before coming around to how he planned on funding his retirement.

'And your children'll take over?'

'No, I don't think they're interested. I had to trick my son into working there.'

'No grandkids?'

'Nope. Wait, yes! I have one.'

That grandkid was sitting very nervously towards the front of a year-level assembly, wondering when her name would be announced and her short film shown. As the end of Moonlight Wang's film was applauded a brief interlude was followed by the appearance in plain white letters on a black background of the title, *Simya*. Her time had come. Annie's eyes bulged and her squeezed stomach tightened as she sat up straight and looked to the rear of the seating, where an assortment of parents had come to watch their child's very first high school achievement.

Her film's music began, one of three songs from Arsen's favourite album that were about bread. Annie's cast of characters moved across the screen in close-up and black-and-white and often in reverse:

There was Denys' wild moustache and tattered vest, the Rain Woman's spell and manic grins, Yuri's high-waisted pantaloons and his knuckles so often at his hips—the taxidermied birds and insects-in-jars of her grandpa's Curiosity Shop, and Arsen's combed silvery hair and his aquatic philosophising—all over the desperate intonation of breadsong. By its end most of her fellow Year-7s were stunned. Her teachers, and even the year-level coordinators, stood at the side of the room in silence.

Annie's eyes searched for the direction of the voice that she was sure was about to condemn her. Then the audience seemed to recall its function, and applauded.

'That was unbelievable,' said one of the coordinators. 'Annie Sukhimov?' she said at the front of the room.

Annie raised her hand.

'That was beautiful, come up here. What does Simya mean?'

'Family,' said Annie as she sidestepped through her classmates. 'In Ukrainian.'

'Family, everyone,' and the coordinator clapped in Annie's direction.

And as the whole gymnasium applauded again, Annie searched for her mother's face.

But her mother was still at the zoo, holding her Peter file above the bonobo forest as though its railing were a lectern, hoping desperately that Dr Katie the animal medium would be able to solve for her its riddles and bring some clearer meaning to her husband's d—.

'Great at breastfeeding?' said Dr Katie, enunciating to make sure she was about to convey to Pedro precisely what her client wanted her to.

'Mm hm.'

'K, give me a second, hun. Pedro? Pedro, hello?' Dr Katie held the palm of one hand to her forehead and closed her eyes. After a moment of staged stillness she said, 'Peter was some kind of manager? Is that correct?'

'A manager? No, he was a paediatrician.'

'You're sure he wasn't a manager of some sort?'

'He was a paediatrician.'

'Did he manage even—Oh, Pedro's telling me he was—yep, he did say doctor. My bonobo isn't great.'

'And the breastfeeding?'

Dr Katie nodded and floated her chin around. 'Pedro says you should say chestfeeding.'

'He what?'

'He says it's less exclusionary of non-gestational parents.'

Fiona shook off an eye roll to say, 'And if it said, "great at chestfeeding"?'

'I'll ask. Wait! Peter's tell me something about travel. That he… liked it? He liked to travel, to… Europe?'

'We met in Europe,' said Fiona, her hope resurgent.

'I'm getting a country starting with an f, or an s—no! A country that has an a in it?'

'We met in Greece.'

'Greece, yes!'

'And—wait, what does that have to do with breastfeeding?'

'Chestfeeding.'

'Katie, I'm going to ask you a question. Please don't be offended.'

'Shoot, hun.'

'Are you really an animal medium?'

'I prefer to think of it as an animal well-done.'

'The bonobo's not even looking up here anymore.'

'No, he's worried about his daughter—she's ill—but he's still talking to me as Pedro. We'll try another phrase?'

With no sense of mysticism towards Katie's profession Fiona raised here eyebrows and sighed: 'The second one is retarded eel magnet.'

'What?'

'Yep.'

'Can I see that?'

Fiona lifted the Peter file from the railing and held it out to 'Dr' Katie. The Peter file waited for a time, as Katie's eyes were still closed, and it was yet to be taken when two suited men came to Katie's side and sprayed Fiona in the face with a stream of liquid that immediately made her face burn. Fiona threw her hands to her eyes, dropping the file onto the top of the hedge. Its cover blew open as at her initial scream Dr Katie opened her eyes. They too were turned on by pepper spray and shortly she, and everyone who witnessed the assault, were rolling on the floor in blinded agony. The Peter file's pages flew into the air as Fiona was grabbed from behind by the taller suited man.

They wafted down into the moat as Fiona's coat was wrapped around her body, which now was carted away.

The Arm Steeler

III

Arsen walked out of the steam room of The St Kilda Sea Baths, leaving his daughter alone with Dale Highview of Kerrigan Construction.

Sweating on opposite higher benches, Dale now slid his bare body along the central bench and swung it around to heave beside Alexa. Sweat flicked from his nose as he turned to her then lowered his lusty voice.

'So once I hire this crane, do these consultations come with the rental? How'd I go about having an even privater one?'

'Hm?' said Alexa turning away from the sour-milk smell of his folds. 'Whatever—' She coughed as she ran through her lines. 'We're talking business, that's all. This isn't a private consultation, it's a business meeting, remember?'

'You know Long Hard Steel's one of my nicknames,' he said and put the back of his fingers to her shoulder.

'Please don't touch me.'

'Not even there?' said Dale and ran three fingernails up her exposed neck.

'Especially not there,' she said, and leaned violently away from him.

'Doesn't it feel nice when your skin's tinglin?'

Alexa slid along the bench until the side of her arm was against the wall; as Dale leaned towards her she turned in until her back was almost flush with it. Then he flunged at her with his tongue out, and banged his forehead on plastic as Alexa strode down the bench and shouted, 'That's it! I'm done!' She grabbed a towel from beside the girls watching the door and wrapped and knotted it around her armpits (the towel, not the door) as she came out to the beach and stormed along its boardwalk.

The combined strength of the two girls outside the steam room were not enough to keep Dale encaged. 'Lexa, come 'ere,' he called out as he hurried after her. 'Look I'm sorry.'

'Go back inside, you grotesque pig-blob.'

Holding his towel up with one hand he shuffled along as quickly as his overburdened knees allowed.

'Leave me alone. Help,' Alexa said, fleeing as fast as she could without running. Somehow Dale caught up with her, and grabbed at the back of her towel. 'Don't you touch me,' she snapped as she turned. 'Help!'

'Now, now, missy—all Dale wants is a kissy kissy. Yelling'll just bring attention. Speaking of tension…'

The river dandy and the travelling salesman had upped from the bench on the far side of the pool and were closing in on their oblivious beloved when two police officers beat them to it. Dale was showered inaccurately in the face with pepper spray and his towel dropped as he put the balls of his hands to his eye sockets and fell to his knees. The officers then turned and sprayed Alexa in the face before falling on Dale's sweating body with all of their knees.

'Not me, you idiots,' Alexa said as they leaned into the fat behind Dale's cage. And as the very last U-Crane customer with whom she would ever sauna was handcuffed, Alexa wiped the spray from one eye then palmed it from the other, then scraped it off her fingers with her towel and watched with barely blinking eyes—for throughout her childhood Arsen had used a much more potent remedy to punish all three of his children for even minor behavioural infractions:

Yuri, aged 7, sidestepped around a penned-off corner of his family's muddy backyard as another kid jumped up and down and prepared to charge him. When shortly it did, Yuri dodged the young goat's head and punched it in the neck as it passed. Yuri turned and lowered his shoulders and re-readied his fists. As he leaned from side to side in anticipation of another charge, Piter—aged 8—stepped up to the pen and hit him in the side of the head with a bunch of dirty carrots. Yuri turned to his brother and wiped the soil from his cheek then hopped the low fence and grappled Piter at the shoulders. As they rolled and twisted, Oleksa, barefoot and 6, pushed them both over and began to wallop them with the carrots until shortly their father came out of the house. The thud of his heavy boots on the wooden floor was enough to halt their quarrelling. Oleksa dropped the carrots and the brothers got up and all three presented themselves before Arsen's sand-coloured fatigues and his dull-green ushanka.

Over subtitles so expensive I had to sell a testicle, Arsen said, 'This is not how siblings behave. Family is all you will ever have. If I hear you are not getting along—all of you—or interrupting the peace that we have here, *this* will be your punishment.' He unclipped from his belt a shining black canister then held it up to them.

'What is it, Papa?' said Piter.

And with one horizontal hiss he sprayed them all in the face with an orange mist. They screamed and stumbled backwards then looked blindly to the sky and scraped at their eyes and screamed some more before in different directions fleeing into the forest, where almost instantly Yuri ran forehead-first into a tree trunk...

Five years later, as the Sukhimovs flew to new lives in Australia, Piter stole Yuri's bread roll as Yuri tried to retrieve his juice cup from Oleksa. Yuri twisted the other way and reached across the row to stop Piter from biting into his roll. So Oleksa stole his jello from his tray. Unable to save either, Yuri fell back in his seat and looked down at his dinner and found it almost gone and growled.

'My sister,' Yuri said in his newly acquired English. 'I am certain I am knowing it is you who is having my jello.' She put the cup to her mouth and squeezed and Yuri pulled down at her wrist as Arsen stood from the seat in front of them and with a prolonged hiss sprayed his bickering children in the eyes.

'Not the spray!' they all shouted in Ukrainian, but it was too late. Oleksa winked and blinked and Piter squinted and shook his head and Yuri snorted and sneezed as the entire cabin wept and moaned and the flight attendants phoned the pilots and told them not to open the cockpit door…

So two weeks out from her 18th birthday party Alexa applied the tiniest amount of pepper spray to two spots that looked like they might become zits and in the Melbourne wintertime Yuri and Peter sprayed it so copiously on their borshch that Arsen was having to order a new canister every week…

And as a large crowd of people writhed on the ground or fled in burning pain, Alexa stood over the sweating and screaming and struggling Dale Highview and with her eyes wide open said to herself, 'No more, Papa. Never again.'

Surrounded by kangaroos and shaded by gum trees, Fiona was hunched over with her coat around her shoulders as she patted her eyes with a water-soaked towel.

'Where's Rodney Dillpot?' said the taller of the two men opposite her—he whom Fiona had seen coming out of the backs of police stations in order to whisper in people's ears.

Fiona pushed a bunched section of the towel into one eye and moaned with undiminished pain. 'I don't know who that is.'

'We *know* Rodney Dillpot's been in contact with you.'

She coughed then responded: 'Look, I don't even want to tell you by who, or what, I've been contacted over the last couple of weeks. But none of them were called Rodney.'

'Then how do you explain… this?'

The shorter agent put a recording device on the picnic table and pressed at its side. Very loudly there played among emus a recording of Fiona being asked beside giraffes about the stealing of arms.

'I'm the Peter file man, keep walking. ... You're who? ... I'm the Peter file guy. ... What? ... I'm the Peter file guy! ... The Peter file, it's me!'

An older mother looked down and frowned at the device and its table of listeners.

'So where's Rodney?'

'That guy came out of the bushes, I've never seen him before. And then he disappeared into the bushes.'

'And the Peter file he's talking about?'

'We need that Peter file,' urged the man with eleven-twelfths of his ears.

'Where are you hiding the Peter file?!' shouted his partner.

The taller officer looked up at the several passers-by who upon hearing the shouting had stopped their strolling. He shook his head and dismissed their confusion with a wave of his hand.

'We know the Peter file's here, Fiona.'

'We know you know where the Peter file is.'

'Good God, people are staring—can you refer to it as 'it'?'

The agents calmed down. 'Is the Peter file at the zoo?'

A mother's uppity eyebrows turned to them.

'I had it with me when you pepper-sprayed me. It must have fallen into the bonobo forest.'

'What's inside it?'

'I want you,' said Fiona, remembering she had questions of her own, 'to tell me how you know that Pete died of a heart attack, when there was no autopsy.'

'Tell us what the Peter file said.'

'We know you've been inside the Peter file!'

'That's an odd one.'

'Look lady—thanks to you there's now a Peter file on the loose in the zoo.'

'Will you stop calling it that, my god!' Fiona cowered as

more eyes turned down to their conversation. 'If I tell you will you let me go?'

'Tell us what's inside it—and yes, you can go.'

She reasoned at last that where the Peter file's contents meant nothing to she who knew him best, they would mean even less to those who knew him not at all. 'There were three phrases.'

'Phrases?'

'Very short fragments, on one otherwise blank piece of paper. And that's it.'

'What were the phrases?' The earful agent readied a pen at a notepad.

'Great at breastfeeding,' Fiona conceded.

'Not chestfeeding?'

'Breastfeeding. Great at breastfeeding.'

The phrase was written down then both agents glanced at one another. 'Go on.'

'Retarded eel magnet.'

'Woah! You can't say that word.'

'I didn't, the Peter file said it.'

A young mother's neck snapped towards Fiona as she pushed a stroller along the gravel path.

'And the third?'

'A juiced scud.'

'Scud like the missile?'

'I have no idea. S-c-u-d. A juiced scud. And that's all it said.'

'That's all the Peter file said?'

'That… is what the Peter file said.'

The agents looked at one another and nodded: 'You're free to go.'

'Really?'

'We need that towel though.'

'I'm done, Papa! No more customer relations, no more

banya—no more being in heat for you!'

'You are overacting, Oleksa.'

'Yes, Arson?' Arsen looked to the grey orb on his desk and decided to ignore it.

'This is only time has happen in very long time.'

'No, Papa! Four times last year. I am more than this, I have skills and dreams! I want to work for myself.'

'Nobody works for themself, Oleksa.'

'Hi, I'm right here.'

'I work for U-Crane, but really for family.'

'And I want to have my own family.'

'We are your family, Oleksa.'

'That's very kind of you to say, Arson, but I'm not quite sure what you mean.'

'Shut up. This family has to work together, we have to *stay* together—we have blue balls!'

Alexa walked to the office's side door. 'Do you understand? I know you are hearing me! Oleksa!'

'Uh huh?'

'You *know* we have blue balls!'

Alexa stopped her exit and stared with uneven eyebrows at her father.

'Blue balls we have.'

And Alexa went outside to the banya, and to the ice pool and the cauldron.

'Might I suggest some pornography, Arson?'

'What?' Arsen frowned at his busybody contraption.

'We all need relief from time to time, I understand. What kind of stuff are you into?'

As Alexa inquired into Arsen's pornographic preferences Alexa sat on the steps of the unheated cauldron and took her phone from her pocket and opened one of its messaging apps. Her closest friends had all lately been preoccupied with the men from her birthday party. As she scrolled through her recent conversations only Fiona seemed a ready ear. She opened their chat and held down its bottom corner and recorded. And Alexa played as though it were clear and chosen music the audio going into Alexa's microphone:

'I just don't know what to do anymore, Fiona.'

'Oleksa?' said her father, looking up then to the side door.

'I was almost raped again today. I'm sick of being army candy for Papa, I'm *sick* of being in heat for him.'

'Oleksa?'

'Hi!'

'You have become Oleksa?'

'I've never *been* so unhappy, Fi. It's like I'm trapped in Ukraine, I know this feeling from my friends. It is no life for a Sukhimov to be a serf, even if she's owned by her father. I want to be free.'

Arsen leaned back from his daughter's voice and fell morosely—soon empathetically—into his armchair.

'If I have to work one more day in the public banya I'll kill myself, I swear.'

Arsen removed his knuckles from his lips. 'I must do what anybody with blue balls must do with his daughter.'

'But Papa just won't listen, Fi.'

'Alexa, call my bank.'

'I know he's done a lot for me, and for us but...'

'Hello, Alexa? Alexa!'

'...I just don't know what to do anymore.'

'*Now* you are not hearing me?!'

Fiona was again both baffled and intrigued as she passed the reptile house on her way back to the bonobo forest.

'Why do they want to know so badly about the Peter file?' she said aloud. She squeezed her eyes tightly then pressed at them with the backs of her wrists. 'And why are the police involved at all? And a heart attack? A gosh-darned heart attack, how—'

'Fiona?'

The Arm Steeler

She looked to the direction from which her called name had sounded. 'Oh God,' she said as a seven-foot-tall koala waved at her. 'Please no.'

Shortly it said again, 'Fiona?'

'Not now, Pete!' Fiona looked to the pavement and walked on. The koala-in-a-shirt followed after her. 'Fiona, it's me—the Peter file guy.'

Still Fiona ignored the giant animal, worried that she had long begun to hallucinate—that after all no cats had winked at her nor pelicans intervened on Annie's behalf.

'It's me, Rodney,' said the koala with greater insistence.

'Mmm,' Fiona almost cackled. 'I was just kidnapped because of you.'

'We have to get out of the zoo, they're prob'ly still watching.'

'Are you *sure* this meeting's a good idea?'

As Yuri went over its probable sequence Mel grew uncertain of whether it would be an adventure or an ordeal.

'This is not one matter of good, this is one matter of finding out who have killed my brother.'

'And are we going to have to kill someone? Because I'm not sure I'm up for that. I'm a gum smuggler and a chair man. Maybe I shouldn't be meeting with arms dealers.'

'Adventure now is seeming scary?'

'It is an adventure though isn't it?'

'I also am not sure if I'm knowing this will be beneficent meeting. It is seeming to me that universe is dancing too fastly. So we consult unbrella.'

Yuri lifted his gilded parasol from its sword rack and presented it to Mel on outstretched palms.

'What's this?'

'A nyangfa is inhabiting this unbrella.'

'None of those words make sense.'

'Nyangfa will speak from unbrella, to man who is wearing

brah malaa.' Mel stared at Yuri as a fancy hat was now placed on his head. 'If unbrella says meeting is safe, is safe.'

'What do you mean, "says"?' said Mel as Yuri pulled down the hat's chinstrap.

'Unbrella was once belonged by Mongkut Phra Siam.' Yuri brought the object closer to himself. 'Rama Four.'

'What the f--k are you talking about, man?'

'Portrayed on screen and stage four-thousand six-hundred twenty-five times by Yuliy Borisovich Briner.'

'All right, do you really think you're Yul Brynner?'

'He have died day before I am born.'

'And?'

'His soul have been reborn in me.'

'And this is Yul Brynner's umbrella?'

'Yul Brynner have played king of Siam four-thousand six-hundred twenty-five times.'

Mel pouted and shook his head. 'I'm still not getting it.'

'You are thinking time is linear?' Yuri handed Mel the parasol. 'Now open.' Mel shook his head as he shook out the umbrella's fabric then flapped open its tiers. 'Now ask, if meeting will be safe.'

'What do you mean, ask?'

'Look to unbrella, and say to it, Is meeting safe?'

'I'm not asking an umbrella a question, Yuri.'

'Ask.'

'No!'

'Stubborn mool. Give to me.'

Yuri pulled forward the hat's chinstrap then placed it on his own head before taking back his unbrella. He closed his eyes and intoned: 'Nyangfa who is protecting whole dynasty of aristocat family Sukhimov across entire globe of human world and in all directions of time—tell to us safety of immediate future for going to meeting with arms dealer for finding out who have killed my brother.'

Shortly the hat, or the umbrella—Mel couldn't discern

The Arm Steeler

precisely which—hissed: 'Yessssss, ssssaaaffffee.'

'What the hell?'

'Is safe?'

'Iiiis saaaaafe.'

'Did that just speak?'

'I have told you.'

'Where'd you get that thing?'

Yuri neatened its silk and retied its ties. 'Unbrella was one gift, from Boryslav from the East.'

'What the hell is Boryslav from the East?'

Yuri stroked the unbrella's gold-lace as he wrapped it as neatly as possible around its pole. 'Boryslav is great and goodly milk brother, who is making worldwide adventures.'

'Adventures?'

'Mm!' said Yuri as he returned it to its sword stand. 'Once to reveal to himself secrets of divine music, Boryslav has caught on purpose one syphilis. But when he have caught one syphilis he is getting down syndrome, which to be rid of he is catching one malaria, also on purpose.'

'Where's this guy now?'

'Where is Boryslav?' said Yuri and momentarily seemed frightened. 'Boryslav is always coming. But we, must be going—and first we sit.'

'Sit?'

'Come.' Yuri strode to the entranceway of his home and sat on its long storage bench, and silently he stared.

'What are you doing?'

'Before leaving to go anywhere we must be sitting down for goodly one minute.'

'Why?' said Mel, impatient of Yuri's convoluted procedures.

'House spirits must stay in house!' Yuri bellowed as he raised an elbow and pointed at the floor. 'If we are leaving when they are with us, they are leaving house with no protection. So we sit, to trick spirit we are not leaving.

Then, we are leaving. It is one Ukrainian thing.'

Mel gnawed at his front lip then informed Yuri of the implication of his ritual: 'You realise this means your house spirit's an idiot?'

'Come!' Yuri nodded and patted the seat beside his. 'Gather thoughts, chair man. You will be finding it most pleasant beginning to present adventure.'

Mel shook his head as he sat beside Yuri. He looked at the blank wall opposite, then across to Yuri, calm in his flamboyant and feathered cowboy hat, before slowly returning his tired gaze to the wall. When his sixty untimed seconds had passed Yuri rose and Mel followed him outside. Yuri took off his, or Yul Brynner's—or the king of Thailand's—who knows really—hat, and threw it into the back seat of his car as he opened its front door.

Rodney threw the head of his koala costume into the back seat of his own car and put his over-gloved hands on his steering wheel.

'They wanna know what you know because I was working on Peter's case the month before he was killed.'

'Killed?'

'I'm sorry. Five years I've been AFP but that whole case felt suspicious—the Peter file was all I felt safe writing down. But then I thought, to have your brother come back and do the investigating for me. That's why I put the gum into his pocket in Singapore.'

'You did that?'

'Tell me, does the word "binocchio" mean anything to you?'

'Pi-nocchio?'

'Hm. Could be. Does Pinocchio ring a bell?'

'It does actually. Pete was having a life-like Pinocchio doll made for his practice. To show his patients that transformation's always possible. He was such a good

The Arm Steeler

man—I miss him so much.'

'And did that doll entail working with an arm thief?'

'An arm thief? What the hell is an arm thief?'

'Someone who steals arms. An arm steeler. You've never heard of limb-harvesting? This has China written all over it.'

Yuri ran his hands over a wooden crate that had 'China' written all over it as he and Mel followed a grey-bearded man into the back room of a Windsor medical-apparatus store.

'So you're the arms dealer?' said Mel and carried a very heavy duffle bag across the threshold.

'That's right,' said the man in a Northern Irish accent and slid the steel door closed behind them. Mel and Yuri were now in a kind of storeroom of steel-lattice display racks. Mounted upon one wall were several lone breasts among dozens of pairs of them. From another hung hollow legs and an array of prosthetic shins and plastic elbows and an assortment of shoulder-to-fingertip arms.

'So which'll it be?' said the Irishman at this last wall.

'These are arms,' said Yuri.

'That's right,' said the man. 'Best I can steal and money can buy. None of that Chinese crap, this's straight outta Ireland.'

'You sell prosthetic arms?' said Mel.

'Sure as not that's why you're here?'

'Wait, you're an arm dealer?' said Mel, hoping to have him clarify.

'Not just arms—legs, eyes, breasts.'

'But you call yourself an arms dealer?' said Mel, emphasising the plural.

'If someone buys two, those are arms aren't they?'

'Why I am told you are doing business with my brother?'

'Your brother? Who's your brother?'

'What have he said,' Yuri whispered.

'Who's your brother.'

'Piter Sukhimov.'

'*Doctor* Peter Sukhimov?'

Yuri nodded.

'Oh yeah. He was building a Pinocchio he was.'

'Did you say building a Pinocchio?' said Mel.

'You are understanding what man is saying?' Yuri whispered.

'Mm,' Mel nodded. 'I see you sell breasts as well.'

'Aye, working breasts. For gestational parents who've had double mastectomies. Gives their babies the natural experience o' chestfeeding. Or for non-gestational parents, for obvious reasons.'

'Do you know anyone who's… great, at breastfeeding?'

'Great at it?'

'Still I am not understanding,' said Yuri. 'Why is one Ukrainian man coming to my… distant relative here—to be asking him for guns?'

'Haven't a f----n clue. Does he sell guns? Do you sell guns?'

'He accidentally have smuggled gum.'

'Gums? That's sure lucrative. Periodontic market's gone black since the tooth famine.'

'Gum,' said Mel, with a hint of juvenile shame.

'Oh,' said the man as he checked the pockets of his tweed jacket. 'Don't think I have any, sorry.'

'No, I smuggled gum.'

'Oh you did?'

'Aye.'

'You want a job then? I know a guy's gum smuggler just got picked up by the IDF.'

'Israel?'

'The Irish Dental Force. Trying to get dentures out of Belfast.'

'You are knowing who have killed my brother?'

'Who's your brother?'

The Arm Steeler

'He is speaking English?' Yuri whispered to Mel.

'He said "who's your brother?"'

'I have told. Piter Sukhimov.'

'Oh yeah, everyone in the industry knows who killed him.'

'In the arm industry, or the arms industry?' said Mel. 'I'm really confused here.'

'If someone buys two—those are arms, aren't they?'

'Yeah I guess so. But we were told we'd be meeting with an arms dealer.'

'And if someone buys two…'

'Well yes. But it's industry knowledge in the arm-dealing industry, or the gun-smuggling industry?'

'He is right,' said Yuri, and crossed his arms. 'I also am confused. Arms or arm?'

'How many times I have to tell ya? If someone buys two,' said the arm dealer as behind him two loud bangs sounded against the hollow steel of the room's door. 'Who else knows you're here?' said the arms dealer (if someone buys two).

'What has he said?'

'Who else knows we're here.'

'Only two Georgians,' said Yuri.

There came another loud bang then a flash of white light before the door slid slightly open and a hand appeared in the new gap clutching a canister—down on which it promptly pressed. The arm dealer (if someone buys one) fell against his wall of arms and squeezed his eyes shut. Mel screamed, 'What the f--k!?' as he slapped the balls of his hands to his eye sockets. And serenely Yuri stood, twitching his nose and shaking his head as four men in dark uniforms, wearing many-compartmented jackets and with triangular goggles over their eyes—all of them pointing machine guns—filed into the storeroom and placed a hood over the arms dealer's head if someone buys two and pulled its drawstring tight and cable-tied both all two of his arm behind his back as they dragged him away.

'Universe is trembling on verge of destruction,' said Yuri, and watched without surprise the extraordinary rendition. 'Between dance of nature and dance of enlightenment.'

'My inhaler,' said Mel, coughing as he stumbled blindly around the room with his face to the ceiling. 'I can't breathe.' He strained to see and continued to lose his breath before falling into and across the wall of arms. 'Inhaler! I need an inhaler!'

The Arm Steeler

IV

Next morning Arsen was at Café Beztsihan awaiting the daughter whom he had demanded meet him there. When she arrived, red-eyed and cuddling a full-length caramel puffer jacket over pyjamas, she could barely look at him.

'Sit, Sashenka.'

'No thank you, Papa.'

'I have news.'

'I don't care. I don't care even if U-Crane's taken over.'

'I give you money for business.'

'Papa?'

'Whatever it is, whatever much you need, it's yours. I will find someone else to take over U-Crane.'

'Papa, really?'

With his fingers clasped and his elbows on the café's bench, Arsen lifted his head and nodded. 'I want only for you to be happy, Sashenka.'

'Oh, Papa!' she said, and leaned over to wrap her arms around her father. 'This is the best news ever! Thank you—thank you, Papa! I have so much to do, plans to make—I have to put some clothes on! Oh thank you—thank you, Papa!'

Arsen tilted his mouth at what he felt was a surrender and thought only about having to find somebody else to take over U-Crane. When finally Alexa stopped kissing his cheek and hurried off to change out of her pyjamas, he stood from the café's front bench and zipped up his Tonny Halfmaker and set off along Fitzroy Street. The shop beside Café Beztsihan was busy with evacuation. A 'sold' sign had been stuck across its front window and hammers and clanking steel banged and rattled within.

'What is happening here?' Arsen asked the two young

men who were removing one of the restaurant's couches.

'Poh pah bah,' said he who was walking backwards.

Arsen scratched his head, for he rarely understood Asian people when they spoke—and had no idea what a pop-up bar was. So he scowled as he returned to thinking about his and U-Crane's future.

Fiona and Mel were side by side on a padded table in the consultation room of their family doctor. Intermittently they blinked and squinted and closed their eyes and shook their heads. As they awaited Dr Reid's arrival Fiona broke the news to her brother:

'The gum was dropped into your pocket.'

'I told you it was.'

'By a federal police officer, Mel, so you'd meet with someone who steals arms? Does that ring a bell?'

'Oh God, no more arms.'

'What do you mean?'

'Do you mean an arms *dealer*?'

'Someone who steals arms,' she repeated. 'An arm-stealer—an arms dealer. That makes more sense.'

'Well he was an arm dealer.'

'He wha?'

'The guy sells prosthetic arms. He's an arm dealer. But he also sells prosthetic breasts, Fi, for breastfeeding.'

'What guy are you talking about?'

'The guy I was meeting with when this happened.'

'You're hanging out with Yuri.'

'The arm dealer was kidnapped, Fi.' Mel lowered his voice and finished his revelation: 'Right after he told us Peter was killed.'

Dr Reid walked hastily into his office and, as Fiona and Mel remembered him having done a hundred times, spun around on one foot to greet them. 'Let's take a look at these eyes then,' he said and raised Fiona's chin.

'Why was Pete dealing with a guy who makes prosthetic arms?'

'Oh he wanted a life-like Pinocchio for his office. To show the kids that transformation was always possible.'

'That explains that one.'

'What one?'

'The arm dealer said Pete wanted to build a Pinocchio. We had no idea what he was talking about.'

'He said Pete was killed?'

Dr Reid broke off inspecting Mel's eyes and glanced back at Fiona. In his very low voice he said: 'I don't need to know how you both got pepper-sprayed on the same day, but it's nothing some lodocortisone won't fix.' He returned his pen-torch to his breast pocket and sat at his desk.

'I *guess* that explains why I was kidnapped and interrogated.'

'They just grabbed you from behind?'

'And the Peter file fell into the bonobo forest.'

Dr Reid's pen stopped looping at his pad. After a moment of blank staring he looked up and across at the two Dixon children. Fiona looked down and shook her head.

'That Peter file was my last connection to the love of my life.'

Again Dr Reid's prescription halted.

'Those three goddam phrases. D Reid do you have a spare notepad?'

He handed her an inhaler-branded one along with their prescriptions and she took a pen from his desk. 'A Peter file by any other name, right?' She wrote down its three bewildering fragments and tore off the top sheet. 'It really was my last connection to my husband,' said Fiona as she and Mel came down the corridor and met Annie in the waiting room. 'Ready to go?'

Lumbering along a busy Elsternwick road, Dale Highview

of Kerrigan Construction squeezed a packet of tomato sauce onto the jumbo sausage roll whose length he in one bite halved. He wiped pastry flakes from his cheek and scraped tomato sauce from his chin then sucked at three of his fingertips. He soon turned his stuffed head as a bald man appeared alongside him and grinned and began to stroll with him.

'F--k do you want?' said Dale as out of the corner of his eye Yuri saw the open door of his own car. 'Would you f--k off?' said Dale as Yuri stepped ahead of him.

Dale finished his sausage roll off in one more bite and Yuri turned around and stopped in his path and put his knuckles to his hips.

'Listen ya bald freak, if you—' Then Yuri lifted a can of pepper spray and pushed Dale back by the shoulders of his shirt as he squirted him in his eyes and shoved him in agony towards then into his car.

Mel and Fiona walked into the school gymnasium and joined the slowly assembling whole-school... assembly—at which Annie's film was to be re-shown then crowned as not only her year-level's, but that of the entire school's, best.

Arsen and Fiona's eyes met and Alexa smiled and waved at them. Annie, with her hair in a halo braid, ran to embrace her mother. Mel said, 'What, no chairs?' as they all came to stand together on the triple basketball court.

'Nastyusha, these are for you.' Arsen took out from his jacket two peaches. 'In case they want.'

'Thanks, Grandpa.'

'I'm so proud of you. Already you are taking on the world, my volyanitsa.'

'Where's Uncle Yuri?'

'He said he'll be here soon,' said Alexa.

Dale Highview was flat on a steel table and unconscious

The Arm Steeler

as Yuri drew thick saddened eyebrows onto his forehead then painted his nose black. Yuri had already run bright red lipstick across Dale's scaly lips after with some difficulty fitting him into his costume. So on either side of Dale's head were now two enormous ears, made of the same brown fluff which encased his face and sheathed his enormous body.

His make-up soon complete, Yuri lowered the table then slid Dale from it, across and into a container that was horizontal on the floor. He made sure Dale's furry-gloved hands weren't dangling over the edges then closed the container's lid—printed to resemble an upright stack of fruit boxes. He lifted the hand trolley on which the decoy coffin lay then wheeled an enfluffed Dale out to the rear of a waiting minivan.

When Annie's film had been re-shown as a projection on the gymnasium wall Annie was applauded by the principal and by her year-level coordinators, and—now compelled to stand—by the entire school. She smiled and put her peaches on her chair and was swarmed by Vajeen Vajones, by Martin Luther Ching, and by the new Brazilian kid, Cornflakes Pereira—all keen on showing off their very new friendship with the school's newly lauded filmmaker. Annie looked to her grandfather, really the star of *Simya,* and to her applauding aunt. Then her eyes lit up and she waved excitedly as her Uncle Yuri, in his I-Crane uniform, arrived and applauded as he stood between his non-gestational parent and Annie's beaming gestational one.

Mel and Annie and Fiona, then Yuri and Alexa behind them, filed through Arsen's living room into his curtainless kitchen.

'Don't sit there,' said Annie with some urgency. Fiona withdrew her hand from the back of one of the chairs.

'Grandpa leaves that space for Grandma.'

'Fiona, you are beside here,' said Arsen. 'This bowl is for Piter.'

'Don't sit there!' said Alexa as Annie pulled out the chair at the table's corner. 'A young woman must never sit at the corner of the table. It postpones her marriage.'

A Ukrainian thing.

'Do you two have hay-fever?' Alexa asked, Fiona and Mel sneezing and sniffing as they circled the table.

'We got pepper-sprayed,' said Fiona.

'Face mist? Oh, there's an easy treatment for face mist. Come to my bathroom, I have hooorse milk.'

The Rain Woman arrived and behind her came Father Pyanenko, scowled at by Yuri as he crossed the living room: 'Him.'

'At last banya will be fixed,' said Arsen as he welcomed them both. 'But first we eat.'

Fiona was bemused when Annie ran to hug the Rain Woman as she and Mel went through to Alexa's bathroom and had horse milk applied to their faces.

'Where's Grandpa?' said Annie to her grandfather, counting the places at the table and finding there wasn't one for her grandpa Geoff.

After fifteen minutes of pea-free sex, Geoff and Karen had changed into their nightwear and began to get comfortable under the covers. Geoff lay back and enfolded his fingers and Karen leaned forward and reached down and took from her overnight bag a large mask, whose strap she pulled over the back of her head. It covered her face from ear to ear and from chin to hairline, and had protruding from its top a plastic tube.

'What the hell's that?' said Geoff, about to turn out the lights.

'My snorkel.'

The Arm Steeler

'Why you wearing it to bed?'

'I *have* to snorkel, or I can't sleep. I told you that.'

'That's what you call snorkelling?'

'Did you think I meant snorkelling in the ocean?'

'No! Why would you mean *that* far more common use of the word? I also can't wait to wear a, snorkel to bed, in Vietnam.'

'Night, night,' said Karen, her teeth clutching at the mouthpiece—and she lay down and closed her eyes.

When eventually Geoff stopped staring at her he too lay back and listened to the amplified sound of Karen breathing. As gradually she fell to sleep the leg closest to him began to twitch. Shortly that leg seemed to begin to shake. Then both of her legs were vibrating as though she were re-entering the earth's atmosphere. Geoff turned his head to her as her whole body convulsed.

'Ahhhhh!' Karen yelled through her snorkel. 'You f-----g arsehole!' she both screamed and mumbled (scrumbled), and she sat up in bed and seemingly was terrified.

'What the hell? Are you all right?' Geoff sat up too and as Karen emerged from a lucid night terror her right leg flailed from its hip and kneed Geoff in the mouth.

'Oh my god, I'm so sorry!' she said through her snorkel and leaned over to check if he was all right. 'My restless leg syndrome is worse at night. I told you I'm a bad sleeper.'

Geoff nodded his head as he listened to the hiss of Karen's breathing and mumbled into his exhausted hand, 'This can not last a long time.'

Arsen stood before a long wooden tray-covering at the centre of his dining table and balanced a glass of samohonka on the backs of his fingers.

'Today we are together in honour of Anastasia, our Nastyusha. With pride of her family she has made movie film for to show school, and which shows to school her brilliant mind. To Anastasia,' said Arsen and raised the back of his hand. All except a beaming Annie stood and Mel and Fiona looked to the others to figure out how to balance a shot glass on the backs of their fingers.

'May our government be always inefficient!' said Arsen, and further raised his elbow. 'Slava Ookraini.'

He turned his wrist and tilted his head back and drank as Father Pyanenko squirted his water pistol into his mouth and Mel gagged as the liquid passed his throat. Arsen slammed down the upturned shot glass and said, 'Now we eat!' He lifted the wooden tray and revealed a steaming length of meat.

'What is it?' said Mel as he sat back down and inspected but failed to recognise the animal.

'It is egg inside pigeon inside chicken.'

'Ah,' said Mel.

'Inside goat, inside sheep, inside pig.'

'Oh,' said Mel.

'Inside cow. Baby cow.'

'Comprehensive.'

'This we eat only on important days. And today is Anastasia's very important day.'

At the knocking of Arsen's large wooden fork against the table Yuri passed Annie a plate of varenyky and all began to feast. While as dusk fell over St Kilda beach...

A stack of fruit boxes stood still upon a hand trolley, ignored or cirsumvented by hundreds of evening strollers. Ignored or cirsumvented, that is, until it began to shake.

The crowd first looked at it, then moved to walk at some distance around it, as now it rumbled and shortly rocked. Then its front swung open, and Dale Highview of Kerrigan Construction, newly awoken from a quarter-dose of elephant tranquiliser, blinked then held up his hands and found them to be covered in brown fur. He looked down at his nose, which he could see was painted black, then touched the enormous ears which protruded from his head.

Seeing ahead that he was at the beach, and sensing he was in a container of some sort, he stepped out and turned to look at the disguised coffin. He stumbled backwards and found that the awakening would not yet allow the full use of his legs. He fell, then tried but failed to remain sitting—and once again passed out.

From both directions the crowd now stepped over the outstretched arms and furry legs of this enlarged Cherubashka—the latest victim of a public vengeance which Yuri called 'cartooning'. Thusly cartooned, Dale Highview had ice cream dripped onto his painted face and pigeon-droppings shat onto his shaggy chest not very far at all from the place in which he had attempted to molest Alexa Arsenovna Sukhimova.

Having shared the news of her new business venture at dinner, all now gathered in the living room to watch Alexa play the piano for the first time in a long time.

Very solemnly she sat at its bench and lifted the fallboard and arched her back. She closed her eyes and slowed her breath; rested her fingertips over the first chords and in a moment went from still to fully bouncing as she tapped her feet and began *Weatherbird Rag*. When shortly Mel recognised the tune his eyes opened with glee and he whistled inaccurately along.

Alexa's right wrist held still as her fingers rolled back and forth over a chord. She leaned down to it then looked across at Yuri and grinned playfully as she rolled the chord on. When it broke she threw her head back and stomped one foot and rattled at the high keys—then drew back her lips and smiled over a pair of candy teeth at all who were standing around her.

As she shot her index finger at the song's last two notes

everyone applauded and Arsen said that it was time.

'Can I watch?' said Annie.

'Ask your mother.'

'Can I watch the Rain Woman get rid of the Bannik?'

'I have no idea what you just said, honey. But yes, you can.'

'Thank you!'

'The film was brilliant, Annie. I'm so proud of you.'

'I love you, Mum.'

'I love you.' Fiona pulled Annie in for a hug then released her to follow the Rain Woman and Father Pyanenko out to Arsen's car.

'Why do we not ourselves be taking one last public steam? Together, as family.'

'I'd love to be in heat!' said Alexa.

'As friends?' said Mel.

'As family,' said Yuri.

'Public saunas are gross though, aren't they?' said Mel. 'They're always so crowded.'

'I've got it covered,' said Alexa and pulled out her phone.

In the floodlit white of U-Crane's backyard, Arsen and Annie watched from outside the banya as the Rain Woman held two hands to its ceiling and chanted while Father Pyanenko pointed into its every corner a golden crucifix.

The Rain Woman took out and shook a necklace of seashells and began throwing sesame seeds at the cage of stones in the banya's back corner. Father Pyanenko shot holy water at the same, and soon a pained hiss came from its recesses. The Rain Woman said, 'Uh oh,' as Annie looked up with frightened eyes. Her grandfather looked down at her: 'That's him.'

Father Pyanenko raised his crucifix to the vocal corner and emptied his water pistol in its direction. The Rain Woman beat the side of her head with the palms of her hands and screamed: 'Hot water burn baby, hot water burn

The Arm Steeler

baby!' Then Father Pyanenko intoned: 'You deaf and mute spirit, come out of here and never enter again.'

Steam began to rise from the banya's stones and shortly its wood creaked all around—until there sounded the deep and echoey cackle which Annie recognised from the day she had let the Bannik in.

'That's it, Grandpa!'

The Rain Woman's screaming loudened—'Hot water burn baby!'—and the banging against her own head grew frantic until after a loud crack the banya fell silent. She stared at the floor and held her head and shifted from one foot to the other as the steam in the banya's far corner seemed to assemble into a vaguely human cloud. Then it wafted towards the banya door, hissing as it floated.

'Maté?' said Arsen, recognising a word, and almost the voice, that now shrieked over his granddaughter's head as the sound and the wind left the banya and flew into U-Crane's front office.

Sufficiently cooled after a dunk in the pool of St Kilda Sea Baths, Mel nodded nervously at the two *Very* Eastern European women guarding the steam room's door as he returned to the heat and the moisture and to forcing himself to not look at Alexa's naked body.

'Siva is dancing mightily,' said Yuri. 'Do you know what is happening when government is taking on role of creator *and* destroyer? It will not be stopping at killing Piter.'

'What?' said Alexa. 'Did you say killing?'

'What?' said her brother.

'Was Peter killed?'

'I only just found out,' said Fiona.

'Wait, you knew?'

'From Mel.'

'*You* knew? Why do you know and not me?'

'Yuri and I were investigating it.'

'Yuri, what the hell?'

'I have told it long ago to Fiona. But even when you are telling to people truth, they are not hearing.'

'I didn't know any of this!' said Alexa, offended.

'Think yourself lucky,' said Mel. 'Less likely to be pepper-sprayed.'

'What will you be telling to girlfriend of where you have lately been?'

'Girlfriend?' said Fiona.

'He is dating one girl who is working at market of socks.'

'Stock, market,' said Mel, correcting him instantly.

'And who was girl at market of socks?'

'She's a friend, I told you. My girlfriend works on the stock market,' he reassured Fiona and Alexa.

'And you have made to her sex-love?'

'Yuri,' said Fiona.

'I am thinking no. But she has given you fishfingers, yes?'

'Yuri!' said Fiona. 'Goddam it, that's gross. I'm outta here.'

'Yep I'm done,' said Alexa. 'I have to start work on Arm Candy.'

They stepped down from the top bench and Alexa dismissed her clothed friends from their posts and went on enthusing to Fiona about her ideas for the new business.

'That really was one hell of an adventure, Yurine. I am kind of glad it's over though. You live a... an eventful life. Arm dealers and Georgian fencing parties—it's a lot of adventure for one person.'

'It is not adventure, and it is not over.'

'It's not?'

'Remember what arm dealer have said about Pinocchio? That my brother was building? Russian Pinocchio, is called Buratino. Buratino also is name of one Russian rocket launcher. It is not difficult to change one U-Crane to platform for rocket. He have never told to me, but I think *this* is why Piter is involved with confusing dealer of arms.

Maybe Piter was gun smuggler after all.'

'No, no, Yuri. Fiona explained that all to me. Pete was having a life-like Pinocchio doll made for his practice, *that's* why he knew the arm dealer. He was getting rubber arms made for a doll.'

'Arms for doll?'

'Mm hm. Someone told Fiona about it.'

'Arms not for rocket?'

'Not for rocket. Lifelike arms for a puppet, so it'd look real.'

'Hm,' said Yuri and sat erect with his fists at his thighs. 'Perhaps it is over.'

'Fun while it lasted... brother.' Yuri looked across the bench and shook his head as a gaunt man came semi-clothed into the sauna. 'You almost said friend yesterday.'

'I have not. And it was not fun, Smell—and was not adventure. I am done here.' Yuri stood and scraped the sides of his fingers-and-thumbs along the fronts of his legs and shook out his hands. As he stepped onto the lower bench he turned and said, 'Has anyone ever telled you you are having most ugly neck?' And he grinned and walked out.

Mel pressed at the sides of his throat as he leaned forward from the high wall beside the door. He rested his elbows on his knees and watched sweat stream from the end of his nose. 'Hot in here,' he called out to the new stranger, who had deposited himself in the high darkness of the steam room's innermost corner. And from that darkness Mel was returned a peculiar revelation:

'Mel Dixon?'

'Yeah?'

'I am here to kill you.'

IN THE NEXT SEASON OF THE PETER FILE…

…Tess finally lets Mel experience her tickles:

In black lingerie she came out of her bedroom and raised her hands and dangled her wrists and bent her fingers into claws as she stalked towards him. 'Here come the Tess tickles!'

'What?' said Mel, looking up from the last of his octopus.

'My Tess tickles are coming to get you!' she grinned, and hunched her shoulders.

'What the hell are you talking about?'

She sang as she chased him around the kitchen table: 'Where do you want my Tess tickles, handsome boy?'

…And Mel, while tracking down the triple and insultingly cheap outsourcing of his own ah-ssassination, falls for a Ukrainian honeypot then accidentally cartoons himself:

Covered in orange fake tan—shirtless and wearing only red boxer shorts—he stumbled drunkenly along a shaded St Kilda street as with one hand he scooped what he thought was honey out of a honeypot in order to lick it from his fingers.

…While Alexa manages a bevy of desperate Ukrainian refugees—and the ghost of her gaslighting grandmother—in order to get Arm Candy open for business.

…Fiona and Rodney investigate Peter's family but can barely have an intelligible conversation with one another:

Surveilling Arm Candy's unfurnished premises, Fiona brought back from the 7-11 their late-night snack and said, 'Do you want sauce or…?'

'A saucer? No, no thanks, it's only a sausage roll. Wait,

The Arm Steeler

did you say saucer or sorcerer?'
'Neither.'
'She'd be a sorceress wouldn't she?'
'Who'd be a sorceress?'
'The sister. If she was a sorcerer she'd be a sorceress.'
'Why a sorceress?'
'Wait, did you say rhinoceros?'
'What?'
'What do they have to do with anything?'

...After being photographed in his royal regalia outside a school Yuri is accused of being a paedophile, then gets kidnapped by his milk brother and taken to the forest— where he's made to eat his—wait! You'll find out.

...And after becoming close friends with Martin Luther Ching, Annie is denounced anonymously at school as a fascist hireling and an enemy of the people.

...At Dixon Hardware a violent turf war erupts between The Soil Baron and The Drill Sergeant on one side and The Pot Dealer and The Weed Killer on the other—both sides desiring total control over aisle 29, the turf section.

...Geoff finds in his basement the family's white kilt, gets locked in a frog-woman's sex attic—then sells Dixon Hardware to the Chinese.

...After inadvertently selling a tank to a gay terrorist, Arsen finds out that the poh pah bah beside Café Beztsihan is to be communism-themed—and has little choice but to become an arsonist.

...And Boryslav finally comes:
The first sign of him was always the music, lilting from

the green button-accordion which hung at his chest. It was the hopak, played with a virtuosity that was the dangerous envy of all of Zaporozhia. Then always came the screaming, as down a shaded St Kilda street young women crouched to catch their falling dresses and young men fled to prevent the repeat twisting of their nipples beneath muscle shirts. And as the crowd of revellers dispersed, and Mel the Pooh rounded the corner, towards the non-existent camera came—with his arms swinging in and out as he played and wearing very baggy trousers held high at his waist by a shining blue cummerbund—and with all of his head shaved except for a long slicked tuft sprouting from its top—came Boryslav, an orphan whose rise from acrobatic shepherd to professor of nuclear physics at Kharkiv's Academy of Skills will be only partially explained in Season Two of...

THƎ PETEЯ FILƎ.

Printed in Great Britain
by Amazon